A TOUCH OF PIGSKIN

DAI BLATCHFORD

Iponymous Edition
First Published in 2013
By Iponymous publishing Limited
Iponymous Swansea United Kingdom SA6 6BP

Design: www.GMID.co.uk

A CIP record for this book
Is available from the British Library

(EBook) ISBN 978-1-908773-21-0
(Physical Book) ISBN 978-1-908773-23-4

www.iponymous.com

Biography

Dai Blatchford has lived in Wales and Cornwall. He received his higher education at Oxford and Swansea. Once upon a time he lectured at one of the UK's largest FE colleges. On returning to Wales he became a freelance writer. Having settled near the sea in Mumbles he wrote for a variety of magazines. This gave him a taste for the craft and after many false starts he settled down to write his first novel. This is it. He divides his time between Oystermouth Castle, Underhill Park (Mumbles RFC) and Café Valance. He is married to Rosie and has two grown up children and a granddaughter. He is very happy in a Celtic sort of way. He is currently working on a sequel to A Touch of Pigskin, provisionally titled Garibaldi's Overcoat.

1

Two rivers run through it

The city of Oxford has two rivers running through it, the Thames and the Cherwell. Because this is Oxford two rivers with one name each would be much too straightforward. Accordingly, the Thames as it passes through the city is known as the Isis. So there are two rivers but three names. Nothing in this city is ever quite as it seems.

The city and the university exist side by side but over the centuries have often been at war with each other. It was one of the bloodiest of these confrontations that led to the formation of that rival university way over there in the frozen wastes on the eastern side of England. Cambridge has always turned to the English for its student body. In Oxford things are much less clear cut. Of course it is an English city and recruits heavily from England as well as everywhere else in the world. In fact there are those who suspect that if the Martians were sufficiently intelligent and quirky then admissions tutors would be issuing invitations to interview to little green men and women. It is a city of students, servants, buildings and rivers and has always had an eye on the Celtic fringe for its academic recruits. In Oxford there is a Welsh college and also a Cornish college, both drawing heavily on students and staff from the appropriate countries. A member of staff of the second of these colleges was currently polluting one of the city's rivers apparently without a care in the world. He was, in fact, exactly that, having lost any stake in the world some days earlier. Professor Petroc Trethewey, repulsive in life, positively loathsome in death, was eddying around a pool in the river giving a reasonable imitation of the well-loved gloomy donkey made famous by A A Milne, a writer though sadly also a Cambridge man.

This particular part of the River Cherwell hosted a very Oxford type of delight in a legendary pool known to aficionados as Parsons' Pleasure. This was a deep pool screened from the river by a system of heavy swinging gates. The sign in Gothic script that had been there for as long as anyone could remember proclaimed 'Ladies Must Disembark at this Point'. It seemed incongruous since the only vessels using the river at this point would be punts usually owned by the colleges. Generations of high spirited female undergraduates, having refused to disembark and walk around the site, were treated to the sight of vicars, dons and a bursar or two in various stages of undress cavorting in the pool. Of the swimmers some went for full frontal nudity, some bathed in long johns or pyjamas and one long retired don bathed in a three piece striped suit with accompanying bowler hat tied to his head with a red spotted handkerchief. Most, like Petroc Trethewey, had spent many happy hours, with, in his case, his attendant blubber allowing a fair impression of the great white whale that once concentrated the mind of Captain Ahab.

On a crisp day at the beginning of autumn his mortal remains eddied around the pool aimlessly as the river crew looked on. At this stage it was assumed that Trethewey was one more casualty of a river that claimed its fair share of victims every term. Michaelmas Term was usually quieter than the warmer terms of spring and summer but it was not unusual to be called to remove a corpse or two from the river in October. The city and the university maintained a small jointly funded group for such activities. And similar to any group involved in such unpleasant, though necessary operations they kept touch with reality through the medium of wine dark

2

humour. The demise of Petroc Trethewey left plenty of room for such dark levity.

"Right then young Ryan me lad, get your boat hook out and try hooshing the floater towards the bank so that Jake and the boys can get some grappling hooks into him." The speaker was a grizzled old soul in his sixties. Having retired from a comfortable position as a bulldog, a member of the university police, Bert Tippings gained a perverse enjoyment from his current post. As the man in charge, or Captain as he bizarrely styled himself, he had his best days indulging his macabre sense of fun at the expense of some of the more squeamish men in the clean-up crew. "Come on Ryan lad, get stuck in. Do some heavy duty hooshing and try steering old Eeyore towards dry land. There's no bloody tide in a river you know. He'll keep circling the pool until he rots or the fish eat him. The police will be here in a minute and they'll not expect to get their hands dirty."

"I'm doing my best Cap'n. But isn't this a job for the police divers? I'm trying my best to push him towards the bank but he keeps slipping off the hook."

"Ay lad. He looks a slippery customer to me," the Cap'n said as he lay back in the small inflatable the team used for corpse recovery. "Now if we can't get him close enough to the bank for the boys to get a grapple on him then you, my lucky lad, will be joining him in the drink where the little fishies swim. And you can forget your police divers. Have you not heard of austerity and cuts? Concentrate, for God's sake lad. You almost had him then. Come on, get the boat closer, and perhaps we can pull him in and row over to the bank with him in tow. We'll be here all day otherwise. Let's face it, the fact that he's floating tells us that the old gases are building up. It's a bit like trying to lasso a mine. If you puncture him with that boat hook he could go off like a bomb and blow us clean out of the water."

This was Bert Tippings' favourite threat to the younger lads in the team. It was all so much hogwash but the young lads didn't know that. Ryan certainly was unaware of it as his face changed from a sea green complexion to a pea green one.

"Look out," Tippings shouted unnecessarily loudly. A startled Ryan threw himself to the bottom of the boat as a long line of rope flew over his head. Without moving from his seat Tippings grabbed it deftly in his left hand. "Right then Ryan, grab hold of this rope and tie it around any part of our floater you can reach. Come on, if you lean out of the boat you should be able to reach an arm or leg. Don't put it over his head for God's sake. I've seen them come right off before. Doesn't help with identification. Come on, shift yourself, it's knocking off time and I've got an appointment with a pint of Wadworths 6X."

It was a credit to young Ryan Simpson, who was made of stern stuff, that by reaching out as far as possible while Tippings held his feet he managed to loop a portion of the rope under the right arm of the floater previously known as Petroc Trethewey.

"Well done lad," came a chorus from the bank after some very careful reeling in of one of the biggest catches ever made in Parsons' Pleasure. With some experienced hands on the rope Oxford's version of the Great White Whale was hauled to the edge of the pool and up on the bank. Trethewey lay on his back in death much in the way he had in life. It was not a pretty sight.

"What's happened to his ears?" Jake pointed at the unlovely head of the corpse. "Don't look at me. I haven't got them," grinned Tippings, who had by now persuaded young Ryan to row them across.

"Ugly old bastard, isn't he?" added Jake.

"Sshh," said Tippings.

"He's got no ears," chipped in Ryan.

4

"You'll do lad," said Tippings with fatherly pride. I think that it is unlikely that this is one of our accidentals or suicidals, mind. I've never come across anyone who has cut off their own ears before taking the waters either because of disillusion or rank stupidity. But this is Oxford after all, so you never know. I've rung the depot and the police are on their way. They told me to cover the floater with an official tarpaulin then we can sign off for the day. I was angling for a bit of overtime by hanging on for a bit but the gaffer was having none of it. Come on lads, the sooner we wrap him up in his winding sheet the sooner we can get ourselves into the Vicky Arms and wrap ourselves around a few pints. I was going to say a little prayer for our floater but assuming he's an Oxford man rather than a visitor it's odds on he's a bloody atheist."

With those prescient words, as it was later to turn out, Captain Bert Tippings and his men dragged the inflatable up the bank and from there onto the works truck parked some way from the pool. They left the earthly remains of Petroc Trethewey, Spriggan, academic and drunk, on the bank covered only by an old tarpaulin. In truth that was a lot more than usually covered him in the halcyon days when he indulged in his second favourite occupation of nude bathing with his chums.

2

By the pricking of my thumbs

Sebastian Slope glared through the window of the house he had rented in north Oxford. He glared at the rain that still poured down, partly obscuring his view, he glared at the mothers bringing their kids home from school: Slope glared at the world. He was in a foul mood, and someone would pay. Slope was a committed and accomplished glarer. In his world there was so much to glare at. There was so much he hated, so many people he despised and this was the city that had done so much to damage his sense of self. Angrily he wondered whether in coming back to Oxford he had made a mistake. He hadn't expected a hero's welcome. He knew what he had done but there was still some room for doubt in the minds of others. Even his favourite phrase, "on the balance of probability" with which he had hoodwinked so many college staff in the past, failed to raise the gloom. He knew there had been plenty who had said of the Prideaux case, "no smoke without fire" and those who should have known better had spouted similar inanities. There are those who are quick to rush to judgement. After all where would the country's tabloids be without the support of the unquestioning brigade? Slope expected better of those who studied and taught at the university. Life was never that simple though. Two of Slope's erstwhile closest supporters had cut him dead in the High earlier in the day. They had pretended not to see him and he wasn't going to give them the satisfaction of calling after them. Still they had been on his side once. What the hell had happened in the interim? Prison was not the Oxford way of course.

There was always someone, with an Oxford connection, further up the food chain. No misdemeanour should be sufficient to lead to incarceration for an Oxford man. This was generally understood. Perhaps Slope had simply let the side down. In any case that bastard Prideaux should have kept his mouth shut and faded away. In Slope's world he had no right to have made the stand that he did. It was unforgiveable. And Slope was not a forgiving man. To him such weakness was an indulgence of the simple minded. There was more to come before honours were to be considered even.

Perhaps other evidence had come to light since his enforced exile. The college pay off had cushioned the blow but the damage to his ego had never healed. He had put up a strong case against the contrived retirement package but concern about the college's reputation had trumped his impassioned defence of his actions. Prideaux himself had never been that popular. He was too forthright for that. And at the time there was a considerable body of people that found him guilty based on nothing more than his long-term membership of the awkward squad. But Slope had been so convincing. Why would they change sides now? It made little sense but the whole business had certainly made him angry. An angry Slope was not a thing of beauty and in one of the swisher suburbs of the city there lurked an angry Slope. His anger was beginning to take on a more practical bent. Such a likelihood had always lurked just under the surface. That surface had been broken and the consequences would be desperate for more than a few now living in blissful ignorance. One such was Professor Petroc Trethewey, expert in the study of Celtic Secret Societies, bon viveur and crashing bore.

Petroc had been an easy kill. It had been Slope's first as an adult, but as he had been told many times by the murderers that he sought for company, and of course, used to carry out their sordid trade for the Spriggans, "only the first one counts, the rest are routine". The only variety lay in the method of despatch and whereas the Spriggans had a rulebook for just about everything, for contracted out murders they left method strictly to the man or woman given the job.

The Spriggans had never left behind their links with violence as a method of control. And where murders were few and far between these days they were still part of the Spriggans' armoury of fear. Petroc had to go because he talked too much. Worst still he was a Spriggan and in what passed for logic amongst this murderous cabal he had to be silenced, suitably punished for what amounted to treachery. All that mattered was that his death could not be directly traced to the organisation. It was vital, however, that those involved knew that his death had been a Spriggans' revenge killing.

Slope knew plenty of 'disposal operatives', as the men and women he employed for such duties were always called. He enjoyed their company and their perfect black and white view of the world. Murder, like prostitution, robbery and banking, was simply a way of earning a living. Feeling anything for a target made no sense. Morality was not an issue. Any weakness would have been dangerous and could lead to poor aim, or poor preparation; the dreaded mistake. It was also a very lucrative pastime. There were those who took a particular pride in their work. Others were very matter of fact and silenced the target whose name appeared on the scrap of parchment conveyed to them under official Spriggan procedure. There was no negotiation. The name and a sum of money would be written down and conveyed to the chosen killer. Slope had arranged such silencing many times. Any special instructions, such as "remove the target's ears" would be written in Ancient Cornish. Thus was the link with a very ancient past kept extant. It was a small and ironical concession from Slope to culture.

In Petroc's case removal of the ears was essential. Anyone who knew the first thing about the ancient cult would know that this was a fate reserved for full members of the Spriggans. It was a warning and this time Slope had decided to administer the particular warning personally. Killing Petroc had taken very little effort. He was old, sick and a drunk. After a few large glasses of Petrus, "Petrus for Petroc" as he continually and tiresomely declaimed, he had no strength to fight and it was as if he welcomed his sentence. He was tired and his course was run. When the sentence was whispered into his ear in the old tongue as he sat in the kitchen of Slope's house it was a blessed relief. A strangely aroused Slope had easily slipped the garrotte over his head and tightened it before Petroc realised what was happening. It took bare minutes to send Petroc slipping and sliding out of this world. Removing the ears was more difficult but since it was an important part of the ritual killing Slope worked at it; the knife was sharp and he achieved the desired result. This was a warning: grisly, certainly, effective beyond question. Carefully, he cleaned the ears, dried them and wrapped them in tissue paper. Placing them inside a padded envelope he could not help but suppress a smile as he addressed it in his best handwriting. The simple act of addressing the envelope was akin to the crack of a starting pistol for the master. The race was on; the quarry blissfully unaware snored loudly in the deepest of sleeps.

All that remained to do was for Slope to telephone a couple of minor disposal men. They would remove the corpse and ensure that not a trace was left at the house. The next time Putrid Petroc would make a public appearance it would be in the form of a bloated corpse eddying round a pool, in style not dissimilar to the doleful donkey who, having been 'bounced' by Tigger, did his best to maintain his dignity while eddying round a very different pool. Petroc's pool was well known to aficionados of nude bathing in the Cherwell. And in death there was no dignity, not even of the imaginary kind. Slope had always been dangerous, now he had made the transition to lethal.

Murder had made him hungry and he had decided to walk to The Eagle and Child for one of their legendary breakfasts. The rain had abated as Slope slammed his front door and walked down the path. Dressed in his trademark dark blue fedora and long black Crombie style overcoat covering a chalk striped Armani suit, Slope looked every inch the successful academic turned businessman he had once been. What he had become was a murdering bastard, perhaps not that far a step. And as in all things in the life of this driven man one murder was never going to be enough, not when there was a score to settle. He had never forgiven and would never ever forgive Prideaux for humiliating him. The prospect of revenge had kept him going through some dark times. In his more lucid moments he admitted that personal vendettas were the province of ignorant peasants, not the raison d'etre for a sophisticated and educated man such as himself. He recognised this but there was a much more powerful and primitive urge that pushed him onwards in search of a visceral settling of an old score.

Opening the rusting gate he turned left and walked towards the pub known affectionately to generations of Oxford students as the Bird and Baby. It was one of the few pubs in Oxford that offered a good cooked breakfast and was open at breakfast time. It suited Slope as he could be anonymous there. It was many years since he had frequented the place as an undergraduate, latterly as Master of St Jude's, but the old place hadn't changed. In fact it had changed little since the days of the Inklings and it gave Slope huge pleasure that he could gorge himself on a full English breakfast in the room where JRR Tolkien, CS Lewis et al. met regularly to drink and talk literature and philosophy. Walking along St Giles prompted the return of memories but now was not the time for the past. Now was about finalising plans to finish the job, started all those years ago, of ruining Prideaux once and for all. In the mind of such a man the fact that Prideaux provided not one iota of a threat cut no ice at all. He had survived, though damaged, and, worse, this upstart crow had spoken against him and done everything in his power to damage his already dwindling reputation. He would pay. But for now breakfast awaited. He ordered what he always thought of as the full train smash. It was a mighty plateful and would carry Slope through the day. He would not feel hungry again until evening. The day could be spent on assembling what supporters he could. The man who was not Mr Rainbow had work to do.

If the victory was to be his, then it had to start somewhere. His first murder had stirred something deep within. He had not given it too much thought previously. There were people who carried out such activities at his command. Yet he could not deny that his first effort had given him an unexpected thrill of pleasure. It was something he could repeat as required. There was the added bonus in his newly discovered expertise that it naturally narrowed down those in the know and it would strengthen his position. The fewer people aware of such crimes, the less likely it was that he would be discovered before he had had his fill. But his revenge needed to start soon and it needed to start somewhere appropriate; that somewhere could be St Jude's College, initially with the bursar Conrad Speight. Speight was a Spriggan clever enough to have hidden his tracks during the plot against

Prideaux. He would be an excellent starting point. Slope resolved to leave a message for him or, better still, to talk to him directly. Pushing his plate away he took out a leather covered notebook. Writing quickly with an antique tortoiseshell Cross fountain pen, using enough old Cornish for Speight to recognise the author, he folded the paper and sealed it with the Spriggan seal. The seal gave a clear insight into the mind of the members of this obscure cult. It was a representation of the mythical creature from which the cult took its name.

Those holidaying in Cornwall would be familiar with the Cornish pisky. Piskies were as distinct from the English pixie as the pasty was from the meat pie, whatever adherents of the red or the white rose might think to the contrary. However, they were generally regarded as benevolent beings, albeit with a penchant for mischief. Spriggans were something else altogether. As white must have its black so good must have its evil and the Piskies had their Spriggans. Believed in by those who believed in such things, Spriggans were held to be dark cousins of the more benevolent Piskies. They embodied the darker side of the world in their malevolent approach to humans. Generally believed to be wizened and twisted, both of body and mind, these evil creatures were at their happiest when playing malicious tricks on their human neighbours. If a cow died or crops rotted on the fields Cornish folk did not launch a witch hunt, they nodded sagely and muttered "bloody Spriggans". If a late night traveller ended up lost on the moor and the body was found days later in a bog, lifeless and alabaster white, it would be "those murdering bastards again". All imprecations were muttered for fear of the "Spivey uns". For it was not simply their offensive physical appearance and vile smell that terrified, it was their reputed ability to suddenly become giants if the occasion demanded. Of course everyone had a second cousin who had told a friend about a witnessed transformation one dark night on Bodmin Moor. It didn't matter that nobody could point to a single individual who could attest to having witnessed the event first hand; the myth persisted and it held the Cornish from Launceston to Land's End in thrall. Whenever Slope used the seal he smiled in recognition of the appropriateness of the twisted wizened creature that summed up so much of the spirit of the cult he headed. It was evil personified and it suited Slope's personality perfectly.

Slope replaced the seal in his jacket pocket, got to his feet, paid his bill and left. There was no tip. Slope saw no reason for the archaic business of tipping. Why should it fall to him to make up wages for those in the catering industry; their career choice after all. Leaving the Bird and Baby he turned left then walked along Little Clarendon Street towards Jericho and the old college.

The college of St Jude's was an odd creation established by Cornishman Jude Blaise in the fifteenth century. Blaise had made his fortune in smuggling and although he had, like a lot of old rogues, been eventually gentrified he was never allowed, nor did he try, to forget his origins. The college had a habit of preferring Cornish students over others and this led to discord and a deal of bad feeling from other Oxford undergraduates. The bad feeling occasionally spilled over into outright violence. St Jude's against the rest was a common situation for many years. Even now it surfaced on the river and the sports fields and was never wholly forgotten. It was often in inter collegiate rugby matches that the violence surfaced most obviously. By tradition Cornishmen were burly and no strangers to hard work, no strangers to violence; consequently they frequently formed the core of any St Jude's first XV. Many a raw boned public school boy representing one of the other twenty nine Oxford colleges had felt, at first hand, or fist, the wrath of a terrible eight, or a furious front five. Contrary to popular opinion it was Cornish rugby men who had perfected the art of the foot rush rather than Scottish Borders players. Not for nothing was the old country motto, "One for all, all for one". A unifying motto that the Spriggans had so shamelessly hijacked for their own twisted rituals. When an incensed pack of Cornish forwards set off on an offensive foot rush the importance of that oft repeated battle cry became clear; strong men were as corn before the thresher, rendered impotent and brought low by the ferocity of Cornish attacks.

There was one other thing that rankled at St Jude's and led to the continuing simmering hostility among sporting types. An archaic rule of the university had decreed that a student representing the university at any sport would need to play twice against the newer university over in the freezing East Anglian wastes before being awarded a blue. There was no justification for this other than general annoyance from the mass of other colleges at being regularly railroaded by hordes of southwest Britons.

Such considerations, of course, did not impinge on the consciousness of Slope as he bustled his way towards Jericho. He regarded himself an aesthete and for the doings of "muddied oafs and flannelled fools" he cared not one jot or tittle. As Master of St Jude's he had indulged heartily in the college's culinary excellence. The master and senior dons dined like emperors night after night with the best that college could provide. All this was washed down with the finest wines that the world's vineyards could produce. His current errand to find a trustworthy soul brought him out onto Walton Street, a thoroughfare that marked the boundary of Jericho. He knew the place well. It was the old working class area of Oxford, part gentrified now but probably still the most vital part of the city.

Just off Walton Street were some cottages still owned by St Jude's. For many years they had been used as accommodation for students. Then for no obvious reason the college had decided to build a brand new block for students, giving the cottages over to grace and favour residences for senior college staff. Speight had been first in the queue. He now lived at Worcester Place in a delightfully refurbished boatman's cottage adjacent to the canal. It was here that Slope was headed. He was fairly sure that Speight would be in. He had no reason to go out. He had all he could possibly want in well-appointed luxury. Anything he lacked, such as company, he could send out for. If you knew the numbers to ring, and Speight had them on speed dial, anything or anyone could be delivered, for an exorbitant fee of course. For a thoroughly miserable bastard Speight was a happy man. He was not expecting this particular visitor at this time of night though.

3

Noblesse oblige

"Who is Mr Rainbow? I am not Mr Rainbow. We are all Mr Rainbow. One is all and all is one!"

Piers Prideaux swore involuntarily. For the hundredth time he wished himself back in his native Cornwall. He was, instead, in Oxford, the city he had first known when, as a student at St Jude's, he had spent three glorious years reading English in the only place there was on earth to study English in the way the language and literature were designed to be studied. Those were special times and he had enjoyed every glorious moment. He had an idea who Mr Rainbow was or perhaps wasn't, but since the stalling of his academic career he would prefer to forget such matters, unless they forced their way into his consciousness. Unfortunately, that is what they had done.

This particular obscure piece of writing was to be found newly scribbled on the wall of the college chapel. Of itself this was not that interesting as a graffito, but taken in conjunction with past events at St Jude's College it took on new significance. It wasn't supposed to be like this. Graduation had been followed by a junior lecturer appointment at the college where he had spent his happiest years. Ten years tenure was supposed to be followed by promotion to senior tutor but it hadn't happened. He'd been over the circumstances in his mind a thousand times and still they made as little sense as they did in those darkest of dark days. As a consequence of his current life he was forced to combine private tutoring with occasional freelance work for the Oxford Record. It was enough, just, but at thirty-three Old Time was still a flying. Something would need to be done and soon. Writing freelance columns for the local rag helped pay the rent but little more than that. And, if nothing else it certainly helped to cement that empty feeling of failure. This wasn't the way Prideaux had planned things.

On this particular autumn morning he sat alone in Brown's. It was a hard habit to break; yet another hangover, even if these days such inconveniences did not rate on the nuclear scale that seemed to govern those of his late lamented student days. Brown's, as the café was still called, continued to serve pint mugs of tea along with the gargantuan breakfasts credited with revitalising many morning students and the occasional alcoholically challenged don. Today, however, he restricted himself to the strong smoky tea that the cafe was deservedly famous for. It was October though the students weren't properly back yet so the cafe was preternaturally quiet. It gave him time to think.

And what he thought was this. His current conundrum bore the hallmarks of his nemesis. Prideaux always thought of Dr Sebastian Slope in these terms. Dr Sebastian Slope, ex-Master of St Jude's and the man who had, with one admittedly Machiavellian plan, put paid to his burgeoning academic career. The man who had led him to the brink of prison as a side effect of his successful scheme to scupper a career to which he had dedicated his life. The man who was possibly one of the Spriggans, a secret organisation that made the Freemasons look like the Pony Club. The man who... he stopped himself, muttering, "that way madness lies" half under his breath.

The quotation in the college chapel reeked of Slope. There was the echo of cleverness. A suggestion of learning and a quotation from...? Where the hell was it from? Obviously it was Victorian. It was definitely

Fanny Ratchford, but which of her novels? The answer would be buried here in Oxford somewhere. But the answer to what? There was no sign of a question yet, but when Slope was around it wouldn't take long. This was personal. Slope would know that even in this city of academics not one in a hundred would recognise the quotation. He would know that Prideaux would spot it straight away though. The ex-Master of St Jude's was back and about to make the world of Piers Prideaux a very dark place for the second time in his life. He shuddered at the prospect as he left his favourite café, heading for his favourite pub. Prideaux left Brown's and walked past the rows of bicycles as he headed for The King's Arms in Holywell Street. This was going to take more than strong tea. He needed something stronger and someone who would understand. He needed to talk to Billy Bones.

Prideaux's oldest friend Bones was at his usual station. Elbows on the bar, sitting on a stool that much like him had seen better days. Receding hair and a receding fortune had marooned William Radleigh de Beaune, third Earl of Mount Charles, among the flotsam and jetsam of the public bar of the King's Arms. His attraction for Prideaux was partly that they had been students together at St Jude's, wholly because he had a mind like a steel trap together with a photographic memory, but mostly because he was Cornish. He would understand. Inexplicably for a scion of one of Cornwall's oldest families with roots going back before the Conqueror, de Beaune had no trace of the clotted cream accent of one of Britain's oldest Celtic outposts.

"Slope is back," said Prideaux.

"And a good Oxford morning to you," replied Bones turning to face his friend. "The bastard is back and you know what that means."

"I do," said Bones in a lazy drawl. "I'm going to have to listen to you banging on until the crack of doom."

"That's not what I wanted to hear," replied an obviously needled Prideaux as, picking up his pint of Tribute, he moved to the back of the bar and sat at some distance from his best friend.

The two knew each other's moods far too well for such a trivial irritation to disturb the air between then for long. And Bones knew full well that the one person able to send Prideaux into such deep despair was: Slope. He knew why too. Apart from Prideaux and Slope he was probably the only one who did. As he made his way to his friend's table he heard Prideaux muttering over and over, "Who is Mr Rainbow? I am not Mr Rainbow."

"Ratchford. Fanny Ratchford if it helps old chap," said Bones as he sat down opposite an increasingly agitated Prideaux.

"I know that you clown. If you can't be more helpful than that then go and drink in the lounge with the rest of the lizards."

"That's what I love about you Piers old friend, your sunny disposition."

With a look that could have cracked granite Prideaux turned back to the notebook in which he was scribbling, and scribbled as if his life depended on something being revealed.

"It was her second novel, The Way of the Spriggan."

"Brilliant. So you're not a total drain on the state then, matey."

"Thanks very much."

"You're fortunate I even speak to a commoner like you Piers. In any case why has this little gobbet of info cheered you up, miserable sod?"

"Because, my little aristo poseur, it may be a clue. I don't suppose you happen to have a copy?"

"My dear Piers, I have this month's copy of Horse & Hound and the latest copy of Debrett's. I may even be able to find you a dusty old Crockford's. But why in the name of the Great Gatsby would I have a copy of some antediluvian ravings by a frowsy, frustrated feminist?"

"You are lovely, Bones. A scruffy unreconstructed old philistine but it's all right. I still love you."

"Can't you borrow a copy from the Bod?"

"Sometimes your ignorance is quite chilling," smiled Prideaux. "If Charles the First couldn't borrow a book from the Bodleian, and he couldn't, how the hell do you think I'm going to get on?"

"Not too well since you mention it, I suppose. Well go and buy a copy then. If there is one thing Oxford is not short of it is books and bookshops. Better still why not nick a copy as you always did. You'll find it's a lot cheaper that way, only for God's sake don't get caught, that would be too embarrassing for words."

4

Dreaming spires
and fish & chips

The equilibrium had been re-established between the two as they wandered out of their favourite pub and headed up the Broad towards Blackwell's. It was a short walk interrupted by the regulation quick pop, as Prideaux had expected. Popping into The White Horse, a tiny pub sandwiched between the two Broad Street entrances to Blackwell's Bookshop, was compulsory whenever the two found themselves on the Broad. A single bar pub with a well-deserved reputation for sublime fish and chips and better still good ale. The White Horse took its responsibilities seriously; the pub provided a haven from the bustle of the Broad at midday. Certainly it was not a pub to be missed on any visit to Blackwell's, or anywhere else on the Broad for that matter.

The single long bar was quiet. A couple of regular drinkers at the bar nodded to Prideaux and Bones as they stepped into the warmth and dark. There were a couple of Japanese tourists drawn by the lure of Morse and the Oxford Murders snapping away with miniature cameras, but that would be the case at any time. Framed photographs of the stars of Morse adorned the walls. It was a pub with the sort of atmosphere that centuries of regular use created rather than designers with inflated budgets and even more inflated egos. In the White Horse, possibly the smallest pub in Oxford, you could forget anything that needed to be forgotten, and you could do it now just as effectively as seekers after oblivion before you would have done it in earlier centuries. It was simply a bar where atmosphere took on the modern upstart now called ambience and gave it a right good kicking. The secret of the place was good ale and a fine dark atmosphere and that indefinable something. The two men ordered pints of Tribute, a fine Cornish draught ale from the St Austell brewery, from Gary the barman and settled into their customary window seat.

"Right then," my cheerless little Cornishman, "wass on? As the boys say down home."

"First of all," mused Prideaux "we need a copy of The Way of the Spriggan, and then we need to put some serious thought into what the bastard might be up to. This is going to need some real headwork and looks to me a four-pint problem. It's not even a proper riddle. Who the hell is Mr Rainbow? And why has Slope surfaced after all these years?"

"Well my Beamish boy, you order us up a couple of plates of steaming fish and chips from Gary, and by the way don't forget the curried mushy peas with mine, and I'll bimble next door to see if I can liberate a copy of Ratchford's book for the greater good."

Bones was as good as his word and in two shakes of a don's gown he was back perspiring and curiously out of breath.

"Had to make a rather sharp exit stage left," he gasped, plunging rather heavily back into his favourite seat, narrowly avoiding sending chips, fish and cutlery flying.

"Possibly not as fit or swift as I was."

"You were never as fit or swift as you were, Bonesie old chap; too much ale and too little exercise, my idle friend."

Finally, the two settled and contented munching sounds were more or less all that issued from the corner for some considerable time. When two plates of the finest fish and chips in Oxford had been licked clean and Gary had brought over another couple of pints of Tribute the headwork could begin.

"Ratchford's second novel," intoned Prideaux in the voice he used when talking to one of the adult groups he occasionally lectured to at the FE College on Oxpens Road, "deals with the Spriggans, a Cornish secret society with links to smuggling and wrecking. Ratchford was what we now call a feminist who was from a privileged background and knew a hell of a lot about what was supposed to be a very secret society. Her level of knowledge was especially strange since the society didn't admit or even acknowledge women. It was usually run by the local squire and you can bet there'd be a mad vicar in there somewhere."

"Don't forget the publican," interrupted Bones.

"Trust you to think of that, Bones. But you're quite right. Everyone knows Jamaica Inn. And the unholy trinity did tend to comprise the vicar, the squire and the publican. Du Maurier knew that and so I suspect did most of her readers. The Cornish ones amongst them would have known for sure. You must remember the Queen's Head we used to frequent in St Austell when we were young lads about town. In those careless days before we became educated."

A blissful smile came over the face of William Radleigh de Beaune. "Ah! Yes. I've lived and died a time or two in that pub. And I do remember it all, especially the underground passage that went from the pub under the town square and came up in the crypt of the Parish Church before going all the way down to the beach. Pretty obvious who was behind that rather obvious attempt at outwitting the bastards from the Revenue. Remember the old cry, do ye? Copper gone, fish gone, clay gone: back to wrecking boys. That's where Cornwall is these days. It'll be a bloody theme park before long."

It was Prideaux who dragged them both back from

dreams of Trelawney, Joseph Angove and other Cornish heroes.

"Let's deal with the matter in hand before drifting off into any pipe dreams, Bones old pal. We got as far as the Spriggans in Ratchford's novel. Now what do they have to do with Slope and this business with Mr Rainbow?"

"I think I can help you there," said Bones in reply. "I was talking to old Petroc in The King's last night. You remember him, Piers. He used to hold the Chair of Celtic Studies at the old alma mater. The college kept him on as a source of amusement rather than anything else until his retirement. Since then he's been a bloody nuisance, roaming around some of Oxford's best pubs and rattling on about the Celtic Twilight to anyone who'll listen and more than a few who won't. As it happens he was in last night and on his fourth large claret when he plucked me by the sleeve and started burbling in my ear. He really is a disgusting old goat. But he does know more than most about Celtic history and particularly Celtic secret societies. One thing of particular interest he did say though, Piers, involved you. He is aware that you have taken an interest in the Mr Rainbow graffito in the chapel. One of his old drinking pals from the college council had tipped him the wink that Slope might be considering a return to the scene of the crime so to speak. I didn't much care for his tone. It sounded more a threat if you ask me. He had that revolting smile on his face as he suggested I warn you that something uncomfortable was heading in your direction. I think he was implying that if you had any sense you would be finding somewhere else to be. You know him, it was if he was lecturing me and for once enjoying it hugely. Bottom line is, old chap, it appears that Slope might well be heading back to Oxford. The chances of him popping in to take a look at the refurbishments in the Bodleian are I suppose pretty remote. He was treating me like a bloody undergrad but he might have been marking your card. Any way you look at it this might be time to circle the wagons, old chap."

"I hope you paid a bit more attention to putrid Petroc's lecture than you used to pay to anything other than loose women and even looser horses when you were a bloody undergrad," grinned Prideaux. "I'm not sure I remember you having attended any lectures unless they were given by that nubile female don that used to specialise in Chaucer. What was she called? Let's see. Abigail Powell wasn't it?"

"My Darling Abi. She was the academic of my dreams. She threw me over for that wimpy so called poet who used to wander round Oxford wearing a cape and spouting incomprehensible poems in Anglo Saxon. I once professed undying love to her on the steps of the Bodleian. She told me that charming as I was I was also as pissed as a priest and that I was in serious danger of being sent down, or at the very least rusticated. But I digress. According to Putrid Petroc the Spriggans were little more than a band of outlaws who terrorised the local communities while engaging in smuggling, wrecking and any other illegal activities that took their fancy. At one time they had connections with the Knights Templar but they split to establish their own organisation that had nothing to do with offering succour to pilgrims crossing Bodmin Moor. In fact they were more likely to rob and kill any of the poor bastards who wandered into their orbit. And in case you think that they weren't that tough, who do you think drove the Templar Knights from their chapel in that isolated hamlet revealingly called Temple on Bodmin Moor?"

"I thought that was one of those apocryphal tales," mused Prideaux. "I know that there was a settlement of Templars on the moor. The settlement is a hamlet these days but quite a few people have told me that there are the remains of a Templar church still visible there."

"That's probably over egging it a bit," Bones answered smiling confidently. You know I have a photographic memory, Piers. I've caught you out many a time and oft with it. I remember it well, and no man should be able to say that after a session with Petroc, but I remember plenty about his little pub lecturettes on how fascinating Bodmin Moor has been over the centuries. It was one of his best stories. There was definitely a Templar chapel sited there and it was in the hamlet of Temple. St Catherine's Church was built on the site of the Templar Chapel. Obviously the original Templar site was there for the reason that most people suppose, offering help and succour for pilgrims braving the dangers of the moor on the way to Europe. What a lot of people forget is that Cornwall has a strong connection with Christianity, particularly in its more militant forms. Some say that the Templars were gone from the site by the start of the fourteenth century and the Hospitallers briefly took over, but little is written about what happened. According to Petroc that is because the Spriggans saw what was obviously a potential money spinner and got in there before the Templars could strengthen their numbers. They then subverted the original purpose of the settlement to their own much more nefarious purposes. Absolutely typical of mankind that. Establish something worthwhile and watch some bastard come along and spoil it."

"You speak the truth, my old reactionary. I had that old cartoon in my mind of two puritans standing outside a house about to go for a stroll. I believe the caption went, 'What a beautiful day, let's go and spoil it for some poor bastard.' Such a thought leads me inexorably on to thinking of the mess successive governments have made of the National Health Service, one of the few institutions this country can feel justly proud of."

"Now Piers, you are sailing desperately close to the reefs of politics. Do not break our longstanding agreement that politics should never be allowed to throw its dark shadow over our friendship. Instead let us focus on the task in hand." Prideaux nodded his agreement in the knowledge that after all these years he could still pull his best friend's wires at the drop of a hat. But he also knew such joys were for another time.

5

The call of the sea

"Well Bones, you've given a fascinating insight into Cornish history but it doesn't get us any nearer working out what Slope is up to so I can't see where it is likely to help us."

"That is where you are wrong, my Beamish boy. Petroc went on to explain that the Spriggans as he referred to them had devised a complete new identity, ritual and all the paraphernalia that goes with secret societies. And, get this, their leader is always called Mr Rainbow. He dresses in highly coloured clothes; all the colours of the rainbow in fact. All the foot soldiers dress completely in black, which is why they are sometimes known by their full title in Cornish of the Spriggans Dhu, in English the Black Spriggans. Apparently their meetings always begin with a chant from the floor that goes, 'Who is Mr Rainbow?' The correct reply from the leader is then, 'I am not Mr Rainbow'. And all the rest of the one for all and all for one cant that goes with it. Bloody load of old nonsense if you ask me. But one thing Petroc did say, this society still exists and they are not very nice people to get on the wrong side of. He reckons the graffito was a warning that Slope, who Petroc feels pretty sure is the leader, is back and up to his old tricks or possibly something even worse."

Bones leaned back and looked at his friend. As he did so Prideaux's phone began beeping an approximation of Theme From The 3rd Movement Of Sinister Footwear from Frank Zappa's album You Are What You Is. Bones hated mobile phones marginally more than he hated the music of Frank Zappa. Prideaux was a devotee of both and this led to some dissension between the old friends.

"Turn that bloody thing off, will you. Is it not possible to have a conversation these days without one of those bloody things bleeping away? And as for that damned music couldn't you get a ring tone or something? At least you might consider something with a bit of class. Something from Beethoven, Bach or Mozart might soften the blow a little. Well answer the bloody thing or we'll be here for an eternity."

Prideaux looked at his old friend with some disgust but did as he suggested. What had preceded the phone call had been nothing more than the regular banter between longstanding friends. Close relationships are often cemented by such behaviour. Between these two, things rarely became serious. Prideaux's face suddenly lost its healthy colour as he listened to the voice on the phone. Bones knew instantly that this was something serious. There were only two emotions that ever made Prideaux lose his colour. One was anger, the second was fear. This was definitely something that had triggered the second emotion.

"I think that the something worse may be murder. That was Mike down at the Record. His source down at the police station in St Aldate's has tipped him the wink that Petroc Trethewey has been pulled from the river at Parson's Pleasure. He was naked as is to be expected at that point on the river. Naked that is except for a rainbow bandana covering his eyes, and his ears have been neatly sliced off."

Bones looked at his friend in disbelief. "If I remember the lesson according to Petroc that very thing is the traditional punishment for an insider who is considered to have betrayed the society. Putrid Petroc must have been a Spriggan."

The silence between them spoke volumes. Both men were now afraid. Talk of violence always frightened

Bones. He was really an unreconstructed old hippy who abhorred violence in all its manifestations. And the thought of the naked corpse of a man who was repulsive enough when clothed and alive really rattled him. For Prideaux it was a relief. He had been harbouring the vague idea for some time that his obsession with Slope had led even those closest to him to suppose that he was losing touch with reality. Now that it was clear that Slope was back it was going to be much easier to get those who mattered onside. Of course, the downside of all this was that it looked very much as if Slope had escalated from being a fraud, cheat and liar to the heady heights of murder. If he was behind the murder of Petroc, and as yet there was no proof of this, then the odds were that Prideaux himself would be somewhere on his to do list. As sure as decrepit old dons and vicars bathed naked at Parson's Pleasure the trail would lead back to the original unpleasantness between Slope and Prideaux.

It would mean going back to a very unhappy time and uncovering things that Prideaux had spent a lot of money on booze to drown. But it was the only way. First he would have to cheer up a rattled Billy Bones.

"Now look Bonesie. It seems obvious that Slope is back in Oxford. It also seems that he is mixed up in some way with the murder of Petroc. Now that may be nothing to do with me. On the other hand it may be that he was killed because he was too loose tongued. There couldn't have been a pub in Oxford where he hadn't spent hours spouting about the Spriggans and their history. Might have been enough to get him killed."

"Come on Piers, you don't really believe that. If Slope is back and, the way it looks, in murderous mood, you will be a target at some time or other. Don't forget the threats he made at the time. He is not a man to give up lightly, but he is one who really believes in enjoying his vengeance cold. He always said he would come after you at some time and I think you would be foolish to ignore the possibility. "Sounds very much to me like vengeance is mine sayeth the Slope. And let us not forget he seems to be the leader of a murderous bunch. They may be hiding behind middle class respectability these days but remember what they came from. Good God man! Back in Cornwall even in the eighteenth century some of them were cannibals. "Remember that cave on Bodmin moor that was excavated when they were trying to find out whether there was ever a Roman settlement there? They found any number of bones scattered around the cave system and most of them were human."

"Carbon dating pinpointed them to the eighteenth century if I recall correctly, and forensic evidence showed that the bodies had been cannibalised. The Spriggans simply used to waylay unwary travellers, befriend them then hit them over the head and butcher them. They even found an icehouse constructed in one of the caves so that they could preserve their human meat throughout the year. I'm sure that short story The Last Cornish Giant must have been based on folk memories of the Spriggans. I can't remember the author though," said Piers.

"I'm pretty sure that the reason nobody says much to their detriment is the cracking job that Ratchford did in romanticising them in her novels. These days people seem to think that pirates were a jolly set of fellows when in truth they were thugs and murderers. Ratchford turned a bunch of murdering savages into folk heroes. If you ask me she probably didn't even write the books. It's probable that they were written by the Mr Rainbow of the time using a female name as a cover," scoffed Bones.

"That would be a lovely irony for the Victorians now wouldn't it, a male novelist masquerading as a woman. Only one thing to do: back to the old country, old friend. We need to do some research, and Cornwall is the place to do it."

"That gets my vote, Piers. A tactical disappearance which will put some distance between us and Slope, could be what the doctor ordered."

"The more we know of the Spriggans, Bonesie, the more we can work out what is going on and what part Slope has in it all. We can stay at my cousin's cottage on the moor. With any luck we should be able to work out what the odds are of my corpse floating around in the Cherwell, and scaring the old dears when they're parading in the buff. I'm OK to shoot off for a few days. I've more or less completed my column for the Record. I can email it in as well from the moor as I can from north Oxford and I'd be mightily amazed if you had anything pressing to keep you here."

"You wound me sorely, Piers. Of course there is much to keep me in the city of dreaming spires and gargoyles. I've taken rather a shine to that new barmaid in the King's. She's Swedish I understand."

"She's also young enough to be your daughter, you old pervert."

"Shame on you Piers, a small touch of the green-eyed monster raising its ugly head, perhaps? Besides she has the capacity to make an old man very happy, and it would be a shame to waste such a talent. I have promised to share with her the source of all my wisdom for the vanishingly small price of getting my hand inside her knickers. And before you start she is twenty three years old and a woman of the world. But alright then, since it's you I'll make the effort. Couldn't trust you out on your own in any case. And I did promise your mother I'd look after you. You must admit I have done my absolute best to keep you out of trouble over the years."

"Bones my old fruit pie I could not fault you in your capacity of my officially appointed mother hen. You have looked after me with more dedication than my mother ever did. Her theory was that if I was with you then I could not get into too much trouble. You always had a nose for trouble and could talk sense into me when no one else can. I remember that time in Lostwithiel when I agreed to be the bouncer for the night as a favour to old Jack. I didn't know that he had banned the local young farmers the previous week. I suppose I shouldn't have talked tough when they turned up to wreck the joint in the return fixture. But you and your silver tongue got me out of a real spot. That was a piece of genius, your reminding that ugly giant who was stirring it all up that his farm just happened to be on your family's land. He went from roaring tiger to pussycat in fifteen seconds. And I've never forgotten the countless times you dragged me home to the family pile to sleep in one of the holiday cottages. My mother used to tell everybody I was spending the night as a guest up at the great house. She never knew that the pair of us were as pissed as pythons. My mother swore blind that I never touched strong drink until I was seduced by those public school wallahs in Oxford. I thank you for it all, old friend."

"It has been an honour and a pleasure to act as unpaid wet nurse to you, Piers, but there is a price to be paid. An old atheist like you should be aware that nothing is for nothing. I've always known that every man has his price, and this is mine. I'm happy to come with you but when the working day is done this particular old aristo wants to have fun. By which I mean in this case some substantial visits to some of the best pubs in the world. As you well know Cornwall is full of them, and I think on this trip we'll start with The Blisland Inn. King Buddha is a man who knows his beer and if there is a better pub on the planet than The Blisland Inn then I haven't been there. I'm quite happy to pay my way, but now I think about it a week of alcoholic and gustatory heaven might set me up for a cold wet Oxford winter. It gets into the pipes you know," Bones coughed in a deliberately exaggerated fashion.

"That's enough of the amateur dramatics, Bonesie. It's a deal. I'll ring my cousin Denzil tonight and tell him we're coming. I've half an idea that he's due to fly out to his trullo in Puglia around now. It doesn't matter if he is away because he always leaves a key with Bert Schirtz in the cottage at the end of the lane. I haven't seen him for a while but he's always said if I'm ever back in the old country I can always stay at his place. Fortunately he lives in the perfect spot for us. There's a real opportunity for a bit of exercise and some first class food and drink."

The two had more or less exhausted the evening and left together, crossing the Broad to walk along Turl Street to the High where they turned right, heading towards Carfax. They turned left into St Aldate's and on to Christ Church before parting ways. Bones headed towards Folly Bridge and the apartment he had lived in almost since his student days. Prideaux walked past Tom Tower and turned right along Pembroke Street heading home to his top floor flat.

Putting his key in the lock he put his shoulder to a door that stuck fast every year at around this season. It was sticking faster than usual and he stepped back into the street to give himself better purchase. It was dark and light rain was falling, forming halos around the street lights. He couldn't be sure but out of the very corner of his eye he was half conscious of a figure slipping down Beef Lane. Suddenly the door gave and as often happened Prideaux found himself in a heap on the floor among the flyers advertising fast food shops, college flyers advertising chamber music, bills and bank statements. Getting to his feet he was aware of one of the ubiquitous padded bags used to deliver all sorts of paraphernalia these days. Picking it up he saw it was addressed to him. Tucking the packet under his arm he made his weary way up four flights of stairs to his flat.

Opening the door he walked in, placing the envelope on the hall table. He would open it later. He walked through to the bedroom, looking out as he pulled the curtains across. Again he had that sense of being watched though by now the rain had increased, making it difficult to be sure. Someone was watching from across the narrow street. It must be his imagination. All this talk of Slope had unnerved him. Some might say unmanned him. He stumbled to the bed and managed to get the top part of his body onto the duvet. Gradually he slipped until his knees reached the floor and he found himself in a position of prayer. It was not prayer that filled his head but an entire swirling panorama of noise and colour.

It continued to fill his head until exhausted, still in the kneeling position he fell into a sleep with his head on his folded arms. Prideaux slept in that position until cramp and cold woke him around an hour later. Starting awake he took some time to compose himself. The alcohol still governed his confused state of mind. He had something he needed to think about but struggled to remember what. He remembered the package. But what had he done with it? It was another half an hour before he remembered that he had left it on the hall table. He managed to stagger through from the bedroom and retrieve the package. In his still drunken state he managed to rip the package open using his teeth. Uncoordinated he was unable to catch the two human ears that fell from the package. He could not remember having ordered anything. And if he had then what the hell had he ordered? In the brief glance he had managed before the contents of the parcel had fallen to the floor he vaguely registered that they seemed to be ears. What would he do with ears? Unless his gourmet pal over at Woodstock had sent him some new delicacy. He knew that Anton had a penchant for pigs' ears. Surely they were to small for that. Unless perhaps they were piglets' ears. Prideaux was no gourmet but with a belly still making swooshing noises because of its alcoholic load that was as far as he could reason. He dropped to all fours. There was one. It had dropped near the hall table. He grasped at it pushing it further and further under the heavy table. 'Fuck it,' he exploded. 'Where's that other bastard?' He rolled over onto his back. Turning his head he realised that something soft was resting against his cheek. 'Got you, you little bastard.' This time he made a successful grab for the ear. 'Better give it a go, I suppose,' he reasoned. 'I've always been a fan of pork scratchings.' Prideaux bit into the gristle. 'Fuck that for a game of soldiers' he thought as he realised that the object was nobody's idea of a late night gourmet snack. 'These chefs have bloody funny ideas about food, not even cooked for fuck's sake' he mouthed as he put the offending article back into the envelope as he staggered to his feet.

He crabbed his way back into the bedroom. Dropping the envelope on the bedside table he measured his length on the bed. Piers Prideaux was asleep as his head hit the pillow. It had been a difficult day. The following day would prove even more difficult as he would spend most of the morning trying to explain to Oxfordshire's finest why he had turned up at the station with two human ears, one of which he had taken a nibble out of the previous evening.

6

Something wicked
this way comes

Slope lifted the old-fashioned cast iron knocker, giving a peremptory knock. Conrad Speight was engaged in his second favourite occupation, viewing porn on the internet. Cursing, he did himself up and limped red faced to the door. One never knew. Though expecting nobody you just never knew. Slope was definitely not what he was expecting which is why he had called. He had intended to catch Speight unawares, in the college bar perhaps, but on mature reflection better still to beard the old bastard in his den. And it would keep one more possible weak link out of the chain.

Opening the door Speight expressed no surprise as Slope swept in without a word. Pushing his way past in the narrow hallway he settled himself in Speight's rather small living room rather grandly named the drawing room. Wearily, Speight closed and double locked his front door. He knew no one left the Spriggans unless it was horizontally and neatly wrapped around by a pine box, and he already knew what had happened to Petroc. He had his own sources and had been at the river when the corpse was pulled out. His description of the event amused Slope mildly but he was not a man to be distracted easily. The scene had unnerved him but anyone acquainted with Slope knew what he was capable of. They also serve who try to ignore the more powerful imperative and run like hell, he thought to himself as he made a half-hearted attempt at looking pleased to see the fearsome Slope.

"You can take that fatuous smile off your face Speight," barked Slope. "You are no more pleased to see me than I am to see you but there is work to do and this is your part of it." Slope handed him the sealed letter. "Don't open it now. It contains a summary of developments since I was forced to leave this city of dreaming drunks. It is of necessity fairly brief as HMP is not that keen on encouraging research unless it is likely to lead to the discovery of clever ways to get stoned on everyday cleaning materials, anything to keep the underclass torpid. You must put flesh on the bones so that I can nail the bastard Prideaux. And don't expect any arcane philosophical justification. I hate the bastard and I want him to suffer and to hell with the consequences. Anybody not with me is against me and that includes you, you pathetic little creep."

Speight knew better than to argue with Slope. He was a man with a terrifying certainty that he was right. He really had no moral compass at all. If he had possessed one it would surely have been set on west, towards the direction of the country that had spawned the bastard Prideaux. Prideaux, the only man with the guts to defy him, would have to pay. Slope did not regard Prideaux as his equal. In truth he did not rate many as his equal, which was all part of the developing megalomania that meant disaster for so many. But for a man such as Prideaux to have stood against him was simply not acceptable.

The only man to successfully defy Slope was blissfully unaware that the man he regarded as his nemesis was currently plotting his demise. Sitting comfortably in the public bar of The Blisland Inn he was draining his second pint of the Cat's Pyjamas, at 6% a fairly powerful real ale from the fledgling Kilhallon Micro Brewery.

"What think you of this?"

The question was, of course, addressed to comrade in

arms Billy Bones who was finishing his third pint of Old Tomkins, an even more powerful brew from the same brewery. He sat on the old wooden settle with a beatific and in truth slightly moronic crooked grin on his crooked face. He had casually mentioned the story surrounding the packaged ears and the perplexed response he had faced when trying to explain matters to the local police.

"No Piers, I think you are going to have to backtrack there a fair way and tell me it again. I'm as astonished as an asthmatic antelope. Ears, you say old chap, what, human ears? What did the polis have to say?"

"If I'm honest Bonesie I'd have to say that they appeared to be a tad perplexed. I took both ears into the station after I managed to dredge the missing one from under the hall table. Ghastly bloody things. I put them back into the envelope, there was no note, and bimbled off down to the polis to report the strange event. The desk sergeant was a right snarky bastard. When I started to explain you could see his face light up. Probably waited his entire career for something like this. He took the envelope from me then started into what he clearly thought was an acceptable comedy routine. 'Hello,' he started. 'What have we ear then? Hello, hello, it would seem to be two ears. This could be a job for Interpol. Looks a case of ear smuggling to me. They look matching ears. Just a minute, this one seems to have a piece nibbled out of it. We might have to refer this to the Anti Cannibalism squad.'

"The bastard went on like that for a while until he was in danger of becoming hysterical at what he thought was his cutting wit. I said, 'OK officer you've had your fun. I came in to report this because I thought it was the right thing to do. Perhaps you could get someone who will take me seriously.' He said 'Right you are sir, I'll get you DC Helps to take your report. He's a bit of a specialist in finding missing persons and reuniting them with their ears. I'll see if he's in.' Some scruffy detective constable took me through to an interview room. He could barely keep a straight face. Obviously he had been briefed by the desk sergeant. I couldn't take any more so I told him unless he took me seriously I was going straight round to the Record and giving them the story. He perked up a bit then and listened to me. Bit of a pointless exercise though. He couldn't offer anything and I didn't want to hang around any longer. Boy am I glad to be out of Oxford for a bit. Can't say I feel at ease, mind."

"Well that's a rum do, Piers, probably some new beef jerky promotion? Go and ask Denzil if he has a packet behind the bar. I'm partial to tidbits, pork scratchings, pickled eggs, pickled ears, all helps to heighten the pleasure of the amber nectar. Can it get any better than this, my old fruit pie?" added the faded aristo. "Back in the old country, beer to burn and not an emmet in sight. Lovely!"

"Let us not forget, old chum, that we are here to work not simply to drink. Tomorrow we must get over to St Blaise to get cracking on some research. I need some more information before I have a chance in hell of working out what level of alert to put the old senses on. Any more of this stuff and I shan't give a monkey's waistcoat what's going on."

The night wore on as the nascent enthusiasm wore off. Well before closing time the pair where joining the locals in beery renditions of Camborne Hill and The White Rose.

There is a moment of stillness in the downhill ride to drunkenness. It is brief and swiftly closes its doors. Experienced topers, and these two were certainly that, were keenly aware of that moment and knew how to react when that moment arrived. Always the sharper of the two, when in his cups Prideaux suddenly realised they were in a pub miles from his cousin's cottage, and had no obvious means of transport in their current state. The Blisland Inn had proved too tempting and instead of settling in at the cottage they had stopped off on the way for a livener or three. No vacancies, too drunk to drive and no prospects of a night in a warm cottage... unless. It was a long shot but Prideaux never backed anything else. Perhaps Ginny and Mark still lived in the village. They were old friends who had moved to the village years earlier. They had lost touch but were the sort of friends that would not mind old friends turning up unannounced even after a five-year silence. Not that he could remember the address of course but surely even in Cornwall a world class potter and a successful writer would not be that hard to track down.

The plan bubbled through the fog in Prideaux's mind as he lifted Bones to his feet and helped him to stagger out onto the green. "I don't suppose there's a point in asking you where Ginny and Mark live, is there Bonesie?"

"Not really," slurred his drinking partner. "At the moment I'm having difficulty remembering where I live. In any case it's all relative."

"What is?"

"Well since I don't know where we are now I don't have much idea of who or what we are looking for. Ergo, it is all relative my old fruit."

Prideaux allowed himself a smile at his friend's impeccable logic. No help from that direction then.

Prideaux pulled his overcoat more tightly around him. It was a sharp night. The moon was up and the lack of cloud cover promised frost and similar unpleasantness for the two. Strange how quickly the euphoria of drunkenness evaporates when darkness and cold have their say. This was shaping up to be a card-carrying disaster and Prideaux did not have the time or the patience to waste. He needed to sleep off the beer before getting back to the cottage and getting over to St

Blaise to begin what he had to if he was ever to achieve peace of mind.

The front door of the pub was shut and the singers had all sung their way back to cottages and the new builds that reminded the Cornish that this Celtic land had to at least admit the existence of the twenty first century. Such a pity really but the way the economy was going the entire UK would soon be back in the fourteenth century. And that would suit the Cornish just fine. Up country they would struggle. They had always had it easy. Down here they knew how to make the best of bugger all. It was in the Cornish nature. Nothing wasted, no opportunity lost and then there was always smuggling. They had invented it and every Cornish man kept a little space in his soul for the old heroes of the smuggling days. But for now Prideaux needed a bed for the night. Walking away from the green with Bones seldom more than staggering distance behind he headed for Cutpurse Alley, even now a narrow and poorly lit cobbled way. Not that it was called that anymore of course. The good councillors of Bodmin Moor had seen to that. It was now called Poplar View, even though there were no poplars for miles.

"Far too poncy a tree to withstand winter on the moor," thought Prideaux. But remembered with a smile the reasons for its earlier nomenclature.

Negotiating the kissing gate at the top of the lane took a little time. A drunken Bones making moues and ridiculous kissing noises did little to lighten the mood, then a glimpse, just a glimpse of a light through the gathering gloom. It seemed to be at the point where the lane turned. It was difficult to tell as the wind had risen and the branches of the young oaks conveyed a flickering effect.

"Shut up Bones," whispered Prideaux. "It looks as if there may be someone further down the lane. They may be able to tell us where Ginny and Mark live or even offer us a bed for the night. Equally it may be the boys out lamping in which case keep your wits about you and do your best to in no way resemble a rabbit. They have hair triggers or, if you prefer, hare triggers, on the moor and I'd hate to see my old pal in pain and leaking his lifeblood like a sieve."

The two walked on. Prideaux sharp and alert despite his earlier intake of strong ale; Bones doing that elaborate creep that actors do when trying to persuade an audience that they are walking silently and carefully. Not unlike a giant cat suffering with painful piles.

At the bend in the lane Prideaux forced Bones to rest against a fallen tree, a failed poplar no less, as he crept up the centuries old hedge to see if he could get a look at whoever was around the corner. What he saw by the poor light of one of those blue light emitting diode torches that make everything look darker went a long way towards lifting his spirits. It was a woman. She had her back to him and was wearing the obligatory Barbour topped by a headscarf. He could see no sign of the striking red hair that would have confirmed his dearest wish. But she was the right height, she had that confident walk and she carried an unbroken shotgun. Everything about her screamed Ginny, but the Ginny he remembered would never walk around in the dark with a shotgun unbroken: unless, of course, she was intent on shooting something or someone. This would need some care. Calling her name might startle her, and at any moment a pissed up Bones was likely to join the tableau, certainly provoking some form of reaction. Prideaux felt around for a pebble. Finding one he launched it over the mystery woman's head. Landing it made no more than a rustling sound and the report from the shotgun shook Prideaux enough to send him slithering down the hedge. He landed on his back and, looking up, stared straight into the light from the torch he had seen earlier.

Behind it was the woman. Pointed directly at his groin was the shotgun.

"Ginny," said Prideaux "am I pleased to see you!"

"Twat," answered the woman. "I am extremely displeased to see you. What the hell do you want at this time of night?"

"Well a cup of coffee and a bed for the night would be nice, and perhaps something similar for our mutual friend and posho Billy Bones if it's not too much trouble of course. Sort us out and I'll tell you a story."

"Well I'll give you that Piers, you always did tell a good story, and it had better be good."

"You know me kid. Remember, we'll always have Truro, and I tell you what my handsome, this particular story is better than ever and it's better than ever because it's true. Not that anyone believes it of course because it falls into that category that sniffy bastards all lump together as conspiracy theories and consequently ignore. I haven't the faintest clue who killed Lady Diana or even whether David Kelly committed suicide or was rubbed out by a shadowy government agency. This much I do know, however. The Spriggans are very much an active force and their current leader ruined my career, spoiled my life and almost drove me to suicide. I'm also fairly certain that he is now back on my trail and intent on finishing the job."

In the full spate of his relief at finding a friendly face coupled with his hatred of Slope Prideaux had failed to notice that Ginny's usually florid complexion had turned deathly white.

"You'd better follow me to the cottage" she said in a near whisper. "Oh! And wake up your oppo over there, he's snoring fit to wake the piskies. I'm seriously hoping that this is a Spriggan free area, but I'm not sure."

Prideaux knew when Ginny was being serious; he had always known. Waking his fallen comrade the two walked silently behind Ginny towards the cottage she shared with her husband Mark. Bed and sleep would probably have to wait. There was too much in the air, and if Mark didn't have a decent bottle of single malt in the cottage that would be an oversight of international proportions.

7

Old friends and shotguns

Ginny had already reached the front door of the cottage by the time the Oxford two had made the wicket gate. Opening the latch she ducked as she entered.

Prideaux watched as she disappeared into the warm darkness. Her athleticism had always attracted him even back in their student days. Back then she stood out among her peers, partly because of her height; she was six foot and a tiny bit in her stockinged feet, but also because of her flashing red hair. On student demos the figure of Ginny Williams, red hair flowing in the wind, red bandana around her neck, wearing the obligatory denim dungarees and chanting Venceremos had become an icon. She had even made the Six O'Clock News way back when the national news was something that attracted nationwide attention, even veneration. They were together then and they were good days.

"Where am I?" slurred a still confused Bones.

"You are in the good old land of Kernow, Bonesie my old Tonka Toy, or if you prefer, God's other country," slurred a less confused Prideaux. "We have passed through the country that dare not speak its name and have come to rest, temporarily, I hope, in the country of our ancestors. Well, all of yours and half of mine. Better still we are entering Guevara Cottage, the current abode of our pals from another time, Mark and Ginny Williams."

"Good God!" gasped the old toper. "How has it come to this, and do you think Mark might have a drop of single malt to bring succour to a drowning man?"

"The only thing you are drowning in, Bonesie old

trout, is booze. And have you ever known Mark, or Ginny for that matter, to be sans booze, though if you don't shift your aristocratic arse you will have given them time to hide the lot in a priest hole or a smuggler's passage. Now come on. Lean on me and let's get indoors before my cock turns into an icicle."

The two staggered on up the path for all the world like zombied bookends, pausing only to extricate themselves from the solitary hydrangea bush that obscured part of the centuries old cottage door before falling inside in an unseemly tangle.

"Plus ca change, plus c'est la meme chose," grinned Mark Leveret Williams as he surveyed the untidy heap of old friends looking up at him from the flagstone floor of his cottage.

"Jean-Baptiste Alphonse Karr, I think you'll find. Parisian born novelist known for his novels and his more than mordant wit. And a Merry Christmas to you too, Mark," gabbled Bones, now lying on his back and waggling his legs like an abandoned turtle.

"If you can manage to find your feet, please employ them for their primary purpose and deposit your good self along with the toper's toper on that fairly faded sofa over there, my good and lovely boy."

The unexpectant host was amused. It had been years since he had seen any of his old friends and these two were amongst his oldest. They were also his most difficult friends as where they appeared chaos came riding along behind, miles in front of that pale horse, with Death right up there in the saddle. Still there was never a dull moment and things were a little quiet in Cornwall at the moment. The Chuckle Brothers adopted a seated position, helped by two large crystal glasses containing generous slugs of Penderyn's finest malt. Always a rebel, Mark Williams preferred to drink whisky made in his own country than that produced in another place. The old friends smiled as they sipped the golden liquid now distilled in the tiny hamlet of Penderyn from the purest ingredients and the crystal water drawn from its own subterranean lake. After some desultory reminiscing Ginny's reappearance from an upstairs room heralded a change of pace and tone.

"Handsome as it is to see the pair of you I am assuming that there must be something you want," grinned Ginny. "I've never known either of you to visit unless there was an ulterior motive; in your case Piers, more than one. And since you have your own personal Sundance Kid in tow I am fully aware that it must touch upon the group that we all hate even more than we used to hate the Monday Club and all its evil works. And before you say anything, whatever Mark the dreamer says, all is not quiet in good old Kernow. There have been incidents here in the village and, more disturbing than that, things have been happening out on the moor."

Ginny jerked her head to indicate the general direction of the vastness of Bodmin Moor that lay off to the north.

Instead of further addling their drink impaired capacities, the two amigos sat up marginally straighter as the golden liquor coursed through their veins. Surprisingly it was Bones who spoke first. Suddenly the drunken slurring seemed replaced by much more controlled and concerned speech.

"We are here because Slope has made a reappearance in Oxford and we are unsure as to what the old bastard is up to. Of all people you will remember what happened at St Jude's. He managed to destroy quite a few lives with his foul and several ways and worst of all almost saw off my old friend Piers for good and all. Men like that do not return to the scene of the crime like dogs to their vomit. There is always a reason. You will remember that when he was sentenced for perjury he vowed vengeance on Piers and all his works. What we didn't realise at the time was the extent of his involvement with the Spriggans and the power that gave him. We thought we were dealing with a crook, embezzler and general arsehole but the truth turned out to be far worse. I for one fear for the life and good health of my favourite of all my drinking buddies. And before you start accusing me of melodrama remember there has already been a murder that is definitely the work of Slope."

None of the four believed in ghosts or spirits but at the mention of the name of the sometime Master of St Jude's an icy silence cut a swathe through the cottage. Ginny was the most affected of the four. Her face seemed to crumble as the memories flooded back in. The brightly lit cottage seemed to have dropped several notches on the dimmer switch.

"Who was it?" she stuttered. "Who died, was it someone we would know?"

"It was Putrid Petroc," answered Bones. "You remember the old soak and part time pervert that eventually landed the Chair of Celtic Studies to help keep him in claret. 'Petrus for Petroc' as the old fraud was given to yell at any given opportunity, even if he was swilling some vinegar suitable only for the industrial classes."

The four friends couldn't help but smile even though there was little enough to smile at. It was Mark's turn and through a grin he repeated words that had been spoken to the people's aristo many a time and oft.

"You really are an unreconstructed old snob, Bonesie my boy, but I suppose it is far too late for an ageing tiger to even think of changing his spots."

"Surely that should be stripes," riposted Bones.

"Look in the mirror Bill," Mark advised. "All that claret has really begun to tell its own tale. If you add in your patriotic addiction to Cornish ale then you, my boy, are on a roller coaster ride to Boot Hill, or whatever cemetery will willingly inter the bones of Billy Bones along with those of his ancestors. And before you trot it out for the millionth time, I am well aware that there are plenty of Bones in the graveyard."

"Now what's all this about Petroc, and although I hesitate to speak ill of the dead the old bugger is not really much of a loss, now is he?" Mark was well aware that Petroc was both a waste of space and of time and lacked any sympathy for him at all.

"Probably not," agreed Bones, "but that's not the point. His death is of very little importance. The manner of his death is most germane to the issue. He wasn't just murdered. God knows such things are not that uncommon in Oxford though happily murder and mayhem are not quite the regular companions that certain novelists and screenwriters would have us all believe. He was murdered in the Spriggan way, Slope is back in Oxford and those two things cannot, on this or any other inhabited planet, be regarded as coincidental"

"Bonesie, it is becoming increasingly clear that Slope is back and he means to take his revenge as he swore at the time. Poor Petroc is simply collateral damage. Friendly fire if you prefer. After all it transpires that he was one of them, even if a particularly ineffectual one. We must get to St Blaise, to Prideaux village in particular, to talk to some of those who know the way the Spriggans work. With luck we may be able to get a handle on what Slope is up to."

"Piers, nobody, least of all me, disputes that Slope is an arsehole, but until his recent return his only real crime had been incompetence and regular harassment within the confines of the groves of academe. Let us be honest, you could accuse most people in the business of such things and be pretty sure you would have a case. Then I think of the thoroughly unpleasant demise of Petroc and it seems to me that some line has been crossed and all bets are off. I could be wrong but this whole business smells to high heaven."

Seemingly exhausted by the effort Bones slumped back in the old squashy sofa, looking suddenly very tired and very old.

"We will solve nothing tonight," said an equally weary Prideaux. "Perhaps it's best if we try to get a decent night's sleep before heading off to St Blaise and Prideaux tomorrow. Should confuse a few of the locals; a Prideaux in Prideaux that is. Dad always said that all the evidence we needed to prove the village had once belonged to the family was hidden somewhere in Bodelva Church. I don't know whether anything is hidden there or whether that was simply Dad's penchant for telling tales of old Cornwall, but if any of it refers to the Spriggans then at least we have a starting point. We have to start somewhere, and that's as good as anywhere, better than many bleak places where we could waste our time and effort.

"There's a decent pub in the village if I remember correctly, so that's something to be cheerful about." Talk of alcohol and licensed premises always seemed to have the magical power of regenerating Bones, however tired and emotional he had become.

"If you don't mind sharing the spare room," interceded Ginny, conscious that the whisky decanter was not quite empty, "then you boys can go up. Mark and I will lock up down here."

8

A Shropshire lad and lass

Sir Gawain Rudyard Cornelius leaned back in his leather chair. His office door was firmly closed. Nobody came to see him without a personal invitation. The uninvited knock was a closed book to him. He expected things to be precise, in fact he insisted on it. His office was a testament to this character trait. His security clearance was so high that senior staff in other departments had never heard of it. Even his title was an official secret. This was how Cornelius liked it. He preferred the shadows to the limelight. It had always been his way. He wore his cleverness lightly but no one ever doubted the power of his intellect. He came from a farming family in Shropshire. The family was comfortable and were real farmers rather than those hobby farmers that blighted the land these days. He knew from his earliest days how hard the work involved in running even a small farm could be. Generations of his family had farmed the land but there was never a suggestion that he would follow his father into farming. His older brother Lemuel was marked out for that role. In any case he had seen the dirt and pain involved with trying to run a profitable farming business. The second son was far too fastidious to even contemplate a life of backbreaking work and the constant smell of manure. This was no horny handed son of toil. From his earliest days he had mapped out a route that would avoid anything smacking of hard physical work in favour of a life of the intellect. He had set out his stall and it wasn't up for discussion.

Cornelius was a voracious reader. He consumed anything and everything as he worked to develop a persona that chimed with his own idea of self. It was a stance that ensured regular beatings from sons and even daughters of the local farming community. Through some mysterious means he avoided the Shropshire burr of his contemporaries. His brother Lemuel, a mere four years his senior was, his speech patterns told the story, of the countryside. Gawain was most definitely not. Standing out as different in any part of society is always fraught with threats. Many of those choosing this path never find any form of fulfilment. Cornelius was made of sterner stuff. Early beatings simply toughened him. He never complained yet somehow he always ensured his revenge on whoever had decided he would make a good punch bag. The revenge was always proportionate and the victim never saw it coming. It was as if he had a guardian angel and gradually such attacks tailed off. The local community simply regarded him as a trifle odd. He made no attempt to correct that impression. It meant that he had time to think, to consider and to create the persona he thought appropriate.

There was one exception to his rule of ignoring the local children and that was in his toleration of a young girl who followed him everywhere. Lola Cutler was bright and she was pretty. She also held the local boys in her thrall. Growing up she defied every accepted piece of wisdom about what a girl should be. For a start she loathed the colour pink with a fanatical zeal. That was evident even before she reached the difficult teenage years. She appealed to Cornelius because she was her own person from the outset. She could run faster than any of the boys in this quiet part of rural Shropshire. She was better at climbing trees, could spit further and was banned from playing football with them because of the focused viciousness of her two footed tackles. She hated all boy bands with an equal passion and would not even acknowledge the existence of bands full of females claiming to advance the cause of feminism through banal pop music. And this is probably where the two moved into a joint orbit. Boy and girl shared a joint appreciation of, and determined attachment to, jazz and blues. If anything more was designed to separate them from their peers then this enthusiasm certainly did the trick. Between them they began to amass an impressive collection of vinyl that began with blues and spilled over into jazz. There were some favourites where the line between the two genres blurred but essentially the music qualified for their approval if it sounded 'real'. It was a shared single word mantra and they used it to exclude any wannabee friend who sensed rather than saw an enviable cool in the individuals and an equal but indefinable relationship between the two.

As they grew older the relationship became closer. In their early teens local wisdom decreed that it had already assumed a sexual dimension. There was certainly some form of connection that some described as electricity. Since most of their waking hours were spent together that would have seemed a reasonable assumption. It would, however, have been entirely incorrect. The relationship was that rarest of things, one based on absolute mutual respect. They enjoyed the same things, they loathed the same things. They loved the outdoors, ranging for hours over the Long Mynd until darkness fell. They loved small claustrophobic places where they could play their records for hours without interruption. This was easily done at Lola's house, not so at Cornelius's family farm where he would be expected to join in with exciting pastimes such as sheep dipping and ditch digging, occupations he deemed below him at the best of times. Nothing intruded when the two met at the modern detached house where Lola lived. The daughter of an absentee father who had once claimed to be a roadie with the Shivering Biscuits and an alcoholic mother,

Lola did more or less what she wanted. Her upbringing certainly accounted for her independence since she had managed to make it to her teens with very little parental support.

As well as music aficionados they were collectors. Because money was uncertain they pooled what they had and over time built an impressive collection of blues and jazz. They were an unusual pair even in this respect as, unlike many more fickle friends of music, they remained loyal to vinyl. Lola's admittedly spacious room held gems from Mississippi John Hurt, Leadbelly, Lightnin' Hopkins, John Lee Hooker, Howlin' Wolf, Lightnin' Slim, The Legendary Son House, Billie Holiday, Etta James, Big Mama Thornton, Ella Fitzgerald, Nina Simone and Little Walter. It was a collectors' paradise and nobody, but nobody was allowed to touch any of it, much less play it.

The two carried on in this vein until it became obvious that Cornelius was intending to apply for a university place. Two years older than Lola he had made no secret of his wish to study politics at Oxford. His performance at Ludlow Grammar had already established him as an ideal candidate. He had a quick mind, was a voracious reader and had complete confidence in his ability. Following interview he was offered a place at Maundering College, Oxford to read PPE. This looked as if the inseparables would finally need to accept that nothing is forever. As always confounding received opinion the two seemed to take the change in their stride. No hysteria, no tearful farewells. One day Cornelius was there, the following day he had packed his trunk in time honoured tradition and toddled off to the dreaming spires he had dreamed of for so many years. They kept in touch from the Michaelmas Term and onwards yet never managed to arrange to meet up. In keeping with their singular personalities contact was maintained through the written word. Cornelius was a confirmed writer of letters. He enjoyed nothing better than settling at his desk with his favourite Visconti fountain pen in hand and some hand finished writing paper. There was nothing that strange about eschewing the advance of digital development at Oxford and he no longer stood out in the way he had in Shropshire. Oxford is probably the last bastion where eccentricity is more highly regarded than normality. So the relationship prospered at a distance. New vinyl acquisitions were discussed at length. And even when Lola took up her place at Cambridge to read Classics nothing much changed.

It was in the Hilary Term of his second year that some indication of the sly old dog changing was waiting around the corner. Since arriving at college Cornelius had kept mainly to himself. He was not by nature a joiner and the word loner could have been invented to describe him. He had shown no interest in any of the bright young female things that adorned the Broad and the High, and general consensus held that this country boy was certainly gay. As always attempts at pigeonholing Cornelius were doomed to fail. Out of the blue he began to leave his rooms more regularly and began to be seen in some of the more popular student haunts. At these times he was frequently to be found in the company of some of the most vibrant and attractive undergrads from several of the colleges. He began to develop a reputation as a brilliant conversationalist and an ideal dinner companion. The accolades began to mount until he became one of the most sought after companions anywhere in this very competitive university town. Gradually the tie between Lola and Cornelius began to weaken. They wrote to each other, phoned each other and saw each other less regularly. He was entering a new stage and so was she.

9

Be careful what you wish for

In a fifteenth century building near Oxford's Folly Bridge an opportunist sat dreaming in a leather club chair as he looked out of his window at the enticing prospect of Christ Church Gardens and the Tom Tower. Despite the incessant rain of this wettest of summers this was a prospect that always pleased. This particular opportunist was cashing in on the gullibility of the general public when it came to his more than dubious counselling skills. He was clever enough to realise that without certainty in their lives, however it was provided, enough people were looking for reassurances to suggest there was a profitable living to be had. It wasn't a particularly good living but then Peter Fisher wasn't a particularly good man. A poor psychology degree from a redbrick had led to the usual stint in advertising and marketing in the sink that Johnson called the "Great Wen" before a return to his native Oxford trailing a failed marriage and a damaged ego between his skinny legs.

He was an unprepossessing individual; now balding and with bad teeth his prospects seemed poor. He had never mixed easily and had no school or other friends that he was still in contact with. Women did not find him appealing and the only sort of sex available to him was the type that came as part of a cash contract. Life did not stretch out before him like a golden road to Samarkand or any sort of fulfilment. It was much more an unmade road that would gradually run out in the boondocks, or possibly the road to hell. He had considered suicide but didn't have the courage or imagination to carry such a project out. This last effort to create a sustainable business was certainly his final hope.

Like many good ideas it had begun in the pub. Not as is often the case as the result of the input of a group of friends or business partners. This Peter Fisher walked alone, but with the inspiration of a good strong pint of Sharp's one evening in the garden of a favourite Oxford pub 'The Head of the River' in the shadow of Folly Bridge it hit him. Sheltered under the protective awning with a table to himself as the drizzle came down Fisher watched the ducks as they came scooting under the bridge far quicker than they had any intention of travelling. The pace of the river at that point was frighteningly quick and Fisher secretly hoped that one of them would crash into the stern of one of the moored boats. He was always amazed by the control they could apply when required. It looked as if they were fitted with their own outboards and the thought amused him. What amused him more was the thought that he could turn his admittedly basic knowledge of psychology into a means of earning an easy living. And so it had proved; once he had added a few part time counselling courses to his degree he was in business. Well not quite. It took a piece of luck in landing what quickly became his consulting rooms in a striking fifteenth-century building in St Aldate's. It was on a short lease and more than he could really afford but the office/consulting rooms gave the right impression. Once he had covered his walls with certificates both real and faked he felt free to open for business.

At first it went reasonably well, even allowing him to employ a receptionist; a plump young woman from the flat Oxfordshire countryside who had managed to slim down her rounded vowels while simultaneously plumping up her already generous figure. Things looked set fair for the latest twister and bullshit pedlar to beset the world of counselling. Given his less than secure grasp on the business of advising those with genuine problems, it could not be long before disaster struck. And strike it duly did with damaging effect. And as a result it was not long before business began to tail off. A messy suicide following a course of fifteen counselling sessions with the newly titled Dr Peter Fisher – he had bought the doctorate – had made a hefty dent in his credibility. Gossip followed and Oxford is a small city so it spread quickly and detrimentally. The student involved had been one of Prideaux's post graduates. Fisher had sought his help in deflecting some of the opprobrium that had deservedly come his way. He had no right to ask but Prideaux was famous for his support of the halt and the lame. In keeping with what many would see as a weakness of character Prideaux had done his best to help out a man who had been an acquaintance in his younger years. His better judgement had whispered to him that he should not touch Fisher with a bargepole. In the event he offered a shoulder to cry on and sufficient support to help Fisher through a self-inflicted crisis. It was more than he deserved and the net result had left Prideaux saddled with a monthly lads' night out that had blighted his social life for far too long. Fisher was something of a pariah at the time but his regular presence around the taverns of the ancient city offered him a form of redemption. His regular nights out with Prideaux were the highlight of a dismal life paved with setbacks and disappointments. But for once in his crabbed and confined life good news had arrived, the letter lying open on his desk was the proof of this. It informed the would-be mind doctor that his consulting rooms were to be graced by a visit from an important personage.

"This is it," thought Fisher. "Get this right and I could be set for life. Never mind these petty minded whingers and critics." He was convinced that he could upgrade the whole scam and make some real money from people's misfortunes, confusion and various hang-ups. God was good, all was right with the world and Peter Fisher was a man on the up. He saw himself in a golden future with consulting rooms all over the city, an expensive car, Armani suits and all the material goods he had ever coveted. His mistake was to tell God his dreams. This might not have made God laugh but it certainly caused some mirthless sniggering from another important personage. And one who claimed the right to life and death whenever it suited.

The important personage whose letter had so energised the opportunist sat at his regular table in his favourite restaurant, Shanghai 30s. This was not anybody's idea of an ordinary Chinese restaurant, but then neither was the man dining alone anybody's idea of an ordinary man. The restaurant was once home to Restaurant Elizabeth and the décor still recalled the 1930s when Shanghai was regarded as the 'Paris of the Orient'. Its food was as opulent as the room that has entranced so many generations of Oxford people and visitors. Ranged in front of the lone diner was what amounted to a feast, with a starter of marinated spare ribs wok glazed in honey and champagne. There was a dish of champagne marinated cod loin with fresh mango and seaweed wrapped in thin pastry and served in a lemon sauce. Shanghai vegetable rice and steamed jasmine rice completed the feast. A bottle of a good French wine completed the picture. Sebastian Slope was not a man to stint himself when it came to good food and good wine. He had work to do, but Fisher could wait until he had thoroughly indulged himself. It was Slope's way.

An unsuspecting Fisher was waiting for his key appointment and indulged himself in some very attractive dreams. Fisher was imagining the things he could buy once it became known that the ex-Master of St Jude's College was one of his patients. There had been that nasty business with Piers Prideaux and the courts and all that but still an ex-Master of St Jude's, even one who had served time, would warrant respect. It would give his practice the gravitas he yearned for. Of course he had heard some of the talk surrounding Slope's activities but Fisher was not one to enquire too deeply into such things. Slope had been found guilty though the case was complex and nobody seemed sure exactly what it was that Slope was guilty of. To those outside Oxford it would appear as a major offence with a fairly serious sentence to follow. Those who knew the place would know that any Master within the Oxford aegis was virtually untouchable. Prideaux had his enemies and also that most dangerous of things, a left leaning philosophy. That was tolerable within the lecture room but certainly not outside, as many left leaning dons had found to their cost. To each his own was a fairly shallow philosophy and Fisher was a fairly shallow personality. The appointment Slope had made was for 6pm on a Friday. It would give Fisher time to read up a little so that he would not be immediately wrong footed by his most valued potential patient. He knew enough to know that Slope had a formidable intellect and was definitely not a man to be trifled with. Fisher, however, was arrogant enough to suppose he could bluff his way through anything that could be thrown at him. It had occurred to him vaguely that 6pm on a Friday was an odd time to arrange an initial meeting. Normally by then he would be ensconced in The Head of the River, comfortable behind a fresh pint of Doom Bar or something similar. It also meant that other occupants of the building would be long gone and, as he always let Melanie leave before finishing time on a Friday to meet up with the girls in The Crown for a night out, he would be alone with Slope. But that would be fine, wouldn't it?

A peremptory knock on the door of the outer office

roused him from this particular reverie. It was one minute to six. Slope was punctual. He walked through from his consulting room to let his caller in. As he did so it occurred to him that his walk had something of the walk of a condemned man on his merry way to hell on the hanging tree at Newgate. Doubt had already begun to flood through his mind even before he met what he thought would be his meal ticket.

If only he had known. Opening the door he felt a frisson of fear. There stood a man dressed in a business suit, wearing a black Crombie overcoat and a dark blue fedora. He was around six feet tall and heavy yet muscular. Without introducing himself he pushed past Fisher and stalked through to the consulting rooms Fisher followed meekly. Slope threw open the windows with a curt, "The air in here is stale. Let's get on with it shall we?"

This simply wasn't the right way round. He was supposed to be in charge, not this man he had never even met. This did not augur well. His initial doubts came flooding back even stronger than previously. Slope had a genius for unsettling people. It was part of his success. Taking off his overcoat and jacket he made himself comfortable in the chair that Fisher had intended to occupy. He had been wrong footed even before he had begun to attempt to blag his way through some of the inanities used by the counselling cowboys.

"You sit over there," Slope ordered pointing to the chair normally allotted to the patient. "You have things you need to tell me and I have the feeling that before I finish with you will tell me anything I need to know. Now, you are not going to be difficult are you?"

For the first time Fisher looked at this man whom he had viewed as his ticket to the good times. Slope was lounging in his chair. In his right hand he held an eight inch lock knife with a wicked looking blade. Bluster was all he had left and in his heart he knew that this would not work with the man he had in front of him. He sat meekly, transfixed by the blade with which Slope appeared to be completing his manicure.

"Now Fisher, I have it on good authority that you are an acquaintance of Piers Prideaux and you remain in touch with him. I understand that he was kind to you some years back and although you are a useless bastard he took pity on you when nobody else would give you the time of day. I wish to know where Prideaux is as we have some unfinished business to complete. Now you can tell me what you know. Let me rephrase that. You will tell me what you know otherwise I shall take pleasure in releasing that watery substance swilling around in your veins and I shall keep on doing that until you turn blue, then white then suitably lifeless. And I warn you, do not begin with stammered excuses or denials because my vengeance will be swift and extremely painful. I'll give you a moment to think, use it wisely.

"Please don't get any ideas about salvation. Tonight is the night you are going to die, unless your responses please me. Nobody is going to save you. There will be no last minute intervention. This is not a B movie. There is no hero lurking outside the door waiting to burst in and disarm me. This is real life, or in your case possibly your real death. All the other offices are empty. There is no caretaker on this floor and in a way you are a lucky man. Most of us have no control over how we die. But I am granting you a real privilege. Die you will, but at least you can choose how, if not when. It will be tonight. Tell me what I want to know and it will be quick. Hesitate even for seconds and I'll make sure you scream like a baby with colic. Even that will bring nobody running because in the pocket of my overcoat," Slope moved lithely to the coat stand, "I have a bondage mask that shortly I shall ask you to slip on. You will die quietly, but trust me you will die."

"I don't know what you want from me. I thought you were coming to me for my help," stuttered an utterly defeated counsellor.

"Do you seriously think a snivelling wastrel like you could even begin to understand me? Wake up and smell the blood, man. I am not expecting heroics from you and I already know that you are stupid, so one last chance. Where is Prideaux, who is with him and how can I get to him?"

"Look, if I knew don't you think I'd tell you? I haven't seen Prideaux for years and he could be anywhere. I don't know."

"Wrong answer," said Slope as he got to his feet, knife in hand. Many hours after he had first walked into the consulting rooms of the wannabe counsellor he left the building. Dawn was cranking up over an Oxford sky as he walked across Folly Bridge and on to Carfax. There was a spring in his step and he looked happy in the sinister sort of fashion that psychopaths often do.

10

Death of a thousand cuts

It was Monday afternoon before they found Fisher's body. The caretaker had tried the door after being alerted by a member of the public who had an appointment and was getting a little anxious at not having been seen immediately. She had patiently waited a full three minutes to get her weekly fix of Fisher. Then she went into full hysteria mode having failed to raise the now slowly decomposing counsellor from the big sleep, well the biggest one he was ever going to get, in this world.

A highly-strung advertising executive, she was not used to waiting for anything. It made her angry and a tiny bit hysterical. Her appointment was at three and it was now six minutes past the hour. Caretaker Martin Green was the first living thing to face the full brunt of the ill humour of Janey Watkin, who was gradually unravelling in the face of what seemed an unwarranted interference with her very closely structured day. She was suffering from a fairly severe case of Obsessive Compulsive Disorder. This was the sort of ailment that was meat and drink to Fisher. He had been stringing out his sessions for weeks. Janey Watkin was a thoroughly dislikeable young woman but she had real problems that were certainly not being helped by Fisher's mumbo jumbo that passed as treatment. He had probably set back her improvement by years and was not even aware of it.

Green knew none of this. He was doing his best to control his initial instinct to smother the bitch when he finally deigned to open the door to his lair.

"Fisher is not answering his door. I demand that you

let me in. You're supposed to be a caretaker aren't you? You must have a bloody pass key or something."

"Calm down love. Why don't you try controlling yourself, I'll see what I can do," Fisher growled.

"How dare you, do you know who you are talking to?"

"All I know is that some hysterical bitch is sorely trying my patience. I neither know who you are nor do I care. If Fisher is not answering his door then perhaps he doesn't want to see who is knocking. I sure as hell wouldn't have answered the door if I had known it was some hysterical spoiled bitch hyperventilating because she can't get her own way. Grow up, woman."

Watkin was unused to being spoken to in this way but with a mighty effort she collected herself, sniffed back the tears, some crocodile and some born of the anger of frustration. Despite this she did her best to collect herself. As she spent most of her life in a fairly uncollected state this took some effort, enough effort to soften the brittle exterior, though internally she boiled and frothed with too many emotions to put a name to.

"Right then love, follow me quick sticks and let's see if we can raise the prof," said Green ironically and in a deliberate attempt at provocation.

It would have been easier to raise the Titanic than Fisher and a lot less messy, but the two were not to know that. Meekly, Watkin followed Green back up the stairs to Fisher's first floor office and consulting rooms. Reaching the door some way in front of Watkin, Green knocked the office door and called out Fisher's name.

"Is that the best you can do," snapped Watkin. "I've already done that, you prat. Use your bloody passkey for God's sake." The brittle exterior was back big time but about to be shattered into a thousand pieces as Green groped in his jacket pocket for the master key that would allow him access to what was now a charnel house. As he pushed open the door his instinct told him something was wrong. In typical fashion Watkin elbowed him to the side and pushed past him into the room. "Mr Fish..." she failed to even get his name out as an unstoppable, irresistible stream of vomit hit the now congealing blood covering the plain office carpet turning it into an approximation of Pollock's early efforts.

Fisher, or what was left of him, hung upside down suspended by a rope tied around his legs and attached to the ancient central oak beam of the old building. His body was covered with what seemed to be hundreds if not thousands of small but deep knife wounds that spread all over his body. It might not even have been Fisher, as the mutilation had not neglected his face. His nose was completely missing, as were his eyes and ears. His throat had been cut so deeply that his head was at an angle never seen in nature. It was a vision of hell that no human could accommodate without serious mental disturbance. Watkins's fragile mental and physical condition combined to do her a favour as she fainted, collapsing delicately to lie in her own vomit.

Ever the gentleman, Green turned on his heel and walked out to the corridor to telephone the local police. There was none of this emergency business favoured by the television police procedurals. In fact had he chosen to walk to the office window that looked out over St Aldate's he could have signalled to the police station to send someone over. Reluctant to pick his way through vomit and gore he chose instead to phone CID.

"Oxford Police," came a voice.

"Could you please put me through to CID? It's Martin Green here, the caretaker across the road. I think you should send somebody over. I have a particularly ghastly murder to report. It looks as if Peter Fisher is dead. Don't worry about a doctor or anything but an undertaker would be good."

In truth it was a team of industrial cleaners that would be required to tidy up after Slope this time. There was, of course, the added complication of a traumatised Janey Watkin, currently helpless and covered in her own vomit. As for Fisher he looked as if he would be more at home in an abattoir than a comfortable office. He had been bled like a stuck pig or perhaps a victim of the exquisite Chinese torture known as the death of a thousand cuts. The sharp stench of vomit and stale blood began to get through even to Martin Green who was forced to turn his back on his gruesome discovery, leaving a gibbering Janey Watkin as company for a lifeless Peter Fisher.

Outside, in the fresher ambience of the corridor, Green leaned out of the open window, drawing deeply on a cigarette as he did so. He noticed that the No Smoking sign was prominent next to the open window and smiled wryly. If ever there was time for a cigarette this was it. He had not particularly cared for Fisher, and had regarded him as something of a charlatan, but nobody deserved to die like that. And the likelihood of the local force tracking down the murderer was vanishingly small. Sadly, he mused that this was not the Oxford where such things were supposed to happen. It was cold blooded murder with a side dish of torture. Whoever was responsible had to be one sick bastard. Naturally, he assumed the guilty one to be a man following the oft-quoted wisdom that decreed that women generally killed with poison where male murderers found the gun and the knife more appealing weapons. Something to do with childhood conditioning perhaps, he thought. Young girls playing with dolls houses and tea sets, young boys insisting on imitation guns and swords; that was probably the core of the whole thing. And like most men who have little knowledge of women – Green was a confirmed bachelor – he simply could not imagine the woman who could torture another human to death.

A scream followed by a gurgling sound brought Green back to the present moment with a start. Turning, he saw the bedraggled figure of the previously imperious Janey Watkin staggering into the corridor. He was forced to restrain a snigger as he saw this wild haired and wild eyed harridan stained with her own vomit, lost for words and desperately attempting to clean herself with the smallest and most ineffectual of handkerchiefs. Defeated, she slumped against the bannister and settled for emitting a low moaning noise. Even that quickly became annoying but Green was not inclined to help. Stepping over her supine body and turning only to flick the cigarette butt out of the open window, he made his way down the fifteenth-century staircase to the relative calm of his small and cluttered haven on the ground floor.

He would await the coming of the CID. It was over to them. In an idle moment he wondered if there was a chance that the local plod would imagine that Watkin had anything to do with the murder. It was a delicious thought but he dismissed it as soon as it formed. At least she would be inconvenienced and the horror of her experience might help to knock some of that haughty attitude out of her. Equally probably it would also undo any possible good that the chancer Fisher might have done accidentally before his untimely impression of a stuck pig took him out of this world and presumably to a better place. Well what the hell! Apart from having to give a statement when Oxford's constabulary at last stirred their collective stumps and got themselves the fifty or so yards to the murder scene that would be him for the day, and he'd be off to The Bear to fill in anyone who would listen on the slow and desperate death of Peter Fisher, Counsellor, now deceased. May he rest in pieces.

11

Her name is Lola

The new stage for Lola Cutler involved research for a PhD at one of the London universities. She prospered there. The relative freedom in academia in the metropolis appealed to her sense of the individual. She did not need to be told what to study by others, she could find her own way; she preferred it to be like that. She found London comfortable and it looked as if it would be the place for her to settle. It was a chance meeting that changed all that and would bring her once again into the orbit of her childhood friend who had already completed his Masters degree at Maundering College. The intervening years had seen no contact between the hitherto inseparable friends.

When she eventually met someone from her old county of Shropshire it was someone whom she had known reasonably well. She shared a country background with Elizabeth West who originated from the neighbouring county of Worcester. They had met on the tennis circuit, both girls playing for their home counties of Shropshire and Worcester. They met again at Cambridge, discovering that they had something else in common. They had developed a more than passing interest in secret societies. In fact Long Liz, as the six foot tall student was called at Cambridge, had included a thesis on that very subject as part of her degree. The thesis was titled Secret Societies and their Influence on European Government from 1850 to 2001. It was a huge study and she got thoroughly swept up in it. The thing that separated Long Liz and Lola was Long Liz's insistence that she was looking for a career with the Civil

Service. Such a structured future held no appeal for Lola at the time so it was something that was never discussed. It remained a no go area between the two. They had not seen each other for a couple of years.

Both girls were acutely aware of the role played by Oxford and Cambridge in the process of recruiting spies for whatever cause, how could they not be? The first team at Cambridge were forever infamous as the Famous Five. Four of these, Kim Philby, Donald Maclean, Guy Burgess and Anthony Blunt are all well known as members of the Cambridge ring of spies. There as many names for the fifth man as there are stars in the sky. Suffice it to say that there was a fifth man though not yet positively identified. This type of intrigue fascinated Long Liz and gradually her research began to yield more information than she knew what to do with. Completion of the thesis did not exhaust her interest. This had been well and truly piqued. It did however suggest to her that not all secret societies were as black and white as many people imagined. The Cambridge Five had been seduced by the Soviet dream of a society that was based on a form of equality. The reality did not turn out to be quite as they imagined. Their actions, however, managed to do a lot of damage to agents of British Intelligence in the heyday of the ring. It was during this intense period of study that Liz took up with a man who claimed to know the identity of the Fifth Man. It was such a wild claim that she didn't really give it much of her attention. Much later she began to wonder as the inevitable what ifs started to accumulate. He could have been telling the truth. His brother would have been at Cambridge at around the right time. He was around the right age, but if he had been the last one of the circle why had he not been identified? She had asked him one night when they were sitting together in the Fifth Column, a popular Cambridge pub.

"Go on then, Ademar. I've heard you talk about him before but you've never explained why if he was the mysterious fifth man his identity has never come to light."

"That is easily explained," he replied, lowering his voice as he did so. "He has never been identified because he left quite early in the piece. British Intelligence was something of a joke. They should have sniffed him out well before he decided that the circle was not for him. He was too clever for them. He was too clever for the rest of the circle too if it comes to that. He would never have escaped if the Stasi had been on his case. He bailed out before things got too hot and he left no trace. Fortunately he had already decided that there was something better to belong to than something dedicated to a political structure. That's alright in films but the real world doesn't work like that. He had a better offer and so he took it and left the four to their fate."

Ademar Speight had never been this talkative before. They had both had a few drinks but there was the distant glint of battle in his eye and he was becoming almost a cartoon German. Still the whole thing was interesting, provided the German bias didn't come to the surface.

"I'd really be grateful if you didn't take off on one of your rants, Ademar. I know Dresden, I know the camps and believe it or not I am well aware of the 1966 final. And yes it was a goal. The Russian linesman wasn't bribed whatever you care to think. What I don't understand is what could be powerful enough to persuade him to betray what must have been a powerful political conviction. Well, are you going to tell me?"

"That's easy," the slightly built German asserted. "Not everyone does what they do for the greater good. He met someone who offered him a position that would ensure that whatever actions he carried out would benefit him directly. He would be protected and looked after as long as he remained totally loyal to the group. Once he became a member of the group that was it. It had quite a bit in common with the Mafia and your Royal Family. There is only one way out and that is in a wooden box. Only the wood will be different. Mafia coffins are much better quality as they love to splash out on funerals. Your effete royals will not spend a penny on such things if they can possible avoid it. I can't remember the name of the group but the leader was a man called, what was it now? I remember it began with an S. That's it, it was Steigung. I can't remember the English for Steigung but someone called Sebastian Steigung persuaded him to join an organisation that he ran as a secret society based in Oxford. My brother left Cambridge for Oxford shortly after that and I returned to Germany. We lost touch. All I know is that he worked at an Oxford College, I think as bursar, and seemed to live very well. We were never close and I have made little effort to contact him since. There. You have what you wanted. That is as much as I know."

The conversation had gone flat as a result of this exposure of something that Ademar Speight clearly did not relish talking about. The two parted shortly afterwards, both going their separate ways. They never met again but the information, slim as it was, began to lodge in Long Liz's mind. She kept coming back to what Ademar had said. It made no sense at all. Why would he leave a spy ring to join something that sounded like a sort of hedonistic society? If it had been the Bullingdon Club it would have made some sort of sense. A bunch of overgrown schoolboys behaving like louts secure in the knowledge that their wealthy families would bail them out. Another restaurant, another bar or a few broken windows. It didn't really matter. There must be more to it. She promised herself that she would find out what her German acquaintance had been talking about before she made her own mind up.

It was research that held her in London. It was a fairly vicious thirst that took her to the Oxbridge Graduate Club in St James's Square. She had been sitting there for a while dreaming about the old university days. The club, founded in 1789, was deliberately designed to induce a sense of loss and longing for the salad days that make such an impression on the mind. All sorts of athletic paraphernalia adorned the walls. Old brown leather rugby balls from long dead matches between the two universities. Oars mounted over the bar with details of whether the winners wore light or dark blue. Lacrosse teams and boxers. Black and white pictures of long dead graduates who had earned their blues in another time. It was a place to wallow. And that is what Long Liz was doing when someone who had entered the club caught her eye. Though it was some time since she had seen her it was difficult to mistake Lola Cutler. She had changed little. She had retained her distinctive masculine walk. She walked directly to the bar and ordered bourbon on the rocks. She nodded at the barman for a refill before the barman had managed to return the bottle to its usual place. Then she turned to survey the room. She picked out Long Liz immediately, smiling and waving as she walked towards her. Hesitantly, Long Liz returned the smile and stood to greet her. The two embraced before agreeing to move to another table further back in the bar. Both women felt more comfortable in what was essentially a private booth. They took fewer than fifteen minutes to catch up with the other's progress since university days back in Cambridge. Both seemed to the other to be guarded with personal information. It was good to catch up with another alumna and the conversation never delved much below surface issues.

It was clear that Long Liz was involved in more than research for a higher degree. Though at first reluctant to say too much it became clear that she had achieved her long held goal of landing a job within the British civil service. It wasn't exactly a desk job either. Lola listened politely as her erstwhile acquaintance related the saga of her graduation, her acceptance for further research and her role within the civil service. It quickly became clear that it was her research interests that had attracted the attention of the inevitable recruiter. It was not until Long Liz inadvertently mentioned the name of her boss within the service that she found her interest piqued.

"That wouldn't be Gawain Cornelius you mentioned, would it Liz?" She heard herself saying the words before they even registered in her brain. "Only I used to know someone of that name when we were both kids. We were in touch for quite a bit after that too, but you know how it is. Could be the same man I suppose."

"If the Gawain Cornelius is what you would call a singular man with an encyclopaedic knowledge of the blues, jazz and the greatest vinyl collection in private hands. And if he is an Oxford man who grew up in Shropshire then you are on the right track. I'd better put you out of your misery. I'm not simply here for the studies, and I'm not in this bar because I'm particularly thirsty. I was expecting you. I'm here to see you and I'm here on the orders of your old friend Gawain. I knew that you came in here from time to time and it was no struggle for me to simply sit here until you did. And for your information he trusts you as completely as he always did. That is saying something for somebody whose current role means that he trusts nobody.

Put this number into your phone and ring him as soon as you can. It is a secure number and he will expect you to ring between 8.00 and 8.15 on a Tuesday or Wednesday morning. He wants to talk to you and between these four walls he will be offering you a position within a unit he currently runs. He is looking to strengthen the unit as he has a major job in hand at the moment. That is as much as I can tell you, because it's all I know. He'll tell you the rest which I gather is fairly top secret. You are the first name on my list. There are others to contact. I go back to active service once I have contacted all the names. It's a bit of a cushy job really. I contact the names on my list then once I've given them the number that's my job done and I can get back to my research. By the way the research is fascinating. I can tell you more if you are free some time. I remember that you had an interest in the field once and the new developments are absolutely fascinating. I think I've said enough now. All you have to do is to confirm that you will contact the number I gave you, then I can check you off the list."

"You can guarantee it. Check it off now. I shall be in touch with him the first chance I get. We were once close and I'd really love to catch up with what he is doing these days." Lola had never been given to idle guarantees and she was as good as her word. The following Tuesday she rang the number Liz had given her. She recognised the answering voice instantly. It had deepened markedly but there was no doubt that it was her old friend and sparring partner from those carefree Shropshire days. He was as welcoming as she had come to expect but with a piquant seasoning of seriousness. By the end of the short phone call she had resolved to meet him the following Monday. Five days later she found herself inside a distinctly nondescript government building in one of the less salubrious areas of the capital.

12

Hunting of the Spriggan

Prideaux was first to wake. He had slept intermittently but felt reasonably well rejuvenated. He left Bones snoring away in his pit, dressed and moved quietly downstairs intent on stretching his legs. The cottage was in semi darkness. He wasn't sure whether Mark and Ginny were up yet. His intention was to slip quietly out through the back door. As he crept down the stairs and tiptoed to the back of the cottage he heard a sound. It wasn't one he could immediately identify but he turned and moved towards it. It seemed to be coming from the living room. Old cottages have their advantages but sneaking around wasn't one of them. Creaking boards and doors meant that unobserved behaviour was a tricky thing to pull off. Prideaux looked up from the shadow of the stairs to spot Ginny sitting there appearing to strain to hear what noise was coming from the living room. She was doing that thing most people do when trying to overhear someone in discussion, cupping her hand to her ear. From his advantage point he could see that the focus of her interest was Mark who was on the phone in the living room. Clearly he was speaking to someone but it was not possible to hear what he was saying. His voice was very low and a conspiracy theorist might well think it was because he did not want to be overheard. But surely he was being thoughtful and trying not to wake anyone who was hoping for that extra hour of peace in bed. He convinced himself that was the case and slipped silently through the back door and out into the morning. Walking quickly along the back path to the point where it joined up with Poplar Lane he headed towards the village green. It was first thing in the morning and there was no one about. It was one of those clear, crisp days that sparkle like a well cut diamond in the gloom of autumn. There was a hint of chill in the air but the sun was up, and when Prideaux emerged from the shadow cast by the plane trees around the south edge of the green, it was shirtsleeve order weather. Prideaux's head was remarkably clear given the previous evening's consumption of alcohol. And it needed to be.

The first thing was to get to his cousin's cottage out on the moor and from there to the village that bore his family name, but what then? He was still whistling in the dark. He knew that the moor had been a stronghold of the Spriggans for many years. He knew that well before people had referred to the empty and often terrifying moorland around the area as Bodmin Moor it had carried another name. That name, Spriggan Moor, linked it to the feared and hated society. He knew that even earlier than that it had been known as Temple Moor in honour of the Knights Templar. That was before they were driven out of their chapel and off the moor by the ferocity of the Spriggans. This was fairly well known history, at least to the Cornish. He had plenty of cousins in the area and they all had a handle on what was going on in a general way but he needed more specific information. Perhaps the answer could be found in the church his father had talked about so often. 'Perhaps' was all there was. Lost in thought Prideaux found himself on the far side of the village green. It was the sound of a couple of shots that brought him back to reality. A shotgun being discharged was nothing at all strange in rural Cornwall, but the second sound was sharper and echoed more than usual. It sounded like a pistol shot. It was close and it came from the direction of Mark and Ginny's cottage. These were not usual times.

Turning, he began to run back across the green. He

wasn't a man given to panic but this Slope business had rattled him and a vague unease had settled on his shoulders.

Reaching the lane at a run he saw two figures facing each other several yards apart. They appeared to be circling one another and both were armed. Bones was facing him, a shotgun at his shoulder. The object of Bones's attention had his back to Prideaux, but there was something in his stance that echoed somewhere in a mind struggling to come to terms with what was becoming a Cornish danse macabre. The figure turned towards him and as he did so he recognised Conrad Speight. His face was contorted and the man was in some pain and favouring his left leg. He was holding what appeared to be a Luger. Prideaux thought back to the war comics he had inherited from a distant cousin. It occurred to him that all the Germans, whether soldiers or not, were always drawn holding Lugers. It also occurred to him how ridiculous this was since Speight wasn't even a German. As far as Prideaux was aware he came from Belgium. It occurred to him that whatever nationality he was Speight was pointing the pistol directly at him. Self-preservation kicked in and Prideaux dived inelegantly behind a convenient hydrangea bush as two bullets whistled over his head. He whipped round to see the Mexican standoff with both men levelling their weapons at each other.

"Well do you feel lucky Speight, do you, old fruit?" drawled a strangely activated Bones.

"Don't be so bloody stupid Bones. A shotgun only has two barrels and with your first one you managed to explode one of the local chickens and with your second you blew the head off the scarecrow" he nodded towards the adjoining field, "clean off" he added incredulously. I, on the other hand, have enough ammunition to do my job and send you and your very irritating friend off to that 'undiscovered country from whose bourn no traveller returns'."

"Well we'll bloody well see then." Peeping from behind the sheltering bush Prideaux was amazed to see the expression on his friend's face. It was pure hatred. He had taken aim and was intent on blowing this man Speight into oblivion. Bones squeezed the trigger as Prideaux convinced himself that his time was up. He waited to hear the anti-climactic click of an empty gun and the ensuing bullet that would come from Speight's Luger. He was not here to mess around. Speight had come to kill and it looked odds on that he intended to carry out his task with some aplomb. The unmistakeable sound of a shotgun being fired energised Prideaux sufficiently for him to leave his hiding place and step into the lane. The Luger lay bent and twisted in the lane with Speight desperately wrapping a handkerchief around an extremely bloodied hand now missing its index and central figure. Remarkably the injured man, driven by fear, managed to crest the hedge and limp off across the fields before Prideaux or Bones could get near him. It was futile for Prideaux to try mounting the bank and chasing Speight, wounded or not. He was out of condition and knew it. Besides Speight was alarmingly sprightly for a wounded man and he really needed to know what the hell was going on. His answer came quicker than he imagined in the more naturally rounded tones of Billy Bones.

"That's it. Run you bastard. Lucky I didn't blow your head clean off your shoulders. Stout chaps one, bad eggs nil. That'll teach you to come snooping around William Radleigh de Beaune. Bloody peasants don't know their place anymore. What is the world coming to? How dare a bloody foreigner quote Hamlet at me. Is nothing sacred?"

Bones followed this with a burst of spontaneous

laughter. More a case of guffawing from where Prideaux was standing, gazing open mouthed at his friend, now doubled over and still clutching an unbroken shotgun and shaking as one badly stricken with a severe case of St Vitus' dance.

"Bonesie. What the hell's going on?" yelled Prideaux.

"Nothing much old boy. Reloaded, didn't I. I found that bastard Speight around in the garden. So I did what any decent man would do and shot him. Winged the snidey little blighter. But that should teach him not to come mooching around here. The only thing is if Speights come can Slopes be far behind?"

"I have no wish to be critical, but couldn't you have locked him in the shed or something? At least we might have had the chance to question him."

"Never crossed my mind, old fruit. Always been a man to shoot first and ask questions afterwards. So I shot him. The cowardly bastard legged it before I could bag him. I've been aching to try out Mark's gun since we arrived. I can think of no better use to put a Beretta to. And I did so enjoy shooting a Spriggan. Beats grouse or partridge all ends up. And at least we know that Slope is definitely on our trail so the sooner we get on the case the better. Good news too on the Mark and Ginny front. They haven't got much on at the moment and thought they'd be our drivers for a while, drive and join in the fun. They've popped into Bodmin to pick up some essential supplies, you know the stuff, and a few bottles of whisky. Oh and some groceries as well I shouldn't wonder. Don't look so glum, Piers. It'll be like the old days again. Loadsa fun and plenty of booze. What could be better?"

In his heart Prideaux knew that what was waiting for them was going to be lots of things but fun was not among them. But at least now they were four. And Prideaux the village might yield some answers even if Prideaux the man couldn't. The return of Mark and Ginny meant an explanation of what had happened in this quiet Cornish village. They wouldn't like it but he knew that it wasn't something that could be kept from them. They had a right to know.

13

Never send to know
for whom the bell tolls...

The village of Prideaux next to the larger settlement of St Blaise was a legacy of the Normans in Cornwall. It had a Norman church, the remains of a Norman castle and a local pub, 'The Parson's Arms', that claimed to date from the sixteenth century. It may well have done but, history apart, these days its main attraction was the oak panelled bar with the roaring log fire that attracted intrepid travellers. There was a scent of old Ireland in the bar from peat added to the logs, an unusual fuel in the Cornish countryside. It would have been foolish, however, to ignore the extensive peat bog right on the doorstep, between St Blaise and Prideaux, and after centuries of neglect and deprivation no self-respecting Cornishman would look a gift horse in the mouth.

The drive from Blisland had been uneventful but the four had not properly dropped their collective guard. There was a palpable feeling of tension in the air. The warmth and some good Cornish ale were helping to defuse some of this but nobody was going to relax fully until they had some answers.

As all outsiders do they eavesdropped on talk at the bar. Four men leaned on the long bar drinking pints of Doom Bar and shooting the breeze. They might have been farmers, or quarrymen. They were certainly manual workers. Try as one might there was no way of getting that look from the gym, not even if you spent eight hours a day there. These men were big shouldered and powerful looking, with the weather-beaten faces that featured so regularly in this weather-beaten part of the world. What talk there was was the usual bar talk, the weather, the fishing, the greyhound results and stock car racing at Par Stadium. Such things concerned locals and nobody much else. Something else caught Prideaux's attention when one of the men casually mentioned a fire over Blisland way. Prideaux's danger antennae began to vibrate and he began to concentrate on what the biggest, most dangerous man at the bar was telling the others.

"My cousin is in the Bodmin brigade and he was telling me. Bad it was. Up on the moor one of the old cottages burned down. Nothing left of it he said. By the time they got there it was too late. It was well alight they couldn't save much of it at all. He said it appeared they found a body in the ashes. Too badly burned to identify. Might have been a tramp squatting there but nobody seems to have much of an idea who it might be."

By this time Prideaux's alarm bells were clanging. It was too much of a coincidence. It had to be cousin Denzil's cottage. But who was the poor devil who roasted to death there? He knew that Denzil was out in his place in Puglia so it wasn't likely to be him. His companions had heard none of this and to Prideaux they appeared too relaxed, given what had already happened. He needed to inject a sense of urgency in case this latest piece of information had a direct relevance to them. Without a word he motioned to them to finish their drinks and follow him outside. One glance was enough to persuade them that something serious was in the air. Outside in the crisp air of a Cornish afternoon he explained, adding that they really needed to seek out his cousin. Bones considered performing some theatrics involving words such as, "Well hush my mouth. How many cousins can one man have?" One glance at Prideaux's expression was sufficient to convince him that this would be a bad time for such a thing. Accordingly Bones kept his counsel. Ginny couldn't help herself however and muttered, "Not another cousin Piers, surely?", which she accompanied with a weak smile.

"Yes, and this one is the black sheep of the family. He's the vicar of Bodelva Church, which is up on that rise at the end of Fore Street. Never had a lot to do with him really. He's a bit too serious for my taste and worse than that he's a Cambridge man. Those newer universities do turn out some awful prigs. But blood is still thicker than water so he'll help if he can. I don't really know him that well and there have always been rumours. Apparently, though you'd never know it to look at him, he was a bit wild in his younger days. I'm not even sure what relationship he is to me. Down here so many people call others cousins that it becomes a courtesy title. If you asked me to track his exact connection to me I doubt I could do it. There was once some talk that he might have had some low level involvement with the Spriggans. I never gave that much thought, mainly because low level involvement with that lot is a bit like being a little bit dead. You are or you aren't. There are no degrees of death. Unless of course you include some of the royal family. I'm pretty sure some of them were pretty much dead years before anyone took the trouble to bury them. But that's another story."

The four walked towards the church with a new purpose. That purpose meant that they were only partly aware of the battered old Land Rover rattling past them carrying four rough looking men. They too were focused on the church but they had a very different purpose in mind.

It was around fifteen minutes later that the four arrived at the lane that led off Fore Street to the church. As they walked up the rutted lane the church bell began to ring. It was a mournful sound that seemed out of sorts, out of tune with everything. It followed no pattern that any of the friends were aware of and there seemed no reason for it. No special service, there were no people in evidence so it couldn't be a wedding or a funeral. But most of all it was completely random as if some sort of heavy weight had been attached to the bell rope. It made no sense. They were already at the lych gate when Prideaux pushed forward and into the churchyard.

"Come with me Bonesie. I don't like the sound of this and I don't mean the bell. You two stay here until we find out what the hell is going on."

Prideaux and Bones walked briskly along the path to the door of the church. It was ajar. There was no sign of life but the noise of the bell had lessened. They stepped inside and found their way to the bell tower. Climbing the stone steps towards the bell room they found their answer. The bell was ringing because the vicar was ringing it but not in any way he had ever intended in this world or the next. The bell rope was wound round the neck of Clarence Carclaze, MA (Cantab), Vicar of Bodelva Church in the Parish of St Blaise, and he was stone dead. His lifeless body still turned slowly causing fewer and now indiscernible noises from the church bell. Bones and Prideaux looked at each other, the unasked question on the lips of each of them. Their answer came as the corpse twisted again until the dead man's back faced them. His surplice answered the question for them. The crude gothic 'S' in scarlet paint on the vicar's otherwise pristine garment left no scrap of doubt. This was the work of the Spriggans. They had struck again and this time a mild mannered vicar, however dubious his past, had prematurely gone to meet his maker. Or if he had not he would have faced a major disappointment.

"That's fucked that line of enquiry then Piers. What the hell would he have been able to tell us if he wasn't dangling over there? He doesn't look as if he has much to say at the moment. Have you any idea what he might or might not have known?"

"I'm not really sure. This is a very old church and it's seen God knows how many events over the centuries. There was always talk about a safe containing documents that could have proved earth shattering if they ever got into the wrong hands. I know that my family was supposed to be involved but I've no idea how. The best I've ever got is that there are secrets stored somewhere around here that date back to the English Civil War. People have come to this church on all sorts of pretences. There can't be anything left that people haven't found or stolen but nobody seems any the wiser. The only clue that made sense that I've ever heard centred on some talk about there being a room somehow built into the walls of the church. Even if that is true, and I can tell you that hardly anybody knows that part of the story, then I can't see how it helps us in our current predicament. Anyway these Spriggans are no respecters of parsons and I think we should exit stage left."

"Well at least he went with a bong not a whimper," said Bones with a weak attempt at black humour. But the tremor in his voice was evidence of how afraid he was. "Shouldn't we try and cut him down? And shouldn't we ring the police? And shouldn't we get the hell out of here?" he spluttered.

"Taking your spluttered questions in order," answered the calmer of the two men, "Firstly I remember reading in Capote's In Cold Blood that hanged humans invariably soil themselves when hanged. Secondly, I'll eat my cat if you can get a signal anywhere around here. And thirdly your plan to remove ourselves from the immediate vicinity is a sound one. So my answers are: no, no and last one to the lych gate is a softy."

Mark and Ginny were surprised to see the two exiting the church door as if the jet-propelled hounds of hell were on their tails. They didn't bother to ask why but turned tail and ran like startled, slightly paranoid grouse back down the lane, into Fore Street and back to the car.

Not one of the four noticed the battered Land Rover that had passed them earlier in the car park of Bodelva's only pub, The Parson's Arms. Had they glanced in through the bar window they would have observed the same four men they had seen in there earlier. Only this time they looked like four comrades in arms celebrating a good job well done. But this was a time for flight not fight and accordingly Mark threw his battered old saloon around the Cornish lanes as if his and three other lives depended on it. He did not stop the car until they were back in Mark and Ginny's refuge in Blisland. Not a single word was spoken during the entire journey. If they didn't know before, they knew now. The four friends were in a rack of trouble, far more than they could ever imagine. Something dark and shapeless was shuffling through the land and it was shuffling in their direction. Unwittingly Prideaux and Bones had placed two of their best friends directly in the firing line. The worst of it was they could not see who was holding the gun and about to loose a volley at their collective heads.

14

Through a glass darkly

Back at Blisland cottage the general air of gloom throughout the Williams household did not look as if it would lift any time soon. There was little optimism to go around and nobody really had a clue what to do next. They had seen but not witnessed a murder and though they were pretty sure they knew the organisation that carried the responsibility for it, they could prove nothing. Even worse, the gentle soul who might have been able to help them had met an untimely end. Poor old Clarence, he deserved better. And even the logical step of going to the police held little or no appeal. There was pretty general agreement throughout the county that there was a strong Spriggan influence throughout the local force so contacting them put them in more danger than ever. It was Bones who was first to break the awkward silence.

"I for one am getting a little fed up of all this skulking around. Lovely as it is to be back in the old country I think the answer to this situation is to beard the bastard in his den. Coming down home has got us nowhere so far. We know Speight has been here. We are also fairly sure that we know that the organisation has had Clarence killed. And to be honest it doesn't take a genius to work out that Slope is intent on revenge and that his main target is Piers. If there's a bit of collateral damage in the process that won't bother him one bit. It's not as if this is Midsomer Murders. They'd have seen at least a half dozen grisly endings by now and that's just in Badger's Drift. So let's not panic. Let us all tootle back to good old Oxenford and face this Slope once and for all."

"Great idea that," said an exasperated Mark, "but I think you forget that until you two turned up Ginny and I were living the life idyllic without a care in the world. And as for doing a little better on the old death counter than the poor souls in Midsomer, Bonesie, I fear you may have taken shore leave of your senses. That is a TV programme; this is what passes for real life and people have been murdered. I don't like being involved."

"Sorry Mark and Ginny," broke in Prideaux, "but the cruel fact is that you are involved. Speight knows who you are which means Slope knows who you are. They also know where you are. He is bound to wonder what I have told you and probably cannot take a chance on you knowing too much in case it impinges on him and his people. I know, obviously, and Bonesie knows and even though, my dear friends, you have no idea of what I'm going on about, you are in the same danger as if you knew chapter and verse."

As usual the calm common sense came from Ginny who, despite the fear she felt at an escalating situation, had a far better capacity for maintaining calm and calculating than the three men put together.

"If as you say Piers we are in the same dangerous situation whether we know why or not then we might as well know. In the circumstances it makes no difference one way or the other. But if I am going to be cut down in what I consider to be my prime by some madman I'd rather go to my grave knowing why. Makes no odds in the end but at least I might be able to shuffle off this mortal coil with a lighter heart if I think that I at least understood why I needed to be killed, since actually I don't really feel that need. I'm as happy as a Celt ever gets and if it is OK with the rest of you I intend to continue in that vein for as long as politicians tell lies and fiddle their expenses."

"A good point neatly made," answered Prideaux, "and

if you are sitting comfortably then I'll begin. Although apart from giving you both an idea of how we got to this point I'm not sure that the knowledge is as relevant as it once was. Too much has happened, but I realise that I owe you this at the very least.

"When I started as a lowly lecturer at St Jude's it was a lovely place to be. I knew the place backwards after my student days there and things seemed pretty straightforward. It all changed when the master at the time, you'll remember Violet Watson, ran off with her secretary. That livened up some of the old buffers in the Senior Common Room. Upshot was that we were left leaderless. Council had to appoint a new master and the whole arcane ritual took an age. You could elect a new Pope in half the time St Jude's took to appoint a new master. The newly appointed Sebastian Slope arrived trailing clouds of qualifications and wearing that year's accessory, a creepy smile. He seemed reasonable enough at first, and he at least appeared to be on the side of the staff. It didn't last long and with the support of the Council he decided to push through some radical changes to our conditions of tenure. It all got very bloody, very quickly and with what seemed to be consummate ease he started weeding out any of the staff who thought his changes were way out of order.

"Obviously I fell into that category, bearing a well-deserved reputation as an awkward bugger. That was enough to make me a target. I looked fireproof, the fireproof prof you might say, for a while but it couldn't last. I was too much trouble. So along with that creep Speight he decided to stitch me up. I don't know whether you remember but there was a really weird student at St Jude's in those days. Now I know that's not much help in terms of description as, almost by definition students at St Jude's tended to dress to the left side of weird in those days. Let's face it they did throughout the system.

Today's lot are like Bambi's security men. This particular weirdo started off with some part time work but in no time had her own office. She seemed to have come from nowhere and there were rumours that she wasn't a student at all but that Slope was having an affair with her. He was a randy old bastard in those days. Probably still is for all I know.

"Effectively she was a sleeper until Slope needed to get rid of the particularly turbulent priest that turned out to be me. She called herself Ernesta Pugliano though nobody knew whether that was her real name or not. I suspect not. Claimed to be married to a vicar too but he was conspicuous by his invisibility. Didn't pay it much heed at the time, nobody did. But that bastard Slope was playing the long game. It was before the long vacation that I had my hundredth argument with him. You know how he used to huff and puff when he was opposed to anything. Now I know that hindsight is a wondrous thing but I can remember his face. He was angry enough to kick a puppy but suddenly, as if he had swallowed a barrowful of bile and needed to void his system, he swept past me, down the corridor and out into the quad. That was the time he had made up his mind to do for me once and for all and it was Pugliano who was going to be his benighted instrument in his twisted scheme. I didn't give it a thought at the time but on reflection what must have tipped him over the edge was that he had found out that I had called a – it wasn't a strike, after all this is Oxford – I had canvassed the staff on a withdrawal of labour, that's more the Oxford way. I suppose I shouldn't have called it for the day that some minor royal or other was visiting the college. The creep was so excited and finding out that a good portion of the staff would not be cooperating must have really got to him. I always had student support too and having contacted the Chair of the Student Union they had also confirmed in writing that they would be mounting a very noisy and inappropriate demonstration to ensure that the visit went with a swing. Small wonder the bastard hated me, but he deserved everything he got. I didn't realise what I was taking on. He had always tied establishing his fiefdom in Oxford with royal recognition of his tenure as master of the college. I took that away from him and he couldn't forget it."

The others had listened intently but genuinely didn't expect what was coming next. They knew bits and pieces about what had gone on but there had been a lot of threats at the time and real information had been hard to come by. What Prideaux said next would explain why he harboured such a hatred and genuine fear of Slope. Clearing his throat he continued.

"Slope called me into his office late one Friday evening. You know I never trusted the bastard so I was wary. The college was quiet and it wasn't that I was really afraid of him. Truthfully I was afraid of what I might do if he tried one of his tricks, and of course he did. He was sitting behind that massive mahogany desk of his, face like thunder, and he handed me a letter. Even had the bloody cheek to have sealed it with the college seal."

"Read it when you get home" he barked. "And don't bother returning to your working class roots and assaulting me. You're already in enough trouble to last you what's left of your life. Security guards are just down the corridor and will escort you off the premises. Don't even try to clear your desk. You are formally suspended from college as of now. Confirmation of your sacking will be conveyed to you when college council meets next Wednesday. Now before I have you thrown out let me update you on how the balance of power has shifted in this particular college. You and I both know that you are not guilty of the offence that has led you to this. The truth is that I am the person responsible for leading you to this sad state of affairs. Well I can't claim full credit for this smartly engineered little plot. I have had the assistance of those members of staff who have had the foresight to be members of my organisation. You were right royally stitched up old chap. You must be aware that college staff hates it when their cosy little world is disturbed. To them it is as if some oik has pissed in the port. It simply will not do."

Piers was generally a reasonable man but as Slope revealed the extent of his chicanery his discomfort increased and he began to steam. In another era he would have taken this man by the throat and choked the life out of him. Instead he had to sit there and take it, while a man he loathed smirked as he unveiled the length to which he had gone to destroy his career.

"All it really took was for me to destroy your reputation. Despite your regrettable left wing tendencies, before I arrived you had a reputation for being honest and moral, if a little misguided. Once I had destroyed that reputation you had nowhere to go. All it took was to persuade someone to accuse you of rape and your goose was well and truly cooked. Remember that one of the most regular aphorisms that the feeble minded or simply cowardly cling to is the one that goes, 'there is no smoke without fire', and Ernesta was more than prepared to blow an inordinate amount of smoke up your arse at my behest."

"Are you seriously telling me that you persuaded a woman to claim I had raped her?"

The smirk on Slope's face said it all. "Don't be so bloody naïve, Prideaux. Of course I did. That sort of thing happens all the time in the business world. It is only you sheltered academics that are shocked by such processes. Thank your lucky stars you didn't end up bobbing up and down in the Cherwell. I could have ordered that, had I so chosen."

"You are fucking totally mad, Slope. You are talking like some sort of Godfather figure. You can't go ordering random rapes or murders. This is Oxford for fuck's sake, not Palermo or Vigata. You must have lost your bloody mind."

"The only person to have lost anything here is you, Prideaux. And you have lost the lot. You've lost your career and for what it's worth you have lost your reputation. More importantly you are out of my hair and will never work in higher education ever again. And you still don't get it, do you?"

"If you mean that I don't understand how a twisted bastard like you can accuse me of something I never did. How you can persuade the governors to sack me for something I didn't do? And most of all keep the police completely out of it. You are supposed to be the master of a place of learning. That does not invest you with the power of life and death."

"Of course it doesn't, my gullible friend, but something else does. I'm sure you will appreciate this, Prideaux, as I understand you are quite proud of your Cornish connections. That something else is my position as leader of the Spriggans. You must know that that makes me virtually untouchable. Want to know how many of the governors are Spriggans? All of them. Would you care to know who else is a Spriggan and therefore at my command? Where shall I start? Well let's begin with the Chief Constable and the majority of his senior staff, practically all the lawyers in the city and the majority of the senior staff in this and every other college in the city. Need I go on? You never had a chance. Once I decided you were an irritant then your time was over. And in case you are still confused, all it took was a few cleverly faked pictures of you with one or two of the students that used to hang around you in the various pubs you frequent. One or two faked emails helped my cause along and you will certainly notice your support melting away once the photos and those emails come to light." This was beginning to get creepy now. What the hell was the man talking about? What photographs? What emails? Prideaux felt panic beginning to rise. His mouth was dry and his mind racing as he did the best he could to process the information that was coming at him in a storm.

"They were well produced and would fool quite a lot of people. I made sure that they did. They might not have fooled real experts but then the real experts were all on my side. It is amazing what one can do when holding all the aces. Ernesta's disappearance merely helped things along. Oh, and don't worry. I know you searched for her without luck. There is reason for that. Your luck ran out the day you decided to make my life that teeny bit difficult. Now I suggest that you kindly fuck right off before I instruct my Rottweilers to give you the kicking you deserve."

He looked at me with that smug face he always adopted when he knew he had the upper hand. I felt pissed without having had a drink. All these images were flashing though my mind. They were going so fast that I began to feel dizzy. I wanted everything to slow down. It wouldn't, it just got faster. Ernesta and I had had a good time together. So I thought anyway. She was the one who did the chasing. In fact at one time when it was getting a bit too heavy I thought of putting things on ice for a while. She wouldn't hear of it. We argued a bit but there was nothing to it really. The next thing I remember was getting a phone call to meet her in the Randolph for afternoon tea. I went along and she had only booked a room for the night. You know what that costs. It was all very enjoyable. The sex wasn't bad and the cakes even better. I did think that her approach was a little on the aggressive side but when one is in the moment that is how it is. None of it seemed to be a problem as far as I could see. But bollocks, the whole thing was a bloody charade. It was a fucking set up and I stupidly fell for it. That bastard must have recognised the precise moment that the penny dropped and he creased himself laughing at me.

"I don't know what I was expecting but sure as hell it wasn't that. Obviously, I wanted to punch him in his smug, vicious little face, but the security men were already filling the doorway and they were big bastards. So I turned on my heel and left without a word. And before any of you says it, yes that was a first for me.

"I walked out through the college gates and wandered through Oxford in a half dream. Small miracle I didn't get flattened by one of our kamikaze cyclists on the Broad. It was sheer luck that I found myself in the back bar of The King's almost by telepathy and wouldn't you know it there was my antidote to gloom.

"Yes, ensconced at the bar was none other than William Radleigh de Beaune. As I remember it he appeared to be attempting some sort of Cornish clog dance to amuse students, drinkers and the odd don, and as you know the back bar of the King's has seen some very odd dons in its time. I managed to catch his eye and he greeted me with a stream of cod Cornish that ended with him leaping salmon like from the bar and ending up to raucous applause in an untidy tangle of aristocratic limbs right at my feet. There is little as comical as a drunk dusting himself down in an attempt at feigning sobriety. Bonesie's efforts would have made a corpse tango. That's as I remember it but, of course, that may well have been another time altogether.

"The point is, seeing Bill took the edge off my depression and cleared my clouded mind sufficiently for me to give some sensible thought to my current predicament. A few pints of Tribute later and I was able to discuss matters with my old pal and drinking partner as he slowly sobered. Since my interview with Slope barely an hour had passed, though it felt like a week, and I had completely forgotten the letter that he had handed me with such certainty. Having given Bonesie the gist of things along with a little time to get his ale befuddled brain into some sort of gear, I opened it. It was starkly concise. Effectively it informed me that I had been suspended forthwith following a serious allegation of rape made by a female student to be known only as P. My dismissal would be (would be, mark you) confirmed at the next meeting of the college council. And I was to mention this to nobody. If I were to be overheard even discussing it with any other employee of the college then both would be summarily dismissed. And it would be that last bit that made my blood and every other bodily fluid run cold. Visions of Hitler's Germany and Stalin's Russia crowded in on me. Suddenly I felt more lost and alone than I had ever felt and it was only the slightly slurred voice of Bonesie that brought me up short. With a prescience that sometimes only the very drunk can summon he slurred, 'I detect the hand of the Spriggans in this. I hesitate to say I told you so but I did.' In the past I would have sneered at his suggestions but this wasn't the first time for Bonesie to suggest their involvement. The old boy had got it right from the beginning; he'd spotted Slope as a Spriggan right off the bat. You know the rest; the council confirmed the sacking and denied the appeal. So after five months with lawyers to the right of us lawyers to the left of us, into the valley of unemployment charged Piers Prideaux, sad of face and mightily pissed off. And nothing's changed. I suppose it was some sort of consolation, later, that my evidence helped to get the bastard sent down for fraud and misappropriation of college victuals and fine wines. I was in court when the judge handed down the sentence.

If there is such a thing as pure hatred then that is what I saw. He said nothing but he looked directly at me and it felt as if he were looking right through me. He really hated me at that precise moment. It was more than a bit creepy and I didn't really know what he was capable of at that time."

The afternoon wore on as Prideaux finished his explanation of why they were all in the particular predicament that circumstances had led them too. A degree of exhaustion, emotional as well as physical, had taken its toll. Ginny had made her excuses and taken herself off to bed for a reviving nap. Mark was in his study listening to Beethoven's Violin Concerto D Major, rather too loudly for Prideaux's comfort. Bones was snoring loudly on the living room sofa oblivious to everything. Prideaux was collecting himself after his marathon of an attempt at explaining what had led them all to this. Nobody, except Mark, heard the tapping on the study window. He looked through to see the oldest postman in Cornwall staring in at him. He was holding a parcel and gesturing to Mark to come to the front door to sign for it. Mark did so without turning down the music so that he had to shout to understand what Old Jobbins was trying to tell him. It didn't help that he was as deaf as a post so a shouting match was the only option. It became clear to Mark that the parcel was not for him or Ginny. But who the hell would be sending a parcel to Prideaux at this address? His face darkened. It made him uncomfortable. The first thing he needed to do was to sign for the parcel in order to get rid of Old Jobbins. He was not a man to tolerate anything unorthodox. After much persuasion he allowed Mark to sign for the parcel and he wobbled off, grumbling to himself, on the last sit up and beg bike still carrying Post Office colours and insignia. Cornwall is another country, they do things differently here, Mark thought to himself as he walked back into the cottage. He felt unsettled. There were things happening that were beyond his control and that worried him. He composed himself as he walked into the living room and handed the parcel to a half awake Prideaux. "It's for you, Piers, though who the hell is sending you parcels to this address I have no bloody idea."

If Prideaux noticed a degree of furtiveness in Mark's manner he didn't think it worthy of comment. They were all overwrought. There was too much happening for any form of calm to prevail. Even Mark's sharply worded, "Open the bloody thing then, let's at least see what's in it," made no impression on the senses of an over tired and confused Prideaux. The contents of the parcel were not calculated to improve matters. Prideaux ripped open the parcel. "What the fuck is this?" Shaking the package vigorously caused two human ears followed by a big toe to fall on to the coffee table. "This is getting bloody ridiculous now. Don't wake Bonesie up, I can't take any more pork scratching jokes, this whole thing is way beyond a joke. And what the hell is someone's big toe doing here? Look at it. It doesn't even have a toenail. Does that look to you like a left or right toe, Mark?"

"How the hell would I know, Piers? I'm not a bloody expert in body parts for God's sake. What are you doing, trying to collect enough body parts to create another human being, or what? I've had enough of this bloody nonsense. I'm going back to my study." Mark stormed off to the study, slamming doors as he went.

"That bugger is as teasy as an adder. What's his problem, Piers?", came a voice from the depths of the sofa.

"I have no idea, but he's clearly not himself, Bonesie. Right now I could do with no jokes and less discussion. I have a nasty niggling feeling I have an idea of who these bits once belonged to. Suffice it to say that I once knew someone called Fisher. He wasn't a friend or anything.

In fact I remember him as an unpleasant piece of work. The only other thing I remember is that he had no right big toe and that he had lost the toenail on his left big toe. Silly bugger fell asleep in front of an open fire when he was monumentally pissed and was lucky not to lose more then one big toe and a toenail."

15
It's a long and winding road

All roads were leading back to the Spriggans. And as Prideaux continued with his exposition on the fate that had befallen him during the original attempt to blacken his name and wreck his career, a high-ranking Spriggan many miles away was venting his anger on a usually compliant member of the lower orders.

"You are a bloody disgrace, Speight. I sent you to Cornwall to keep an eye on things, not to alert that bastard and his allies, which is what you have done. This time I'm not able to take the academic route to nail him. I can't even think about that as I no longer hold an academic position. Then again, neither does he."

Speight's best course of action would have been silent acceptance of the filleting he was to receive. He knew Slope's temperament and that opposition merely inflamed him, but after all he was a senior and loyal member of the organisation he was not prepared to take it lying down.

"I merely did what I thought appropriate at the time. I had an opportunity and I took it. It didn't work out but at least I gave it my best shot. Just so happens that Bones turned out to be a better shot. And anyway he got lucky. I sometimes wonder what it is you want from members. I've done my best for you and the Spriggans for years. You wouldn't be living in the lap of luxury if it wasn't for my skill in fiddling the books. I'd appreciate it if you treated me with a bit more respect. After all I'm not one of the minions that you enjoy ordering around so much."

"Alright Conrad, you needn't splutter. My decision is

final when it comes to Spriggan policy. We've been made too visible. What it requires is some obvious sacrifices that will re-state our control without alerting outsiders to our existence. After all, what is the point of a secret society if everyone knows it exists? That's where those Masonic clowns and Order of the Rosy Dawn and all those other religion based groups have got it wrong, so bloody wrong."

Slope's colour was rising now. He had saddled a favourite hobbyhorse and was intent on riding it off into the sunset or into the valley of death. He was a committed atheist and hated all the semi-secret religious secret societies with a focus that bordered on obsession. His main line in hatred was their pathetic attempts at becoming inclusive once their covers were blown. Whether it was some intrusive journalist writing an expose or a gazillion selling novelist doing the exposure job it was all irrelevant to him. It was cowardice in the face of the enemy. Secret meant secret and any means to keep the status quo was justifiable. After all the Spriggans had never been based on any sort of religious belief or any ethical standpoint. They were founded on the old crimes of smuggling and wrecking; crimes that didn't even figure as crimes in the dark days when Cornwall was even more neglected than now. And it never mattered if the local vicar was involved, he generally was, since he was a Church of England man he was perfectly able to do the job without ever troubling his conscience with a belief in a supreme being, unless it was the leader of the Spriggans of the time.

He managed to recover himself and row back from a certain self-induced stroke. He turned his attention back to Speight, who seemed to have shrunken considerably under the full blast of Slope's ire. He remained standing and showing a creditable resistance to someone who was a force of nature when in full flow. But nobody stood up to Slope for long. He had that dangerous combination of plausibility and menace that had served many a tyrant well. Slope was in full swing by now, but despite the tough talk it was not immediately obvious what was possible in terms of administering the punishment he had saved up for Prideaux.

"I've decided to call a meeting of the 'One and All Caucus' in order to devise a fool proof plan for exacting revenge on Prideaux. It's not that I need any form of consensus; they will do as I tell them. But the Caucus is made up of some seriously disturbed bastards and there is a good chance of one of them coming up with a devious and vicious plan, but best of all one that does not leave a trail of muddy footprints all the way back to yours truly. Send in the psychos, Speight. That'll be what the man who is not Mr Rainbow ordered."

"What do you mean?" Speight asked.

"Talking to you is like trying to teach a jellyfish to arm wrestle," Slope spat.

"Surely in an organisation dedicated to self-preferment and the eradication of any and all opposition we will have a smattering of card carrying psychos. One will do, for God's sake. Only I don't just want some sicko who has persuaded the shrinks that he has paid for his crimes and is now safe to be allowed back into the community.

"I want what I call a virgin sicko, by which I mean one that has no form at all but a sufficiently twisted personality to make him useful to me. And in case you are not already aware, a seriously disturbed personality need not mean that its owner is stupid. Stupid people are of no use at all, something you should probably take note of, Speight. Accordingly, I intend to call a meeting of the Caucus for next Wednesday evening. You make the arrangements. Tell them only that the meeting is an emergency one. Tell them nothing else but make sure that all twelve attend. The meeting code is black.

They will know that there are no accepted excuses for non-attendance, except of course death. He smiled his sinister smile. The meeting will take place in the usual place and will last for precisely one hour. At the end of it I will have in my hand a piece of paper bearing the name of the man who will initiate the practical aspects of a plan that will put paid to the bastard Prideaux."

Blissfully unaware of his intended fate Prideaux finished his exposition and, since it was a Friday, suggested adjourning to the pub. The pub on Friday night was, of course, a sacred ritual as any wage slave will testify. And Blisland's village pub held more than the average attraction; the log fire, proper Cornish pasties rather than those abominations that masquerade as the real thing outside the county, sadly in some spots inside the county as well. You know they're not authentic when even the seagulls won't eat them. These beauties though were made in the pub's kitchen with short pastry, skirt beef, onions, potato and turnip. This was the way that pasties had been made for generations. Prideaux had exhausted his patience long ago in explaining to emmets that to the Cornish the turnip was what they knew as swede.

This was another point of difference between the Cornish and everyone else. Small difference perhaps, but on small differences events may turn.

But the point now was; what to do next? Living in the moment the famous four were content to eat pasties and drink real ale in God's other Country. Many believed that Cornwall had acquired the soubriquet God's other Country because of the number of villages or towns named for saints. In truth you couldn't fire a cannon filled with grapeshot through Cornwall without hitting a Saint Blaise here or a Saint Austell here, but that's not really it. The reason is that Cornish folk really believe their county to be blessed. Take a look at the scenery, the climate, the best of the food and all the rest. And of course they all know that Jesus came to Cornwall with his Dad. Anyone unaware of that should take a trip to the achingly beautiful St Just in Roseland. Of course Jesus came to Cornwall, it says so in the pretty little church by the creek. But with the ale coursing through his veins and some sort of confidence forming, Prideaux was beginning to work out what best to do in the current circumstances where forgiveness lay pretty thin on the ground. A Christian faith would not be much use in these circumstances, not, that is, unless it was resolutely Old Testament involving eyes and teeth, with pale horses charging about in numbers.

So far two people were dead. Not many would miss Petroc. He had a cousin somewhere in Northumberland but nobody really knew where, or cared. Clarence, however, and his untimely death, would raise one or two eyebrows. On top of all that it wasn't just him in the frame any more. Prideaux's three companions shared his precarious position. Slope was not likely to let any of the four live. He knew where they were now and even if they returned to Oxford it wouldn't take a heartbeat to track all four of them down. Then there was the shadowy world of the Spriggans that meant nobody could be trusted. They did not go in for funny handshakes, rolled up trousers or secret tattoos, and were so well absorbed into everyday professions that it would be next to impossible to be sure whether an individual was a member or not. It could easily be that even longstanding friends or close acquaintances of his could be members. You could never tell, and four hundred years of brutality would not vanish in a dream. What he needed was a bolthole for all four of them. At least the other three could be trusted, couldn't they? He would have no problem in turning his back on any of them, but where was there to hide? It was what the sainted Sherlock would doubtless declare to be a two-pipe problem.

16

The silent valley

In a wooded valley in the depths of South Wales, at the end of an unmade road that turned into a stream in the rainy season, was a stone built longhouse dating from the late eighteenth century. Its low roof with the undulations of many years of pressure from the heavy hand cut slate seemed to snake its way along the landscape; it might have been the lair of the last dragon in Wales. In a way it was. For the sole resident of this remarkable testament to the resilience of the Welsh was himself that very same thing; he was a survivor.

Still here and now in his eightieth year, Rhys ap Dafydd, known to all as the Black Prince, stood as upright as he had when as a young man he had served as a stretcher-bearer, though under age, in the Great War. He had seen the worst that man could visit on fellow man at Ypres and the Somme. He was a warrior who reserved the moral right not to kill. He had seen enough of that and he knew that it was never the way. Yet at six foot three of solid muscle topped with a beetling brow and a stare that could stop a charging rhino, there were few occasions where he was called to even simulate violence. He was a man of peace but like many with that inclination he had killed.

To a fireside philosopher like the Black Prince that knowledge upset the equilibrium of his mind. He was at peace with the world, never with his mind. The mind is only partially rational and some say, in a Welshman of the pedigree of the Prince, hardly at all, so he remained unable to rationalise the killing of the Germans and the English officer. Self-defence was too weak an excuse though that is what it was. He should have stuck to his principles. Had he done so he would not be here now. Here, that is, to offer shelter to his grandson and those friends of his who needed a form of sanctuary. And he looked forward to seeing Piers again. It had been a long time. There had been no falling out, it was simply that their paths had diverged, that is what paths do. It is the individual who must decide which one to travel. He would have kept in touch but, having graduated, Prideaux never really came home except for high days and holidays and the inevitable funeral. But there was a bond; there always had been. From the days when the Prince taught him the old ways to the day Prideaux left for Oxford the two had been inseparable.

After that they had inhabited separate worlds. Prideaux had relegated the old ways to the seventh circle of his consciousness. He no longer needed them. He was in the real world of study, thought, debate and argumentation. The old world was gone. If the old man was hurt, he never showed it. He carried on with the life of the seasons, the woods and the cleansing fresh rain and he never forgot his grandson. Now after all this time his grandson needed him again. He had waited for this time. He knew the old ways never go away. They could lie buried by dusty academic study, by immorality or even by plain material envy but they always surfaced. The old ways were too deeply rooted to be bested for long by materialism or the trivia of modern life.

The old man knew and Prideaux knew too. His only problem was he hadn't known that he knew until now. Going back wasn't that simple though. The old man eschewed modern communication. He had no mobile phone, no computer or iPad. Had never needed them then; didn't need them now. If anyone needed to contact him they could come to the house. Phone messages could be left at the Morning Star, the pub so high up the mountain that visitors needed oxygen to reach it. Not that there were ever many visitors. It was very firmly a locals' pub. They never called it The Morning Star; to them it was always The Top House. It wasn't even a pub as such. It was the front room of the house where old Rhian lived on after her parents died. She continued their tradition of always having plenty of home brewed beer on tap for callers. It was simply the old way again and needed no explanation. The beer was brewed from locally harvested barley, hops and woodland herbs. It tasted heavenly but like heaven it was an acquired taste. It had none of the cold tasteless quality of the latest designer beers. And it was never, never served cold. Nor was it ever served in glasses. It was a drink that sat well in the old china mugs that had been used at the house for years beyond reckoning. And it was strong. Any unwary walker who accidentally happened upon the Top House was limited to a single pint, laughed at a little bit then sent on their way to the floor of the valley. Some got there quicker than intended. Somebody had once erected a notice that read, 'Beware of Rolling Drunks' that had amused those locals more than accustomed to a 'tidy drop'.

The purpose of the Top House these days was to provide liquor and conversation for the scattered population of the valley. In truth that was what it had always done but these days a physical place for the people of the valley to meet had assumed a greater importance. Modern technology isolates as much as it unites and these were people who knew the importance of community. They had no need for entertainment; their default mode was talk and drink. They had no time for other things. Quiz nights, karaoke, and music were all things that others did. And the others had no place or business in the comforting dark of the Top House. Best of all Rhian paid no tax to the Revenue nor observed any licensing hours.

Like all the scattered houses in the valley the Top House had been constructed in as difficult and desolate a place as possible. It wasn't really accessible in the accepted sense. Even the battered old Land Rovers mostly driven here could only get so far up the tracks that tended to lead to the houses of the people. Nobody could get within a mile of any of the houses of this strange community without being seen. Revenue men and the police never bothered to make the effort. It was pointless. A group of men loudly discussing politics at 2am would be a private party helping the landlady, or the bushy bearded Rhys, to celebrate his birthday. Rhys played the role of companion to Rhian and did most of the odd jobs around the place that needed to be done. By anybody's reckoning he'd be around 140 by now. This was a way of life that had resisted all modernisation for generations and this was a way of life that a thankful Prideaux and friends would gratefully embrace until they could come up with an answer to the threat of Slope and his deadly Spriggans.

For Bones with his love of decent claret the fear was that it could be a long sojourn. Although even this hardship could be alleviated by the presence of industrial qualities of what those outside the valley would probably refer to as moonshine. It wasn't, it was wysgi. These people had been distilling the good stuff since long before the Scots and Irish entered the business. It wasn't random either. They had their own strict quality controls and there was only one still allowed in Silent Valley. Silent Valley single malt was a little taste of the warm south with a granite finish and not a sign of peat to be tasted anywhere. The Scots could add their own peat. The taste of this area did not run to such frippery. This wysgi must have had some sort of health giving quality because the people of the valley seemed to live forever.

It was dusk when the four friends reached the house of

the Black Prince. A single light burned in the longhouse. Prideaux knew it would be a decoy. Rhys would be nearby in the woods. He would know they were coming. He would also be aware that their presence could bring the sort of unwanted attention that needed to be dealt with, summarily. He tried the front door. It opened with a creak that echoed through the valley like a gunshot.

"Where the hell is the old bugger?" gurgled Bones. The sentence choked in his throat as he felt the knife cold against the side of his neck.

"He's right behind you, Bonesie, and he still takes exception at being called old."

"I didn't mean anything by it," spluttered a patently rattled Bones.

"Neither did I," smiled the old man. "But point taken, I imagine. You had no idea where I was, or who I was and that very fact can mean the difference between life and death. It's the sort of thing an out of condition old city slicker is going to need to know until this is all over. Now Croeso to you all and get inside and you can tell me all your experiences and how I can help to get you out of what sounds a tightish spot."

17

The black prince

The telling did not take long. Old Rhys had a logical mind and he followed the fairly tortuous tale with a real glint in his sharp flickering eyes. He would brook no interruptions or circumlocutions and did not speak until the story was up to date.

"Right then, first of all open a bottle of the golden stuff and we'll do some thinking."

The instruction was directed to nobody in particular but Bones shot to his feet like a startled grebe and filled five glasses of the smoothest malt he had ever tasted.

"Now there's two ways of looking at this," Rhys said with relish. "We could take the Crocodile Dundee model and take the bastards on here in the hills. Choose our own ground to fight as you might say. But the trouble with that picture is that it's not our ground, it's my ground. That means I would have to take anything that Slope sends against us on my own. That shouldn't be a problem, or it wouldn't be if I knew his strength. I don't and from what I already know there could be dozens of otherwise normal people who are secret Spriggans. There is no way of identifying them. It would have been easier," the old man glanced at his grandson with a smirk, "if you had upset a bunch of zombies. You can tell them a mile off. Groaning and bleeding and dragging their feet like escapees from the naughty step at an old folks' home. I could outrun them carrying a gas stove on my back. But trust you. You had to go and upset a whole hatful of bastards who could pass for normal anywhere. One of you might be a Spriggan for all I know."

"Don't even joke about that, granddad," said Prideaux.

"You've been away too long, Piers my boy. If you had stayed around you would know I never ever joke, especially where the matter is one of life and death. But I have had an idea. We'll be safe here tonight but tomorrow morning I want us all to go into town. I still have a lot of friends there and I never gave up the old town house I used to live in there. It doesn't look much but there's plenty of room for four and I can start talking to some people who will be able to help in all sorts of ways. That's my decision and that's what we are going to do. Any dissenters?" Bones looked at Prideaux. Words were unnecessary. The look meant simply 'It's your family, mate. If that's what he wants then who are we to argue. Please tell me that he is all there though. Just for my peace of mind, you know how it is.' Without any formal vocal response acceptance was assumed. "Right, off you go and get some sleep. The accommodation is fairly basic but it's clean and we should be fine here for the night at least."

The following morning was bright with a touch of air frost. By the time the four had managed to struggle down to the kitchen the Black Prince had been up for four hours. Training and instinct had meant that he had already checked the perimeter and, with a woodsman's cunning, ascertained that there was no evidence of any unwanted visitors in the immediate area. There was a roaring fire in the grate and an old cauldron suspended over it. It might have been a witch's house or more likely a wizard's. The slippery, meaty smell filled the cottage.

Of course it was lamb, home reared and gently killed then jointed and cooked with wild garlic, onions and root vegetables. Voluptuous slippery cawl, the food of angels. Not normally taken at breakfast but then these were not normal times. Good food would sustain them longest and Rhys's homemade cawl was a thing of legend. A pig looking in through the cottage window would have been impressed with the slurping, gurgling and glugging sounds of his human counterparts. Of course it may have been the condemned eating a hearty breakfast, the world was changing so fast anything could happen.

With five appetites sated and the sink filled with greasy dishes, one by one the group gathered round Rhys ready to listen to what the old man had to say. It was succinct, as the four listeners had already come to expect.

"Trouble will follow you so we need to be prepared. There was a time when I knew and trusted everyone in Wild Horse River but that time is gone. My house there is set apart from most of the others. It is built into the cliff at the back and sides so it is easy to spot anything out of place. We'll go there now and I'll settle you in."

It was 11.30am when the group headed for town. There was none of the chatter that one would expect in such a situation and, let's face it, this lot were talkers. It was commonly said of Prideaux and Bones that they could talk about anything for an hour, two hours if they knew anything about it. But this was different. There was this looming sense of something that nobody really understood. It was always there, ill defined, nameless, but like a dark cloud that might rain down fire and brimstone at any moment. Worst of all there was no knowing where the threat may come from. That was the worst part. It is always the worst part. If the threat is visible at least it can be faced. Then at least the hope is to go down fighting, but such a luxury would never be on offer where Slope's secret soldiers were involved.

18

Pour encourager les autres

A hundred miles or so from this particular bout of soul seeking Slope was indeed planning his next move. He still resembled a human version of one of those old fashioned pressure cookers where the steam is building and nobody is entirely sure whether the release valve will work or not. In short he was about to explode. It was around a month after the Wednesday that Slope had dictated should be the date of the emergency meeting. That fact had fuelled his current evil mood. He knew that the longer this went on with Prideaux and his pals on the loose the more dangerous his own position was becoming. Friends in high places was all well and good but he knew better than most that when things got a bit sticky such friends could melt like hoar frost on a bright spring morning. Slope was not a man to wait on action, if it were done then it would be well it were done quickly, he thought to himself with a smile resembling a freshly sharpened stiletto.

Speight looked at him with the air of a tethered goat awaiting the matinee appearance of the leopard. "The twelve will be here by 5.30pm," he said in a reedy voice. That he was in Slope's bad books there was no doubt at all. People in that position tended not to be around for long, and frequently when they reappeared it would be as a bloated floater in the Cherwell or the Isis. He shuddered at the thought of Petroc who, though loathsome, had met a pretty unpleasant end. His only hope was that Slope's newly rediscovered blood lust had eased. It didn't look much like it though. Slope's response didn't even elicit a nod. "They had better be," was the expression on

115

his face as he sat in the throne reserved for the man who was not Mr Rainbow. Eschewing his customary black Slope was dressed in the customary rainbow coloured robes demanded of his position. Strangely he exuded even more than his usual menace. It was a quiet menace that in no way chimed with the beauty of the room where the two men sat. It was highly decorated with priceless frescoes and furnished with a long refectory style table. Placed on the table, in front of each chair, was an ugly bronze representation of a Spriggan. The bronzes were twelve inches in height and seemed to embody the spirit of evil in the twisted, contorted face of each figure. Leaning against each of the ghastly figures was a card in a colour of the rainbow. From Slope's right the cards read red, orange, yellow, green, blue, indigo and violet. The remaining five cards were buff and had supplicant written on them in old script. They were for the five members who had not yet gained full membership of the highest level of the society. They would always need to be present even at an emergency meeting. It was the Spriggan's wild idea of democracy to include beginners in the process of decision making. In truth they had no vote but it amused Slope and the higher echelons to pretend that they did.

The twelve started to file into the old chapel with the elders first, followed by the supplicants. They all stood behind the appropriate chairs until Slope gave the sign for them to sit. "There is no agenda," he announced in the soft voice that he took to be his reassuring voice. It wasn't. It was the more terrifying for barely being above a whisper and usually betokened bad news for somebody. Nobody spoke, all being aware of the infamous Slope temper. "There are, however, two items for discussion." He smiled at the word discussion. "That is to say two things must be decided today and they are as follows; number one, the impending death of Prideaux, Bones, those two slackers they have with them and that Welsh bastard who likes people to call him the Black Prince. And two, the sad fact that someone in this room is a traitor and has, I believe, been betraying some of our secrets to outsiders."

The silence was palpable. The senior members had been through this type of thing before and it always ended badly. The supplicants had never experienced the real thing but knew enough about the organisation they had joined, thinking it would help their careers, to want to be anywhere else in the universe rather than where they were, the college chapel of St Jude's.

None of the twelve seemed to notice the slim man in a business suit, although he must have seemed incongruous in the midst of the plethora of flowing black gowns, with Slope at the head of the table decked out in all the colours of the rainbow. Had they noticed the man they would have felt at ease as he looked as if he were the organisation's accountant. Not only was he slim but he was also short, wore quite thick glasses and looked particularly harmless. He was, however, more than that. The irony was that Scratcher had qualified as an accountant several years previously and had prospered in that capacity. Ultimately, though he had made money whether through work completed or through occasional bouts of light embezzlement, the profession lacked the excitement he craved. He had discovered when still a young man that killing gave him pleasure and he had developed attributes and skills that made him the perfect assassin. He was quick, ferocious and merciless whether in the operation of knife, garrotte or gun. Despite his slim build his wrists were enormously strong, making strangulation one of his favoured methods of despatch. As the delegates took their seats he lurked in the shadows, his face giving no indication of the horrors he could visit on the unsuspecting.

Attention focused on Slope as he rang the antique ship's bell that tradition dictated would announce the commencement of business. It had a dolorous sound peculiarly appropriate to its purpose, and whomever it was tolling for today was shortly not going to ask for whom this particular bell tolled ever again.

"There is a traitor in our midst and for that reason I shall address the second problem first. I have decided to make an example of two of you." His eyes swept the room, his familiar smile playing around his thin lips. "As yet you know not who you are, that will soon be rectified. But first let me say a word about the theatrical value of what is to happen. Some people may think it a little melodramatic but in my experience murder most foul tends to concentrate the mind. An organisation such as ours can only prosper when its members strictly observe what the Mafia call omerta. Most people think that means silence, and while it incorporates that concept it is at the same time a much bigger word than that. It is not enough to refuse to betray the organisation when under pressure or duress or even torture. It is much more important that you should remain alert at all times and never drop a single word that may give outsiders any access to this organisation at all."

Slope was warming to his theme now. He had the complete attention of the room and he knew it. It was this form of absolute power that attracted him and vindicated his sense of self-worth. Since he had no moral compass it was useless for anyone to even attempt to persuade him that his actions were cruel, brutal even. For him murder was the action of the furnace in purging any impurities that could taint the organisation rendering it less effective in any of it nefarious activities.

"You will be aware of the recent death of one Petroc Trethewey who recently logged out for good as a putrefying heap of flesh in the Cherwell. The elders here will be aware that he had been a Spriggan. He is a dead and discredited Spriggan now. And do you know why he died?" The silence in the room was suffocating as he moved towards his theatrical climax. "I'll tell you since it is apparent that you all seem to have lost the will to speak. At least that spares me any last minute appeals for mercy; there will be no mercy. That is not the way of the Spriggans. Putrid Petroc talked too much. Not that he was an inveterate gossip, though he certainly was that. He died because he discussed the business of this organisation in public places in the presence of non-Spriggans. And for those who are interested you should know that I killed him myself even though he was my brother in arms as well as my natural brother. He was my stepbrother in reality but our mother always insisted we were closer than full brothers. How wrong she could be. We had the same mother, that's all. It doesn't mean I had to like him and I didn't. I didn't even know him until he arrived to stay with us. He was three years older than me when he turned up on the doorstep. It's fair to say we didn't hit it off. He was a lazy bastard then, even in his attempts at bullying. He tried to give me a hard time once or twice. Curious thing really. He was always afraid of the dark. At the time we were renting a large and decrepit old Victorian pile. One day I waited until he was ensconced on the loo. The bathroom was huge. All I had to do was reach inside the door for the switch and turn the light off. Poor Petroc screamed his head off. Strangely he never bothered me again after that. He never went into the bathroom at night time either so I think he learned a lesson. Didn't mean I let him off the hook though. Poor bastard became neurotic. They started taking him to all sorts of doctors, both quacks and the other sorts. He was always coming out in a rash and the general opinion, both medical and otherwise, was that he suffered from nerves. You bet he did. I never let him rest. If he had a weakness I found it. Spiders in the bed, that was me. A rat in his toy cupboard, that was a good one. They were thinking psychiatric help was needed after that one. I had great fun and in the end he was terrified of what I might do next. The threat is often enough to get the job done. But one should never make idle threats. To be honest I never have done, not even in those far off days. It was a bit like attending a prep school specialising in the arts of terror and violence, I suppose. Didn't do me any harm in any case. I suppose killing him was bit further up the scale but such things are not that unusual, now are they?" The question was left hanging as there was a bout of synchronised concentration of the table immediately in front of the assembled members.

"Oh! Come on. Don't look so surprised; there is plenty of precedent for such a deed. Anything common enough to need a word to describe it can hardly come as a surprise even to the least knowledgeable of you all. Fratricide is not a big deal and for anyone amongst you foolish enough to be Christian it is well documented that Cain took care of Abel when it suited him." At this point Slope had got to his feet and pushing back the great chair, traditionally the throne of the man who was not Mr Rainbow, he walked casually towards the seated supplicants.

There is a point at which all hope dies in the human mind, that point had been reached and was visible on the faces of all those present, except Slope. Not one even turned in his chair as Slope reached his apparent target. He had begun chanting a curse in ancient Cornish that became louder as he moved closer. Images flashed through the minds of the five. Images of past conversations, perhaps some gentle boasting, some showing off, a loose tongue here or there. It could be any one of them. The worst thing was that each of the five knew that any form of resistance would be futile. Death was about to visit and two of them would never leave the chapel, not under their own steam at least.

The move when it came was brutal and mercifully swift. Ending his curse, Slope's wiry arm slipped effortlessly around the neck of novice number five. There was a crack as he twisted and, showing no more emotion than if he were killing a chicken for the pot, he allowed the lifeless body of the novice to slump in the ornate chair he had previously occupied in blissful ignorance. Simultaneously he had nodded towards Scratcher who moved silently from the shadows. A thin steel wire lasso emerged from the sleeve of his jacket and with expert precision was slipped over the head of the totally unsuspecting Speight. He gasped as the killing wire cut deeply into his neck. Blood started to drip from his neck as it tightened inexorably. It was impossible to free the grip once the killing wire was in place and the struggle was not long. "Say not the struggle naught availeth," muttered Slope, smiling at the irony as Speight slumped forward onto the table, his head on his arms at a crazy angle as life drained from the body.

Scratcher removed the noose, wiped off the blood on what was left of Speight's hair and stepped back into the shadows as Slope slipped effortlessly back into the big chair. It could have been choreographed; it was the choreography of death. Slope the Showman would not miss a trick.

"We shall continue as if nothing happened here, because in effect nothing has. I have simply taken the appropriate steps to purge the organisation of weakness and incompetence. You will have heard the old saw, 'What doesn't kill us can only make us stronger'. I suggest you keep the emphasis on 'us' because those corpses that will keep us company until the end of this meeting didn't. And, of course, if any word of what happened here reaches the outside world there will be the appropriate measures to be taken. Now with your permission I shall proceed with today's major item, which is the final solution. I am fully aware of the emotive nature of that phrase, which is why I have used it. This organisation has developed from an ancient self-help group into a powerful force for evil and I intend to keep it on track.

"The secret of our success has been to gradually winnow out the original members and replace them with men of a different hue. I have lived in many places and I am not enamoured with the natives of any of those places. Many of you in this benighted place you so laughingly call the United Kingdom pretend that this is a great country with the unqualified support of all its citizens. Sadly for you the real truth is that there is only one thing that unites this place and that is the reciprocal dislike of every defined part of the country for every other part. It is a unity based on mutual and intense hatred, and pretending that it is not the case has been raised to an art form.

"In my experience the worst of the lot are those who live in the extreme west of the country. There is nothing worse than those who cling to a mythical golden age that never existed. Of those the Welsh and Cornish are by far the worst. They insist that they are the descendants of Brutus and are related to the ancient Britons and it is all bollocks. Even if it weren't it would not matter. In the modern age painting oneself as one of the 'dreamers of dreams and singers of songs' is some sort of hippy indulgence that should not be tolerated. I am descended from the Vikings, the race that ripped up this place for generations and as far as I am concerned the only way to progress is to take whatever it is you happen to want and ensure that you keep it. If some of our weaker brothers go to the wall in the process then it is simply natural selection doing its best work. And never forget I reserve my most terminal vengeance for those who betray the interests of the organisation. We have friends in high places and I intend to keep it that way."

Slope was on his feet by this point in his tirade. His face was a terrifying shade of puce, his lips were flecked with spittle as the venom bubbled and vomited from a hate filled soul. This was megalomania in full spate and the listening group sat transfixed. Questions that might have offered another interpretation of history were suppressed as the extent of his anger became clear. What none of them knew was that Slope held that type of hatred peculiar to one who had so hidden a background, one that did not chime with his own idea of who he was, that not even Speight, who so recently had breathed his last, had any idea that Slope had Cornish blood. He had not been brought up in the county though had visited when young. His father and grandfather had been navvies – they weren't all Irish – and had moved around the country. He felt no roots anywhere and had listened with poorly disguised contempt to stories of the old country from his father. He was uninterested in tales of a Celtic twilight. He regarded the Celts as barely civilised and had set his face against all their works. All, that is, apart from the one that exercised his every working thought these days.

He had become familiar with the history of the Spriggans from visits to the Central Cornish Library in Mount Charles, not from any misguided sense of belonging but more to feed the contempt he already held for the county and what he held to be its bloody-minded inhabitants. But Slope was nothing if not a planner. As a child he knew that he would never be a manual worker, he was too clever for that. He had seen and smelled the desperate sweat of the day labourer and even when young was far too fastidious for that lifestyle. He had no sense of specific direction except that he suspected it would need to be outside the traditional professions. He knew that he could make money in any profession he chose, but of itself that would not be enough.

What appealed to his perverse sense of individual success was the opportunity to have a façade of respectability behind which he could rip to pieces any moral law or ethical construct that even the most civilised system could invent. To him that was the way of the Spriggans. He would become one of them, better, he would become the man who was not Mr Rainbow and then bend the relatively harmless secret society to his more than malevolent will. He had the best qualification of all, the psychopathic disregard for any form of truth or justice that was independent of the individual. This Slope did not observe any law, moral or otherwise. He devised his own laws and woe betide anyone who was not a strict observer of Slope's Law.

His plan, though already there in outline when he was little more than a child, began to take a more solid shape as he aged. The final impetus came when as a teenager he was awarded a scholarship by St Jude's in Oxford. He had already established himself as something of a big brain at the local grammar school, though he loathed the place. He was a loner and refused to take part in any of the sports or organised activities. He may well have been the target of local bullies except for an indefinable stillness that unsettled even the most brutish. One occasion more than any other crystallised this in the minds of the local population. Having transferred to a local school in rural Wales he became an immediate target. He had an English accent, he made no attempt to fit in and was dismissive of all things Welsh. A farmer's son called Evan took it upon himself to teach this upstart a Welsh lesson.

An impassive and unresisting Slope took the mother

and father of all beatings in a copse at the edge of the farmer's land. Not a word was said and Slope spent two weeks away from the school. There was nobody to appeal to. His father would have told him that he deserved everything he got, of that he was fully aware. This was the beginning of his transformation into the independent force he would gradually become. He returned to school. Again it was never mentioned and he never referred to it, but he became even more withdrawn.

Two weeks after he returned to the school Evan, the farmer's son, disappeared. He was a self-reliant lad of around fifteen and initially nobody was too concerned. He ran the woods and knew that he would take over the family farm so was not too bothered with academic achievement. On the third day his father was doing his usual check of the farm's perimeter when he became aware of something blocking the flow of the stream that ran through the copse. It was the area where Slope had taken his beating a couple of weeks earlier. From a distance he could see an old coat lying half in the stream. As he got closer intending to clear the blockage he recognised his son's jacket the one that he wore all the time. Breaking into an uncontrolled and uncontrollable run he dropped to his knees next to the bundle. It was Evan, his head in the stream, and it was obvious that he was dead.

The subsequent enquiry and inquest could only establish that cause of death had been a broken neck, and that the boy must have slipped and, twisting in a failed attempt to save himself, caught his head on a rock. The awkward fall would have led to a broken neck. Nobody believed it, not the investigating officer, not the coroner and certainly nobody at the school. There was no proof otherwise so an open verdict was handed down. What was indisputable was that no one went anywhere near Slope after that. The sense of menace was overt, palpable and always present. Slope had found the power of fear, something that would remain one of his favourite weapons throughout the rest of his life.

It was a weapon that had taken him to the pinnacle of power for a man who loved the feeling of control that such a position could give. He had the perfect disguise for a power hungry psychopath. In adulthood he became urbane, cultured, and had the capacity to exude charm. He was able to lie without blushing and would have walked right through any lie detector test without blinking, certainly without sweating. He was amoral and lying was simply one more technique in his bag of tricks. By such means he had progressed from supplicant to eventual leader of the Spriggans. And he had achieved this through political machinations that would have left Niccolo Machiavelli speechless and doubtless envious. His current purge was designed to return him to what he saw as his rightful position as head of a lean and mean secret organisation. He had protection in high places, and this recent exercise in choreographed murder would soon reach the ears of any of the great and good currently reconsidering the cloak of silence they had been so ready to spread over the shoulders of this most evil of men. Speight and his most recent companion in violent death would soon turn up bobbing in one of the Oxford rivers. Ears in the pockets of two bloated corpses would confirm that Slope was approaching a return to his murderous best. It was not a happy situation for an unsuspecting Prideaux and friends, currently some hundred miles away and still pondering a sensible next step.

19

Is this the way to Wild Horse River?

The four set out for Wild Horse River in the old man's battered Land Rover. Rhys followed on a Royal Enfield motorbike and sidecar at a discreet distance. He never wore a helmet and with his long white hair flowing in the wind he looked, for all the world, an Old Testament prophet. This part of the world wasn't short of Old Testament men. There were plenty here who thought that an eye for an eye and a tooth for a tooth was a pretty pacifist cop out. Rhys wasn't one of them but where family was involved he tended to deal with things summarily.

To an outsider he simply looked like some old buffer who had managed to sneak out of the coffin queue. To mistake old Rhys for a coffin dodger would be a terrible mistake to make, and if an outsider had any form of evil in mind it could also be a last mistake.

As he clattered down the mountain track leading to town his mind was racing as fast as the old machine he threw around as if it were an extension of his body.

Because he knew the mountain and the tracks he arrived in town before his four visitors. What he knew and they didn't was the whereabouts of the tunnel that led directly into the house he had lived in for so many years before the death of his wife. He was in the house before the four had parked the Land Rover and walked up the gravel path to the front door.

The effect of the old man opening the front door as Prideaux put his hand up to put the key in the lock was electric. The four leaped back in a way that would have earned them a hatful of points in any synchronised leaping competition and it amused the old man that he still possessed the power to unnerve. Well at least, thought Rhys, it looks as if these townies are on guard.

"Welcome to the house of pain," said Rhys with a smile that stayed the right side of menacing. The four tumbled in through the front door giving a fine impression of a Feydeau farce. "What the hell is this?" spluttered Prideaux.

"This is what you might describe as a redoubt; a place to make that last but one stand before pulling back to the hills. You've seen Zulu; it is a tactical move before pulling back to the last resort or, in this case, my house in the woods. Do you remember the old philosopher?"

"You mean Ray Guevara," answered Prideaux who remembered him well. Ray wasn't his real name, neither was Guevara, but it is what everybody in the area called him because of his political views. It was Ray who had warned, years before anyone had given it a moment's thought, of the importance of water in the future of the United Kingdom. "Future wars are not going to be about oil," he would say, "they will be about water. It doesn't take a genius to work out that when there is a genuine shortage whoever controls the supply will be in a powerful position."

Such talk was met with plenty of scepticism even in a naturally rebellious country such as Wales. Ray would always counter with 'Cofiwch Dreweryn" in his native tongue.

"You will recall Treweryn, when they flooded an entire valley because one of the English cities was short of water. It didn't matter that the residents didn't want to go, they were forcibly removed and that was that."

"I'm sorry to stop you," interjected Prideaux at the risk of upsetting his grandfather, "but my immediate concern is not Welsh history, fascinating as it undoubtedly is, but my current difficulty with Slope and his crew. Reminiscing about dear old Ray Guevara doesn't help me at all. How am I going to deal with the fact that what appears to be a homicidal maniac is on my trail and that of three of my friends? Oh, and by the way, you will be on the list too by association, if nothing else. And lest we forget, our ecumenical cousin the vicar has already been sent swinging off to meet his maker. The bell tolled for that poor old soul for certain. I always had my doubts, and if truth were told I still do, but that doesn't alter the fact that he didn't deserve to die in the way he did. I have to say that I feel sorry for him and it merely highlights the danger that the Spriggans present. They don't seem to care what they do and so far I have seen little evidence that there is anyone who gives much of a damn."

"My dear boy, I have been on that list for years. I have known the Spriggans and their leaders since your mother first brought home the Cornishman who was to become her husband and your father. Your father told me all there was to know of the Spriggans and how all decent Cornish folk would have nothing to do with them. The fact is that it all went wrong in the last century. A lot of these secret societies started out with good intentions. Masons, charcoal burners in Italy, even the Mafia, had some sort of moral standards to begin with but it all gets lost. Once the naturally criminal mind sees some advantage in having the support of the local people they start to see pound signs as well. Remember that the smugglers in Cornwall and Wales originally tried to make subsistence living a little more palatable by bringing in goods for personal consumption rather than profit. Even the tobacco smugglers were originally after a bit of baccy for them and their mates when duty was unreasonably high. Remember there is nothing new under the sun.

This Slope of yours is the latest in a long line of crooked bastards to wheedle his way into the Spriggans when he has no natural right to be there. The organisation has been bent for a long time now but there is a difference. Slope is intent on turning it into some sort of Mafia organisation with him in complete control. It is pretty much that way at the moment but what you may not know is that he has support that goes a long way. In the hope of not sounding too paranoid it goes as far up as the cabinet."

It was beginning to appear a bit too much a poor soap opera. Something American perhaps shown on an endless loop on daytime TV. There would be a doctor who would drop everything in the operating theatre and shoot off to investigate a murder, only keeping the police informed when it suited him. But this was different and Prideaux knew it in his heart.

The old college had been a great place to study and its left wing tendencies coincided pretty neatly with Prideaux's own. But there were plenty there who, despite all evidence to the contrary, had membership of the establishment in mind all the time. Sure, they would turn up on the inevitable demo where they would often carry the red flag and be the most vocal of the lot. But underneath the bluff and bluster it was politics, and specifically the politics of power, that interested them. Prideaux had featured in plenty of arguments masquerading as debates with the ravening left-wingers who had one eye on old Karl Marx and the other on the bigger prize of government. He loathed them and they reciprocated. Their careful scheming didn't always survive his skilled and combative filleting of their pathetic justifications and in some cases they became invisible for a while after graduation, only to reappear some years after in a junior government role. He hadn't given it a lot of thought, as it tended to be too depressing. What was even more depressing is that some he had regarded as comrades might even have been long-term members of the bastard organisation that Slope now fronted. It made him grow cold. This was no two bit soap opera, it was real, and the threat of violence was bubbling along too near the surface for comfort.

His reverie was interrupted by the consoling and comforting voice of his grandfather. "Don't take it to heart, Piers. We all get fooled again and again. What counts is what we do about it. We already know that Slope has killed recently. He sent one of his men to Cornwall in one attempt to get rid of all of you. He failed. Experience tells us that he will try again and he is not going to give up until he succeeds. We need to prepare for his next attempt. We need to be ready and I can guarantee you it will not be pleasant."

20

Together again

Cornelius knew that she would come. He had not yet offered her the post that he knew would strengthen the team he was assembling. Once and for all he would put a stop to the remorseless rise of the Spriggans and put an end to that bastard Slope. He had assured her that the trip would cost not a penny and that it would be worth the small effort involved. If nothing else it would be an opportunity for two old friends to catch up and to rekindle a bond that had once been an unbreakable one. With peace of mind on one front he returned to the irritation provided by Slope and his minions. As he did so he felt his blood pressure inexorably rise to an unhealthy level. This was part of the job but it was also personal; he hated the man and all he stood for with a real passion. Most of all he hated the fact that influential voices in the cabinet protected Spriggans in general and Slope in particular. Cornelius had come close before. He had uncovered the scam that Slope had organised at St Jude's. It was staggering in its simplicity and depended on what Cornelius always thought of as 'The Emperor's New Clothes' principle. Among the ruling classes there is an assumption that among the better class of alcohol, jargon for wine and port, knowledge is absolute. Nobody, whatever their background, would admit ignorance of the finer points of civilised drinking. Woe betide the undergraduate at any of the colleges who was unaware of the custom that the port must be passed to the left. Similarly, not to recognise a premier cru in a blind tasting was regarded as a faux pas as heinous as belching in front of a dowager duchess when it was her turn. What all this means now and has always meant is that duping the pretentious is easy meat for the criminally inclined. Those outside the dreaming spires would never guess the extent of the cellars held by individual Oxbridge colleges. The value runs into many millions. It's not difficult to see how much money can be made in this way when you know that the average price of a standard bottle of Henri Jayer Richebourg Grand Cru, Cote de Nuits runs at over £10,000, and even a Petrus Pomerol comes in at an average of £1,800 per standard bottle. Each college runs its affairs as though the college were the personal fiefdom of the master. This was certainly the case where Slope was involved. An unholy trinity of Slope, Speight and Scratcher ruled the fiefdom with scant care for their presumed mission of educating the young of the great and the good of Britain.

The scam was simplicity itself. Working on the basis that around 80% of any given group of people will be so eager to fit in that they will not rock the boat even if the thing is sinking, Slope decided to siphon off some of St Jude's best wines. Not literally, you understand. The Spriggans and their leaders throughout history were far too clever for that. All he needed to do was to contact wine lovers on whom he could rely to keep their mouths shut, except when drinking the best wine known to man or woman, and hey presto. Obviously he chose only those who could afford premium prices, albeit with a seemingly generous loyalty discount. The second part of the scam was to employ Spriggans with the knowledge and equipment to place inferior wines in convincing bottles. Add in a fake label and the die was cast. It carried a risk for obvious reasons. Guests at college feasts were frequently wine experts. However with the 80/20 rule in place most could be relied on to keep their mouths shut lest they revealed themselves to be philistine in their appreciation of wine. The scam was well on its way to making north of £3.5 million per annum for the coffers of the Spriggans when a college official made the mistake of inviting one Piers Prideaux and William Radleigh de Beaune to one of the frequent dinners that the college held for staff and graduates.

In normal circumstances the two would not have gone. In normal circumstances the two would not be invited. But, with the bluebird of mischief twittering merrily on Bones's shoulder, turn up is exactly what they did. Slope was crafty enough that the right wine was served to any of those likely to uncover his carefully structured scheme early in the piece. That meant that, by the time the progression from soup to nuts had been accomplished, anyone suggesting that everything was something less than ticketty boo could feel the full force of the dark sarcasm of the privileged classes. It was a powerful weapon. Bones and Prideaux were probably the two men in all Oxford who were unlikely to be silenced by such an obvious technique. Given that both were masters of the power of sarcasm in their own right it was never likely to work on them. Bones was particularly vocal until he, together with Prideaux, was exported from the Great Hall by two of Slope's heavies. Thus began a long series of disagreements, turning to arguments, turning to mutual dislike, turning to mutual hatred that characterised the relationships between Slope and the two men ever after. Piers's refusal to back down had led to an uncomfortable sojourn at Her Majesty's Pleasure for Slope for which he would forever hold Prideaux accountable. Even those friends in high places in whom Slope placed such store had been no help this time. Aware that the man was on a sticky wicket they hurriedly left the field and left Slope to face his fate. Slope's personality was such that not only was Prideaux a target from now on but so became everyone who associated with him. He was not a forgiving man and prison was the ultimate humiliation. He would be avenged.

Cornelius permitted himself a smile as he lifted down the massive file that he held on St Jude's College. The individual file on Slope was even bigger, and the comprehensive file on the Spriggans in general the largest of all. Each file contained timelines of significant events that were explained in further detail among the many pages. As a way of easing himself into the task of perusing the documentation for the umpteenth time, he began lazy gazing at the Spriggans' timeline. All this information was contained in encrypted files on the office computer. Cornelius did not entirely trust modern technology so he kept paper versions of everything there was to keep. This he locked in a safe, the combination of which was known only to him. Even a casual glance sufficed to remind him of the extent to which the pernicious organisation he was tasked with eviscerating had penetrated every level of society for generations past. The development of the Spriggans seemed to have gone in a pattern. From its inception as a self-help group for the dispossessed it would develop into a brutal and efficient criminal organisation. Eventually there would be a backlash, followed by a witch hunt, and the whole circle would begin again. It served to fuel his hatred that Slope was merely the latest in a long line of leaders who had subverted the original intentions of an association for his own nefarious ends. Slope was not the first, he would not be the last. That is unless the unit that Cornelius was assembling could bring him to book and stamp out the influence they wielded for good.

He poured himself a generous slug of Dalmore 1974 Single Highland Malt Whisky as he settled down to skim through the timeline:

Spriggan Timeline from 1119 to the Present Day

This is not intended to be exhaustive and a fuller exploration of the timeline can be found in files currently stored under highest security classification: ASU/14/KERNOW. This file gives a general sense of longevity of the organisation we now know as Spriggans and charts its decline into the criminal organisation of today.

1119: Knight's Templars Founded by Hugues de Payen in Jerusalem. Originally a group of nine knights formed to protect pilgrims making the most important of pilgrimages. They were poor knights without property or even proper armour yet by the time of the Council of Troyes in 1129 they were regarded as heroes of Christendom. By 1145 the Pope had issued three papal bulls that made the Templars answerable to nobody and virtually untouchable. They also had become fabulously wealthy and it is likely that this had a major part to play in their downfall.

1123: Templar Church founded on Bodmin Moor believed to have been founded by a descendant of Bertrand de Blancfort (1156 – 1169) the 6th Grand Master of the Temple . There is a record of one Frederic Blancfort described as a mason having an involvement in this foundation.

1130: Knight's Templar driven from Bodmin Moor by loose association of farmers, fishermen, peat diggers and charcoal burners. No named leaders known and group loosely referred to as brigands. Although one Frederic Blanchfort was purported to have had a hand in the insurrection. It was common for Norman names to be gradually anglicised so this may well be the same descendant of the 6th Grand Master who looks to have changed sides, joining those regarded as insurrectionists. This may suggest that Templar power in Cornwall was on the wane and that said Frederic Blanchfort knew which way the wind was blowing.

1150: (approx.) Evidence of the Cathars in Britain. No known record *of a presence in Cornwall.1307 to 1314. In March 1314 Templar Grand Master Jacques de Molay was burned for heresy. He was tied to the stake and forced to sit on a pile of faggots. His last words reputedly were, "Regardez Maman le toit de la Monde." Again there is no verification of this though this has never stopped Hollywood film directors hijacking the sentiment.*

1200 to 1490s: Rumours of an organised group now well established at Bodmin Moor site once operated by the Knights Templar. Possible that group has taken the name Spriggans after a particular malevolent piskey blamed for most bad fortune by people in these parts. Difficult to disentangle truth from myth during this period as written sources are both few and doubtful. From this period to the Cornish Rising there is only sporadic reference to an organisation operating outside any laws, local or central, playing havoc on the moor and in surrounding towns and villages. Unexplained deaths on the moor are frequently linked to the Spriggan name. Whether this implies some human agency or is a superstitious reference to some invented magical creature is usually obscure. Although anybody's Aunt Alice will tell you of an occasion when a strange apparition appearing through the Cornish fog was responsible for tearing her favourite dress. In Cornwall and particularly on the moor it is commonplace for all sorts of strange events to be laid at the door of the spriggans. It is more than likely that as often as not this is a convenient excuse for horseplay that has gone to far. It also may be convenient to latter day spriggans who appreciated the opportunity for a little low level sexual assault secure in the knowledge that the imagined beings would take the blame.

1497: Cornish Rising: An uprising by the Cornish people against Henry V11 and authority exercised from London. Led by Michael Joseph An Gof (An Gof - blacksmith in the Cornish language). Marched on London. With lawyer Thomas Flamank who joined the march at Bodmin around 15,000 made as far as Blackheath. Outside the gates of London they were met by 25,000 of the King's troops. What followed was inevitable and both An Gof and Flamanck were hanged, drawn and quartered on 27th June. This was despite a promise from the young king that if the men withdrew an agreement would be reached and the leaders would not be harmed. In the English civil war Cornwall was generally on the side of the cavaliers though there are still more than a few hamlets that remember the perfidy of the king on that day. The descendants of Thomas Flamank are still pursuing a case through the judicial system for compensation from the king for his actions on the day. It is not generally known that there remains a law on the statute books that any Cornishman found after dark in Blackheath can be arrested and brought before the courts. That day is still celebrated in Cornwall as An Gof day. Some old Cornish sources resurrect the idea that adherents to an organisation known as the Spriggans had limited involvement in the rising. At that time it is believed that, if it existed in anything other than the imagination, the organisation had not gone rogue. There is very little evidence other than colloquial records for anything that would constitute an organisation with similarities to the Mafia preying on those unable to defend themselves.

"I wish to God the bloody organisation had never gone rogue," thought Cornelius as he flicked his way through the mound of papers on his desk. He stood up to stretch his back and then walked across the room to the cabinet against the far wall. On top of the cabinet were ranged half a dozen crystal decanters filled with the best spirits that money could buy. "Must be some perks" he thought as he poured another generous measure of the Dalmore. As he took a first mouthful, swilling it around for the full effect, his office phone buzzed. "Bloody typical. The minute I leave my desk some bugger wants me." He walked back to the desk and put down his glass of Scotch. "What is it?" He sounded angry though it was more irritation than anything else. A man and his Scotch are not soon parted. It was his PA, as he had expected. "There's someone to see you, sir."

"Well, send the bugger in, Johnson. Don't faff about.

I'm assuming that they have clearance, otherwise I shall have your guts for garters."

"She says that she's an old friend of yours and that you asked her to call in."

"Well that's all right then. Send the lady in. Before you do so, Johnson, isn't there something you've forgotten?" There was an extremely pregnant pause on the other end of the phone. "Well, come on man, I haven't got all day. Yes? What is it you have forgotten, apart from the fact that you are wasting the time of a senior intelligence officer? That's right. If she is a friend of mine there is every chance I'll know her name. Have you asked the lady her name? Aah! So you have. Well done. And what did she say that name was? Lola Cutler. Well what are you waiting for?   Send her in immediately. And by the way. Where the hell did we get you from?"

"You were at school with my uncle, sir, Gridlock Morgan the Town Planner."

"Old Gridlock, eh. Well how is the dear old chap? I haven't seen him for yonks. Give him my regards the next time you see him. And Johnson, sharpen up a bit, there's a good chap."

The door opened and Lola walked in. It was as if she had never been away. The attraction was as powerful as always. She was understated, he more overt. All the pieces were in place for a relationship that transcended the platonic and then some. There was an unseen barrier that meant when they embraced it was with the genuine warmth of old friends reunited. When the small talk was over Cornelius adopted his usual serious mien. "This is the situation Lola. What I am about to tell you is outside even my remit, which is pretty broad, I can assure you. I am offering you a role within a specialist unit that operates from this building. Once you have agreed to listen to my offer you can discuss it with nobody. If you turn the position down and subsequently tell anyone that you have even been to this office you will be in serious trouble. If you accept and then tell anyone that you have been to this office then you will be dead. That is the area within which I and my unit operate. So what's it to be?"

"I think you know me well enough to know that I have never been one to prevaricate. I haven't changed since you saw me last. Perhaps a little more jaundiced about what a bastard life can be, but essentially still the same Lola Cutler you knew back in those summery Shropshire days. So give it to me straight and I'll tell you what I think of your offer. But don't get over excited and leave anything important out. I need to know what I might be getting myself into. It sounds as though it might be a teensy bit dangerous. So, go on Gawain, do your best to frighten the hell out of me. You know you want to." She giggled as she realised that the old bonds were as strong as they ever were. She was the only person who could speak openly to Cornelius.

It took a while to update Lola with details of Slope and his permanently open file. She found the whole thing with Bones and Prideaux fascinating but there was more to it than that. She had known Cornelius for a long time. She knew him well enough to know when he was being completely open with her. It was a feeling, but she was sure he was holding something back.

Best of all she enjoyed listening to Cornelius when he was genuinely passionate about something. It was like the old days when he had found some new source of vinyl, or was on the trail of a previously unheard Robert Johnson song. He became absorbed and all the more fascinating for that absorption. There was a difference this time. The passion was there, but this time it was driven by a visceral hatred of his subject. She could understand Slope's reaction to Bones and Prideaux. They had been responsible for his loss of face and he was not the sort of man to take that lying down. He had been confident in the days leading up to the trial. His defence barrister was certainly a Spriggan and he in turn had done his best to ensure that the case would be tried in front of a sympathetic judge. It would have come to pass too, were it not for that 'simple twist of fate' Dylan once sang so eloquently about. In this case the initial judge, Sir Hartley Whitney, merely happened to fall off a ladder and break his ankle while clearing bird's nests from the antique guttering at his stately pile in Oxfordshire. Despite his insistence when lying on the ground, having been attacked by several rather militant seagulls, that it was, "merely a flesh wound, bandage the bugger and I'll be as right as a trivet", the much respected judge was nevertheless carted off to hospital by Bert Loam, his gardener and lifelong companion. A replacement was urgently sought to avoid postponing the case and a distinctly less sympathetic figure, in the person of Colin Viner, was appointed.

At the trial it was obvious from the beginning that Slope was not only lying but lying under oath. His barrister did his best but the jury took fewer than three hours to find him guilty of embezzlement compounded by perjury. The judge handed down a sentence of ten years without the option, and Slope was carted off to prison with his plans in tatters. And all because of the involvement of Bones and the bastard Prideaux. If Slope had any consolation it came from the fact that his actions had already dished Prideaux's career before his arrest. He had acted swiftly to activate the college's disciplinary procedure that culminated in the college governors relieving Prideaux of his post before Inspector Knacker came along to feel Slope's collar. What had evidently really got through to Cornelius was that Slope served a mere three years of his sentence. It stank, and, although everyone was aware of that, Slope was back in Oxford in no time. There were vague references to prison overcrowding and time off for good behaviour but this action must have been authorised a long way up the food chain. Cornelius was convinced that Slope was being sheltered by his well placed friends. He was absolutely positive that among them were high ranking Spriggans. He could never prove it, but there was more than a probability that the Home Secretary herself was one of the Spriggan High Council. It had to be that. If not, why was he continuously told to lay off any pursuit of Slope? If Slope had a parking ticket his commanding officer would be down on him like several ton of bricks. If he wanted extra funding to authorise obboes of Slope and Speight the money was denied. Frankly he was getting royally pissed off with banging his head against a brick wall that showed no signs of movement at all. He counted his bollockings from the most senior officers in the force in tens rather than single numbers, and it became clearer with every warning he received that Slope's law went a long way through a corrupt government. He could not control his visceral hatred of Slope and, try as he might, he could do nothing to stop this abuse of power. It was a lonely place to be, with the consolation of his new unit the only bright spot in a grey career.

Lola had listened with fascinated concentration as Cornelius highlighted the many ways he hated Slope, the Spriggans and all they stood for. At first she had smiled, then giggled but, as it became clearer that here was a man determined to break through the miasma of corruption, her admiration for him simply grew. Their relationship had always been based on admiration rather than love. Amor platonicus is frequently quoted as an alternative to the love dependant on physical attraction and sexual passion. What existed between these two was the melding of twin souls, established and maintained by the purest of pleasures, the unerring pursuit of intellectual satisfaction. Nothing had changed. The excitement in such a pursuit remained and was palpable. Yet there seemed to be something more than a mutual admiration society developing between the two.

Cornelius's expression as he looked up from his desk confirmed for her that her thoughts were reciprocated. What he was offering was the mother of all intellectual challenges with the added frisson of some physical confrontation. She was not so naïve as to suppose that all Spriggans would be equal intellectually. Some would, of necessity, be thugs and enforcers. She would relish the opportunity to surprise such types with her physical strength and capability for serious aggression when the situation called for it. If somewhere on the platonic scale there was a little stop off point for something peeping around the corner in the general direction of sexual love then this could be its opportunity. For the immediate present she would wait to hear details of the offer he was working towards making to her.

Cornelius took off the glasses he wore for close work. His eyes looked tired but the old smile was there. "I don't even know if I have the right to put this to you formally. In any case I've already said too much and probably enough to be removed from my post should any of this get out. You now know enough of the situation to present a security risk so what I....." He tailed off as she jumped from her chair and stood bolt upright.

"For fuck's sake Gawain, spit it out, will you. Of course I'll accept. I'm not that bothered what the post is as long as I can do some serious research. I am bored with London. I want to get really stuck into something that will be a proper challenge. What you have outlined so far more than fits the bill. Where do I sign? I've just thought of something. You're not asking to marry me or something equally daft, are you? You're making such

143

a meal of it that it sounds like you're either pissed or you've been smoking that stuff you used to play around with back in those days when you were naught but a Shropshire lad."

Her response caught Cornelius off balance. He paused for a second then burst into such raucous laughter that would have brought the ceiling plaster down had he not controlled himself. "Of course I'm not asking you to marry me, because I'm entirely sure of what your reply would be. Let me put this in terms you will understand. I'd like you to do for me what Robert Johnson did when he met the devil at those famous crossroads."

"You mean you want me to sell you my soul. To be honest, if it will make me a guitar player with half the talent Robert Johnson had, then the answer is yes. Since I have known you long enough to know that it's unlikely you are a particularly well disguised old Nick, then I must assume you're asking me to come and work for you. And I never said that marriage was out of the question." The coquettish smile on her face as she looked directly at him unnerved the poor soul.

"Spot on as usual. Except I don't want you to work for me, I want you to work with me. There is a difference and this is it. You will work directly under my command but with unlimited discretion to take any action that you feel appropriate in any given circumstances. You will have executive rank but will work as an operative in the field. This is an arrangement strictly between us. Everything you need will be provided for, but you must accept that you will be carrying out a vital service for me that will inevitably place you in the firing line. You are the only creature on God's earth I would trust with this responsibility. Once you accept the offer and take up the position you will be completely alone. Nobody else in the unit or MI6 itself will know that you exist. When you leave this building you will leave through a secret door and through a passage way that will bring you out at the rear of the building.

"The only person that knows you came into my office is Johnson and I have already sent him off for lunch at his club. He's a loyal old thing. Claims he was once a mayor of somewhere or other, but sadly he is a bit of a buffoon. I only keep the clown on for his comic value. So there you have it. All the details you need plus financing, a secure phone and the obligatory Walther PPK in pink are inside the case. Sorry, the pink pistol was my idea of a joke. Special edition. They only ever made two and I have the other one. Are you in, Cutler, or are you out?"

"Of course I'm in, you dozy twat. It would help if you mentioned, even of only en passant, where it is you would like me to go for this very taxing assignment of yours."

"As always, Lola, you have identified the mot juste, because I want you to go to Paris. And I expect you to be there for around a year or so, depending on what happens in other places." Her expression gave him the greatest pleasure. She smiled her widest smile just as he knew she would. Paris was her favourite place in the world, and spending time there for any reason would make her "very, very, happy".

"You sly old dog, you. You really know how to treat a girl, don't you. I shall get on it right away. I'll do my best to cope with such an onerous posting in such a terrible place, boss."

"Right then. Now this is where the fooling stops. I couldn't be more pleased to have you onside but this is no jolly. By agreeing to do this you are putting your life in jeopardy. As I've said, all the information and special items you need are in the briefcase. But please do not underestimate what you are undertaking. What I want you to do is to merge with everyday life in Paris.

While you are there I know you will have no trouble communicating since I am aware that your French is better than the average Parisian. You will at all times keep your ear to the ground. Effectively you will be my eyes and ears in Paris. Once you are embedded there, and it shouldn't take you long, you will be informed of those targets we wish you to keep track of. Anything you discover, however small, must be reported to me directly. You are not to get involved. You are to follow nobody unless I expressly authorise it. Of course, such authorisation will have to be given to you personally. This means we will be seeing quite a bit of each other over the coming year or two and, depending on how successful you are, it could become a lot longer than that. I know that I can trust you completely. My only doubt is that you will take it upon yourself to take unreasonable chances. You must promise me here and now that there will be no heroics. Come on. I mean it."

It was obvious to Lola that Cornelius was serious. She obliged, though a serious Cornelius always made her want to giggle. She managed to hold it together and left the office, having solemnly promised she would behave with propriety. In her briefcase was a return ticket to the city of which she frequently said, 'Paris. I'd die to live in Paris.' How hard could the assignment be?

21

Bows and arrows
of outrageous fortune

The weather in Silent Valley had the feel that warms the soul. The sky was clear and the ground was beginning to warm up. The wild garlic was beginning to flower and in a few short weeks the air would be full of that wonderful wild garlic scent filling the air. The past few weeks had been a difficult time. Life in the valley had fallen into a routine, and routine in these circumstances could be a trap. Once the miasma of familiarity shrouded everyday activity people would relax, defences would drop and danger would become suddenly real rather than simply a distant unpleasant prospect. Sitting outside the Morning Star on a Sunday afternoon, Prideaux and Bones, together with Mark and Ginny, were enjoying the peace as well as a few glasses of their favourite local brew. As a group they were mellow and looked for all the world like a group of tourists on a walking holiday. Something lay between them though; it was the silence of near despair. Nothing was happening and there was no obvious solution to their dilemma. They knew it would be useless to pretend that Slope would go away. They knew nothing of the threats that faced them, and uneasy lies the head whether it wears a crown or not when there is an obvious threat in the offing. They were in check and the black queen was uncomfortably close. How close they could not know.

A sudden swishing sound, one familiar to all devotees of the longbow, split the silence as the pint mug directly in front of Bones shattered, spilling ale all over the surface of the table, splintering the wood and skittering off into the rhododendrons that grew in profusion outside the ages old pub. "For fuck's sake," gurgled Bones as he spat out more than a mouthful of ale. "What the hell was that?"

"That, my friend" came a stentorian voice from the edge of the woods that backed onto the old pub, "was an arrow with a barbed tip that, had I chosen, to would now be buried deep in old Bonesie's chest cavity, and he would be in the arms of Morpheus, never to sing, drink or fornicate ever again."

"That's all well and good," shouted an upset Prideaux, "but you almost initiated four myocardial infarctions in one go over here. What the hell are you playing at?"

"I am playing at nothing, Piers," answered the old man. "I never play. I am pointing out to you four, in a practical way, since you seem to think you are on some sort of extended jolly, just how easy it would have been to kill one or all of you quickly and silently. Now if an old man like me could do that how easy do you think it would have been for Slope or any of his foot soldiers, incompetent as they can be, to carry out the same straightforward task? It so happens that I am adept at the use of the longbow, a most efficient agent of whispering death if there ever was one. Slope's men could have used a rifle with a silencer, or, to be honest, simply walked over and shot each one of you in the back of the neck with a pistol. You are looking that dozy."

The Black Prince emerged from the woods carrying his hunting bow, a quiver of hunting arrows swinging from his waistband. He looked like the old man of the woods. Fitting easily into his surroundings, he could have stepped directly out of the fourteenth century. His exhibition was a little melodramatic but had without question had the desired effect. The shock on the faces of the four was obvious. They knew that they could all be another set of ticks on Slope's to do list. It was a frightening if sobering thought.

"Right then, get me a pint in and I'll tell you what I have discovered and what we are going to do."

There was a cracking noise as he walked towards the table where the four sat. Then the sight of an arrow flying over the heads of the seated friends. Not a soul moved a muscle. Fear does many things to the uninitiated. Immobility is one of them. Not so the Black Prince who spun on his right heel at the sound of the crack, the bow coming up into the firing position as he knocked an arrow and let it fly directly at the woods. It was poetry in its own way. It was a man completely in control and at one with his surroundings. The arrow flew straight, defying the sharpest eyesight to follow its trajectory, and buried itself into the chest of the bowman in the woods. At that same instant he loosed his bowstring, resulting in his arrow flying high and harmless into the air. It was powerful enough to have penetrated him completely, entering some way into the tree that the impact had forced him against. Running across to the woods it became apparent that one of Slope's killers had not done his planning very well. The body slumped forward, a neglected rag doll held upright by the arrow that had taken his life. The dead man was Scratcher. It would have been difficult to criticise the man's ability to multi task. One day a bent accountant, one day a hitman, another a hitman with a bow and arrow and a message. Sadly for him, reverting to a weapon that had its heyday in the middle ages had not done him any favours. The warning message was at least delivered even at the cost of his life. There would be no happy retirement to Thailand for this particularly unpleasant individual. Similar to many of his type he led a conventional family life with two kids and several wives scattered around the globe. None of them would ever know how he met his end. For a reasonably successful assassin it was probably just as well. To be outshot by a man of the Black Prince's vintage would have proved a little embarrassing at the annual assassins' ballroom bash. His absence would be noted, however, and at the end of the evening the assassins' prayer would be recited in his honour. Any assassin not attending the annual knees up was naturally assumed to have failed and therefore be pushing up daisies or woodland plants in some part of the world or other. As senior members of the Assassins Guild the Spriggans had a table nearest the stage at such celebrations. Scratcher would be notable by his absence later in the year. A senior member of the Spriggans would be tasked with reciting the assassins' prayer:

May your aim be true, and you never rue
A malfunction of your chosen means
Whether gun, rope or knife
May you take the target's life
And safely leave such murder scenes.

It would be a fitting end to an amoral life to be celebrated in such doggerel. Strange as it was the assassins present would raise a glass and chant Scratcher's valediction and there would not be a dry eye in the house. For now there were more pressing matters.

"Good God," Mark stammered. "He's dead. You've killed him."

"Well done that man. Obviously steeped in the major skill of stating the bloody obvious. Would you have preferred it if I had allowed him to shoot one of you, because that's what he was doing here?"

"For God's sake, you can't go around killing people when it takes your fancy. This is not bloody Deliverance." It was Ginny who spoke and who looked most shocked.

"Let me explain something to you," said Rhys, leaning his hunting bow up against the tree that currently held up the would be assassin. "I have been following this man for around an hour. I have tracked him through the woods and I knew why he was here. Scratcher is a Spriggan assassin and his instructions were to maim one of you as a message to the others. It doesn't matter which one. That is because Slope has a particularly unpleasant fate waiting for you, Piers and you, Bonesie. But because he is a sadistic bastard he wants you all to suffer as much as possible before finishing you off. I used the arrow to wake you up a bit but also to put his assassin on the back foot. He wasn't expecting it and I knew he would try to rattle a shot off as I walked towards you. I knew where he was and that I could put an arrow through him on the turn. And as you can see I was quite right."

The old man was flushed with his triumph. Age hadn't withered him to the extent that he had lost the ability to respond with accuracy to a genuine threat. He knew that the assassin's brief was to shoot one of the four yet not to kill. His guess was that the target would have been Ginny and that the shot would have been designed to induce suffering rather than death. Slope was a vicious bastard, of that there was no doubt, and special circumstances required a special response. This was the second Slope inspired attack on the team and like the first it had come to nothing. He would not continue to fail; it simply was not in his nature. Driven by hatred of the most obsessive kind he would have his way.

"I think we had better start listening properly to Granddad," Prideaux said after an awkward silence. "We've had a lucky escape and this situation is getting out of hand. I'm not sure what we should be doing but I can't go on living like this and I'd take a large bet that the rest of you can't. It strikes me that we have no obvious way out. The bastard has a long reach and if he can get to us here he can get to us anywhere. We don't know whom we can trust and we can't go to the authorities, just in case. So what do we do?"

"As I said before I was so rudely interrupted," the old man smiled, "the man I have shot is one of Slope's assassins. Slope didn't send him here specifically. He has put out what amounts to a fatwa. Scratcher has simply taken the responsibility on his own shoulders. If he had succeeded it would have put him in an extremely good light with the Spriggan hierarchy. It's another one of the lovely resonances between the Spriggans and the fundamentalists. The main difference is that a job like this would have earned Scratcher a fee of around £50,000. Since he failed the money will go into the Assassins' Widows and Orphans Fund. Nice irony, but Scratcher was one of the trustees for that fund and had been embezzling money from it for years. Perhaps it's karma in action, or perhaps simply a random and indifferent fate. I suppose you pays your money and takes your choice. Be that as it may I have not been idle even while you bastards have been. I have been in touch with some of my contacts in Cornwall and in case you are not sure what you should be doing next, here it is. Slope's Spriggans have outraged the boys from Kernow. They can be an insular bunch down there as you know, but they are very proud of their country and not a bit keen on anyone hell bent on bringing the old place into disrepute. So pin back your shell likes and listen to a story that I shall tell, then get your bloody selves organised." It was typical behaviour for the old man. If he belonged anywhere he belonged everywhere. There was something of the prophet about him but, coupled with his clear ability to look after himself and anyone else he chose, there was a timeless dimension that surrounded him, an aura. When the Black Prince spoke people listened, at least they did if they had any sense.

"We all know where the Spriggans originated and we all know what they have become. That current degeneration is down to one man and his malign influence on the evil bastards who have clamoured to be his fellow travellers. Slope was not the first to infiltrate the organisation but was preceded by another master of the long game, one Jon Spine. He was older than Slope and they had met when both were teenagers at a school somewhere in the Midlands. They stuck together as they were both scholarship boys from ordinary backgrounds. They subsequently found out that they had a lot in common which is why they got on so well. I gather they both had a penchant for being spanked that was probably a legacy of regular beatings from a parent. I gather such a preference can often be a sign of a mildly disturbed mind. However, I digress. The top and bottom of it all, no pun intended, is that they got on well with each other and not with many other people at all. They both suffered from what psychologists call the Napoleon or Emperor Syndrome. It is nothing to do with restricted height or the wish to keep one hand inside one's jacket, simply a general belief in effortless superiority and an attendant sense of entitlement. Neither man ever regarded other people as having any intellectual worth at all. In fact they regarded most people with total contempt and as members of a subnormal species. Since that particular syndrome came as a package with an amoral personality, it made both of them men to be avoided at any and all costs."

Prideaux was gradually regaining some composure after the shock of sudden death and the even more disturbing realisation that their whereabouts were now known to any half cracked follower of Slope who fancied a little light murder or mutilation. Much as he loved and respected the old man he was unsure whether the current lecture was going to advance their position significantly. He knew more about Slope than he cared to. He had heard vaguely of Spine, enough to know he was a dangerous man, but found it hard to imagine how an 'are you sitting comfortably?' could possibly help matters that had got this far. This is what he thought though he tried to hide it from his grandfather. He did not succeed.

Fixing him with a gimlet eye the old man said, "Now Piers, I know what you are thinking, but put aside your natural scepticism while I finish what I was saying. I guarantee it will clarify things for you." Prideaux nodded as the old man continued.

"Spine it was who conceived the idea that the Slope could be a likely vehicle to help him in a plan, initially to infiltrate, and then to take over the organisation, then to bend it to his will. Over time, and it took a long time, the two bastards gradually changed the nature of what the Spriggans were. It's an old technique still used in politics all the time. Make minute changes often enough and they pass without anyone noticing, then before you know it the organisation is nothing like it was. And of course Slope had the added assistance of Spine at his right hand. Spine was a master of the long game. He realised as a young man that if you greet everyone with a smile and a hearty handshake mostly they will accept you as one of the good guys. The advantage that gives to a naturally criminal mind is incalculable.

"And when it comes to the criminal mind Spine is way out there on his own. He cut his teeth on disinheriting his own family. Planned it twenty years in advance and ripped off his own mother who ended up penniless and living in a home. You know the expression: 'The evil men do lives after them, the good is oft interred with their bones'. Marc Anthony knew how to sway a crowd, and never did words apply more accurately than those, from his speech over the bleeding body of Caesar, when applied to Spine and Slope. What they have overlooked though is the essential balance that seems to exist in the world. Don't worry, I'm not getting spiritual on you. But there is always a response to such extremes, and by this roundabout means I finally arrive at the information I have for you. One thing I have learned in my long life, with its fair share of hardship and general unpleasantness, is this. If you have an enemy, the more you know that enemy the greater chance there is that you can defeat him.

"I've recently been in touch with an organisation that has provided a home for a whole hatful of disgruntled Spriggans. It had to happen and it has; the spin off from Slope's machinations was always going to create a backlash. In this case it is a group that style themselves the Sons of Dozmary (Mebion Dozmary in Cornish). They are a group of quite powerful folk drawn from all over Cornwall. Their original raison d'etre was cultural, in the sense of defending the unique quality of Cornish culture. They have all sorts in their membership and it is not restricted in any way, provided you are interested in the county and its history and are prepared to defend it. I think I'll leave it to your imagination to work out their views on the current behaviour of the Spriggans."

Silence, when it is deep enough, can be a powerful force. The silence following the old man's pause for breath and a whistle whetting slurp of ale was deeper than the pool that this breakaway group had taken as a name. It was Bones who was first to speak. "Obviously, I speak for myself, but I fail to see what a cultural organisation located deep in the heart of Kernow can possibly offer to Slope and his psychopaths. Short of scaring them to death with a demonstration of full contact old Cornish clog dancing, I do not see that it is that way our salvation lies. Now you can call me an old cynic, and you'd be right to do so, but if you had told me that we had teamed up with the Cornish branch of the SAS I'd sleep a lot easier in my chair. Sorry and all that, but that's the way I feel."

As always, from out of the mouths of old aristos and ageing soaks came the odd spot of wisdom. At first glance a cultural organisation would not offer much of an umbrella defence against Slope and all his works. However, as in all things Cornish, there is always something hidden. In this case the something hidden was that within the Sons of Dozmary a sleeping giant had already begun to stir. It wasn't political, it wasn't cultural, it was double headed and it was deadly.

The brothers Job were twins who ran a farm on Bodmin Moor and were both as strong and wiry as you would expect subsistence farmers to be. They had grown up on the farm and had worked on it practically since they learned to walk. In the process they had grown hardy and athletic with an easy and confident grasp of everything country. Starting with catapults, they had graduated to airguns and then to shotguns. Membership of the local Territorial Army unit in nearby Bodmin had helped to hone their military skills until the Job twins were something to be reckoned with.

The twins, for some reason always known as the two twins, shared a wicked dark sense of humour and best of all enjoyed a good fight. When the boys were quite young if nobody else was available they would fight each other. They often claimed, falsely though typically nobody ever argued, that Bob Fitzsimmons, once Cornish heavyweight champion of the world, was a cousin. The aggression gradually moderated until it mutated into a fierce bond between them so that each would defend the other to the death. At around this time they liked nothing better than to spend a Saturday night fighting at one of the rougher pubs in St Blaise or St Austell. It was not unusual to see the two, all blood and snot, flattening any tough guy or loudmouth foolish enough to try it on. Some of the mid Cornwall towns in those days resembled Dodge City more than quiet rural backwaters, especially when the Job boys came to town. There was even a time when the boys took a trip over the Tamar to visit Bristol. They came away from that one with an award, unofficial of course, from the local police for sorting out one of the most feared Bristol biker gangs. The Bristol police did their best to avoid this particular crew but fate would have it, as fate often will, that inadvertently the boys were enjoying a late breakfast in a biker café. Most of all the twins shared a deep-seated hatred of anyone from up country who had the temerity to criticise their beloved country in any way. Many a tough guy had regretted tangling with the twins; they always came as a pair.

The meanest half dozen of the Redland Gang had been haring around the Bristol road system putting the fear of God into law abiding road users. Stopping for a refill for the bikes and one for themselves, they kicked open the café door to see that fate had presented them with an opportunity for some excellent sport. The leader of the gang, known to all and sundry as Rat, made a straight line for the café counter, taking care to kick the chair on which Bob sat in a piece of perfect timing that meant Bob's mug of breakfast tea spilled all over the table. "'Ere boy, I don't think you meant to do that and I expect you are sorry and would like to say so." Rat's response in pulling a knife from his jacket was exactly as the serving staff knew it would be, and they quickly moved into the kitchen out of harm's way. The predictable sounds of violence, smashing crockery and glass followed until there was complete silence.

"I don't think that was very friendly of these boys, Janner."

"No Janner, I think they need to brush up on their manners. They're not up to much at fighting either, in my book," Robert replied.

One of the braver of the café staff eased open the kitchen door to be greeted by a sight familiar to all fans of B movie westerns. Not much of the furniture remained in a usable state. Four of the hardest tearaways in Bristol lay unconscious in a heap inside the café, the other three had obviously been thrown one at a time through the plate glass window. Judging by the state of him Rat had gone through first, which was only fitting for a man calling himself the leader of the pack. Police and paramedics looked after the worst of the wounded, the walking wounded were being arrested and charged. Chief Inspector Everley walked over to the twins and stuck out his hand.

"I'd like to shake both of you by the hand. That lot have been making my life a misery for months now and I am grateful that you seem to have given them the mother of all hidings."

"They started it," said Robert.

"I'm absolutely sure that they did," replied Chief Inspector Everley. "And I'm equally sure that they will have learned from your lesson in self-defence. If you are ever in Bristol again please call in at the station and I'll take you out for a drink to say thanks. All the very best to you."

Smiling, the twins walked to the old Range Rover they had parked in front of the café and took off back to the old country, with the praise of the senior policeman ringing in their ears.

The twins had been christened Bob and Robert by truly unimaginative parents though they often referred to one another as Janner. The name is often claimed by Plymouthians but is very often found in Cornwall, and in this as in all things the twins were no ordinary sons of the soil. Both had been educated at the same Oxford College as Prideaux and Bones though they were not there at the same time. Some ten years younger, the pair had been a handful as students. Whilst at Oxford, though they had not proved to be naturally studious, they had shown a natural intelligence that took them a fair way in their studies. Where they starred was in the college first XV. There the twins fitted effortlessly into the second row of a team that became all conquering in games between the colleges. They were never to achieve their goal either academically or in sporting terms. They had a reputation that scared selectors and both had been red carded for retaliatory violence more than twice in a season. This made the authorities wary of picking them for the Blue that their performances genuinely deserved. Again it was the old problem; the boys came as a pair. An offence against one was an offence against both and the scale of retaliation could be biblical in its scope. Many Cambridge men had cause to thank their lucky stars, or whatever God they prayed to, that they never had cause to come up against the Job twins.

Missing a Blue was a minor irritation but what rankled more was the way they were treated by some of the more privileged denizens of some of the richer colleges. A private education gives a massive advantage in life, but rarely prepares the young gentlemen who benefit from such a head start in life to deal with the likes of Bob and Robert Job. It took less than a term for the message to spread that any attempt at belittling either twin with some form of approximation of a country accent would meet with a swift and immediate response. The result was never in favour of the taunter who, like as not, ended up spluttering his weed adorned way out of the Cherwell or Isis, permanently chastened to within an inch of his life. Sending for reinforcements never worked as a policy either, as more than once the twins had faced down double figured groups of vengeful students intent on returning these Cornish upstarts to their proper place in society.

This was not the Wild West, not the American version at least, though it could easily have been. Overseas visitors had scattered like chaff in a westerly one wet Wednesday, as the two fought with a group of rowers who had decided to teach the twins a lesson on a slow evening in the King's Arms. They fought back to back and it was less dreaming spires than Armageddon. Beefy rower after beefy rower was levelled by fist, foot or chair as overseas visitors scarpered to the back bar for safety. At the end they burst into spontaneous applause at one of the most comprehensive examples of choreographed violence since the Seven Samurai got a little upset and decided to do something about it. The twins shook hands and settled down to a pint or two of Trelawney's best bitter while the erstwhile vigilantes crawled off to get the physical damage repaired. On these twin towers the hopes of Prideaux and his allies would be placed. Always democratic, the twins never minded whether it was Bristol thugs or well educated gentleman; if they wanted some then by all that's Cornish the twins would oblige.

22

The bottomless pool

"Dozmary Pool looms large in the legend of old Cornwall. As most people know Cornwall is a place replete with stories and the county's very otherness lends a sheen even to some of its wilder places. It has strong connections with King Arthur as so many places in the county do."

The speaker's presentation was worthy from the beginning but dry. She had the facts, if facts they were, at her fingertips and imparted them to the small, bored looking group facing her in the lecture room of Truro Museum. At the back of the room, where you would expect them to be were Bones, Prideaux, Mark and Ginny.

"She's not telling us anything we don't know," interrupted Bones in one of those stage whispers that can be heard several buildings away. "We all grew up knowing Dozmary and the stories that Excalibur could be found there. At least, it could if the pool wasn't bottomless. And we all know of the legend of Jan Tregeagle, the giant who was condemned to bail out the pool with a limpet shell for eternity. His suffering as he tried to complete this uncompletable task is well known."

"It might be well known to you, matey, but I am here to listen to the lecturer rather than to you." The tones were purest Oxfordshire, as redolent of that county as the warm honey coloured stone of the cottages. Bert Tippings was holidaying in Cornwall at the insistence of his wife Myrtle, who had been agitating for a seaside holiday for some years. With his usual genius for getting things wrong they had fetched up in Truro; a lovely place, but not one's idea of a typical seaside Cornish town. Bert had an interest in watery matters, born of his full time job of relieving various Oxford waterways of their human detritus. He was one of the few to be interested in what the lecturer had to say and Bones's noisy commentary had annoyed him more than somewhat.

"I'm not sure I care for your tone. And by the way I am nobody's matey; I'd thank you to remember that."

"I'm damn sure that I don't like your tone. You've been rumbling on disturbing this poor lady's lecture for too long now, why don't you give it a rest? Or would you prefer I give you some assistance in taking a long rest?"

"This is provocation up with which I will not put," bayed Bones in Churchillian tones, cleverly channelling one of the great man's more famous quotes. "You jolly well mind your own damn business. Bloody emmetts coming down here. Bugger off back to the midlands or whatever landlocked county spawned you."

It was beginning to get out of hand. Bones wasn't likely to withdraw and Bert Tippings showed an inclination for fight rather than flight. It took all Prideaux's skills of diplomacy to broker an uneasy truce enabling the lecturer to continue. In truth she looked as if she welcomed the intervention in something that she did not really have her heart in. Bones at least reduced his mutterings to a faint roar as he continued to chunter on.

"In the end," he continued, in a real whisper rather than a stage one, "it was supposed to have driven him mad and into howling despair. I expect the devil would have been in there somewhere too. If you take the devil out of the equation then all of this smacks of the Greek legends that they drummed into us at school. What I fail to understand, though, is what on God's earth we are doing here in a lecture by some sort of local harpy. This is stuff we absorbed with our mother's milk. I say this in full knowledge that the back bar of the Red Lion in Boscawen Street will already be open to those who know the appropriate knock."

Prideaux looked at his old friend with a look that only the fond can give to those designed by nature to annoy the hell out of them. "Bonesie, my handsome, I love you as a brother but sometimes your exasperation quotient is off any scale known to man."

By this point the lecturer had totally lost the attention of the class, some of whom were physically wandering off; others, though physically present, might as well not have been. It was that moment when what had seemed to be some form of structured lecture imploded, and there was no going back.

"I'll explain once more before I run naked and screaming down Fore Street having set my hair on fire in utter frustration. We are here so that we can talk to the grey and exhausted lady, currently with her head in her arms and resting on the lectern in complete despair. And the reason we are here is not to listen to one of Dr Joan Thripp's admittedly turgid lectures but because she is a distant aunt of the Job twins and should be able to tell us how to contact them. The other thing is that she is a respected authority on the Spriggans and I believe is in the process of writing a book on them. It's supposed to take an historical perspective, but I've heard a few murmurs that she might know more than is good for her regarding the organisation's current incarnation. Since all this Spriggan stuff reared its ugly head they are apparently very difficult to get hold of. Since my tad-cu took the trouble of pointing us in their direction I am understandably keen to get in touch. I'm hoping that they may be able to help us with a task only marginally less difficult than Tregeagle's eternal stint of pool emptying with a limpet shell."

"Well why didn't you say, boy?" whispered Bones,

with a smirk on his face that only a mother could tolerate. "If we toddle on down to the Red Lion, pop through Gropetit Alley and knock appropriately on the back door all will be revealed, even though it is several minutes shy of ten in the morning."

The look that Prideaux flashed at Bones would have curdled even the best Cornish cream. "What in the name of all that is good and holy are you talking about, Bones?"

"Simple," replied a smiling Bones. "Whenever the boys go to ground, which they do from time to time, the place you will always find them is the smugglers' bar in the Red Lion. I thought everyone in Cornwall knew that. Both of them have a fancy for Rosie, the barmaid there. In fact they have both been courting her for around ten years. She likes them both but can't make up her mind which one she prefers, so on it goes. But I guarantee you they'll be there now." In the certain knowledge that he had taken the wind out of Prideaux's sails, Bones sat back with a sigh of satisfaction.

"For fuck's sake, Bonesie, you sozzled old tart. Why the hell didn't you tell me this earlier? It would have saved a hell of a lot of buggering about, here and back in Wales. What is the matter with you?"

"Nothing wrong with me, old chap. I thought you would know such things. Cornwall is only a small county and I imagined that everyone knew the Job twins."

"Of course I know about the Job twins. What I didn't know is where to find them at this time of day. That is privileged information that you have been keeping to yourself. We could go on batting this back on forth all bloody day. It's not good enough, we must get on or we'll get nowhere fast."

"My thoughts exactly, my old fruit pie. Let us, as you say, get on."

"OK my handsome," said Prideaux through gritted

teeth. "I suppose you are able to get us into this magical place even though it is not even near opening time yet, or is that a bit too much to ask? I take it that you are aware of this special and possibly magical knock that will open doors for us, or is that lost in the mists of Cornish time like so much else?"

"Of course I remember the special knock, my old fruit pie," grinned Bones. "What you do is this. When you have worked your way along Gropetit Alley you boldly approach the back door, it is of course green, then you tap out the tune of Camborne Hill. When you get to the bit of the tune where the horse is stood still the door will be opened unto you. Alternatively you can look up at the CCTV camera above the door, wave to Rosie and she will let you in. That is always providing she recognises you, of course. Simple but effective, and you don't get in unless your intentions are honourable."

By this time Dr Joan Thripp had wandered off to the museum café for some caffeine and to muse on why it was that these days nobody seemed happy to listen to her lectures. Admittedly she had lost the fire she had displayed in her earlier years. Her subject still fascinated her but the job was getting harder, that she could not deny. Perhaps it was because she was comfortable, perhaps because she was in love. She would think about it later when back at home and nursing a cheering gin and tonic.

Shortly afterwards this pleasing prospect disappeared, as she stepped out of the museum and, when barely halfway across the road, was comprehensively hit vertically into the air by a nondescript Land Rover. Its windows and licence plate were both obscured by mud and, probably, pigshit. Absorbed with thoughts of retirement and a quiet contemplative life in a cottage on the Roseland Peninsula with her much younger girlfriend, she didn't hear a thing. Briefly she tried to make sense of why she seemed to be floating some ten feet in the air and heading unerringly for the unforgiving tarmac. Just before lights out she wryly reflected that this was possibly the most exciting event in her long and carefully ordered life. Like the iceberg that did for the Titanic, the Land Rover carried on as if nothing had happened. It was a random act of violence carried out by a Spriggan supplicant. This particular supplicant had been present at the meeting where Slope and Scratcher had committed murder in such a casual manner. The killings and the ease with which they were carried out left an indelible imprint on his mind. As a supplicant he was aware of the fatwa and had decided that a £50,000 cheque would pay off a lot of debts to a lot of unpleasant people. That would still leave a substantial amount for the finer things in life like sex, drugs and chastisement. This small man, who was as unpleasant as he was insignificant, was doing his very best to curry favour with the man who was not Mr Rainbow. This self-same supplicant would surface in the river mud nearby at Malpas, having received the appropriate punishment for rashly drawing attention to the cause. He was too insignificant to warrant any special treatment but had simply been routinely beaten to death and his body committed to the water. Another hefty sum would be transferred to the widows' and orphans' fund. He would not be missed. One more victim of an unforgiving organisation.

Bones, Prideaux, Ginny and Mark were at that instant enjoying a coffee at the same table that Dr Joan Thripp had so recently vacated. They heard the sirens of police car and ambulance, briefly reflected that this inevitably meant trouble for some poor soul, then continued with the matter in hand. Practical as ever, Ginny wondered fairly abstractly why, as by the time they finished their coffee it would be opening time at the pub, they could not go in through the front door like everybody else? The explanation was a simple one and it was that the Red Lion had a large public bar that opened onto Boscawen Street. Regulars would use that entrance as well as the thousands of visitors that flocked to the city every year. Truro was a popular holiday hotspot in the theme park that Cornwall was rapidly becoming.

The snug bar, though, only opened onto Gropetit Alley and consequently only those known or vouched for were ever granted access to that small yet secure room and to where it led. Not even the local police could gain access to that room unless by invitation. If that sounds unlikely then it was at least partly because the local Chief Constable was a keen member of Mebion Dozmary. The whole set up was a legacy of the great Cornish industry of smuggling, and it had been the entrance to a private room for occasions where such a thing was a necessity, in past centuries just as it was becoming again. Smuggling may well have been a distant memory, but the skill with which the room had been incorporated into the fabric of the building was of the highest order. From the public bar it was impossible to tell that a completely hidden room lay behind the interior wall that faced the Boscawen Street entrance. The Revenue men had never found it, and the green door was not the giveaway that it might have appeared. That door only opened into a small storeroom. The snug lay behind a cleverly counterweighted section of wall operated from behind the bar. When open this led through into an ante room where a similarly disguised trap door led to a set of old, well-worn wooden steps leading down below street level. A dimly lit passage then took entrants old and new into a large room hewn from solid rock. This was the journey undertaken by all four of the friends as the lifeless corpse of Dr Joan Thripp was being ferried off by ambulance to Treliske hospital. There would be a very sombre visit scheduled to her long-term companion and junior school headmistress, Loveday Cornelius.

Entering the subterranean bar the four were struck by the heat that was unexpected in such a buried place. Moisture and cold seemed to characterise underground rooms of any description, but in its day this had been Smuggling Central and was capable of housing many men and women without any discomfort. Cornish miners were world renowned for their mastery and skill below ground, and this had led them to create a room heated by thermal energy and completely self-contained. The only modern addition was the sensible installation of a permanent generator. The room's existence could therefore not be traced on any national system and gave an almost totally secure place for those who wished to meet unobserved. The generator had been the final cog in the wheel of secrets. It was now the perfect hideaway. The occupiers of the room were mindful that more than one cannabis factory had been traced and broken up by official traces showing unexpected spikes in electricity use in the small hours. That was sloppy, and this legacy of what was, frankly, the dirty business of smuggling deserved more care than the possibility of being discovered by those with alliances to groups with respect neither for the past or present of Cornwall. It was, if you like, the very definition of a safe house. You were risking a lot if infiltration was your game and, truth to tell, that was the only way that this particular inner sanctum could be exposed. And those who despised the Way of the Spriggans were alert to such a threat. Access was by invitation only and retribution had not been necessary for many years. Its existence was a fairly open secret but so was the involvement of the Job twins, and there was not a man throughout the county who would willingly upset 'the two twins'.

The 'twins' were discovered leaning on the bar at the

far end of the cavernous space as the friends entered. They were chatting to the barmaid Rosie. A few others were seated at the bar on stools and one or two groups sat in loosely arranged groups in leather armchairs. It looked for all the world like a gentleman's club designed by the cartoonists who had drawn The Flintstones.

Nobody looked up as Bones led in his three compatriots. There was no secret handshake, no form of words as no such subterfuge was necessary. If these four people were in the subterranean bar then they were entitled to be there. It was Rosie who greeted Bones first.

"Well, well, you old bugger. Where you been for the longest time? I should have thought your membership would have expired by now."

So saying she ran around the corner of the bar and threw herself into the arms of William Radleigh de Beaune, planting a great big sloppy kiss on his cheek as she hugged him. The twins straightened as Bones coloured. There was something feline in their movement that combined athleticism with menace. Bob looked at Bonesie with a wicked smile and drawled in a deep baritone,

"It's alright, Bonesie, we knew you were on your way. The Black Prince sent word from his old army oppo, big Andy Wenmouth from up Mount Charles way. We know who your companions are too. You are welcome. Any enemy of the Spriggans has friends here."

Faces turned towards the companions and softened as they too smiled a welcome that held within it the implicit threat that could make blood run cold.

"Come over here, you lot, and have a good pint of draught Trelawney, then we can fill you in on what we intend to do to finally deal with the excrescence that is Sebastian Slope. And please relax. You would not be anywhere near this place except that we have a common cause in an enemy of Cornwall."

The day stretched from late morning to late in the evening as Prideaux told his half heard tale. Many Cornish folk, especially alumni of St Jude's, knew elements of the story, few were fully aware of the level of Slope's murderous degeneration. It was after eight by the time the twins were satisfied that they knew enough about Slope's perfidy in framing Prideaux, his subsequent return to Oxford and involvement in the death of Petroc Trethewey and the fact that his hand lay behind the bizarre murder of the vicar of Bodelva. The room remained unaware of the double murder choreographed by Slope that had seen off an unnamed initiate and Conrad Speight. For someone who had previously been an amateur Slope had taken to the ranks of the professional killers with alacrity. The tentacles of Slope and his Spriggans spread far and wide and it seemed impossible to get close enough to the man with any certainty of success.

A tired and extremely emotional Mark, his arm around Ginny, summarised the situation as the conversation was degenerating into a general hubbub. "Since this all started we've been chased, menaced, threatened and frankly scared half to death. What I would like is to go back to a quiet, uneventful, though to us ultimately satisfying, existence back on the moor. It may not sound much but we have the best real ale pub in Cornwall, the only village green in Cornwall, and Ginny has her pottery to run while I have my books. I appreciate that we are targets because we know Piers and Bonesie but if anyone here can think of a way that we could return to pick up where we left off then I should be eternally grateful. I'd never let my friends down but you only have to look at us to see that Ginny and I are not cut out for this sort of life."

By virtue of having been born two minutes earlier than Bob it was Robert who took it upon himself to adopt the role of elder statesman. "I appreciate your honesty, Mark and Ginny, and I appreciate that this is none of your doing, but you are in an impossible situation. The fact that this is none of your doing is by the way. Slope knows where you live so returning to your cottage on the moor is out of the question as long as he remains a threat. Equally, we know enough to be aware that he has the resources to track you wherever you go. He got close in Cornwall and he got close in Wales and if we were to leave you to your own devices you would not last long. The irony is that you are of no consequence to him; he is simply intent on hurting anyone with a connection to Piers or Billy Bones. Our problem is that we need to take him out of the equation.

"Sadly, this is not old Cornwall and it is not as if Slope is one of the Revenue men and we a group of wreckers. If that were the case he'd be somewhere off shore by now being nibbled down to his wishbone by the little fishes. When we take care of this particular bit of business, however, there is not to be any part of it associated with us as a group or you as individuals. We have three options as I see it. Options one and two, buying him off and threatening him with severe repercussions, are not going to work with a man like Slope."

Before the older twin could get to option three the fruity tones of Billy Bones floated over the assembled company. "And option three is we kill the bastard and drop him in the sea which, let's face it, is where the slimy bastard belongs."

The murmur of approbation that followed Bones's interjection neatly summed up the feelings of the Sons of Dozmary. It was clear that the threat of Slope was sufficient to have prodded reasonable men a long way towards murder as a solution.

"There is another way," came a sweet voice that sounded out of place in this cavern where dubious deeds

171

had been planned and, no doubt, carried out successfully over generations. "Surely if we kill this man we are no better than he is and chances are we will get caught and some of us, perhaps all of us, will spend a lot of time reflecting on that fact." Rosie was in full flow now and chasing a hare she felt it important to catch before some of her greatest friends did something they would regret for the rest of their days. "What if someone were to infiltrate the Spriggan hierarchy, and get close enough to Slope to find evidence of his crimes that would send him down for the foreseeable future? Surely he is such an arrogant bastard that he would regard himself as untouchable, but nobody can go committing murder without there being some evidence, or somebody who could give evidence against him. That must be worth a try."

"And who would you suggest should be the suicide jockey to make this brave foray into the lair of the murdering bastard, as if I didn't know," asked Bob? The vein on his forehead was standing out and beginning to pulse ominously. "I'll be damned if I let you get anywhere near that madman."

"And who the hell do you think you are, telling me what I can and or can't do, Bob Job? And you can kindly shut up before you start as well," she added, casting a withering glance at Robert, who knew better than to argue with her when she had the bit between her teeth.

"Slope doesn't know me so why should he suspect an innocent barmaid who makes casual acquaintance with one of his lackeys? Once I have been on the scene for a while he will take no notice of me. From what I hear he is not really that interested in women in the first place. I'm pretty good at getting men to tell me stuff they wouldn't even tell their wives, so if I could get the evidence to put him away for good then the rest would soon crumble. From what has been said today the organisation is based on fear of Slope and not much else. The underlings will find some other criminal activity to save them having to work for a living if we take out the head. My old aunt always told me, kill the head of the snake and the body will writhe for a bit but it will die. And this way nobody human has to die. It is a perfect solution."

It wasn't the Gettysburg Address, it wasn't Henry V on the eve of Agincourt, but the impassioned speech of this tiny young girl cast a spell over a roomful of men who, minutes earlier, had been on the verge of taking up cudgels and battering any living Spriggan available for sport and enjoyment.

The spell was broken by Piers Prideaux who, after thanking Rosie for her kind and courageous offer, continued, "There is no way that I can let you put yourself in danger on my account. This whole mess revolves around me. Slope hates me and wants me dead. Sadly, he has extended his hatred to include my friends and more or less anybody who has any connection with me. Brave as you are, Rosie, I think you are underestimating this man. He heads an admittedly small organisation but within that killers and sadists are two a penny. If he found out you were a plant you wouldn't stand a chance. Mercy is not a word in his vocabulary. Apart from that he has a network of minor sympathisers who seem to be inordinately well informed. Some are in deep cover and for all I know there may even be one of them here. We simply couldn't take that chance."

"Ah! But that is where you are wrong," replied Rosie. "You wouldn't be taking that chance, I would. And I am prepared to take it. For your information I am not simply the barmaid here, I own the entire building and a few more properties besides. I can also look after myself if things cut up rough, as they occasionally do. I lived in China for a while when my father was ambassador there. He made sure that I learned self-defence. Not that choreographed stuff you see in the films but the lowdown dirty stuff used on the streets. I fear nobody, and if you want to check that, admittedly unlikely, boast, then ask Terry and George over there."

She nodded to two men at a corner table who were making the most obvious attempt to look invisible that Prideaux had ever seen. "Go on ask them about the time they were pontificating that men would always be superior to women because they were stronger. Men would always beat them in a fight. Ask them how I suggested we put it to the test, and ask them how they got on. Well, Terry?"

"She is not like other women," answered Terry, his discomfiture clear to see. "She is too fast, too violent, and whatever they taught her in China should carry a health warning. We were only kidding around and she put poor old George here in Treliske hospital.

"She knocked you spark out before you even got your hands up," said a visibly disgruntled George. "Until I saw her perform I thought all that jumping in the air and kicking people in the face was faked, but she can do it and, once she starts, it's a force of nature. She can do a lot of damage to a chap," he mused, before falling into an embarrassed silence.

"So you see, I'm not the shrinking violet you apparently think I am. Would you care to put it to the test, Mr Prideaux?"

"I would not, Rosie. And I can see that you are far better prepared to look after yourself than am I. And that is part of the problem. I don't have the equipment to deal with Slope. I am not a fighter. I am an academic. The point is I am an academic who lost a promised tenure because Slope set me up. Now I can rationalise my feelings but essentially I still want to punch his stupid face. Unfortunately, I know that I am not simply dealing with a completely incompetent ex-master of an Oxford

College. God knows there were plenty of simpletons and incompetents on the staff at St Jude's, but we are dealing with someone who has already proved he is capable of committing murder and has me fairly high up on his to do list. If I could walk away I would, but there is not a chance that Slope will allow me to. He will not rest until he has taken personal charge and a whole lot of pleasure in ensuring my demise. Whatever my feelings I cannot allow someone I barely know to put herself at risk on my account."

"That's settled then," said Rosie in her sweetest little girl voice. It was a way she had of winding up quite a few very strong men who thought she needed their protection, when if you get right down to it the reverse was the case. "What we need now is to identify a minor Spriggan who is likely to fall for a pretty girl with her own pub. Any ideas, anybody?"

"There is no talking to her when she is in this mood," chorused Robert and Bob. "I suggest we sleep on it and decide what to do next tomorrow."

"It's not really my business," piped up the previously embarrassed Terry, "but if anyone asked me I'd say that Rosie is better able to look after herself than most blokes I've come across. To be honest she laid me out fair and square. I never saw it coming. She is not only fast but she's also bloody lethal. I don't know whether it will help but there's a bloke down in Falmouth. I drink down there a bit when I've been out fishing. He's a regular in the Captain's Finger. Man by the name of Johnson. Not sure of his first name, James or John something like that anyway. Binky Jago will tell you. He's landlord of the Captain's Finger. Goes fishing with me when I'm down Falmouth way. He's a good old boy is Binky. I've had some laughs with him, I can tell you. Long story short, anyway, he knows this Johnson bloke. Binky reckons he's a queer old fish. He's never quite sure of him, bit of a bullshitter, but I've a feeling he could be your man. Binky reckons he goes on about all sorts of stuff. Disappears from time to time up country. When he's a drink or two taken, he has let slip something about seeing somebody murdered in some sort of meeting he was at, somewhere up that Oxford way. I've heard that he likes to drop hints that he has some sort of Spriggan membership. I hates them bastards, so if this helps then that'll do me. He can talk tough but I wouldn't fancy his chances against our Rosie there."

"Thanks for that, Terry. I think I'll take a little excursion down Falmouth way to see what I can see."

"I bloody knew it," chorused the twins in unison.

23

The man who stepped
into the mirror

Back in north Oxford, Slope was relaxing in a hot
bath with a glass of twenty year old malt in hand as
he washed away any traces of his victim. He had been
careful and had already destroyed in an incinerator the
clothes he wore to commit his latest atrocity. He was
always careful. There was no point in being caught for
the murder of a nonentity such as Peter Fisher. Sure, he
had enjoyed the torture, but felt a vague irritation that
the man did not have anything of interest to impart. A
vague idea that Prideaux was somewhere in Cornwall,
based on little but supposition, was the story Fisher had
stuck to through the beginnings of what Slope thought
of as the process. He was a methodical man and, since
his conversion to the pleasures of murder as a hands on
hobby, rather than something ordered like some bizarre
takeaway, he had come to realise that it was the smell of
fear and of blood that he enjoyed in a sexual way.

He had always been pretty sure that he was a sadist,
but for years had subordinated the impulse to do physical
harm to the pleasures of harassment within the world of
academe. There was plenty of scope there as it was often
the last refuge of the halt and the lame. Incompetence
was rife and his rapid rise through the ranks, giving
him power over those with better degrees than he had
managed, meant he had the power to bully the weak
unmercifully. He had cheerfully driven several lecturers
to breakdowns with his unjustifiable habit of sweeping
uninvited into their lectures and intimidating them to

such an extent that the only response of those targeted was to take sick leave. Such a course was the beginning of the end, as when the inevitable return to college had to be attempted Slope would upgrade his standard of psychological bullying until the victim simply bailed out in an attempt at retaining some sort of sanity. He was good at it and he knew it. He had willing lieutenants who were themselves adept at psychological bullying and knew where their bread was buttered.

Only one had ever stood up to Slope for any length of time and that was the man he always thought of as 'that bastard Piers Prideaux'. Sure, Slope had got rid of him, but the act had not satisfied his sadistic streak. Prideaux had not suffered enough, and although Slope decried this desire for total revenge as a weakness he was powerless to do anything about it. Even he was aware that this search for revenge had reached a tipping point. He was aware that his support base was weakening. Followers were beginning to melt away as things became too hot for them to face. Fear could only go so far as a motivating force. Slope's precipitant descent into savagery was an open secret amongst previously committed Spriggans. Perhaps his greatest mistake was the murder he had enjoyed even more than the slow torture of Peter Fisher. His choreographed indulgence in the murder of the acolyte and Conrad Speight had proved a watershed. Spriggans had begun to disappear. Addresses were changed, phone numbers removed as previous supporters covered their tracks, some even leaving the country. Slope was not an enemy to take lightly and he now seemed, to many, to have turned on his own. This could not continue unless he plotted to go out in some form of conflagration, perhaps like Cagney's Cody Jarrett in White Heat. Somehow "Made it Ma! Top of the world!" did not seem the sort of epitaph for a man like Slope. Perhaps it would be more appropriate for him to go to ground until such time as he could formulate a sensible plan. The thought had occurred to an increasingly haunted man. Like many loners, Slope was fine when things were going in his favour. When they hit any sort of buffer he had nobody to turn to. There was nobody to inject that important dose of realism into any situation. Therefore he brooded. The morality of what he had done thus far troubled him not one jot or tittle. So what? Some nobodies died. People died every day. 'Woo hoo I'll make you famous'. He would never have admitted to having heard of 'Young Guns" but there was an element of the Billy the Kid philosophy in his general attitude.

"You have been summarily executed by Sebastian Slope, academic, leader of a very effective secret society, writer and philosopher. Your name will forever be listed when future journalists write the story of a man who achieved so much in a short time and very kindly included you in his plans. You didn't die in a random accident, nor writhe in the throes of some ghastly unnameable disease or breathe your last in some stinking and understaffed nursing home. None of that applied to you. You had the distinction of being summarily thrown out of this life by someone who mattered. Your pathetic existence was raised several notches as a consequence. You should be grateful. Nothing in your life was as important as your leaving it at the hands of someone who not only enjoyed the process of murder but was also bloody, in every sense of the word, good at it."

Psychiatrists probably spend their lives debating the concept of evil and its attendant atrocities. Something happened is the explanation in this particular case. Yes, Slope had a history of cruelty, impatience and cruelty. This description, very probably, applies to every chief executive, college manager and small firm boss in the country. It doesn't lead them all to the altar of murder.

Not all of them cheat on their taxes either, perhaps only their partners. But Slope was the man who had stepped into the mirror. He was now looking in on humanity rather than being one of the boys in the band. His advanced sense of entitlement had made him a dangerous adversary before now. Now he was a danger to anyone and everyone. There was a real storm on the horizon and Slope was in the eye of that storm. Prideaux's position at the top of his to do list was now threatened by every other sentient being in the country. Chaos was to be loosed on the world and it came in human form. For the second time in fourteen hours Sebastian Slope smiled to himself, only this time he was smiling from the wrong side of the mirror.

He was distracted by his phone. Only important calls came through on the phone he kept with him at all times. This particular ring tone alerted him to the fact that this call came from the highest level within government. His smile vanished. If Sir Wilbury Burford was contacting him then it could be trouble. No cabinet minister would take the trouble to contact him at this time of day. It was close enough to lunchtime for all self-respecting cabinet members to be taking their customary three hour lunch break. Sir Wilbury was sufficiently senior not to let government business interfere with the serious matter of lunch at his club.

"Now listen Slope old boy, a word to the wise. I'm warning you in recognition of our previous working relationship as it is a matter of some importance. I think you should be aware that this blasted unit that Cornelius has put together has been given the green light to take you out of the equation. I'm afraid it's rather been taken out of my hands. Seems you and some of your chaps have been making too much noise of late, if you get my drift. As you know the wheels of government grind exceeding slow but also exceeding bloody small. Best if you avoided the grinding wheel in all its horror if you ask me. Made efforts to intervene, old fruit, but no progress made I'm afraid. Best advice from the top is that you take a bit of a long vacation. I mean a long vacation too, Slope. Only so much a chap can do, don't you know. Superhuman effort and all that but no business resulting if you get my drift. Best for everyone if you toddle off into the sunset and find yourself something less demanding to pass the time. Take up art or something. Get a couple of young gels to model for you. That'll be the ticket. Some obscure island somewhere the sun shines all day and half the night, that'll be the badger. Well, good luck, old chap. Must dash. I've to meet one of my many young nieces at the club in half an hour. Mustn't be late. Destroy your phone after this call. Will be no trace of any conversation anyway. Clever chaps these IT wallahs. Pip pip." The phone went dead.

"Destroy the phone. I'd cut your bloody throat given half a chance", yelled a furious Slope. He was furious because he knew things were beginning to unravel and that drastic steps would be the only thing to meet the case. "Damn you all to hell," he thought as he mused on the unreliability of his fellow man.

The rest of Oxford luxuriated in the first real sunshine of the summer. For once kamikaze tourists, many of them Japanese, strolled rather than sprinted from shop doorway to college doorway in failed attempts to avoid the persistent rain. Instead of filling up every coffee shop, fast food outlet and pub in the city they lounged on the steps of the Martyrs' Memorial, they headed for the river, for Christ Church Gardens. Outdoor living had become the order of the day. Perverts licked their lips as attractive teenage schoolgirls dressed in the most provocative of 'Lolita come to academia' influenced styles. Businessmen unaccountably felt the need to adopt a strange uniform of suit jacket and the most outrageous shorts as well as the British staple of sandals with socks. Jeeves would have been singularly unimpressed. Oxford became its summer mash up. Locals attempted to carry on as usual but were grumpy as hell, overseas school students carried on as school students do everywhere once released into the wild. And despite the inevitable bustle there was a summer torpor in the air.

The place to be was on the river. Salter's was prospering with its river trips as visitors battled to join return trips to Abingdon. Canoes began to proliferate and the braver ones attempted to rent punts. This was perhaps the favourite spectator sport for locals and those students over-summering in the city rather than returning to the family estate, or increasingly, in these more democratic times, the council estate. And the best vantage point to watch the hapless first timers underestimate the tricky nature of the Oxford punt was anywhere on or near Folly Bridge. Coincidentally, when Slope was Master at St Jude's he insisted that a college punt be permanently kept moored at Folly Bridge for his exclusive use. Woe betide any student with the temerity to attempt to use it, whether Slope needed it or not. Rustication was the very least that student could expect. As you might expect Slope was as accomplished in the use of the punt as he later became in the prosecution of his murderous designs.

For now the man who had stepped into the mirror was mulling over his final effort at doing away with the turbulent lecturer who had blighted his total control on St Jude's. He was not going to entrust it to minions. From now on he would walk alone. Only he had the power to formally disband the Spriggans, or at least to stand them down for the present or until the wind started to blow in a more favourable direction. Unusually for him the recent phone call had rattled him more then he cared to admit. He forced himself to recognise the quandary in which he now found himself. What was the best course of action? There were options, but his problem was that others were now making decisions that affected him. This conflicted with his desperate need to hold all the aces. He was pathologically addicted to power. To him it was not something to be shared. If he wasn't in complete control, he was nowhere. He forced himself to remain calm. He would find a way through all this. He had to. But how could he best deal with the organisation he had headed for so long? It had become more of a hindrance than a help in recent times. With the organisation out of the picture it might prove easier for Slope to get close enough to Prideaux to finish him off, and so much the better if he could create the opportunity to give him the Fisher treatment. How he had enjoyed torturing Fisher. How that pathetic little man had squealed. His dearest wish was that one day he could inflict that sort of pain on Prideaux. Once he had removed this irritant he could disappear. He had contacts abroad, particularly in southern Italy, where he knew he would be welcomed with open arms. Money had never been a problem for Slope. There had always been shrewd investments and he had used his position in the Spriggans to maximise the take for his own purposes. His investments were spread throughout the world and he relished his numerous bank accounts. Dodgy bankers are nothing new. Slope had always sought out his own kind, and bent bank managers protected his wealth as if their own lives depended on it. Given Slope's current frame of mind that was probably closer to the truth than any of them imagined.

The latest intelligence reports showed that Prideaux was somewhere in Cornwall. He was moving around a lot, obviously deliberately, but it could not be beyond Slope's powers to find him there. He had the knowledge and skills to ensure he could achieve this without his own presence being discovered. If he made a big fuss disbanding the Spriggans and fed that news through to Cornwall then Prideaux could get careless. He might assume that Slope had given up the struggle. But Slope was not a man to deal in possibilities; he needed certainties.

Sure, the end of the Spriggans would have obvious benefits. The downside was that a network of informants and minions would no longer be available to him. So what! He didn't need them, he had never needed anyone. He could be the man who walked alone because he was better, cleverer, richer and sure as hell more murderous than any of them. The idea became more appealing to him by the second. He would begin planning the ultimate solution then, having carried it out, he would vanish before surfacing again with a new identity and in a part of the world where a man of his special talents would be valued.

24

Under the radar

Slope was a meticulous planner, and now the decision was made he began putting things in place with a focus and determination that was obsessive. He began by clearing out the Oxford house. He called in a final favour from two Spriggan disposal operatives. Used to covering their tracks, the two men who had worked for Slope many times cleaned the house to forensic standards. When they had finished it was as if the man who was not Mr Rainbow had never existed. It would be three months before the bodies of the two operatives were accidentally discovered in the cellar of a derelict house several streets away from the north Oxford base that had been Slope's since his return to the city.

His next step was to change his appearance sufficiently to wrong foot any but the most observant. His clothes having been disposed of by the now dead operatives he had adopted a much more casual style of dress. For the first time in his life he bought a couple of pairs of jeans and several T-shirts. He had always regarded such clothing as suitable only for the lower classes, particularly those who did manual work. The very thought of the words forced his lip into a sneer, though he was pleasantly surprised that having dressed himself in such garb it instantly changed the way he looked and to some extent the way he walked. He looked much less purposeful and would pass for an idler without anything of major importance in his life. He had become ensconced in a back street bedsit in the Jericho area of the city. This was an area where people didn't ask too many questions. This was where people were too involved with their own lives to care too much for one more slacker who minded his own business and whose very appearance suggested that he was not interested in establishing any relationships.

Never one to do things by halves, Slope had even invested in a completely new hairstyle. He had also grown a moustache and, of all things, had indulged himself with a very convincing fake tan. Slope's own mother would have had difficulty in recognising him, particularly with the piece de resistance. Applying his considerable powers of application through exercise and diet he had managed to reduce his weight from a fairly hefty sixteen stone to a positively waif like twelve stone six. It was the final cog in the machine and gave him the conviction that his plan could work.

His next step was to ensure that the organisation he had headed for so long was formally reined in. This was a move that had been forced on him and, though it was an easier process than might be supposed, Slope was as angry as hell at having to do it. The group of twelve that comprised the central council of the Spriggans, minus, of course, Conrad Speight and the unnamed novice, were responsible for carrying out any command that came from the leader. Slope only needed to compose the official notice and forward it to the man who bore the soubriquet Brother Red and it instantly became his responsibility to call the deep cover meeting which all Spriggans and any remaining supplicants would attend.

The words to be used were these: 'By the order of the Man who is not Mr Rainbow, the Spriggans organisation is now formally ordered to refrain from any direct action until such time that full involvement is directly declared. Any member who disobeys this command can expect the full force of the displeasure of our current leader to visit them as Death riding a pale horse. From this day forth the Spriggans are officially stood down, with the sole exception of the Man who is not Mr Rainbow. Until such time as the order is received to fully regroup he shall remain the one, the only and lasting Spriggan even until the end of recorded time'. Confirmation would then be passed in writing to Slope at a prearranged spot near Magdalen Bridge, and an underground organisation that had existed for generations would position itself even further underground. The bulky package that was accepted formally by Slope on a particularly gloomy Wednesday evening from Brother Green contained comprehensive contact details of the homes, family and businesses of the novices that had been present at the winding up, and the brothers that made up the council, with the exception of Brother Red and Brother Green. It was so like the man to take no chances. Now that he was a lone wolf and had achieved the feat of fading very effectively into the background he needed insurance.

The action of placing the organisation into deep cover was not one taken lightly at any time. This was only the third time in its history that such action had been sanctioned. During both world wars the presiding individual who answered to the title 'The Man Who was not Mr Rainbow' had been forced into the position of side-lining the organisation he headed. Neither time had the action been taken in the interest of the country. Spriggans never thought in that way. It was simply that in times of national emergency conducting the business of the organisation became difficult, when spies and fifth columnists were suspected everywhere. Putting the organisation into cold storage served to preserve its secrets and the identity of its adherents, allowing reactivation when the time was more conducive to its aims. Slope knew the organisation's history intimately and it was this knowledge that fed his cold anger of the moment. It had taken two major worldwide conflagrations to push the Spriggans into deep cover in its entire existence. The third time such action was deemed necessary it had been because of the actions of one man. A psychiatrist would have had a field day studying Slope. He was a man of many complications. He could appear rational and normal in almost every regard but when baulked in any way it was if a switch was turned. Now it was clear that Prideaux had interfered in his plans even to the extent of forcing him into issuing the deep cover option. It was now that the irrationality began to swamp his consciousness. A cool and clever planner when stable, his mind currently whirled with hatred. He must crush Prideaux. He would crush this man. He would do so with the application of as much pain and humiliation as humanly possible. Prideaux would pay and he would die slowly and painfully. How dare this insignificant bastard force him into doing something as significant as standing down his Spriggans?

Slope felt that he had been pushed into a corner, and by Prideaux of all men. Obviously he had covered his own back in ordering the deep cover option. The information he held gave him the assurance that, should strange things begin to happen – he was not a believer in coincidence – then he could easily and quickly track down any or all of those who may be trading their knowledge for gain or even for immunity from prosecution. What neither Brother Red nor Brother Green knew was that he already held the necessary information on both of them. He would, of course, use it without the slightest qualm should it become necessary. His plan was proceeding at some pace. He could move around, even in Oxford, a city where he was known, pretty much undetected. He had presided over the dissolution of the organisation and he had established for himself a new base and a virtually new identity. His next task was to decide how best to carry out the business end of the plan. He already had his backup plan in place and knew where and when he would disappear when the final coup had been delivered. It would not be that long until the existence of Piers Prideaux would no longer intrude on his heightened sense of self importance. Sebastian Slope was, for the first time in years, a happy and contented man. The man who stepped into the mirror was now more dangerous than ever. Piers Prideaux was edging ever closer to discovering how dangerous for himself. Though as yet he did not know it.

25

Friends reunited

It was later that evening that an unexpected phone call from Cornelius attracted Lola's attention away from the box set of Inspector Montalbano episodes she was currently ploughing a very merry way through. She recognised his voice by the silence. He was hesitating again. "Is that you, Gawain?" She knew it was as he confirmed instantly, prompted by the undercurrent of irritation her voice betrayed. "I wondered if I could come around to your place and tell, well, brief you, a bit more clearly, Lola. There are things that you won't know and I think I must tell you before you take off to Paris. Would it be OK if I came around tonight?" Torn between a fictional investigator and a real one there was no contest. Not that Montalbano wasn't very nice to look at but she could put him back in the box for now.

"What time were you thinking of, Gawain?" she asked.

"How about now?" was the reply. "If you look out of your window you will see that I'm at the entrance to your building. You could buzz me up. You'll have no problem seeing me. I'm the smartly dressed chap carrying two bottles of vintage champagne."

For a second she was going to ask how he knew her address but she realised he would smile and say something evasive. She was secretly pleased and, having returned one investigator to his box, she prepared to welcome another to her flat.

Lola was unsure what she expected from what had every indication of a social call, perhaps even more. The old ideas of friends or lovers as immutable opposites didn't really cross her mind. What crossed his she was never quite sure. He arrived, the epitome of the lover bearing gifts of the seducer's favourite fizz. Within minutes she was clear that there was something weightier on his mind than any possibility of seduction. His kiss was peremptory and, of all things, he was carrying a well stuffed briefcase. He wasn't afraid to use it either, as he started laying out dossiers and files all over the artfully distressed kitchen table. It was obvious the way this was going. It really meant no odds to her, as her feelings for him remained in that tricky area where friendship didn't quite overlap into something more exciting. She resolved to adopt a professional approach, with perhaps a little light flirting thrown in as a distraction when things got too serious. She handed him a glass of champagne as he continued to arrange files and papers in neat piles.

"Thanks Lola. Here's to us," he toasted, taking a long draught from the crystal champagne flute. "I am looking forward to a long and rewarding relationship and this could be the start of a beautiful friendship."

"I bet you say that to all the girls, Gawain," she replied, biting her lip as she did so. What had started in her head as a light and flirty reply emerged from her lips sounding flat and trite. Gawain would expect a lot more than that, she thought. He appeared not to notice and nodded at her to sit next to him at the table. He indicated the mass of files with a rueful smile. "I'm here to explain what I expect of you, Lola. I should have felt comfortable enough to tell you more in the office. The fact that I didn't is a comment on the nature of the intelligence business. You know the old joke that goes; history is one damn thing after another. Well, in the intelligence community there is a similar saying. I'm sorry to admit that it is based on sour experience and the fact that the entire intelligence community mainly consists of psychopaths, sociopaths and alcoholics. It is true when they say that intelligence work is plugging one damn leak after another. I thought that this place would be a good place to meet as it is not tainted with any electronic listening equipment. I had it checked out to be on the safe side."

"Very thoughtful of you. I suppose that is your roundabout way of telling me that you have leaks in the office and that you are not sure who is responsible."

"You are partly right. There are leaks in MI6. That lot leaks like a sieve at the best of times. The thing is that various arms within the service specialise in different areas. As you know I specialise in keeping a weather eye on the Spriggans. My remit extends further than that, but essentially it is that specific organisation and any offshoots it may have. I often liken the Spriggans to a smouldering volcano. You know they are there and every so often they erupt into much more lively activity. Not many people are aware of how far they are embedded in public and private life, though. The really frightening thing is that they have a presence outside the UK. They are active in Europe and the US. At least, they have been at various times."

"Gawain, I have no wish to interrupt your flow, which I must say is both fluent and manly. I have a gathering feeling that you are about to break the bad news that I won't be going off to Paris after all."

"Not as such, Lola. You will be going, but not before you have done some important preparation for your new role. I didn't bring a bursting briefcase with me for the extra exercise of carrying the thing, bloody heavy as it is. What you have here," he indicated the files now covering the table where they sat, "is some case histories covering events where Spriggans have been involved at some level. It's best if you look through two or three of the case histories to make sure you are up to speed on the unit and what our function is. There is no pathetic business jargon involved. Nobody has a mission statement unless it is something like 'to root out the bastards wherever they raise their ugly heads.' The files with a green sticker are the ones I'd like you to start with, as they are histories. The red stickered files are current and I'll come on to that later. For the time being I'll pour you another glass of champagne and put my feet up while you do some serious and necessary research."

Cornelius smiled as he noticed Lola adopt her studying face. She had always been brilliant at absorbing and retaining large amounts of information. Once she had adopted that specific face that she always brought to the process of information crunching he knew she would be absorbed for as long as it took. He left her to it and started looking through one of his own active files.

The first few pages of the file she chose to start with seemed to echo what she expected from a government department file. After that it started to get interesting. She vaguely remembered the fuss that surrounded the events at the time. This wasn't something lost in the mists of time. Far from it in fact. It was something that had come to prominence within the last ten years. Mention of global warming tends to polarise people and reliable information can be hard to understand without a scientific background. Fertile ground for the machinations of an organisation that has always profited from sewing seeds of misunderstanding and panic. According to the file a whole range of seemingly respectable scientists have encouraged climate change deniers in recent years. Strangely, any evidence of long term study of climate patterns has been conspicuous by its absence. The gang of three, as three senior government scientists were styled, were influential in playing down the role of man-made pollution in the process of global warming. Their influence was pernicious, and investigations by the predecessors of Cornelius's unit proved that each of them had Spriggan connections. The real conspiracy lay in the fact that, although the file contained names and enough evidence to convict all three, the file had been pulled by the Minister for Secret Societies and had never been made public. In the margin, neatly written in Cornelius's copper plate, were the words: 'Not only are scientists A, B and C members of the Spriggans it is also clear that the minister is also a member of that organisation and is abusing his position in protecting them'.

Having read this together with a good deal of corroborating evidence and some fairly imaginative speculation, Lola got up to stretch her back. She was rubbing her eyes that were beginning to strain, despite the fact her reading light was provided by an Alex lamp. There were still two more files to go. She refilled both glasses and, blowing a kiss in Cornelius's general direction, she settled down to the second file. This was a very dog eared file where the English was quite difficult to read, partly because it had faded quite significantly and partly because in structure and vocabulary it was archaic. She gave a wry smile as she settled down to read.

The file was controversial from the beginning and it pulled no punches. In modern English it read: Though generally believed to have been a Popish plot, evidence obtained at the time of the torture leads me to conclude that the conspirators had been infiltrated by a dissident group of disparate folk hidden inside a secret society. The Spriggan Folk was the contemporary name for the group that had provided the best known of the conspirators in Guido Fawkes. He had been serving in the army of Spain in Flanders and had been recruited there. He was a Yorkshire man by birth and was able to convince Robert Catesby, the most prominent of the Catholic conspirators, that he was as devout a catholic as Catesby himself. In fact he was, as evidence cited in the file made clear, a high ranking Spriggan. Since the plot took place in 1605 the file gave a good picture of the longevity of the secret society that the modern Spriggans continue to be. What is also evident is the callousness that came to define this group from their earliest days. They never shied away from violence. In fact at many times in their history the use of violence was applauded for its efficacy. Neither did their leaders at any point show any real sign of the loyalty to ordinary Spriggans that they demanded from them. This was never as evident as in the fact that the letter that betrayed the plot and listed the names of the conspirators has been shown to have come from the man who was 'Not the Mr Rainbow' of his day. Fawkes had infiltrated the group on behalf of the Spriggans to ensure that the plot went ahead successfully. Catesby was a charismatic figure and the rest of the group trusted and relied on him to carry out the plot successfully. Fawkes, however, had worked as an engineer when in the Spanish army and knew gunpowder. He knew how to use it and how much to use, both skills desperately important when dealing with the notoriously unstable gunpowder in use at the time. Because of this he was invaluable to the success of the plot. His instructions were to ensure that the explosion would wipe out as many of the protestants as possible, leaving both Catholics and protestants at each other's throats as usual but with both groups significantly weakened. This is what Fawkes believed his role was. It made sense, as a successful explosion would have perfectly suited the secular ambitions of the Spriggans. It seemed a reasonable plan in the context of the times. The apparent reality that intervened came in the form of an anonymous letter delivered to Lord Monteagle who took it to James's First Minister, Robert Cecil, Earl of Salisbury. The letter, of course, came from the Head of the

Spriggans at the time. A facsimile in the file showed that it was a warning to Lord Monteagle to avoid the official opening of parliament on 5th November. For years it was claimed that one of the plotters, Francis Tresham, was responsible for the letter. He was a cousin of Monteagle and would have known the likely consequence of sending such a letter. Whether Tresham himself was a covert Spriggan or whether the letter came from another source is still the subject of debate. But there is no doubt that Fawkes was sacrificed on the altar of expediency. He had played an invaluable part in getting the plot to the stage of being a believable attempt by extreme Catholics to decimate parliament. The discovery of the plot would ensure that the persecution of Catholics would continue for a long time and at all levels of society. Fawkes never knew that he had been betrayed by his own leader, and even under the extremities of torture suffered by him and all the plotters he never revealed his true allegiance. Fawkes was subsequently hanged, drawn and quartered in January of the following year. For some time it was an effigy of the Pope that was burned in the bonfires of thanksgiving traditionally lit on the 5th November. Gradually the Pope was replaced by the Guy Fawkes effigy that is so familiar in the present day.

"So was he a Spriggan or not then, Gawain? I know you well enough to know that you will have a view."

"The point in getting to read some of this stuff is to make it clear to you what we are dealing with here. In fact it doesn't matter that much whether Fawkes or Tresham, or both, were Spriggans. The involvement of the organisation is what is important. It shows that in many historical events that seem to have been researched half to death there is often some form of involvement by the organisation that Unit S has been set up to seek out and destroy. The problem is that in this country and much further afield the general public love a conspiracy theory.

I've already mentioned global warning and you can add in the death of Diana and dozens of other events. Trying to get people to understand that there is an organisation that is corrupt and that frequently can be traced all the way up to government is much more difficult. The Spriggans have managed to infiltrate the higher reaches of the civil service. They are active in the Commons and more so in the Lords, and they have support in royal circles too. I know that Unit S was set up to fail. The Minister for Secret Societies is undoubtedly one of them as well as being a bloody nuisance. He obstructs me at every turn and is determined that anytime I get within a whisker of Slope doors start to slam in my face. That is what you are getting yourself involved in and you must know that. Sorry if this all sounds a bit preachy, but you know how much I care."

"Gawain, you old softy. Of course I know you care. I'm very fond too but I'm a big girl now. I can make my own decisions about whether I work with you and whether I go to bed with you." She smiled as she said this, knowing it would make Cornelius blush. He was easily embarrassed and she seemed to have the knack of hitting that particular nerve."

"Lighten up. I'm teasing," she added. "I have every intention of joining Unit S, as you have been so kind as to invite me. But right now I'm knackered and heading for my bed. There is a very comfortable sofa there. It'll turn into a bed if you can be bothered with the mechanics. Or of course you could come with me and share my lovely king sized bed. I can't promise I'll be awake for longer than a minute or two but I trust you to behave as a gentleman would and not take advantage of a lady who is tired and emotional."

"You should know, Lola that the Boss never sleeps with the help. It is simply not done and I'll be perfectly comfortable here. But I appreciate your kind offer of a bed share and, who knows, in the future I might well take you up on it." Lola blew him a kiss as she walked into her bedroom, leaving the door conveniently open.

Cornelius smiled as he settled down on the sofa and began to think. There was too much running around in his head for him to sleep, except fitfully. He kept waking and thinking through his reasons for getting Lola on board. Were they as honourable as they first seemed? She was an attractive woman and he loved her dearly as a friend. In truth his record with women wasn't a good one. Like a lot of driven men he often failed to find time for whoever the woman in his life was. But Lola, well, she was something else. Unfortunately that something else was a friend. He had an old saying circling around his mind, in the way things do when you have no real idea of what to do next. 'Men can be friends with men because there must not be sex, men cannot be friends with women because there must be sex.' It was ridiculous. What could he offer Lola, anyway? He lived for his job and had never factored in any long term relationship when considering the future. He got up, doglegging his way around the flat in the dark. He did not put on any lights for fear of waking Lola. The last thing he could handle now would be an in depth discussion of their relationship. For the present he must keep things as they were. He was the boss and, of course, she would get special treatment while working within the Unit S set up. For anything else to happen some form of change would need to take place. That was in the future, and the present was the only place he felt comfortable. Still, there was plenty of time for a relationship to develop. If it was meant to be then perhaps he had best leave that to the Fates. The thought consoled him and, feeling his way back to the sofa, he lay down and was asleep within minutes. But in that sleep some very strange dreams did what dreams do. They came, and they came, not single spies, but in battalions.

26

Paris

Liz Bennett sat outside her favourite café near the Gare du Nord. She wore her customary black matching her favourite sour expression. She had always been dislikeable and age and experience had changed nothing in terms of her personality. She was not old, perhaps around thirty eight now, but looked older. There was certainly no attempt to halt the march of time through human intervention. She wore little makeup and seemed careless of her appearance. Life had not been kind to her and she had never been over fond of life in return. It had dealt her very few good cards. On a spring day in Paris all life was burgeoning and looking to the future, while she stared into her café noir and thought of the past. Part of that past was the only man that she felt able to trust. This was a contrary view, since there were few others who would have turned their back on this man or, indeed, wished to confront him in a dark alleyway. And only a fool would ever trust him, as many had found to their cost. In those days she had gone under the name of Ernesta Pugliano. It suited her purposes then. Reverting to her real name, Elizabeth Bennett, seemed the right move when she left the old life behind her.

There had not been many men in her life and those who had dallied had not stayed long. As a result her view of the gender was pretty much silted up. The one man that survived her jaundiced view was, ironically enough, the one who had so recently stepped into the mirror. Life frequently throws up strange bedfellows and there had been none stranger than these two. Sharing little in common there had been nevertheless some form of bond between them. That bond must have been cemented by the one commonality they did manage to share; both these misfits bore innate superiority feelings towards, and hatred of, the bulk of mankind. As a consequence the two made perfect bedfellows. They also formed a formidable alliance that for the moment was not actively in operation. It would not remain that way for long.

Bennett finished her coffee and walked off towards Rochechouart. She did not notice that she was being followed, at a discreet distance, by a figure that she would have struggled to recognise. That was not because she did not know her follower. She knew him too well. But she would struggle to recognise Sebastian Slope in his newest incarnation. Experts in disguise argue that there are all sorts of ways to become a different person. Some are ruinously expensive and only suitable for gangsters, or bankers wishing to put some distance between themselves and an avenging angel or two. Other disguises are more modest and work only at a distance and with the benefit of low lighting conditions. Slope, however, had always had inclinations towards the acting profession and he had immersed himself in becoming somebody else, somebody completely different. Perhaps not such a stretch for a man who was accustomed to insisting that he was not Mr Rainbow as the head of one of the world's most lethal secret societies.

Slope was not a man to stint on effort. His current disguise had taken time, while he lay low in the Oxford suburb of Jericho. All trace of the hyper confident Sebastian Slope had been expunged. The combination of extreme weight loss, complete hair makeover completed by a straggly moustache tinged silver, and old fashioned glasses presented a man a world away from his previous appearance. Since Slope was a man of some perseverance he had gone to the extent of having his ankle broken by an obliging thug. He then waited for several days before attending the Radcliffe Hospital to have it set. He had suffered agonies in the meantime but when he was told that it had not set properly and would need to be re-broken he allowed himself a quiet smile. He would need to wear a cast for several months and at the end of that his natural gait would differ completely from his previous way of walking.

Private investigators and spies will tell you that the way someone walks is akin to a signature. It is the biggest giveaway there is and the hardest thing of all to disguise. Slope had achieved that task through perseverance and a natural bloody mindedness that confirmed his ability to walk through the world as his new creation, a man of no fixed abode and one of apparently small consequence.

None of this was known to Bennett as she continued to walk along the Rue de Maubeuge. She was conscious of a presence some way behind her but the street was busy and she had never felt threatened in this part of Paris. At most times of the year this area of the city was thronged with visitors, so it is not as if she was tramping through some of the shadier parts of St Denis. After around thirty minutes of constant awareness of an obvious follower neither quickening nor slowing his stride, she felt a slight twinge of discomfort. She had no intention of looking back. In truth she was not really afraid. She was, however, aware. She knew this area and rather than quickening her pace she simply computed the optimum time to step into one of the myriad of side streets and wait for her follower to pass by. He would soon realise that he had made a life changing mistake if murder or rape was what was on his mind. Her face flushed slightly as the adrenalin began to pump. Whoever this was, he was about to get a shock he would never forget. With practised ease she shimmied into Rue Lentonnet. Stepping back into the doorway of a block of seedy looking apartments she quickly checked her pistol, ensuring it had a full magazine.

"This bastard had better be a terminally lost visitor or he can wave his balls goodbye," she thought to herself as she pressed further into the dark of her chosen doorway. The footsteps echoed as the man turned into the lane.

"So he was following," she said to herself as they drew nearer to her hiding place. She never tired of the excitement that came with this sort of situation. She had the whip hand and knew it. She would wait until her pursuer walked past then pop one of the small calibre bullets into the back of his neck. He wouldn't know what hit him, not until the next two burst through both his eyeballs exiting at the back of his head as he lay helpless on the ground. It was a scenario that appealed to her twisted instincts. The sudden realisation that the follower was taking too long to appear made her uneasy. There was no way he could have passed unseen, or got behind her. She was convinced he had turned into the alley just as she had done, so where the hell was he? She fought for as long as she could against looking out. Such a move would reveal her hiding place and could, she knew, prove fatal. Curiosity is such a powerful force that it has accounted for more humans than it has ever done for cats. Eventually she yielded. Of course it was against her better judgement, something that became obvious as a much larger hand locked on to her gun hand as she took a tentative peek out of the shadows. The hand of the unseen assailant was black gloved and strong enough to send the pistol spinning from her grip. What happened next was something that startled more than frightened her.

The potential assailant locked his mouth on hers and pulled her close, kissing her violently as he did so. Hating most men as she did she felt sick, yet recognised something from the past. After what seemed an aeon he allowed her to breathe, but did not release his grip. Now that the surprise had passed she began to fight like a cage fighter, using every part of her body in an attempt to damage the man who had taken such a liberty. He was strong and seemingly oblivious to every blow she landed. When the temper had tired her she subsided and seemed beaten, yet still he held her in an iron grip.

"I'll let you go if you promise not to try to kill me, Liz." He knew her name yet she did not recognise the man who stood in front of her. There was something about him, but what was it? "It's me, Sebastian," smirked the liberty taker. "Don't you recognise me?"

"Of course not, you fucking clown. The only Sebastian I know is twice your size and is not painted working class orange. Neither does he wear stupidly affected facial hair or walk as if he's just shit himself. So who the fuck are you? And I'd advise you to answer your starter for ten with due diligence or I'll do what Jeremy Paxman does metaphorically to idiots with the extremely sharp knife that is now hovering tantalisingly around the area of your worthless bollocks."

"I should have known you would have a knife, Liz, but it is me. I have had to change my appearance, my name and my walk. It's a long story but I am still the Sebastian Slope you once knew, and, to be fair, who knew you more than once, in the biblical sense of course. There are good reasons for my change in appearance which I'll tell you about over coffee. Now if you still insist on removing my bollocks then you will be closing off an avenue of pleasure to me and to you. If you take a closer look at my face then perhaps I could be tempted into opening up your own avenue of pleasure for me to take a nostalgic stroll or two." Slope removed his gloves as he spoke. "If you remember anything you will remember the fact that I have a low boredom threshold and a temper that Jeeves would describe as a trifle sudden. So fondle my balls by all means but put that knife away before I take it off you and cut your fucking head off."

Bennett did as she was told, reasoning that if this man was out to rape and kill her he would have begun the assault by now. If he was really Slope then it was more dangerous to annoy him, as she knew what he was capable of. Their relationship had been based on sex pure and simple. Well, if she were honest it was never pure and rarely simple, but by God it was always thrilling. She pocketed the knife and stared intently at the man who insisted he was Slope. There was something about him, except that he was so changed as to be almost unrecognisable. Could it be him? She had neither seen nor heard from him for years and in the old days she had been his guilty secret. She had never been more than a clandestine fuck to him. He never took her out in public but turned up at her flat in Jericho when he was feeling horny. But he did come back from time to time. And the sex was as she liked it. Usually she preferred women but she was happy to take it where she could get it. Rough and uncompromising as it was it suited her precisely. It was nasty, brutish and short and usually left her exhausted and in some discomfort. But so what? There was no commitment and she harboured no ambitions of becoming the next Mrs Slope. It was wham, bam and never so much as a goodbye ma'am. But he always came and often came back. Except that one day he didn't. All she knew was that there was some unpleasantness at the college where he was master and he had disappeared under a cloud. There was a vague memory of having helped him to stitch up some awkward bastard from within the college. She could barely remember his name. Began with a P and sounded a bit poncey. She couldn't remember much more. Those days were something of a haze. Sex was easy and plentiful. Nobody cared much about things like commitment. Then there were the drugs. There were always the drugs. Something had gone on but she hadn't stayed around long enough to find out what it was. Sometimes the best way was to cut and run. So that is what she did. She heard no more. But if this really was him she was not going to miss out on some decidedly rough and ready sex. Not in this world, not on your life. And despite his apparent lack of interest in her, apart from the obvious, she couldn't shake the feeling that on some level he cared for her.

"If I tell you why I suspect it may be you after all, Sebastian, you are not going to be best pleased." A raised eyebrow suggested it would be probably be better for her in the long run. "I remember many things from the Oxford days, but most of all I remember the particular feel of your skin. You probably won't be aware of this but your nickname among college staff was 'pigskin', on account of those having been unfortunate enough to have shaken hands with you always reported that your handshake resembled the touch of pigskin." Bennett had barely got the words out before the back of Slope's hand crashed into her mouth. As the blood ran down her chin and began to drip on to her left shoe she felt the beginnings of the old arousal she once took for granted. "How nice to feel the touch of pigskin again," she spluttered, spraying globules of blood into the air. What followed was very like the woman herself and was indeed not an example of humankind at its imperious best. It satisfied both parties on a level that would have proved the norm in any self respecting farmyard.

"Will I see you again?" Bennett murmured the words as she wiped the blood from her mouth and shoes using her torn knickers. "I'll let you know," answered a disappearing Slope who had already buttoned up and was disappearing further down the alley way. She had a look of satisfaction on her bruised and bloodied face, Slope had his usual look of disgust. For him it had been a purely animal experience. Bennett had long expected nothing else from this cruellest of men. She couldn't explain it especially to herself but it was what she enjoyed and she suspected that the reappearance of Slope heralded some refined enjoyment in the near future. He would not have found her unless he had more in mind than simple sex. He was up to something and the chances were that giving full vent to her nascent sadism would have a part to play in whatever twisted conspiracy he had in hand. It was much later that she remembered his offer of a coffee and explanation. How bloody typical of the man. There would be another time. There was always another time.

27

You go your way, I'll go mine

Mark and Ginny Williams had taken the advice of the two twins, both one at a time and in stereo. They left Cornwall partially for their own safety but mainly because the pair had already suffered enough. The euphoria of meeting old friends had evaporated in the glare of the recent deaths. Prideaux and Bones were always good for a laugh and a spicy slice of controversy was always in attendance. Wherever they went excitement was never far behind. Recent events, however, had shaken the couple to such an extent that they needed to leave the whole mess behind them. Fortunately for them the twins were looking to scale down their responsibilities, giving them the chance to bail out of the current situation. Bob and Robert felt responsible for the two and they knew how dangerous that could be when things got bloody. Taking an eye off things in the current circumstances would give an advantage to the enemy. This was no ordinary enemy and, left to their own devices, they would have charged in with the fraternal cry of 'boots and saddles' regardless of the strength of the opposition. Their suggestion that Mark and Ginny should take shelter for a while was a godsend for them. The problem of where to go was solved by Bones.

"Much as I hate to see the back of you two, I have already rung my maiden aunt who lives in Cheltenham. She has a fine town house in Pittville Lawns, very near the racecourse, and would be happy to accommodate you until the current situation is resolved. I warn you she can be an irascible old biscuit but has a heart of oak. Unfortunately she is as deaf as an adder, and in a typical piece of well established maiden auntish behaviour she blames everybody for mumbling. I advise you both to enunciate as well as possible and nod at her as often as Wemmick does to his Aged P in Great Expectations. Now get yourselves packed and I'll drive you to the station. I've bought the tickets as a form of apology for all the trouble that Piers and I have put you through recently. No need to thank me, the least I could do. We'll be in touch when things settle down a bit. I'm sure we'll all get together to have a drink and laugh about the whole thing one fine day."

"I'm sure we will," answered an unsmiling Ginny. Ginny was a veteran of many demonstrations and standoffs against various fascist incarnations and was not used to retreating, even for tactical reasons. But, albeit reluctantly, she saw the sense of removing herself and Mark from immediate danger. "I've already packed our bags," she continued. "I hoped that someone would see the sense of getting us out of the way for a while. In a way I'm quite looking forward to leaving the ground clear for you to sort things out. I'm not sure whether I feel safer or not when things are as quiet as they have been recently. It isn't possible to relax and it's a bit similar to having an invisible rain cloud following you around. You suspect it is there and you know that it's going to piss all over you, you just don't know when. I find all that deeply unsettling."

The group was sitting around outside the twins' farmhouse. They were drinking glasses of the farm cider that the twins had earned a reputation for. It vied with the vastly more famous Lerryn cider made not far away but typically was far stronger. Prideaux had banned Bones from partaking as he was deputed to drive Mark and Ginny to Bodmin Parkway to pick up their train. An hour or so later the two emerged from the farmhouse with their bags. "Now you two," said Bones "there is absolutely no significance in the fact that I have bought you one way tickets. It is simply that I have no idea what is to happen next. Obviously you are not being confined to Cheltenham for the duration. But I for one will feel a lot happier with you both out of harm's way. After all this is our mess not yours, well, I suppose really it's Piers's mess. I'll get the old Land Rover loaded up while you two say your goodbyes, or do I mean au revoirs?" Minutes later Bones was driving a tearful Mark and stoical Ginny down the farm lane towards the Bodmin road.

It was something of a climactic event as the Land Rover vanished into the distance. It marked a sea change in the dynamic of a group that had been yoked together for some considerable time.

Prideaux felt the need to take charge of a situation that was in danger of becoming maudlin. The alcohol had done its job, releasing inhibitions but bringing with it a dangerous ennui. "Look you lot, I'm not appointing myself leader of this motley crew, but sitting here feeling sorry for ourselves isn't just indulgent, it's potentially dangerous. Just because things are quiet at the moment does not mean it is all over. That bastard will not give up until he has sated his bloodlust and he could make a move at any minute. I rather liked Ginny's storm cloud analogy. At some time, now or in the future, we are going to get soaked."

"For fuck's sake. It's not just Ginny's analogy. Give it up, for fuck's sake. She chose Mark, not you, and hanging on her every word like a mooncalf is bloody embarrassing at your age." The twins had voiced what had been nagging at Piers for far too long. Piers and Ginny had been together before Mark's arrival and in the end she had chosen Mark. Prideaux had never really recovered from that blow and had struggled to form another relationship since those dear, dead college days. He knew that they were right. He also knew that his best friend, Bones, was always attempting to bring him back to the real world. Mooning after a lost love would pay no dividend at all. They were still potentially at the mercy of an evil bastard whose sole motive was revenge. There was no arguing with such a creature and his current invisibility made everything as bad as it had ever been. The twins took it as hard as anyone. Not for them the approach of the tethered goat waiting on the convenience of the tiger. They were far too gung ho for that approach. A full frontal attack was what they had always favoured. Their problem was that you cannot confront that which you cannot see. It made them unsettled to the point where they became teasy as adders, a fine Cornish saying that encapsulates that uncomfortable feeling perfectly. But it was not a good state to be in for two men who could be efficiently violent when the occasion demanded.

The return of Bones rattling back up the farm lane broke what had become a fervid silence. "Home is the hunter," he shouted as he jumped from the cab. "Two chums safely deposited and waved off to pastures new. Now what the fuck is the matter with you miserable bastards? Our friends are on their way to a safe house and we are now a lean, mean fighting machine. I am put in mind of the A-Team. What we need now is a plan. A bit of logical thinking will do no harm at all. And rather than this splendid cider a few mugs of steaming hot black coffee should be the drink of choice. I don't know about you lot but I'm thoroughly pissed off with living life in a vacuum. I'm a chap who wanders at will, without the concern of catching a sock in the neck with a two by four or whatever it is these artisan murderers tend to wield in anger. We are certainly going to solve absolutely bugger all by hanging around here, however comfortable it is."

"A stirring speech, Bonesie. As usual from the heart and well appreciated by us all. In your absence we have been chewing the fat and trying to decide what possible next steps to take, and if you say big ones," continued Prideaux, "I shall be tempted to allow you to feel the back of my hand. Now as I see it, and the twins agree, there is nothing happening at all where Slope is involved. He has gone to ground and, from the little I have been able to glean, the Spriggans have more or less ceased to be. I can't see what sense that makes. He will never give up in his quest to make my life hell and to take as many of my friends down as he possibly can. There is one glimmer of light. I've had a call from the lovely Rosie at the Old Red Lion in Truro. The little bitch has ignored us and gone off on a quest of her own to find a Spriggan to infiltrate. I'm not sure that she understands the concept but as we all know she is impossible to deflect from a course of action when her mind is made up.

"She has managed to take up with some lowlife from one of the pubs in Falmouth, who has been making some fairly wild claims about his membership of the society. Unfortunately, he is the one who seems intent on infiltrating Rosie and not in a good way. The twins are already arguing about which of them gets first dibs on ripping his arms off. It's impossible to know whether he is telling the truth or is just a local chancer. Now the boys are up for paying Falmouth a visit and politely asking this cove what he knows and how he comes to know it."

"What Piers is attempting to explain in his overly polite way, Bonesie, is that we intend to track down this scroat and demonstrate some scrummaging techniques, using his bollocks in lieu of a rugby ball. The bastard will tell us anything, I can guarantee you that. And of course if he has so much as touched Rosie, Janner and I will fight each other to a standstill for the right to rip his fucking head off."

"Hold your horses there for a moment," interjected the current Earl of Mount Charles. "Much as I am in sympathy with your aims and objectives, and if you have one I should no doubt applaud your mission statement, I am unsure whether this is the way to proceed. Torturing and killing folk with whom they disagree is the Spriggan way rather than ours. Could we not allow the fragrant Rosie to explore every avenue before adopting a scorched earth policy? I have this vaguely unsettling feeling that I have slumbered and woken to find myself in the Wild West of America. Surely, a more thoughtful approach is possible."

It was stalemate between the four men. They all knew what was at stake and Bones had a point. This was not the Wild West. There was a rule of law, crooked as it was, being bent in favour of those with power and influence. It would doubtless land on their heads like a ton of blocks if they pursued a course that was other than law abiding, but inaction was not an option. The twins were getting restless but their regard for Rosie was strong enough to control their more explosive instincts. Essentially, if she was cultivating this would-be Spriggan then she could be in serious danger. Charging in to such a situation would inevitably cause collateral damage. That would be fine with them as long as the damage done wasn't to the love of both their lives. The struggle between their natural instincts and a more cerebral approach was exhausting to watch and Prideaux couldn't stand to watch it any longer.

"Now listen for a minute, chaps, and if you don't like my idea then we'll do it your way. What we need to know is the whereabouts of Slope and whether this lowlife that Rosie has focused on is any use to us at all. How would it be if we contacted someone in Falmouth who could give us chapter and verse on any Spriggan activity down that way? You know Falmouth. Anyone there who is not a sailor will be a foreigner, anyone who is a sailor will be known to everybody. I don't know whether either of you two has a contact? It doesn't matter that much because I reckon if Bonesie and I ensconce ourselves in one of the harbour pubs down there we are bound to find out something." Such as it was this was the plan that the four agreed on after some heated debate and a lot of cooling homemade cider, the black coffee option having been voted down. Bones had done the decent thing and abstained from the vote, leaving the result as a three to nothing landslide. As a consequence of this tentative exploration into the world of democracy it was well after noon on the following day before they fetched up in the busy town of Falmouth. They booked into a B&B in nearby Penryn and, while Bones and Prideaux took the short stroll to harbour side Falmouth, the twins promised to stay indoors and away from any controversy that would bring them any unwanted attention. They were naughty schoolboys promising with many effusive gestures, but somewhere in the recesses of their minds fingers were metaphorically crossed, so promises made held no force at all.

On a crisp, dry afternoon the two old friends wandered into a busy port that was not yet overrun with the thousands of tourists that would change the character of the port in late summer. Falmouth was a working port with a shining maritime history. It had seen its hard times but of late a move to concentrate on what it did best was paying dividends. There was the maritime museum to focus the attention of visitors on its illustrious past. Restaurants were opening, the pubs were thriving and the prestige of the area had been given a massive boost by the addition of a new university. It had always had a cosmopolitan feel but the addition of thousands of students to the mix had intensified the bohemian atmosphere of the place. There were plenty of shiny new boutique hotels, wine and coffee bars and bijou fashion shops. These catered for the needs of the newcomers, but in the darker back lanes still squatted some of the sailors' taverns of old. One such was The Captain's Finger, an ancient establishment that was so ancient that no two residents or indeed denizens of the tavern could agree either on its age or the meaning of the pub name. Its major attraction was its dark single bar redolent of old sea tales and usually sprinkled with a selection of old sea dogs. Some of these had spent a life at sea, others had never set foot on ship or boat, not even the King Harry Ferry. Entering here would not necessarily cause all who entered to lose hope completely, but its interior would certainly put a dent in the optimistic outlook of any glass half full jockeys. This was where the devil left his shovel and if the old sea cook himself had been hopping around behind the bar nobody would have been the least little bit surprised. It held, of course, a massive attraction for the two Oxford men. It was akin to a return to the womb, and a hand pump sign on which was written 'Doom Bar' was the clincher.

The point at which the river Camel meets the Atlantic on the north coast of Cornwall has a treacherous sand bank, known to sailors for centuries as an unforgiving foe unless treated with the utmost respect. Sharp's Brewery, founded at Rock as recently as the nineties, had cleverly named one of their premium beers after the natural feature. It too was something to be treated with circumspection and respect but was so good that it had already achieved cult status. Its reputation extended a long way beyond the Duchy and was a more than welcome sight to two itinerant Cornishmen.

The Finger, as it was known locally, was one of those places where putting the lights on made the place look instantly darker. As a consequence the lights were rarely switched on. Instead they relied still mostly on oil lighting from refurbished ship's lanterns. It gave the tavern a menacing look as the oil lights flickered, casting monstrous shadows on the walls. As a concession to the world of light outside, the walls were whitewashed, and if ever someone from up country wanted the full pirate experience then 'The Captain's Finger' would give them the thrill of a lifetime. The thrill of a lifetime was not what Bones and Prideaux were in search of. What they came in search of was not tales of the sea and pirate treasure but a pint of Doom Bar and a proper pasty. Simple tastes, perhaps, but there was a task in hand and no guarantee that this was the place to begin that task. "Come on, Bonesie," shouted Prideaux, though the third Earl was only feet away. "There is only one way to enter a tavern of this type and that way is confidently."

"Happy to oblige, my old pasty muncher," sniggered Bones. "I shall show plenty of confidence in the face of the enemy once I have at least a quart of the sainted Doom Bar, and a regulation homemade pasty, fortifying body and soul. Come along, Piers, screw your courage to the sticking place and we'll not fail." It would not be easy to keep a low profile with Bones in this sort of mood. Stepping out of the strong sun into the darkness of the bar was like stepping through the portal into another world. The darkness appeared total and Bones stood stock still. It took him a moment or two to remember he was wearing sunglasses. Removing them didn't help a lot. This was a pub that took its atmosphere seriously. The bar could be dimly discerned to the right. There were no garishly lit pumps advertising gassy foreign lagers. There were beer kegs on stoops behind a bar that looked as if it had been made from planks recovered from a sunken ship. That's because they were, and there were still locals who recalled the names of those who sank that ship. This is, after all, the land of legends, myths, smugglers and wreckers.

The two made their way over to the bar. As their eyes became accustomed to the gloom they realised that the bar was empty "I strongly doubt that this is a self service bar," opined Prideaux. "In fact it looks like one of those places run for the convenience of the landlord and nobody else. Hang about, there's a ship's bell over there. Perhaps a couple of tinkles would bring someone running."

"You of all people, Piers, should be aware that we are in Cornwall. In Cornwall nobody runs anywhere. Not unless they are from up country, that is. You can't have forgotten that the Cornish invented the concept of 'dreckly', one that you take lightly at your peril. It makes the Mexican 'mañana' sound like a call to arms. And another thing, there is a note here. I'll read it to you, it says, 'You cannot imagine how much it will piss me off if someone, who is not a regular, rings this bell to attract my attention'. It is signed Binky Jago and there is a drawing of a skull with a snake crawling through one of the eye sockets. It is my opinion that we should await the arrival of a regular or get the hell out of here a bit swiftly."

Prideaux was in relaxed mood and, being back in his native county, was much less wired than he was when in his usual state. It was as if his reason for being here had slipped his mind. He had stepped back in time and for the moment life was a little bit more uncomplicated than he was used to. "I don't think we're in any hurry, Bill, are we? Surely we can spare an hour or two for a sit down and to enjoy a couple of pints. After all we are here for a purpose."

"I'm well aware of that, my old Tonka toy," replied a wound up Bones. "This particular old posho is in need of a pint or two to whet the old aristocratic whistle. However, I do not currently feel up to ringing the bell that will bring forth this Binky Jago from his lair. I'm sure a regular will be along in a minute or two. Surely, we can amuse ourselves until a passing regular feels the need for a quart or two of the old neck oil." The two sat together on one of the worn wooden settles that provided the basic seating arrangements for what was very obviously a drinkers' pub. There was no sign of any fripperies such as snacks or more substantial fare, much less the ubiquitous Cornish pasty. "Right then," began Bones. "What we are doing here is looking for some sign of Rosie and this lowlife she has taken up with in the hope of finding the whereabouts of the creature Slope. Now how successful are we likely to be in this noble quest sitting in an empty pub without a pint of Doom Bar to console us?"

Bones knew how to needle Prideaux and in this case he had hit the spot. "Don't be such a twat, Bonesie," was the nettled response. "We haven't been here for ten minutes. Somebody will be in shortly. It is a pub after all."

Bones nodded towards the open door of the pub.

Framed in the doorway was a man dressed from head to foot as a Cavalier from around 1642. As he stepped inside his flamboyant hat brushed one of the pub beams, and in a seamless move he removed it from his head and swept a bow towards Bones and Prideaux. The two suppressed sniggers as the Cavalier spun on his heel with an exaggerated gesture and moved to the bar. Placing his befeathered hat on the bar he shouted across the bar, "Binky, where the fuck are you? Cavalier here in need of a drink. Killing Roundheads is thirsty work as you well know, you lazy old bastard." He leaned the small of his back against the bar and looked towards Bones and Prideaux as if for approval. The two were completely fazed. "I'm telling you now, Piers, if any more of those bastards come in I for one am fucking right off. I know, of course, that they will recognise my aristocratic bearing and no doubt offer their protection to one of my breeding. But you are a natural Roundhead, old pal, and I suggest that you follow me in a sharpish disappearing act should this strange place suddenly fill with the king's men."

Prideaux's response was to hoot with laughter at the ridiculousness of the situation. This was after all the land of legend, and the odd Cavalier dropping in for a fortifying pint was not that untoward. "It'll be fine, he's probably one of those weirdos that dress up to recreate long dead battles to avoid doing anything useful. What if his pals do come in? As long as a bunch of Roundheads in a revolutionary mood don't follow them in then all will be well. You worry too much, Billy. We are in a pub in the middle of one of the leading towns in Cornwall. We are not ensconced in some weird establishment on some empty and blasted moor in the north, for God's sake. Heads up, it looks as if our Cavalier friend over there has roused Binky Jago from his slumbers. Looks to me as if dear old Binky has been asleep for a hundred years."

Bones followed Prideaux's gaze. A door had opened at the back of the bar and through the door ducked a giant of a man, his arms covered in tattoos. Wearing only a vest over stained jeans, he scowled at the Cavalier, completely ignoring Bones and Prideaux as he began to tap a pint from a barrel behind the bar. His presence was unsettling, more so as he hadn't uttered a word. If this was Binky, it was not the image the name suggested. Bones had in mind some sort of effete theatrical who would doubtless call everyone darling. What had appeared looked more like someone who had vacated a primeval swamp in pursuit of something to kill, for sheer pleasure rather than food. Serving the Cavalier was a case of slamming the tankard down with his left hand whilst holding out his right for the money. Nothing approaching conversation passed between the two. The Cavalier took up his tankard containing what beer was left in it after the rather violent way in which it had been served, and returned to sit not far from where Bones and Prideaux were sitting.

The Neanderthal remained at his post, glaring in the general direction of Bones and Prideaux. His expression and stance screamed out a challenge to the two. "Go on then, Bones," Prideaux whispered in a stage whisper. "We can't sit here all day. Go up and get us two pints of Doom Bar while he's still there. I have this feeling that if he goes out to the back room we'll be lucky to get a drink before next Trevithick Day in Camborne."

"Why me?" mouthed Bones in answer. "Why can't you go and get the ale in? After all, you're the bloody peasant here. I am the one of aristocratic birth. I know it has been a long time since the world went totally mad but surely it is your place to wait on any remaining aristos not driven to penury by you and your Marxist friends. Look at the size of the bastard. He could eat me alive, if he wanted to."

"He could do that for certain sure, but he won't. You needn't worry about old Binky, he's OK." For the first time the Cavalier had spoken directly to the two. "It's alright," he continued. "I know he looks a bit terrifying, and to tell you the truth he was a street fighter in his day and can still look after himself. He's a bit of a gentle giant really but we'll all be fine as long as none of the Roundheads come in to the pub. He used to be the leading light in our little group of re-enactors. Least, he was until his missus ran off with a Roundhead, must have been five years ago now. Worse than that. The Roundheads are played by Devonians and the man who cuckolded Binky was from Exeter. He hates Roundheads as much as he hates Devon dumplings, which is how he refers to all Devonians. Now if you two are Cornish at all you will be aware that it is a matter of pride to hate anyone who comes from that place immediately the other side of the Tamar. They say it dates back to Athelstan, when he decided to massacre all the Cornish from Exeter down to the Tamar in a practice bout of ethnic cleansing. I've no idea whether that is the real story or not but it still justifies a bloody good punch up, even today."

"I'm not sure whether that is completely reassuring or not," said Bones, "but I suppose I could give it a go. Nothing ventured, nothing drunk I suppose. At least the fact that I am Cornish should go in my favour."

"Get the bloody drinks, man. I'm dying of thirst here and I really have never heard such a performance over buying a couple of drinks in my life." Drawing himself up to his full height Bones walked the width of the bar in what he thought was his best aristocratic manner. Prideaux cringed when he heard Bones say, "two of your finest pints of foaming Doom Bar, landlord, if you please, and one for your good self." The reply shook the two friends as the behemoth smiled and said, "Thank you very much sir, that's very kind of you. I'll have a half with you." The Cavalier had dissolved in helpless laughter at this point, to be echoed by the noisiest bout of belly laughter Bones and Prideaux had ever heard. "Just a little joke we play on emmets. No offence, but often brightens up the day. Binky there is a mainstay of the local shanty singers and I don't think he's ever been in a fight in his life. He's the mildest mannered chap between here and St Ives. And his missus hasn't run off with anyone. In fact she's down at the harbour getting hold of some fish as we speak. What are you doing in Falmouth then, my handsomes?"

"Nothing much," Prideaux answered. This was, of course, true but he was still sufficiently wary of saying anything he may regret later. "We're taking a short break. We're both originally from Cornwall but we've been living up in Oxford for years now." The conversation wandered as conversations in pubs tend to do as gradually the bar began to fill with a variety of drinkers. Gradually Bones and Prideaux ran out of things to talk to the Cavalier about and he wandered off to join a small throng of similarly dressed men. "Thank God he's gone. What a boring bastard. I was beginning to lose the will to live, Bonesie. Now is there any chance we can achieve anything today or is getting totally trashed the only adventure left to us?"

"Listen to your favourite old aristo, my friend. I think that we would be best employed hanging around here for a bit. While you have been politely listening to the most boring man in the world I've been keeping my eyes open. Sure, there are the last remnants of Charlie's army warming the settles over there near the bar. But the majority of those who have come in recently look to me to be locals. In fact they look to be some of the most unsavoury bunch of locals I've seen in a couple of months of Sundays. It does seem to be the place where Rosie might well turn up with that lowlife she has supposedly taken up with." Mollified and encouraged in turn, that is what Prideaux agreed to do, though there was tacit agreement that the intake of Doom Bar needed to slow otherwise the two would be neither use nor ornament.

28

Shadowland

In a café within the Pompidou Centre a disconsolate Sebastian Slope toyed with his coffee. It was not the sort of place he usually frequented. Far too trendy and therefore too common for his taste. The coffee was nowhere near the standard he expected either, but it suited his current mood. Sex with Bennett had been a minor diversion. It had been simply a case of blowing the froth off. Several weeks had passed without feeling the need to revisit the scene and there were plenty of Parisian prostitutes catering for extreme tastes. He kept the beast inside more or less chained most of the time. It was not sexual frustration but more the inevitable ennui that will afflict anyone resident in Paris sooner or later. Things were not going his way. He had not killed anyone for at least six of the seven months he had lived in Paris. He was concerned that he was growing soft and losing his focus. After all he was not in Paris for his health or for a holiday. He was here to give himself time to think. He had little respect for the police or indeed authorities of any kind. It was unlikely they would be looking for him. He had been careful to cover his tracks, and besides his current appearance would easily fool all but the most determined.

A fluent French speaker, he read Le Figaro regularly and never missed televised news. Nothing suggested that he was even a minor topic of conversation. Yet he could not continue in this fashion. His hatred of Prideaux had not diminished and that hatred remained all encompassing. Anybody not with him was against him, so any friend or acquaintance of Prideaux deserved a similar fate. He would have been apoplectic had he been aware that

Bones and Prideaux were having a high old time in a tavern near the harbour in Falmouth. It is probably as well that human beings are not blessed with second sight as such a thing would probably reduce any human relationships to chaos. This was not a thought echoing through the canyons of Slope's mind at this moment. Those canyons were beginning to darken though, as he struggled with the position in which he found himself. Pushing the bistro table away he stood up and walked towards the exit doors and onto the piazza.

Immediately opposite the Pompidou Centre was a café he had recently decided to frequent. It was clean, good value for this expensive area of an expensive city and thronged with a mix of Parisians and large numbers of visitors from around the world. In a curious way he harboured some vague idea that this would be the place where he would meet someone who could galvanise him into action. This was so unlike the man that he found it difficult to explain the change to himself. He was aware that such a radical change in appearance and lifestyle carried its own risks. But never for a man like him.

He was the epitome of the alpha male. He planned, organised and acted. He had reached the highest level of academia in an Oxford college. He had lied, schemed and bullied his way to the top. Now he looked, acted and was beginning to think like a dropout. It made no sense that simply dropping into character as part of his plan to disappear could turn him into a different person. But that seemed to be the way things were beginning to turn. Ordering yet another black coffee he sat at his favourite table with the Pompidou Centre in the background. Humanity of all colours and creeds flowed past the café. He never took his eye off the passing hordes. He had convinced himself that the catalyst to shake of this damned ennui would surface. He saw himself becoming desperate with the attendant danger of carelessness and he hated himself for it.

Salvation of a sort presented itself from an unlikely quarter in the person of an obvious tourist. He was obvious to Slope as he had the wide eyed wonder coupled with childlike excitement that operated as a badge identifying those new to Paris. Perhaps the fact that he had three cameras dangling from his neck and was one of a party of Americans doing Paris in a day helped with the identification. The walk was led by a tall, thin American who made a good living by leading walks. He was an academic who had lived in Paris for years. He was very good at conducting the walks as he knew what note to hit to suit his audience of the day. He ran walks around literary Paris, Revolutionary Paris and for those of the appropriate persuasion or the simply curious, Gay Paris. The walks subsidised the research he was doing into his next novel that was planned to be a historical novel set at the time of the revolution. He was always somewhere on the streets of Paris and was someone Slope recognised. Someone Slope didn't recognise was the large, florid faced American who had dropped off the walk and was advancing towards him with an ingratiating grin on his face. Sensing that this could be awkward and realising that there was little chance of escape Slope started to get to his feet, only to be enthusiastically motioned back into his seat by what had to be a Texan, who was far too far away from Texas for comfort and far too close to Slope.

"You really could not make it up," thought Slope as the American wiped a brow dripping with sweat. "I really do not need this." "Why, hi there, Buddy," the American shouted in the most Texan accent Slope had ever heard. If he had followed his greeting with a shout of "Remember the Alamo" he could have not drawn more attention to himself. Slope hated Americans, particularly Americans abroad. He hated their brashness, their assumption that their country was the only one that mattered. At the moment what he hated most was this particular American's insistence on talking to him. Slope was irritated by the level of attention that was focusing on him as a result of the big ugly American's enthusiastic approach. There was only one thing for it, Slope would pretend to be French. That wasn't much of a stretch for him as he was fluent in the French of Paris. His problem would be keeping a straight face in the process of dealing with what he had decided was, in the language the American would have used, a Class A lunkhead.

The American sat down opposite him, shouting, "Coffee, garcon" as he did so, and for the first time Slope saw the cliché in action, as the American really did add insult to injury. "Well now" the big man continued, "I think we two could have a little talk." "In for a centime, in for a franc" thought Slope ignoring twenty years of European integration as he did so. "Pardon Monsieur. Je suis Francais. Je ne parle pas Anglais ou Americain. Je parle Francaise seulement." As he spoke the words he adopted a mien of haughty indifference that many Parisians wore as a badge. He sniggered but managed to control himself. If it wasn't so public and such a sad waste of his time he could have enjoyed this encounter. It had suddenly begun to lift his mood. Slope's unwelcome companion proceeded to babble inanely as he informed him of his love of Europe and Paris in particular. He learned that his name was Henry though everyone called him Hank and he was from Lubbock in Texas. He was a Baptist, a lay preacher and a supporter of the NRA.

"What a fucking surprise," thought Slope as he continued to stonewall, his impression of a truculent Frenchman gaining refinement as he studiously ignored the Texas bore who seemed singularly unaware of the effect he was having. It was already becoming tedious and Slope began to feel people in the café turning to look at the noisy Texan. It would probably be best to end things and move away. He stood and, with every indication of polite leave taking, moved swiftly away. He had walked for some little time before the irritation got to him and his mood became much darker.

The tiny tableau had caught the attention of Lola Cutler who had been at the back of the café. She had been in Paris now for some three months and was following Cornelius's instructions to the letter. Her brief was to keep an eye on Slope, to track his movements and establish a pattern. General feeling within Unit S was that while it would be helpful to know that he was no longer a threat it was unlikely, given his personality and past record. Lola was under strict instructions not to approach him but to continue to shadow him and ensure that any intelligence was reported regularly to Cornelius. Wandering around Paris and indulging in people watching was something she would happily do for pleasure. She was clever enough to be aware that Slope was no fool. Drawing attention to herself could prove to be a very dangerous error. But providing she maintained a discreet distance this could prove her most enjoyable posting for some time to come. She watched as Slope limped into the distance. Now was not the time to follow. He was obviously irritated by the American's crass approach and she was pretty sure that he would be headed for his flat to calm down. She would leave him to it. Anyway there was a performance she hoped to catch at Shakespeare and Company. It began in around an hour, giving her plenty of time to walk to the venue. Walking around Paris was a pleasure in itself that she never tired of. Her second favourite pleasure in Paris was anything taking place at her favourite bookshop.

Cutler was not the only one in Paris to find the bookshop an enticing prospect. It was not simply for its extensive and eclectic collection of books that Parisians and visitors were attracted. The place offered much more than that. On this particular evening a much garlanded writer, Nathan Englander, was there to talk about his latest collection of eight short stories, 'What We Talk About When We Talk About Anne Frank'. The shop was thronged with an appreciable and appreciative crowd who, if not actually hanging from the bookcases, were certainly relying on them to keep them upright. The crush was the result of a sell out crowd, with close to a hundred people hanging on Englander's every word. At the book signing that followed Liz Bennett and Lola Cutler were unwittingly within feet of each other as they each bought a copy of the book the writer had read from. Queuing at the till to pay was important. More important was receiving the coveted stamp of the bookshop that proclaimed sophistication. Bennett was immediately behind Cutler, both reaching the till simultaneously. Cutler politely stood to one side in Bennett's favour. She received no acknowledgement for her consideration and took her turn as Bennett moved away.

It was then that Cutler made a basic mistake. Enthused with the reading, she began chatting with the assistant who was one of George Whitman's 'tumbleweeds', and she temporarily forgot why she was in Paris in the first place. The tumbleweed, a fresh-faced young New Yorker with writing ambitions, was doing what all tumbleweeds do, simply passing through. She was a chatty and enthusiastic young woman who was clearly an Englander fan. She was also new to the city, and the chat quickly turned to social matters with Cutler dropping her guard. It wasn't the content of what she said that attracted Bennett's attention but the manner in which she expressed herself. Bennett was well attuned to inconsistencies and there was something in the way she spoke that didn't quite seem to gel. Many frequenters of the bookshop had gone there in search of a book and romance. Some emerged with a companion in tow. In more cases than seems feasible such initial attractions resulted in many engagements and a significant number of marriages. On this occasion, however, Whitman's romanticism had worked in reverse in fixing the existence and appearance of Lola Cutler in the mind of a very dangerous woman.

29

The Captain's Finger

Slope remained a threat to Prideaux and all those close to him. In the current situation where that threat was muted he was probably more dangerous than ever to those closest to the old enemy. Closest of all to Prideaux at the moment was his oldest friend Billy Bones as they sat together in The Captain's Finger. The re-enactors had returned to the field of battle. They would spend the rest of the day simulating violent death and serious maiming as part of an enjoyable day out. Most of the pub's remaining denizens looked as if they had spent most of their lives in Falmouth, most of that time having been spent on the very spots they currently occupied.

It was dropping dusk when the sacrifice of spending most of an afternoon in a gloomy pub looked as if it may have been about to pay dividends for Prideaux and Bones. Yet again the pub door creaked open before banging shut, something this particular door had been doing for centuries. The latest two entering the place where all those entering should swiftly abandon hope were an odd looking couple. He was a washed out and stooped grey haired man with a face full of randomly arranged teeth. His thin hair was scraped back in a sad attempt at a ponytail. She was bright, young and vibrant. She wore a navy blue coat over a dress that accentuated her trim athletic figure. She looked young enough to be her companion's daughter. Her smile froze as she looked across the bar to focus on her worst nightmare. There sat Bones and Prideaux.

As a scion of the de Beaune line the third earl was well used to embarrassing situations. He had the insouciance of all aristocrats that allowed him simply to pretend things he didn't care for or approve of simply weren't happening. Consequently he looked preoccupied as if nothing currently happening was any of his concern. This approach, known in the family as the 'ostrich ploy', had worked many times during social occasions where gaffes were unavoidable. A determined refusal to recognise anything remotely uncomfortable usually results in the problem melting away. This probably explained the high proportion of aristocrats eaten by lions over the centuries. The stiff upper lip approach in the presence of a ravening lion would, of course, be to pretend the predator wasn't there at all. Bones would have justified such a ridiculous course of action in terms of the unflappability of the ruling classes. Prideaux, being possessed of much more refined survival instincts, would have classed it as the inbuilt stupidity that follows hard on the heels of generations of inbreeding. The fact remained that neither of them had a clue what to do on this tricky occasion other than wishing for the earth to swallow them.

Such a thought was not as outlandish as it may appear. Cornishmen were famous for their skills as miners and there was barely a square metre of the old country that was not honeycombed with unregistered mine shafts. And for years countless poor unfortunates breathed their last having fallen three hundred feet when an unrecorded shaft gave up the ghost, claiming yet another victim. Sadly for them this was not likely in their current location. Some other strategy was obviously called for. It fell to Prideaux as, short of whistling tunelessly, Bones was doing everything in his power to reprise the acting skills of the amateur actor trying to appear invisible on stage, having forgotten his lines whilst in the full glare of the spotlights.

Fortune smiled on the pair however, as Rosie's

companion veered off to the left heading for the pub toilets, leaving Rosie centre stage mouthing the words, "What the fuck are you two clowns doing here?"

"Charming," muttered a relieved Prideaux as she walked warily across to them. "Shut up, and get the fuck out, Piers," she sweetly replied. "And take the jolly posho with you. You are about to muck up some rare work I have been doing for some time. I reckon that this tosser I'm with is genuine and I'm getting close to persuading him to spill the beans on Slope's whereabouts. And before you give me any of that macho guff, I do not need your help in dealing with this idiot. So far he has not laid a hand on me, which is fortunate for him. It is fortunate because the minute he does I shall rip off that arm and beat the slimy bastard to death with it. I only appear to be sweet, as you should be well aware of by now. So piss off. I'll be in touch when I have something to tell you. Go and look at the boats in the harbours or feed the seagulls chips, anything, only get the hell out before he gets back."

"OK Rosie, but please be careful. I think you should know that we have Bob and Robert in tow and I'm not sure we will be able to keep them quiet for very much longer. We're going, but get in touch as soon as you can because if those two get wind that you are in the slightest danger they are likely to raze this town right down to the ground."

The two got to their feet a little unsteadily and made their way to the exit. They left without looking back, letting the pub door bang behind them. Of course Prideaux knew that Rosie could look after herself, that wasn't the issue. What was the issue was the presence of the Job boys, both absolutely stuffed full of the finest testosterone known to man and simply spoiling for a fight. It was a consummation devoutly not to be wished. God alone knows where the Jobs on a mission could lead them all. And what would be achieved? They needed to get back to the B&B in the fairly vain hope that the boys were safely ensconced in the TV room watching a soap or two. So off they toddled. It wasn't the most direct route back to the B&B that they took. The Doom Bar had done its mazy work so there were very few solid objects they didn't bounce off on the most circuitous route possible. They fetched up in a heap in the front garden of the house vaguely near their original target. One of the saddest sights in the world is that of two intelligent humans attempting to make sense of the world when they have had just that bit too much to drink. Blank looks, stuttering, muttering and false starts were the order of the day as they desperately sought some form of sobriety. The twins would know they were drunk. A blind rabbit could have established that. What they could not do is to let the twins know that the girl they both loved was currently attempting to extract information from a man who may well have been a closet Spriggan. They needed a plan, something that did not come easy to a couple of drunks. But the human mind can be a persistent little blighter and valiant efforts were afoot to cast off the powerful influence of strong ale. Bones had the idea of lying by pretending that they had been surveying the scene, a scene that had not repaid their efforts with anything approaching interest. It wasn't much, but the best these two minds could muster. And it wasn't as if the pair didn't have a reputation for enjoying the conviviality of the tavern in the first place. In any case, desperate circumstances demanded desperate measures.

The front door of the house suddenly opened as a bemused householder looked out to see two very drunken men apparently at rest in her front garden. Loveday Cornelius was in no mood to deal with a couple of drunks. It had taken her a long time to come to terms with the apparently random death of her long term lover, Dr Joan Thripp. In truth she had made little progress in that direction. The cold horror of that visit from an unsympathetic policeman chilled her to the bone then, and that feeling had not left her since. There was no sense to it. Joan was a careful woman. She was certainly not the type to skip across a busy road oblivious to oncoming traffic. It was a hit and run, the bored young policeman informed her in official terminology as if he were informing her of a parking violation. There was little hope of catching the person responsible, said the young PC. He might as well have been reading it from a card. When he left she cried for a long time. There was nobody to turn to. They had been a close couple and kept to themselves. They both loved the cottage but it had quickly lost its appeal at the realisation that Joan was never coming home again. She could never say how she had got through the funeral arrangements, but in the darkest of hours people cope. So she coped. Support from senior staff at her school eased the immediate pain and she was allowed time off to grieve. But she could not stay in the cottage; there were too many memories. She was offered a deal that allowed her to leave the school with a small pension that would allow her to get by until she could get back onto an even keel.

The cottage had been jointly owned, though it was Joan who had the money. Selling it had been the final act in her failed attempt at coming to terms with loss. Selling seemed a betrayal of all they had planned for and dreamed of. The sale had been unexpectedly quick as it was not a good time to sell. The money allowed her to buy a small terraced house in Falmouth where she hoped to rebuild a life of sorts. In line with her personality she kept very much to herself, spending most time in her garden. The small front garden was an immaculate small scale version of a typical cottage garden. This was the front garden where Bones and Prideaux were attempting to recover their senses sufficiently to function at any level. As Cornelius looked at the two men her long barely suppressed hatred of the gender surfaced. She wasn't in the mood for such nonsense and the drunken sots had already trampled over some of her precious planting.

"Get the hell out of my garden, you pathetic excuses for human beings," she screamed. They were the first words to have formed in her head. As abuse goes it was on the weak side of mild but it had a transforming effect. It must have been the tone of extreme exasperation that had penetrated the fog surrounding the men's response. It is never clear what it is that can return drunks to a form of sobriety. Obviously time is an important factor, but on occasions something unexpected can have an immediate effect. This was the case with Bones and Prideaux, who suddenly floated back to earth when faced by a woman at the end of a quite short tether and teetering right on the edge of hysteria. Neither man was completely at ease with the opposite sex and both realised that a mumbled apology would not meet the case.

Prideaux managed to pick himself up and decided to take charge of a situation in urgent danger of running out of control. "Excuse me, madam," he began. "My friend and I have had a little too much to drink and have mislaid our lodgings. On leaving a convivial tavern down near the harbour we appear to have misconstrued a boulevard or two on our way back to where we are currently hoping to lay our weary heads. There has been no intention on our part or parts to upset, distress or annoy you in any way at all. I apologise on behalf of my humble self and further on behalf of my aristocratic chum the third Earl of Mount Charles in the kingdom of Kernow and the county of Cornwall." In support of his friend's words Bones had struggled to his knees, doffing his hat as he did so. The effect was somewhat diminished by the fact that he was not wearing a hat. However, this small performance changed the dynamic between the men and Loveday Cornelius who, despite herself, could not suppress a smile as she looked at two grown men behaving for all the world like two small and quite naughty boys. "How the hell did men ever come to rule the world? If you two are typical examples of the male gender then God help us all. Look at the state of you. Have you any idea of where you are supposed to be?"

"We are, lovely lady, supposed to be at the Cosy Nook Guest House on Fore Street, though I suspect that we are anywhere but at the front door of that esteemed establishment."

"Your suspicions are completely correct," was all that Cornelius could manage before dissolving into giggles. It was the first time she had laughed, the first time she had smiled since that dreadful day when she had lost the only person she had ever cared for. She did what she had sworn all her life never to do. She proceeded to invite two complete strangers into her home. Worse still, these strangers were still hovering in the outer reaches of drunkenness and there was no telling what they might be capable of. For the moment she did not care.

Several very black coffees later, with sensible introductions completed, a type of dawn began to register in the head of Prideaux. He was always the slightly sharper of the two in such circumstances, and there were often such circumstances. "Just a minute," he managed to stutter burning his tongue on his third cup of coffee, "aren't you wossname?"

"If you mean, aren't I Loveday Cornelius then I should answer yes, indeed I am. As for wossname, whether that is a given name or an honorary title, I should be forced to answer no, and I know nobody of that name." It is always interesting to watch realisation shed a defining light on the mind of the befuddled and so it was for Cornelius as she watched Prideaux drag the appropriate words into the light. "You must be Dr Thripp's partner. I knew her. In fact I was attending one of her lectures on the day she died. She's an aunt of the Job twins, isn't she? What happened? Hit and run, wasn't it?" The words tumbled out as Prideaux began to return gradually to the land of the sober. Their effect on Cornelius was cumulative. She had promised herself she wouldn't cry. But her resolution deserted her and the tears came, leaving a baffled Prideaux at a complete loss. Roles were reversed as he tried to comfort a woman who had spent too long living a country mile beyond comforting. He did his best but made little progress until, with the resolution that was a natural part of her character, she straightened her shoulder, and wiped the remaining tears from her face with the palms of her hands.

"I'm sorry. I always promised myself I would never do that. I've coped pretty well but mostly I've avoided company, particularly male company. I'm afraid I can't answer your question about how she died except to say that, apparently, it was a hit and run. I've never understood how such a thing could have happened in the middle of a busy place like Truro. Someone must have seen something but the police have obviously closed the case. It looks as if there were no witnesses, or if there were they are not prepared to come forward. I have to rebuild my life in any way I can and try to forget everything else. Except I can't. I can get by from day to day but that is literally all there is. Don't worry, I'm not going to start weeping again. What will that achieve? Perhaps you are in a condition to tell me your story, and I hope that it is a bit more uplifting than mine."

Prideaux was absolutely in the frame of mind to tell his story. He did so to growing interest from Cornelius who grew more tight lipped as he went on. As she learned

236

more about the Spriggans and their leader her face began to lose its defeated look. Instead she began to take on a look of angry defiance. There was no evidence of any Spriggan involvement in her lover's death but she needed a peg to hang a recovery on, and this was as good a peg as any. Joan had indulged a particular interest in Cornish history and had developed something of a reputation as an expert on Spriggan history. Initially she had taken an academic historical approach. This was her background and training. Though as her research proceeded she became much more interested in the modern role of the Spriggan organisation in public and private life. She retained her academic rigour but her approach mirrored that of an investigative reporter more than a serious historian. It was beginning to make sense. Initially Joan had chatted over dinner about recent discoveries she had made in the archives of Mount Charles Central Library. If she were honest Loveday would have admitted that her research was not quite as fascinating as Joan clearly believed it to be. She listened dutifully nevertheless. But as the research and note taking proceeded Joan became less communicative and a little bit secretive. At the time Loveday hadn't given it much thought. She was well aware that relationships wax and wane like the moon. They were never constant. If they were that was usually because there was no longer a relationship anyway. But it had to be faced. Joan had become much less open and, though always timid, had retreated further into her shell. The book with all her notes had been on Joan's lap top. But where had she put the lap top? She did not want to forget Joan so had been reluctant to get rid of everything, but for the life of her could not remember where she had put the lap top. The book. It had consumed so much of their lives. It had led to arguments between them. It was the only thing they argued about. Writing the book had changed Joan. She had never been particularly outgoing. For someone who earned her living lecturing to students she was surprisingly introverted. But it was obvious that the book had taken on a life of its own. In the early days it had been a worthy if interesting account of the development of the organisation in historical times. All that had changed when she moved to the second section of the book. She had begun to research the modern day organisation and its involvement in the affairs of state. It had become increasingly murky, and had begun to absorb her so completely that she had little time for anything else. Her occasional comments convinced Loveday that she had literally lost the plot. The book was becoming a cut and shut job. Worse still, she had argued with her publisher so violently that he had washed his hands of the book completely. This had thrown her for a while, and initiated a foul mood that lasted for three weeks until she landed a new contract with a small but successful campaigning publisher based in South Wales. Prossper Press was much more suitable as a publisher to the new direction her research had taken, and her mood lightened. She pruned the historical introduction she had already written so savagely that it practically disappeared in favour of a focus on the way the organisation had infiltrated public and corporate life at the highest level. She had changed the title from 'The History of the Spriggans Past and Present' to 'Stripping the Spriggans Bare: The Story of a Murderous Cult'. This was only a working title but it showed the way her mind was working. It was to be more like investigative journalism than historical research, but Loveday was pleased at her improved mood. There was one niggle that would not go away and Loveday attempted to remove this by the one act that can be death to any relationship. She knew that Joan's password was Sappho13 and, against her better judgement, took the opportunity to access her lap top while Joan was down at the harbour buying freshly landed mackerel. What she found confirmed her fears. Joan had been digging deep into Spriggan activity. She had obviously been in touch with quite a number of people, as her inbox showed. They were not names that Loveday recognised but there was a huge quantity of information from those claiming to have the inside track. The one who emailed most regularly always signed off with the initials JJ. Whoever he or she was seemed to know a hell of a lot about the Spriggan hierarchy. It all seemed a little adolescent in style, though. It had the sense of someone trying to impress but without revealing an identity. Loveday knew that she could never discuss what she had found with Joan. She would never be forgiven for such a breach of trust. So she kept quiet and, as casually as she could, tried to steer Joan away from too much research that could prove dangerous. Her only course was to bottle up her fears, hoping that at some stage Joan would see sense. It seemed an unlikely outcome though, as when Joan had the bit between her teeth she would become completely absorbed.

For the first time in a long while she felt some sort of enthusiasm for life come pulsing back. Whether he liked it or not Prideaux was quickly acquiring a follower. A spot of gardening was fine in its own way but nothing could equal the energy of a just cause. If the Spriggans had been involved in killing Joan then, sure as hell is a little warm in the summer, she would follow them to the ends of the earth in search of her revenge. She had not thought about it for months, but given recent events she began to muse on the possibility that Joan's research had led to her asking too many questions of the wrong people. She couldn't really countenance the thought, but if there was the slightest chance that the Spriggans had been involved and revenge was all that was left to her, then that would be her course. As Prideaux reached the present day in his story there was a stirring from beside him on the sofa as Bones made his gurgling return to reality. A bit of huffing and puffing followed by some determined focusing, then a gravelly request for, "the hair of the dog, any old dog", meant that the old aristo was back in the game.

"I'd like to be as hospitable as possible but I'd hate to waste the industrial quantities of black coffee you have so recently poured down that aristocratic neck, so on this occasion the answer is no. However, I have listened to your compatriot's story and I think it is time you contributed your take on recent events."

It took a heroic effort but Bones managed to get into his stride, after all he had many years of practice under his belt. "Sorry. I closed my eyes for a second or two and there I was, gone. I wasn't asleep, just not awake. I'm sure that Piers, my friend and trusty ally, will have filled you in on how we got to where we are now. As far as I'm concerned the pressing matter, as always, is where we go next. The meat and veg of the situation is that we have Rosie grooming a possible Spriggan down in the town, and somewhere in Falmouth, possibly Penryn, we also have two forces of nature in the form of Bob and Robert Job. As I see it our main task is to ensure that group one and group two in this little scenario do not meet up any time soon. As to how we achieve this very testing feat I can assure you I have not one bloody clue."

30

Rosie Takes a Hand

Rosie and her target sat quietly in The Captain's Finger. Rosie was relieved that Bones and Prideaux had left before her companion had returned from the gents. He was no conversationalist so Rosie was forced to do most of the talking. She had hedged around the subject for several weeks and had made very little progress. Having volunteered for the job she felt obliged to see it through, but she had many much better things to be doing. She had a pub to run back in Truro if nothing else. The time was close when she would have to grasp the nettle. A couple of beers for Dutch courage and it would have to be straight in, feet first. She had no idea what the response would be. It didn't matter that much one way or the other. She could look after herself and this was a public place. "Were you ever a member of the Spriggans, Jim?" Her companion wrong footed her immediately by not replying. "Did you hear what I asked? I wondered whether you were ever a full member of the Spriggans or just a hanger on." She looked at him full face, making her best effort to appear winsome. This time she did draw a reaction.

"What's it to you if I was? I been a member of lots of things. Spriggans is no different to any others. I might have been, but that's my business. Got nothing to do with you now, has it? Seems to me that you are asking too many questions. I've spent a fortune on taking you out and what have I got for it? A peck on the cheek, that's what. I'm beginning to think you're one of those there prick teasers. Now since we're on the subject, are you going to sleep with me or not?" "I'm so sorry Jim,

I didn't realise that sex with you was the price I owed for my part in the twenty trips we have recently taken to three different pubs. So far today you have already spoken more than on our previous outings. And as for sex, what makes you think that I have any desire to waste my time in bed with a repulsive object like you?"

This approach drew a more extreme response as Jim's face darkened. He had never had great success with women but this direct approach was new to him and he was unsure how to deal with it. The momentum was taken away from him as Rosie stared into his eyes at her most coquettish. "Well Jim. It looks as if I have not been keeping up my side of the bargain. A couple of halves of beer and a few bags of crisps equals the opportunity for you to ferret around in my knickers. Well, fair is fair, as they say. You want sex. I'll give you sex that you'll never be able to forget." This was said in a low husky voice that, if only Jim had known, tokened bad news. "Come on then. I know a place down near the wholesale fish market. If you're up for a knee trembler then I'm your girl."

A look of pathetic gratitude suffused Jim Johnson's pockmarked features as he followed Rosie out of the pub and into the dark of a salty Falmouth evening. "Come on then, don't dawdle. Do you want it or no? It's down Fish Street and around the corner into Crab Lane." The ill starred Jim Johnson hurried as quickly as he could, hampered mainly by an erection that made walking difficult. He turned into Crab Lane mere seconds behind Rosie to find her pressed back into the darkness of an empty shop doorway. It was quite a private area and Johnson could not imagine they would be disturbed. "Come on big boy," came a whisper from the doorway. "Don't be shy, lover boy. I can see you are pleased to see me from here." She grabbed at his belt and stared to undo it. "Right then. Let's see what all the fuss is about."

As his jeans slipped to the floor she grabbed his erection. Johnson thought her grip a little fierce as he winced in pain. "That's the way, you revolting little prick. Squeal you bastard, only not too loudly. Then forget any notion you have ever had of having sex with me. By the time I've finished with you you'll be lucky to be able to shag a blancmange in future. That is if I allow you to have a future."

Jim squealed, his balls catching his throat.

"Now down to business. Sadly for you it's not the business you anticipated. And I warn you not to struggle too much. If you answer my question truthfully then I'll set you free to limp away. In the pub back there I asked you a question. I'm going to ask you that same question once more. Are you now, or have you ever been, a member of the Spriggans? You can nod your answer. Shake your head and you'd better start looking for someone to sew your bollocks back on, because I'll have them off quicker than you can say knife." Johnson nodded. The turn of events had baffled him, leaving him speechless. This changed immediately as Rosie put further pressure on a rapidly deflating penis. "Not such a big man now are we, Jim? I accept your nod and raise you one further question. This is the big one, Jim boy, unlike that thing between your legs. And in case you haven't noticed I am holding this rather sharp scaling knife under your left testicle. Now then, ready?" Another nod. "Good boy. Here it is. Where is Slope and who are the members of the Spriggan High Council? The clock is ticking and I have never been known for my patience." Johnson was a defeated man. Tears of fear and pain ran down his cheeks. He looked a disappointed orphan on Christmas Day having been ignored by Santa.

"Don't hurt me again, Rosie," he pleaded. "I'll tell you what I know. It's not much but will you let me go if I tell you?"

"Unlike you, I am an honourable human being. You tell me what you know and I'll let you go. That's how it works. Lie to me and I'll have your bollocks for earrings. Your call, matey."

"All I know is that things were getting too hot for Slope in this country. In fact the last I heard he had disbanded the Spriggans. Stood them down was the term I think. I believe there was some collateral damage as a result. I was among the highest ranking Spriggans. I attended the inner sanctum when policy was decided and punishment meted out. I had a title at one point. I was known as Brother Red. What changed it all for me was one particular meeting when Slope and one of his assassins killed two men without a word. Conrad Speight was one of them. I'm not sure whether they had done anything wrong or whether it was a warning, but it was pretty horrible. I stayed at that level when the Spriggans were stood down. I was party to a lot of incriminating information but Slope trusted me for some reason. Later I wasn't involved because of the order to stand down. I still give people the impression that I was more important than I was though. You know the way that some articled clerks pretend they are really solicitors. I was never questioned because of the power of the Spriggans. Apparently, Slope radically changed his appearance. All I know is that he lost a lot of weight. He was somewhere in Oxford but I heard recently that he had gone to France, intending to lie low there for a bit. He speaks fluent French and loves the country so he might never come back."

Rosie gave a viciously sharp squeeze to Jim's testicles and he groaned, "The Spriggan High Command comprises most of the cabinet, a good portion of the Church of England, seven Chief Constables and three of the older royals. If you didn't have me by the bollocks I'd add, and a partridge in a pear tree. I think you know what I'm saying. They're all at it. Well across the board anyway. Pick up any public school yearbook and it will be a rogue's gallery. Look, do you really need this information? You must know that Slope will have me killed if he finds out I've told you anything." Rosie's face said it all. There was no space for discussion and it was now clear to Johnson. So far he had told Rosie nothing she did not already know.

"If Slope chooses, then the Spriggans will just disappear. Without him in charge the organisation will not exist. I've told you all I know. Honest to God. Now will you please let me go?"

Rosie's reply was physical rather than verbal as she brought her right knee jerking up into Johnson's testicles. The force of the blow forced air from his lungs, making a sound like that of a rapidly deflating balloon, size large, as he slumped to the ground, curling up into a ball and looking for all the world like a giant hedgehog resigned to his fate as road kill.

"I do believe you have been a truthful little Johnson," said Rosie with a wicked smile on her face. "I hope for your sake that you have been because if I have to come back to ask you any more questions you will regret it more than words can say. Don't forget to do your zip up before walking back through town. I know that Churchill said once that, 'dead birds don't fall out of nests' but that tackle of yours is looking pretty miserable at the moment. I'd put a little Germolene on it if I were you. Well toodle pip. I hope you never see me again, for your sake of course." Johnson was still moaning as Rosie began the walk back up through town in search of Bones and Prideaux. She was blissfully unaware that soon she would be in the company of two men who loved her dearly while jointly driving her to distraction.

Fortunately for Johnson's health and for Rosie's peace of mind both men were asleep, tucked up in their beds back at the Cosy Nook. Before long, if precedent were a reliable guide, they would be up and looking for mischief wherever it could be found.

It was the following morning as the sun was trying to break through some light cloud with the promise of a warm day with occasional showers. At least this was the hopeful prediction of the local weather man, attempting to reassure locals and holidaymakers alike. In fact the rain was coming down horizontally, driven by a wicked onshore wind. It battered the windows of Loveday Cornelius's terraced house. It clattered against the twin bedroom at the front of the Cosy Nook. And it made a general nuisance of itself throughout Falmouth, Penryn and in small villages throughout the Caradon area. The noise it made stirred a bleary Bones and Prideaux, who surfaced in the front room of the house where only hours previously they had made a holy show of themselves. "Wake up you lazy bastards, breakfast is on the go," came the voice of Loveday Cornelius. "I'm assuming a pair of wasters will be rampant carnivores so you can probably smell the bacon, sausages and hog's pudding already dancing grease like in the pan. She broke into a chorus of, 'You're the one that I want...'. There's a pot of coffee ready too. But if you seriously think I have any intention of waiting on you then you will be sorely mistaken. Get yourselves washed and generally cleaned up as best you can. Breakfast will be on the kitchen table in ten minutes. If you aren't here by then it will be in the bin. Up to you my lovely lads." She could not explain it to herself but for some reason having got so much off her chest the previous evening had helped her to feel more at ease than she had since losing Joan. Perhaps it was time to move on. Nothing was being served by wallowing in pity. She had always known this but acting on such knowledge was something else again.

Bones and Prideaux needed no second bidding.

They were both serious trenchermen and the call of a Cornish breakfast was a compelling one. They tumbled to the bathroom and, following some rudimentary sluicing, tumbled back down the stairs and were seated at the kitchen table, as ordered, in eight minutes flat. Tousled and marginally cleaner they sat like naughty schoolboys in trouble with the headmaster, or in this case the headmistress. Two plates of food that would warm and probably challenge the heart of any carnivore were placed either side of the kitchen table. Four rashers of best back bacon, three sausages, two eggs, beans and hog's pudding mounded on two large plates were a sight to warm the cockles. There were cockles too but these were optional, sitting comfortably in a separate blue and white striped dish as not everyone is fond of the gritty little additions to a traditional breakfast. "Go on then, tuck in. It's all local, all fresh, especially the cockles." Cornelius smiled again without knowing why. The two tucked in knowing full well that the only real cure for a hangover is a classic full Cornish breakfast. "I must say Loveday," mumbled Bones through a mouthful of bacon and egg, "you certainly know how to cook a decent breakfast. This is the ticket to revitalise a chap after a night on the sauce. My compliments and heartfelt thanks and compliments to the chef."

"Seconded," announced Prideaux, but before he could add anything more he was interrupted by the haunting strains of Albinoni's Adagio. "Change that obscure ring tone," muttered Bones, grimacing at his friend.

"There is nothing obscure about that piece of music," interrupted their hostess. "It just happens that Albinoni's masterpiece was not only my favourite piece of music, it was also Joan's favourite. This is the first time I have been reminded of it without bursting into tears. Perhaps the presence of you two clowns is toughening me up. Piers, perhaps you had better answer that."

Prideaux smiled as he extricated the phone from his trouser pocket. Looking at it he turned the face towards Bones. "It's Rosie. Answer it, for God's sake, Piers. We don't want to incur the wrath of the Rose. We're in enough trouble as it is." Grimacing in mock terror Prideaux answered. From the other side of the table Rosie's voice could be heard loud and clear. "Where the hell are you, Piers? If you tell me that you are in some den of iniquity known only to sailors, fishermen and painters I'll skewer you and your aristocratic pal. The last thing I need at the moment is to have the twins moping around me. I managed to find the Cosy Nook and the woman who would be your landlady if you had bothered to return to the place last night. She thought I was looking for the twins. Fortunately, I realised they were there before she woke them up. Now I need to see you urgently. I have some information for you. It's not much but I also need to not be in Falmouth at the moment so let's have it. Tell me where you are and I promise not to extract your lungs through your armpit."

"Piers, old chap. A word to the wise," counselled a smiling Bones. "Do not under any circumstances say anything to inflame the situation. No use of 'calm down, girl'. No mention of not making a fuss. Tell her the bloody address and let us finish this wonderful breakfast by paying it the respect it deserves. Any other course of action will, I fear, end in one or both of us wearing said breakfast." "Point taken, old chap," whispered Piers out of the side of his mouth. "Sorry Rosie. My fault entirely. We got lost and were very kindly offered shelter for the night and sustenance for the morn by the lifesaving Loveday Cornelius. The address is, what is the address, Loveday? I must say I didn't notice when you let us in last night."

"It's 23 Fore Street," shouted Cornelius who by this time had gravitated to the lounge where she was reading the Packet and enjoying a cup of the finest coffee available from the Frog Street deli. "Did you get that? Sounds as if she did," Piers explained as he returned to the remains of his breakfast.

It was only minutes later that the doorbell of number 23 rang with a persistence that was suggestive of impatience. "That'll be for you, Piers. I don't get any visitors," Cornelius shouted through. "Better get that, Piers," added Bones with a smirk. Prideaux walked to the front door with the air of a man who, having had his last meal, was now getting on with what naturally follows that. Head bowed in anticipation he opened the door with the air of a defeated man, to be greeted by a flushed and furious Rosie. "Right then, you total twat. Get me a cup of tea and start explaining before I start rearranging your features to resemble Tweedledee, then I'll start on Tweedledum over there. Stop pretending you are not there, Bonesie. I know wherever Piers happens to be you will not be far behind or, indeed, in front." A Rosie roused was a force of nature and she was ensconced in the kitchen before the presence of the householder began to figure on her radar.

"Do come in, and welcome to my home," said the householder with as much sarcasm as she could muster. "My name is Loveday Cornelius. I assume that yours must be Rosie. There's some coffee in the pot, do feel free to help yourself. I'm having a little me time, having spent yesterday evening sobering up your naughty little chums now cowering before you. And as a matter of interest I've spent this morning making sure that their stomachs are once again fully stocked. We must look after the inner man, after all." The cutting edge of sarcasm took some of the edge off Rosie's anger and, pouring herself a cup of coffee, she sat down at the kitchen table to face Prideaux. "And where do you think you are going?" she said to a rapidly retiring Bones as he attempted to duck out of the kitchen into the relative sanctuary of the living room. "You and Prideaux are in this together, so sit." Her voice had the timbre that would have made a stroppy bull terrier sit and stay sitting. Bones sat, as directed.

Once Prideaux had explained, with various apologies and prevarications, some of the anger began to dissipate and Rosie was able to tell the two what she had managed to discover prior to her emasculation of Johnson. Both men winced audibly as she described her actions and his response. She was heartened to hear a frank outburst of unrestrained laughter from Cornelius who had remained in the living room. "Now you know as much as I do. What you intend to do with the information is none of my business but I suggest you tread warily. If you intend involving those two madmen currently sucking their thumbs in the Cosy Nook then make sure you damn well look after them. I've told you roughly what Slope looks like currently. It is also fairly plain that he is in Paris. Over to you. Either you pop over the channel and do your best to find him in a pretty busy city or you come up with some sort of plan to entice him back here to the old country. Whatever you decide you will need to do it without me. I'm off back to Truro while I still have a pub to run. You are on your own, boys."

Bones and Prideaux looked at each other with the kind of expressions that suggested it might be a cold day in hell before they managed to come up with a manageable plan. It was the unmistakable sound of a front door splintering that jerked them back into the real world. The Job twins had not been asleep after all. They had followed Rosie to Fore Street and this was their way of effecting an entry. "Jesus, not the Chuckle Brothers. That's all we need." Rosie looked skyward with every sign of helplessness. The Job twins had arrived.

31

Keeping it in the family

"I think that we need a plan," said Bob Job, stating the obvious. He was good at that. The twins, Prideaux, Bones and Loveday Cornelius sat in the comfortable living room of her Falmouth home. Loveday Cornelius was at last feeling that there was a future before rather than behind her. It had become plain to her as she had listened to the story of the Spriggans and the gradual descent of Slope into as near pure evil as is humanly possible, that he might well have had a hand in the death of her lover. There was no hard evidence to justify this belief but then, why would there be with such a man and such an organisation? The organisation, she was in little doubt that it existed. After all Joan had been an expert on the subject. If she had stayed with her original intention of writing a book focused solely on history then perhaps none of this would be real. It didn't seem real anyway. She could not believe what had happened to change her life completely. She had told her time and time again to lay off the investigative stuff. Joan was an historian not an investigative journalist, but the organisation had got to her. She was possessed by all things Spriggan and could not let it go.

Slope the man himself moved in the shadows. She had heard rumours. Everyone in Cornwall had heard rumours. And while there are many who dismiss those who listen to such talk as conspiracy theorists, there are always rumours of this type that persist. There are conspiracy theories simply because there are conspiracies. There have been since the dawn of time and the modern age had probably done most to ensure that they remain a threat to the unwary. Suddenly for Loveday Cornelius life had become exciting once again. She would do everything in her power to help bring to justice any and all who might have had a hand in the death of Dr Joan Thripp. Never mind the rest of their transgressions, like Shakespeare's mob In Julius Caesar, she was prepared to kill Cinna for his bad verses. She smiled at the thought, imagining the bard would have approved. This was the new Loveday Cornelius. The old one would not have approved but this was a chance to follow a new dream and she intended to follow it until it petered out or turned into a nightmare.

The Job twins had arranged for a carpenter to fix the splintered front door. It meant paying for a new one but when the Job twins splintered a front door it tended to stay splintered. The twins looked angelic as they did their best to contribute to the fairly convoluted conversation that was winding its way around the living room. There was general agreement that now they had a fair idea of where Slope was they needed to decide on a next step. There was, however, an added ingredient to the mix that meant the group would receive some firm direction. Of course it would come from Loveday Cornelius, a woman who was well used to organising the recalcitrant, the lazy, the incompetent and the dreamers. It went with the territory; after all she had been a teacher for fifteen years, a head for five more and a good one at that. The motley crew currently indulging heavily in saffron buns and coffee were a little bigger, or in the case of the twins a lot bigger, but the principle remained the same. And this was the new life that was growing out of the ashes of the old.

"I'd pretty much say that I am up with the story, having listened to you all for some time." Cornelius's voice had an authority that encouraged each one of the group to attend in his and her own particular way. But attend is what they did. In some cases despite themselves, in others because of that empty feeling of having been through it all before. What they all had in common was a desperate wish to see some form of resolution to a murky situation that still did not look as if it would go away. "What I suggest is this," Cornelius continued. "The best information we have tells us that Slope is in Paris. He has been there for some time so no doubt will have established some form of support group. He will also know the place or certainly the area where he has based himself better than any of us could in a short time. So the best chance we have is to attempt to flush him out and to give him a pressing reason for returning to the UK, other than the obvious one of wanting to slice up Piers here and all his chums.

"This is what I propose. I think that we need to tempt him onto ground that we know as well or better than he does. I am aware that we all know Cornwall but if there is a place we all have in common then I think Oxford is where we would be best placed to take on someone with his cold approach to life and death. I can also tell you that we have something of an ace in the hole. There is no reason any of you should know this but my uncle is Sir Gawain Cornelius, a senior officer in MI7. In fact he is the senior officer. We fell out some years ago over that, well that and the fact that I preferred girls to boys. He hasn't really come to terms with that yet but he still sees me as his little girl. If I contact him he will probably have the resources to entice the wretch back to Blighty.

"The only thing to be aware of is that if he suspects that Slope is any sort of real threat to the State he won't make it back here alive. So it depends whether you would like the opportunity to enjoy your revenge on this bastard personally or you simply want him to be no more. I'm listening. I'm probably speaking out of turn here but although I'm not sure how important my uncle is I know that he has a lot of power. Contacting him would be a start if nothing else."

"Well chaps, it's not often that a fellow is presented with an offer this good." Bones was first to speak. "And moreover I think that we should avail ourselves of the facility of dear old Loveday's uncle to make the unmentionable one disappear for good. Can't see even the tiniest problemette with that. Seems to me exactly what the chap deserves, unless we are to enter into some discussion of the efficacy of the death penalty. We all know that the bastard is a murderer so what is the point in attempting to rehabilitate him? A bullet in the back of the neck would be the kindest thing. We could always get Bob or Robert to wring the bastard's neck of course, and place the good news on one of those social networking thingies, pour encourager les autres as they probably say in Paris."

"Spoken like a true aristo, Bonesie," Prideaux grinned. "I'm surprised you haven't been ringing Madame Guillotine to see if she is available for a spot of light decapitation on the weekend. That'll teach the plebs that they should know their place. What about the rule of law? I doubt if anyone hates that bastard more than I do but surely he's entitled to some sort of trial."

"Don't worry your pretty little head, Piers," Cornelius interrupted. "If my uncle decides to take the job on I'm sure Slope will get the fairest of trials. One of his men will appear as if by magic one dark night. Slope will then be asked to confirm that he is who he is supposed to be. He will then be fairly tried and fairly shot. In uncle's game there are no excuses and no messy trials by jury or anything else. The only thing is that my story, I mean your story, will need to be sufficiently convincing. He has to play the game after all. He can't go slaughtering people on the whim of his niece. There'd be a mountain of corpses if that was the case, I must admit. However, the next step is up to you. Any other comments, or should I get cracking?"

"Before you go any further," Prideaux intervened. "Much as I am tempted to join the lynch mob assembling here I am finding it hard to reconcile lynch mob membership with a fairly woolly belief in fair play. If the power of speech is what distinguishes us from the animals then surely the quality of mercy should be what distinguishes us from the likes of Slope and his ilk. And before you start quoting Shakespeare, Bonesie, shut up and listen for a minute." He turned to Cornelius, addressing her directly. "If you can persuade your uncle to engineer the return of Slope to Oxford and allow us to corner him before handing him over to the proper authorities to ensure he gets a fair trial, that would sit a lot easier with my liberal conscience. All this guff about assassination squads within government agencies is surely the stuff of fiction. There's no such thing as operatives who are licensed to kill. Surely all that originated in the fertile imaginations of writers like Fleming and the rest."

"You might think that. I couldn't possibly comment." The words were Rosie's. The pub landlady who had been smoking a cigar in the back garden while this discussion was taking place smiled enigmatically and joined the group in the living room. "I was hoping to avoid this but I've heard a lot of what has been said whilst I've been having a quiet whiff in the garden. What I'm about to tell you will mean that you all automatically become subject to the Official Secrets Act with all that implies. You are old enough by now to know that you should never take anything at face value. Loveday does know what she is talking about. The twins are the only ones among you already subject to the Act. I am the unofficial contact for both of them. I notify MI7 of any actions locally that might have a Spriggan connection.

The reason they are both based in Cornwall is that here is where the Spriggans had their original power base. Mebion Dozmary is a group set up by MI7 and well funded by Government. The initial idea was to give a rational outlet for the Cornish identity and to establish a group that was effectively opposed to the Spriggans. It hasn't been as successful as we had hoped but it has put a good deal of intelligence our way which, as a faithful member of the group, I have sent through to a contact in Whitehall. She winked at Loveday Cornelius, leaving no doubt as to who the recipient of that information was.

"For example we know that Slope has ordered the Spriggans into deep cover. I also hope that we can bring Slope back to Britain under his own steam. That is the limit of my powers. Somehow though I feel that a proper trial with all the coverage would be more effective than his sudden and unexplained disappearance. That is what I shall be suggesting to my contact in MI7."

This wasn't what the group were expecting to hear from Rosie, who was clearly a bit more than merely a barmaid and it certainly put a completely new complexion on things. "How much do you know then?" Prideaux looked directly at Rosie. "You must know what we are dealing with. Slope is no ordinary man. He is not likely to come quietly and if he gets the slightest whiff of what is going on then there will be mayhem." "You needn't worry, Piers. I can tell you that Loveday's uncle has had a watching brief on Slope for a long time. I believe we have an operative at this moment keeping a watchful eye on his activities. I have done as I was asked. The thing is that Slope wasn't lying when he claimed to be well connected. I'm pretty sure that the connection extends to the highest level in government. I've no evidence for this, but I'm pretty sure the rumour is true that there is the tricky matter of one of the minor royals having some involvement. As a member of Mebion Dozmary I do my best to present the county in a good light. That will help investment and perhaps some funding that will help to keep our brightest and best down here. It's an age old problem that to succeed in a career our young people will inevitably move away. That is no good for the county and my local group is trying to improve local opportunities."

Mention of royalty was always a red rag to Prideaux, who had always had republican sympathies. "Come on, Rosie. You are not telling me that this bastard Slope has some sort of involvement with that dysfunctional family that has the brass neck to pretend superiority over the rest of us. If that's the case then I've heard the bloody lot. There really is no bloody hope for any of us."

"Calm down, Piers," came the languid voice of William Radleigh de Beaune floating through the room. "There really is no need for you to go all republican on us. It has been common knowledge, well perhaps not among the common people, for years that one of the Queen's close relatives has not been, well, in fact not very well behaved. It's never been a constitutional issue but out of deference and respect for the institution certain things have been hushed up. Nobody has been hurt or anything but the immunity that Slope likes to rely on does come from the top of government with more than the occasional nudge from the palace. To be honest I don't know all the details but it's one of those things that people are aware of that is simply not discussed in polite circles. Sometimes it pays to say nothing. You know, somewhere along the lines of 'whereof one is ignorant one should not speak', or whatever it was that philosopher Johnny said."

"If by that philosopher Johnny you mean Wittgenstein then I agree with the sentiment. But if you are seriously telling me that, for the sake of saving the embarrassment of an unelected bunch of idlers and ne'er do wells, people have lost their lives and murder has been hushed up then

I very much take issue with you. This is appalling. From reading between the lines it appears that you are trying to justify allowing a sociopath to cut a swathe through civilised society without check to save embarrassment. This is way beyond the pale. And in any case, what the hell has changed now?"

"I'm afraid that I don't know much," said Rosie, "but to put your minds at rest the matter might have resolved itself within the past few days. That is an impression I have and all I am prepared to say. And the simple reason is that I don't know any more than I have already told you."

"And that amounts to sweet fuck all," growled Prideaux, before subsiding into a state of suppressed fury. The rest simply sat in silence, pondering the weird construction that is the British constitution.

It was the sort of silence that seemed to go on forever. In fact it was less than a minute before Robert Job stood up. He walked to the window, appearing to be focused on something outside. It was his way of collecting himself before speaking. He turned to face the group. "If it helps," he began, "I am no happier than Piers with this bloody mess. People have died unnecessarily, careers have been wrecked and a madman has been allowed free rein to kill as he pleases. It is a national disgrace. However, the recriminations can come later. And let me tell you I shall have more to say than many. You are not supposed to get a whiff of this but I was on that bastard Slope's trail before poor old Petroc got his and ended up floating in the Cherwell. I could have taken Slope out at any time. In fact my original orders were just that. They were countermanded on the request of the palace and you know the rest. Modern democracy, don't make me laugh. We are still living in the Dark Ages where that lot are concerned. But that is for another time and another place. For now we need to organise ourselves to complete the job that I should have carried out years ago. Bickering amongst ourselves will get us nowhere. Now this is no longer my shout but it seems obvious that to stamp out any further threat from Slope we ensure that we lure him back to Oxford and take whatever steps are appropriate. We have the resources and, against my better judgement, I think that a major trial followed by a high profile conviction would meet the current case. But that is up to others; along with my brother I'm just a foot soldier who happens to be handy by. And for my part I intend to do whatever it takes to bring the bastard down."

In all the time those present had known him this was the longest speech they had heard from Robert. It had the power of conviction and achieved his aim. It strengthened the resolve of all involved to do what he had suggested. The next step was agreed. No more hesitation. Everything would be geared to support the return of Slope to home soil and the reckoning. The hope was then that this most evil of men would receive the punishment he deserved. The concern was that men such as Slope rarely did receive their just desserts. More often than is proper in a civilised world, some grubby deal is done that lets such men off the hook in the name of political expediency. It was ever thus, and there was no sign that the tide was likely to turn in the immediate future.

32

Shakespeare and Company

Slope's energy levels were beginning to rise as he spent longer in Paris. The city had the power to drain energy from the most energetic of people. Yet the opposite of that was that it also had the power to re-energise the most jaded of individuals. Slope was too wary to allow things to slip too much and not prepared to take any chances. The morning sun was breaking over Montmartre as he sat in the Chez Marie café drinking his morning espresso and idly leafing through Le Monde. His attention was taken by a short paragraph on page thirteen of the newspaper. The strapline read, 'Les Spriggans et Finis'. Such a piece was the only thing that would focus his attention. What followed was a fairly routine rehashing of some generally known facts about Slope's former organisation. There was one line that really made him sit up though, and that was that an ex-member of the organisation was currently talking to Oxford police concerning some of the activities of the now disbanded organisation. The man concerned was described only as Brother Red which, it was explained, was how he had been known within the organisation. He had experienced some sort of conversion when in Falmouth. He would say nothing about what had happened there but was prepared to wax lyrical on the matter of Spriggan organisation and membership details, which he had been party to for years. "Batard!" The expletive had escaped before Slope could apply his usual cold control. He threw down his paper, overturning his chair as he stormed off in the direction of Rue Gabrielle.

This was one angry Slope as he quickened his pace,

determined to get away from the throng in Montmartre. He couldn't think straight when surrounded by people. He needed to be alone in order to concentrate. This was not something he had expected or prepared for. If Brother Red decided to tell the police everything such information would be swiftly passed to the anti Spriggan unit within MI7. They would be on his trail like the hounds of hell. Just when things were beginning to settle down the waters were being muddied again. Brother Red knew too much and it appeared that he was already sharing it with all the wrong people. Paris, or anywhere else for that matter, would no longer be a safe place for him to linger. Against his better judgement he was going to have to return, to Oxford of all places. The place kept dragging him back. It was a bloody magnet, for God's sake. He had always planned to return to the country at some point, but not now, and not there. There was nothing for it, he must start planning. As he walked his mind began to find its normal controlled tenor.

By the time he had reached the Left Bank he was his old self. He would need to arrange transport and to do it quickly. The authorities, he knew, would take a time to process any information they were being given. Once they found out he was in Paris he would need a new identity and that would be expensive. He couldn't afford to "let 'I dare not' wait upon' I would', like the cat in the adage". It was obviously a case of "if it were done it were well it were done quickly". Strange how frequently the Bard has the answer. He had reached the area of Paris where he had last seen Liz Bennett. With his organisation in deep cover, on his orders, Slope needed an ally. If only someone to use as a sounding board for his plan to delete Brother Red and wipe Prideaux and his friends from the face of the earth. Following that blessed day he would engineer an effective disappearance, stopping only to ensure that the next leader of the Spriggans was in place before taking a well earned rest in a town and country of his choice. His final act before disappearing would be to reactivate his organisation. Every Spriggan leader, unless removed for an offence, and it had to be a major and memorable one, was entitled to lifelong membership of the organisation. This only applied to leaders, the rest were disposable. Once he was gone they could sort themselves out. But he would have his revenge before he moved anywhere.

Slope had always planned to retire one day, but not now, and he certainly couldn't step down until he had overseen the death of Prideaux and as many of his friends as possible. The memories would keep him warm and entertained in what was looking increasingly like a forced retirement. That bastard Prideaux would, however, not have the satisfaction of gloating that he had had a hand in Slope's demise. He must share this determination to play out the endgame with Bennett. It was curious how close the line had always been between love and hate where Slope was concerned. He would willingly sacrifice Bennett if she ever became any sort of threat but, despite himself, he had a mild affection for her. This was something he would admit to nobody and barely recognised the feeling in himself. But it explained his need to seek the woman out when the world seemed to be biting back.

He had no number for her but he knew roughly where she lived and was familiar with some of her favourite cafes and bars. It could take a while to make contact. Then he remembered something that she had said to him the longest time ago. They had been talking distractedly about places where they felt both safe and comfortable. Neither had reason to experience either of these feelings, given the machinations they had both been inextricably bound with. He had talked of his all enveloping love of the darkness of the backstreet cinema late on a winter weekday afternoon. There was something womb-like about that experience, particularly if the rest of the audience comprised a couple of deaf pensioners and the usual sprinkling of perverts; something of a cross section of society in the twisted labyrinth that passed for Slope's mind. He remembered that Bennett had found the thought tacky and beneath someone of his intelligence. She had countered with the darkness and damp book smell of the second hand bookshop. That was it. Now where in Paris was the type of secondhand bookshop that Liz Bennett would frequent? There could only be one. In fact there were two but Slope knew where he was to head if he was to renew his recently revived acquaintance with the woman who had been his more than willing accomplice in his original plot to discredit Prideaux. She had not needed much persuading. Sex carried no implications of commitment to her. She was also a consummate liar. Since her role in what had become known in Oxford as the Prideaux Affair, her involvement would not even involve physical intimacy. She would dance to Slope's tune; it was the only tune she would dance to. In this case a simple entrapment operation would be all that was required. The poor fool would not see it coming. It was her first realisation of the power that Slope could wield through his undercover organisation. This power appealed to the controlling sense that had always been a prominent part of her personality. The only time that element of her was subordinated in any way was in her, admittedly infrequent, associations with Slope and the resultant sex that usually followed their meetings.

There can be few more magical places in all Paris than the bookshop, Shakespeare and Company. It sits right in the heart of Paris on the Left Bank opposite Notre Dame. It is much more than the humble bookshop it appears to be. Over the years it has grown into something more akin to an institution yet without losing its particular shabby chic appeal. This is the Latin Quarter which for centuries past has attracted the academic, the thinker, the philosopher, musician, the eccentric and, most of all, the writer. Since 1951 the bookshop itself has held a particular appeal to the writer and to the reader. George Whitman's experiences in South America convinced him of the importance of hospitality. As a consequence there are estimates that as many as fifty thousand writers, readers and those in need of a roof and bed for the night have availed themselves of that hospitality over many years.

George Whitman himself would doubtless have been less than pleased that two devotees of his institution were the likes of Slope and Bennett in whatever incarnation they chose to appear. Intellectualism, however, is no bar to evil, whatever those with a simplistic view of human psychology may believe. None of this occupied the mind of Sebastian Slope who, though his appearance had been radically changed, was still wary of attracting unwanted attention to himself. He was intent on finding Bennett and was backing a hunch that she would be somewhere in the labyrinthine passages of the most famous bookshop in Paris. Wandering along the Rue de la Bucherie he arrived at the famous Paris institution with the air of a flaneur. She was not outside though the sun shone and as always the bookshop was besieged by visitors. Many of these were intent on having their photographs taken with the bookshop's famous facade in the background. True Parisians, and Slope had sufficient remaining arrogance to place himself amongst this class, despised such beings. Unfortunately he did not currently have the luxury of time to spare, and despite his distaste for those he regarded inferior, most of mankind as it happened, they had to be controlled while he dealt with the case in hand. Hoping that

Bennett was there he brushed past the group of Chinese tourists more or less obstructing the entrance without a word of apology. If they thought they were dealing with a civilised human being they were much mistaken. Not much progress for East-West relations there. He pushed his way through to the back of the shop. He knew that she would probably be upstairs browsing. There was so much to see in this tumbledown mountain of books that anybody could be anywhere. On the first floor the shop was less crowded and the noise levels generally dropped. Those new to the bookshop tended to enjoy the haven of the ground floor whereas experienced users knew that real treats often lurked higher up. There were gracefully aged chairs dotted around for the convenience of the regulars, and this is where he expected to find her, if she was here to be found. It took a little while before he spotted a figure dressed in black sitting in a dark corner concentrating on a copy of Hemingway's The Sun Also Rises. Since this place was Whitman's baby, and this was Paris, it was likely that the copy in which she was so engrossed was a first edition of the classic of the Lost Generation. Hemingway's masterpiece was a book dealing with the disillusionment of the generation that followed the war to end all wars. What a joke that worthy ideal had become. Women readers often had a problem with Hemingway. If you can divide authors into those who appeal to women and those who appeal to men then Hemingway was definitely in the second of the two camps. This book, regarded by many as a work of genius, examines the bonfire of the illusions in the whirl of 1920s Paris nightlife. Disillusion with the chosen route of society certainly appealed to Bennett, as it did to Slope. Too many people weren't listening. They were not doing what the likes of Slope and his followers thought they should be doing. It was boneheaded indifference that was leading the world to hell in a handcart. What they needed was strong leadership rather than the vapid posturers that they had landed themselves with. But that was for another day. For now he must re-establish his links with Bennett.

His approach was silent. He always wore thick soled shoes, not quite brothel creepers, but certainly along those lines, the better to approach as close as possible to his target. It was yet another facet of the man's character, something he had developed in the much more staid surroundings of the college of St Jude's. Lecturing is a peculiar practice and tends to attract the halt, the lame and the plain eccentric. There are wildly differing views on how best to conduct oneself when involved in such an occupation. Slope had developed and refined his view when a young and practically penniless junior lecture at St Jude's. As he watched Bennett, apparently lost inside the world created by one of the great American novelists, he remembered the disagreement he had had with a young contemporary. The argument concerned the best way to approach the young and unsuspecting undergraduates wherever they were in the college. His acquaintance, whose name Slope had long forgotten but whose appearance he could conjure vividly in his mind's eye, favoured hammering segs into the leather soles of his shoes. The resultant tapping echoed through college corridors, his approach giving a clear and present warning that he was approaching the lecture hall, junior common room or any other place where undergrads could be expected to gather. The theory he espoused was that any unscholarly behaviour would be nipped in the bud by the persistent tap, tap of his approaching footwear. In reality he tended to sound like Blind Pew in search of Billy Bones, if that fictional character had the energy and eyesight to break into something approaching a trot. Slope's favoured approach would always be silent and could be deadly. In this way he would be spared the worst excesses of boorish undergraduates en masse. Slope favoured the silent approach so that any undergrad foolish enough to be behaving in an unacceptable manner would hear nothing until it was too late. Suddenly a looming and furious lecturer would be directly in his face, and at that stage of his career a furious Slope was not something to be trifled with.

He should have known better with Bennett who, without looking up, threw a, "I know you're there," over her shoulder. "Stop pissing about. There have been some developments." Bennett was not given to hyperbole. Her world view was simply that the world was there to bend to her wishes. Slope could detect something unusual in her voice. She did him the honour of looking up from her Hemingway and facing him directly. "Before you say a word, listen. I realise that will be difficult for an ego like yours but for once let someone else have the floor." Slope indicated that he would do as she had demanded. She was probably the only person in the world capable of having such an effect on him.

"I came here because I love it here. No more complex motivation than that. I thought that I could lose myself for an hour or two in one of my favourite books. And yes, you are right, it is a first edition but it has been doctored. What sort of philistine messes with a first edition Hemingway I cannot imagine, but that is what has happened. Somebody knows more than I ever imagined. They know that I come here, for a start. And they know that I know you. They also know that we are in contact. More concerning is the fact that the message embedded within each odd numbered chapter of the book is a message for me to pass on to you." It was this last that grabbed Slope's attention. "You heard me correctly," added Bennett. "It took me a little while to work it out but essentially I am to tell you that one Sir Gawain Cornelius, some sort of mandarin within a specialist anti Spriggan group, Unit S within MI7, is offering you an opportunity to discuss a deal that will let both of us off the hook. Me for the original plot against Prideaux, and other assorted crimes, you for a fuck-load of plotting, murders and general pissing about. That of course is not a literal translation but you get the gist. It's up to you, but I don't think it's a trap. Someone has gone to a load of trouble to place the message inside this particular volume in this particular aisle and I don't believe they would bother if they simply wanted us to disappear. We seem to have an opportunity to wipe the slate clean. In your case that is one hell of a dirty slate. And if you ever find the vandal who defaced a first edition Hemingway let me know and I'll make the bastard suffer."

Slope looked thoughtful as he digested the information Bennett gave him. "I know that bastard Cornelius. He's been out to get me and destroy the Spriggans for years. We'll need to tread carefully with him. He's clever and ruthless. A man after my own heart really. If we weren't on opposite sides we could probably work together. He's hard to get at, unless we can find a weak spot, that is. I know that years ago he was very close to a woman who was on the fringes of MI7. Some sort of academic as I remember it. There was a time when Cornelius and I were fairly close. He recruited me at Oxford. I reckon that he recognised my dislike of humans as a race. It was Cornelius who recommended me for specialist training as an assassin. He didn't do the training himself but he was always hovering in the background. He supervised a couple of my training runs. You know the sort of thing, a bit of practice with the SAS over at Hereford. I never did actually kill anyone, though I came close on the odd occasion. The training is peerless but having benefitted from it I realised that in the field it would be a dangerous game to be involved in. It wasn't that which put me off so much, it was the fact that the salary was an insult. I was never interested in all that Queen and country nonsense. Risking my life for for some concept that has never meant anything to me doesn't work. So I decided to take what was on offer, the training and all that, but to go into business on my own account. If I was ever going to risk injury or death in the pursuit of removing some target from this vale of tears it was going to be on my terms. I also feel it is best to kill the ones you hate. Where's the fun in murdering someone you don't really know? It's a philosophy that has worked particularly well for my current, shall we say, more self interested organisation. In the end I left, to pursue other interests, as they say. I wish I could remember the name of that woman. I have the feeling she was from Shropshire. Some sort of rural backwater or other I'm fairly sure."

Bennett's face broke into an approximation of a smile. It was her opportunity to prove her worth to Slope. "Lola Cutler is the woman you are thinking of. I know what she looks like. When I tell you where she is at present I assume you will be pleasantly surprised."

"Unless you can tell me that she is in Paris, preferably a short walk from here, then your information is not likely to be of much use."

"Come over here, Sebastian." Bennett was leaning on the sill looking out to the area at the front of the bookshop. "You see that group of three women sitting around the table to the side of the entrance. The one in the middle is the lovely Lola. Happy now?"

"It'll do for now, but as you know I live by the maxim, 'call no man happy until he is dead'. I wonder how Cornelius will deal with the loss of Cutler. Before we leave Paris I'd appreciate it if you would take care of this small task for me. You can have as much fun as you like killing her and frankly I'm not that interested in how you do it. Throw the body in the Seine when you've finished with it. Only two caveats, do not get caught and make sure that you cut off both her ears. I'll send Cornelius a small reminder of who he is dealing with. Now off you go, there's a good little murderer." For the second time in an hour Bennett's face contorted into what passed for a smile. Bennett had been trained by Slope and this was the opportunity for the pupil to excel the master. She would grab it eagerly. She had never attempted to control the pleasure she took in inflicting pain on another human being. The pleasure had a sexual dimension that grew more powerful with repetition. Best of all she enjoyed ensuring that her victim was helpless and knew what was coming. That was, for Bennett, the real kick. She had been given permission to enjoy herself and there were no limits.

It was a week later when Lola Cutler disappeared. In such dangerous waters an absence of two days constituted a disappearance Two days without contact with Cornelius would raise more than questions, it would raise the roof. It would be much later that Cornelius felt the pain. Halfway through day two the entire Paris section were on full alert. It was unlike Lola. She knew that she was on dangerous ground. Slope was capable of anything. If the Paris section couldn't find her then he would fly out himself and put a rocket up the lazy bastards. This was not just any operative. Any missing operative would get blanket support in such circumstances, but this was Lola. Cornelius raged around the Unit S offices like a gorilla with psoriasis. She must be found and immediately, or he'd have someone's guts hanging from a lamppost. It took the combined efforts of the senior staff to persuade him that he should leave things to those on the spot. Charging in would be the last thing to help Lola. He could not know that Lola had been beyond anyone's help from the moment that Slope had given Bennett authorisation to dispose of her.

Elizabeth Bennett was not one to let the grass grow. She was a country mile from any type of vacillation. She had already formed a plan. Lola continued to follow Slope and that was where her concentration focused. She was unaware of the slight figure shadowing her in perfect text book style. Ask any operative who they fear most and they will always answer, 'those trained by our own side'. It was a rainy Paris evening as Lola left her favourite bookshop heading towards Notre Dame. She turned right before she reached the famous old building to stroll down an unnamed side street that she knew operated as a shortcut to her flat. She was tired but happy. Slope did not seem to be putting in an appearance at his usual haunts. This left her free to be the tourist in Paris, a delightful position for one with a love of Parisian culture. Better than that, she was getting paid for the privilege. Her guard was down and she was to pay a heavy price for forgetting one of the unit's primary rules, 'an operative is never off duty'. Bennett had followed her for some days. It had been her idea for Slope to drop out of sight for a while. She reasoned that it would put her off guard. It did just that. Bennett had planned thoroughly. She was aware that the street lamp that gave a muted illumination to the lane was broken. The lane, jokingly known to locals as Rue de la Morte, to mark the murder of a young French singer some years earlier, was avoided by Parisians. Nobody had ever been convicted of the crime and Parisians, sophisticated as they are, do not take unnecessary risks. Everything was in favour of the predator. Lola walked past the derelict stationers without a glance. Her natural reactions kicked in as Bennett's hand slipped round her neck. She kicked backwards and heard the crack of contact with Bennett's shin. The grip loosened slightly though not enough for her to break free. She was able to turn as Bennett brought the cosh crashing against the side of her head. She made no sound as her legs refused to support her and she fell into a crumpled heap on the muddy road.

When Cutler regained consciousness she was unable to raise her head. She was cold and her head throbbed in the ways heads do when their owners had taken them on an extended tour of Paris night spots. She had been on her way home, though. What was she doing here and why could she not lower her arms? She ached all over. The lamp on the rattan table to her right emitted little light as she painfully opened her eyes. It made no sense. She seemed to be suspended from a beam by her arms.

"So the sleeper awakes." The voice was accompanied by the switching on of a strong industrial light that cast sharp shadows around what appeared to be a basement room in some state of disrepair.

"Don't trouble your pretty little head. You are in the basement of the abandoned stationery shop that you passed when I gave you the blow that rendered the beast unconscious, as I believe the famous Mrs Beeton once instructed. Not really appropriate except that I am the hunter and you are my prey. Then there is the fact that I am the last person you will ever see on this earth. Don't worry, I'm not some cannibal. I am not going to cook and eat you with some beans of any description. However, I am going to kill you...slowly. Please don't bother with all the pleading and asking, why me? I'll save you the trouble. You have become a nuisance and so you must be removed. I have been given the pleasant task of killing you. Don't bother screaming. I always prepare thoroughly. This road is virtually a no go area and this cellar is soundproof. Screaming will only heighten my pleasure and increase your pain."

"I wouldn't give you the pleasure of screaming, you twisted bitch," Lola spat with as much disgust as she could manage. The ties attaching her to the beam were wire and were cutting deep into her wrists. Only now did she realise she was cold because she was naked and her arms were sticky with blood. She noticed that on the rattan table was a copy of Hemmingway's 'The Sun Also Rises' lying open. She felt sick and dizzy.

"Oh you will scream all right. You'll scream until you can scream no more and then you will die." Lola looked at her with mute resignation as her killer approached, her face contorted with lust, and with an already bloodied knife in her left hand. Bennett was right on both counts. Lola screamed, a lot and Bennett was the last thing she saw before she died.

Two days later French river police removed the body of the woman from the Seine. It was nothing unusual, the Seine was frequently the last resting place for the dead and the desperate. This corpse was naked, had obviously been tortured and was missing both of her ears. It did not take long to identify the body of Lola Cutler. Slope had his trophy, Bennett had her pleasure. Slope would send the last mortal remains of Lola Cutler to Cornelius by registered delivery.

33

The rovers return

Two weeks later Slope and Bennett were back in the UK. The return to the old country had been roundabout and it had taken a little while to organise appropriate identification documents and passports, but there are always ways. It had cost, but Slope had reluctantly paid the exorbitant prices that fugitives always have to pay. The next step for them would be to confirm that they would attend the suggested meeting and that they would do so without prejudice. Neither was stupid enough to think that they held any real cards. The odds were against them but there must have been some chance of a deal otherwise the fish shoals in the channel would have enjoyed a right royal feast on the bodies of Slope and Bennett. Any chance was better than no chance. But they were certainly not walking naked into any conference chamber. Plans would need to be made. Both needed to get out of the rural backwater they had landed in. It was useful simply because nobody really knew where it was. As city folk the country held little appeal for the two, and increasingly they rubbed against each other, causing friction rather than sparks. In fact anything that could be construed as sex or animal coupling had gone by the board in the few days that they had been marooned in the land of the Barbour and the casual shotgun. The mighty had fallen and it did not feel good. They had fulfilled the first part of the bargain by returning to the old country but now they cooled their heels waiting for the approach that would take them to London or wherever else it would be that contact would be made.

Country walks did not appeal except as a means of

clearing cobwebs from increasingly cluttered minds. Alcohol proved useful insofar as it dulled some of their worst imaginings, that they had been set up and before long would be found floating in the Thames or buried under some newly built relief road. The ways of the intelligence services and those of the underworld are depressingly similar. Slope did his best to contact some of his friends in high places, those who had enjoyed the fruits of their relationship with Slope and his organisation for many years. They had always been there for him as he had been for them. Now suddenly, when he most needed some high level support, the silence was deafening. He had the numbers. Nobody had more direct line access to people in high places than Slope. The establishment had simply done what it had always done when under any sort of threat. It closed ranks. Slope after all was not one of them. He did not have the breeding, and although he had plenty of genuine wealth it all had the whiff of trade about it. Worse still he had become unpredictable. There was too much circulating concerning his behaviour. For them he had ceased to exist. Slope was not surprised at this. He was angry and frustrated but definitely not surprised. What raised his anger to boiling point was his inability to contact any of the Spriggan High Council. Their instructions were to always remain alert for a call from his one specific phone. It was untraceable yet he was unable to contact any of the highest placed Spriggans. Heads would roll for certain. He needed a plan and he needed it quickly.

Though Slope and Bennett believed themselves to be in some way aesthetes, they proved immune to the countryside charms of this particular part of Oxfordshire. The waiting is what proved frustrating for the pair. They were killing time in one of the most attractive parts of the British countryside, yet could not be tempted to embrace the towns and the area surrounded the small village where they were staying. Apart from the seventeenth century cottage they were currently holed up in there was nothing much else apart from a pub and, of course, The Red House of William Morris in Kelmscott. The cottage was one of several bolt holes purchased over the years. The idea was a sound one. Houses would be maintained in various parts of the country to operate as safe houses for important Spriggans when needed. Slope had felt that an immediate return to Oxford would leave him far too exposed. Kelmscott, though remote and quite isolated, was an ideal staging post and would give him time to think and plan before engaging with Cornelius. He knew the mettle of the man. He also knew that by now Cornelius would be aware that he was involved in the brutal murder of Lola Cutler. Such a man could not, would not let that lie. Since the murder he had done some research of his own. He was now well aware that the late Lola Cutler was a lot more than simply an acquaintance of Cornelius. He had pulled the tail of a tiger. And while it added spice to life Cornelius was not a man to be taken lightly. He would need to be very careful.

"Good God, man. Surely the world has not come to this. I knew that standards had slipped but any man who does not know that the port is passed to the left surely should not be within the walls of any Oxford college."

The speaker was Sir Gawain Cornelius who after one or two generous glasses of crusted port could be relied upon to revert to type. He was, in this case, responding to a story regarding the ignorance of a recently appointed don who had not yet absorbed the totality of arcane ritual that defined membership of an Oxford college. There were plenty who harboured the serious complaint that Cornelius, although knowing full well which way the port was supposed to travel, usually showed a marked reluctance to allow it to stray more than the odd couple of inches from either hand. Yet despite this and other failings he always managed to keep a clear head when matters of security were being discussed. This particular day he made full use of the acting skills that had helped sweeten his path to the higher echelons of the intelligence services. There are few who have the capacity to maintain the hail fellow well met profile when they are dying inside. Cornelius was one of the few. He had been told what had happened to Lola Cutler. He had received the vile envelope that confirmed his worst fears. He had always disliked Slope but now it had become personal. He could maintain an equilibrium while the current situation needed to be managed. He also recognised that, with some judicious planning, he could gain his own personal revenge once he had manoeuvred Slope into a corner. It was chess with human pieces. He had no qualms at all in mixing business with pleasure. The motley crew attending the meeting would serve his purposes well and with luck they might all survive.

Cornelius had convened the current meeting where the crusted college port was doing the rounds, in the correct direction of course and at a respectable rate of knots. He had requested, in his case always a euphemism for demanded, the presence of Prideaux, Bones, his niece Loveday Cornelius and the Job twins. Highly irregular in terms of the appropriate procedure in such cases but Sir Gawain Cornelius had always been a maverick. There were rumours that he knew where so many of the bodies were buried that he was in pole position to open his very own private enterprise graveyard should the wish take him. But such rumours were whispered rather than being bruited abroad. He held the highest possible clearance and that in itself was enough for him to run his organisation in whatever way he chose. Under his command MI7 more or less did what they pleased.

Within government of whatever persuasion the only watchwords are efficiency and results. Cornelius was good at what he did. His masters would indulge him for as long as he continued to turn out the results. People like him were, after all, the last bulwark between the people and whatever evil currently lurked around every corner. Currently it was terrorism although not in its most obvious form. The current threat came from close to home. In fact the threat was so close to home that only a sharp operator, something Cornelius undoubtedly was, had a chance in hell of exposing it. And if it opened the way to settling a very personal grudge then so much the better. Everybody wins.

He had chosen to hold this particular meeting in the Great Hall at St Jude's partly because he was an alumnus of the college, and partly because he was confident of the security arrangements, which were more secure than they ever could be in London. This was because he ensured that year on year a significant proportion of staff at the college would be of his own choosing. His writ ran through academics, management and all the way to the humblest college scout, bulldog and porter. This was not popular with the hierarchy within MI6. The members of that organisation hated him for the very existence of MI7 in any case. Cornelius, though, was a charmer who lived a charmed life. A man who got results in this business was generally pretty much fireproof. And Cornelius got results. "Right then you lot, let's get down to it." Perhaps not the opening remarks one might expect at a meeting of such magnitude but they did the trick. "The message has been delivered to Slope and his equally ghastly partner in crime. My sources tell me that they are no longer polluting the Paris air but to date we do not have a forwarding address for them. Although I have a shrewd suspicion of where they may be. I have ordered a small squad to check out the various safe houses within reasonable distances of Oxford. To date they have cleared Burcot, Witney and Woodstock. That only leaves the cottage at Kelmscott. I am expecting a call from there at any second and then we will know what we are dealing with. I suspect they are lying low. My operatives are on the case but as yet no business has resulted. The reason I have called this meeting, apart from the quality of the surroundings and, of course, the quality of the crusted port, is to ask you to help me out. Yes, I shall repeat that a little louder, I should appreciate your help.. You are all allowed to contribute but let us not make the mistake of assuming that any form of democracy is at work here. I shall decide on all aspects of policy. I can order action covering the complete scale from a mild rebuke to a jolly good thrashing; we'll park that as I suspect both of these miscreants would thoroughly enjoy such a thing. And of course if I decide to remove the bastards from England's green and frankly unpleasant land then that too is a mere heartbeat away. Please be under no illusion how far my jurisdiction extends. I have no need to tell you this as it is in fact none of your business. Slope has been my business for some time. Sadly he has now made himself my personal business too. If he were some ordinary psycho with no powerful contacts he would be already dead. I am not at liberty to tell you who but someone very close to me has been touched by his evil. For this he must pay. I need your help to ensure that he does." It was only by a magnificent effort of will that Cornelius kept things together. He was slowly curling in on himself but would not give in to the boiling emptiness and rage that threatened to possess him. He kept reminding himself not to lose control. He needed to stay calm if he was to have any chance of concluding the current business, he must allow his training to take over until he could find an opening for the revenge he felt he owed to Lola.

Sitting in the Great Hall surrounded by oil paintings

of the great and the good, who had all had contributed to the success and, of course, some notable failures of the college, was an odd experience even for those who were alumni. What seemed not unlike the meeting of a local book club, albeit chaired by an eccentric with powers of life and death, felt anachronistic. Bones of course was in his element, and the port passing had become a little too competitive between him and Sir Gawain. Emboldened by his possession of the port decanter, Bones decided that there was too good an opportunity to miss circling the hall. "If I might be allowed to offer a considered opinion," he began with just the right amount of condescension, "I think that you should execute both the bastards forthwith and save the taxpayer, and I am one, a fortune. No excuses, no mitigation. They are both beyond the pale and deserve no consideration at all. Pour encourager les autres if you like. A phrase I repeat often, you might note. And I'm not in favour of keeping such wastrels living in the lap of luxury. I've always believed that that particular lap was the sole preserve of the aristocratic backbone of this country. Here I rest my case," he finished as he poured himself another glass of port, hanging on tightly to the decanter after he had filled his glass.

"A pretty speech, Bonesie my old toper, but we must remember that we are not supposed to be barbarians any longer. There is the rule of law even if I am personally above such ridiculous concepts. And you needn't worry your little aristocratic cockles one little bit. These two will not be settling for a cosy stay at Her Majesty's pleasure. They have incurred my displeasure and I am a swift and jealous god when such behaviour eats into my leisure time. This bastard has taken away the only person I have ever really cared for. Worse than that, it is my fault that she was killed. I should not have sent her to Paris. She was too near the most murderous creatures it has ever been my misfortune to deal with. These adherents of weird ancient cults are supposed to be harmlessly dancing around standing stones at midnight while they expose their wobbly bits to the moon goddess, or some such nonsense. What they are not supposed to be doing is concocting conspiracies, and committing murder and mayhem on the Queen's highway. Well, not on my watch for certain sure."

The impassioned utterance of Sir Gawain would have gone down a storm in the Lords, although few would have been aware of the personal grief that was threatening to overtake this private man at the moment. Prideaux was sitting to the left of the self appointed chairman and right next to the Job twins. He had already registered the rising annoyance in Robert, who sat next to him, at the tone of the speech, and was conscious of the trouble the twins could cause when upset in any way by such old school arrogance. He could not deny himself a wry smile as he noted Robert digging his left hand into Bob's thigh. He had seen this before and was aware that it was often the prelude to an explosion that would dwarf Krakatoa. His only thought was to defuse what would undoubtedly be an unproductive and potentially bloody outburst.

"We are all in agreement that these two people should be subjected to special measures, but let us not forget that there are so called underground or secret societies that are not composed of phantom Morris dancing aficionados and white witches, Sir Gawain," he began. "You were a student here and you of all people should appreciate that the customs and practices are a little different to most of the other colleges. That does not make them wrong; it makes them different. Just as those of us who come from the western and south western fringes of Britain are different from those who hail from the Home Counties and selected parts of England to boot. If we are to cooperate then I suggest we bury our differences for the foreseeable future, until the matter in hand is resolved to the satisfaction of all."

"Well said, Prideaux, my lad. Just pissing about as usual. No harm intended and my apologies if anyone here feels slighted. I'm still a little cranky at having had to postpone a longstanding arrangement to pop up to the Highlands and slaughter some bird life, so the quicker we get on the better as far as I am concerned. And as you have probably gauged by now I am simultaneously nursing a personal grief that will take some assuaging. Now shall we continue? This is where we are at the moment. I have a budget that is more extendible than the arms and legs of Inspector Gadget. What this means is that I can offer the toxic twins a pardon and a one off payment to seek succour on another continent. I call this option one. Option two I refer to as 'liquidate without prejudice'. I'm sure you have heard some of that bollocks you find in books about spies where they have some sort of licence to kill. Doesn't happen. There is no such thing, though I sometimes wonder whether it would make my life a lot easier. Why in hell's name would you want a spy to hold a killing permit? They are spies after all. The clue is in the name. What I have is a shortlist, and it is a shortlist of names of professional executioners. They are men and women who have been trained within the unit to elicit violent death where such an event fits the circumstances. I am the only person in this country authorised to issue such instructions. These people are kept on a tight rein and live very ordinary lives. They are not very ordinary people. You are probably aware that killing people is easy. At least it used to be, in the good old days when the odd drowning or broken neck could automatically be classed as a sad accident. All this technical bollocks with investigations and DNA evidence has made us look again at our portfolio of killers. Now I am about to tell you something that you will tell no one outside this room. I expect that I am the only person here who, when he says,' I could tell you but then I'd have to kill you', actually means it. Don't worry, you will not attract my unwelcome attentions unless one of you blabs. Then you won't know what or who it is that hits you. Just be aware that from this moment onwards there is a dark angel who will always be just over your shoulder. If any one of you would care to leave now I'm afraid you have missed the boat. You already know too much, and I'm sorry Loveday, that includes you, even though you are my niece. I never was much of an uncle but then I never did get the hang of uncling."

It was clear that he was an old ham really as he paused for effect, topping up his glass as he did so, having wrested the decanter from Bones's hands. The overacting was his trump card. It allowed him to compartmentalise private worries, in this case, the murder of Lola, and temporarily bury them under a performance that would deflect too many questions and, God forbid, any expressions of sympathy. He could not face that. He filled his glass and took what could only be described as a slug of port that from any importer would cost in excess of £500 a bottle. Collecting himself for the coup de grace he looked pleased at having such an attentive audience.

"I've only mentioned two options so far as that is all I can rationally see. There is a third one that I believe is too risky to entertain. Such a course would mean attempting to bring one of our most effective executioners back in from the cold, so to speak. For the slightly hard of thinking amongst you, now looking at me and doing a fair impression of a haddock who has just been told that his wife of ten years had been cuckolding him, I shall clarify. Yes, Slope is one of our top executioners, I know how good he is because I trained him. Sadly he chose to ply his trade outside the unit. In turn though, he trained Bennett, and if anything she is marginally more effective and dangerous than him. It is because of that simple but possibly life preserving fact that I am aware of how deadly both of them can be. So you see the first two options look like being the only ones. I'll give you a short break, during which you will not leave this room, to think things over before I start to outline where we go next. Don't worry, I'll have some food and drink brought in. I'm afraid it will be fairly basic as these are austere times, and we're all in it together. Well I'm not, but these accidents of birth can happen to anyone. Now is everybody happy? You had all better bloody well be."

At the climax of his deliberately structured grandstanding speech he swept from the room and along the corridor to a private office that was always kept ready for him. Slamming the door behind him he sank into his favourite club chair as he started to sob, vainly attempting to stifle the noise with a blue spotted silk handkerchief. Gawain Cornelius, Head of the Anti Spriggan Unit, was crying like a baby and there wasn't a single thing he could do about it. It was more than twenty minutes later when his secure phone rang and a vaguely familiar voice greeted him. It was Sebastian Slope.

"Don't bother trying to trace this call, it is simply not possible, and your team got to Kelmscott a little late, bad luck. Now I suggest you listen and listen carefully. You know me well enough to know that I never bluff and I never negotiate. These are my terms. I want immunity from any possible prosecution and I want it in written form. I know that you hate me and I'm not inclined to take your word so I want a document signed by the PM and endorsed with the royal seal. My other demand is that Prideaux should bring the document to me and that the package includes a compensatory payment of £4 million. Prideaux should be responsible for £250,000 of that amount. That should comfortably bankrupt him and ensure he ends his pathetic life in penury. In return I shall take myself a long way away from this small windswept island and you will never hear from me again. Now, do we have a deal?"

Cornelius struggled to control himself. The Slope arrogance was there in full flow. The bastard who had murdered Lola was now dictating terms to him. It was more than he could bear. He had been trained in a tough school but controlling himself now was the hardest thing he had ever done. He knew what a slippery bastard Slope was. After all he had trained him. He would need time but he would cry vengeance somewhere down the line. He forced himself to speak to the man he hated most in the world.

"OK Slope. You win." The words sounded as if they came from somewhere outside himself as he struggled to maintain equilibrium. "I can arrange this but it will take some time. I shall need to persuade Prideaux but I'm pretty sure I can do that too." There was a silence. He stopped himself from talking irrationally to fill that silence. No hostages to fortune where Slope was concerned. And Prideaux would have to take his chances.

"I'll be in touch, Cornelius. Oh, and so you are aware, Lola screamed before she died. She screamed a lot."

"Bastard!" yelled Cornelius as he smashed the handset to pieces on the rosewood desk. It took many minutes before he could control himself well enough to return to face the others.

34

The Cornelius perspective

The group had managed to consume a good portion of the sandwiches that had been brought in by a college servant. Digesting the sandwiches had proved a lot easier than digesting the information Sir Gawain had so recently provided them with. Bones had immediately plucked Prideaux by the sleeve as the refreshments were being brought in. "That's not so bad then, Piers. He can kill these two busters and we're all off the hook. Job done. Everybody's happy, you bet your boots we are."

Prideaux looked thoughtful. "I take your point, Bonesie, but sadly we are not living in Colombia or Mexico. We are not really at liberty, and I use that word advisedly, to begin massacring those with whom we disagree and dangling their decapitated heads from the Bridge of Sighs. The university simply wouldn't stand for it. Hardly cricket, now, is it? I think we now need to tread more carefully than we have ever done before. We are in a minefield as far as I can see. We have been introduced to a man who has the power of life and death over anyone in the country, from the way he is talking, up to and including the Queen. Of course he could be exaggerating but looking at him I doubt that he is. We are now complicit in all this and I really think we need to be onside for safety's sake. He's not absolved his own niece. I don't think he is the type to bluff."

Cornelius announced his return with a regal clap of the hands, indicating that the break was over. "I left you with a bit of a bombshell and I reckon you have had long enough to mull it over, but I'm sure you will have questions for me so I am allowing you fifteen minutes to ask them. I shall answer them if I deem them to be germane to the issue. If not I shall completely ignore them. But before you say anything let me enlighten you. The person you know as Slope was trained in my unit. I was particularly involved with Slope's training. That means I know what he is capable of. What I didn't foresee was Slope turning rogue. With hindsight, that is what he had in mind all along. Once he completed training and had acquired all the skills and knowledge he needed he jumped ship. He spotted an opportunity and took over an existing organisation that had a weak leadership and no real direction. By the time he had restructured the Spriggans and established his own agenda he had a powerful force under his command. The only saving grace I can think of is that he modelled the organisation using knowledge he had acquired through Unit S training. That is why he is so dangerous." "Listen to me, matey," interjected a furious Robert Job. "You talk a good fight, but I wasn't trained by you and until recently had never met you. I find it hard to believe you are as important as you claim to be. You say you have some sort of God-given power over the lives of anyone in this or presumably any other country. That sort of thing is not sporting and especially not in a democratic country like Britain."

The response of the apparent Lord High Executioner startled the small group, who had suddenly begun to look physically smaller as their confusion increased. A sudden burst of laughter that appeared born out of contempt rather than amusement was not what anyone was expecting. "Who the fuck told you that this was a democracy? For your information this post of mine existed under Henry VIII, although it was never documented. He was quite fond of a decent execution and he had men to carry out the dirty business, but they were all directed, taught and controlled by someone very like me. There cannot be accountability for someone in this sort of post. And as for answering to those cretins and halfwits who spend most of their lives fiddling their expenses, or indeed, fiddling with each other or worse, I hold them in the highest contempt. They are only there as a sop to those who might otherwise make a fuss. They have as much power as you lot do. And as a demonstration why don't you, Robert Job, take a look at the forehead of your twin. You know weaponry and I'm sure that you recognise the red dot currently adorning his forehead as a sighting spot. The weapon projecting that deadly dot is completely silent and if I say the word his head will explode into somewhere near three hundred pieces."

The room suddenly became very quiet as the enormity of their involvement gradually dawned on all those present. The spot was there alright. This was suddenly very real. Apart from the explicit threat of death, instantaneous if they chose or a lingering threat whatever path they preferred, this was a challenge to all the liberal ideas that any of them had ever espoused. If it was true and it was all a sham then where the hell did all the certainties go? Collapsing banks, imploding economies, breaking up of old alliances, respected figures in the media and politics being revealed as having feet of clay. All these things were terrifying in their own way. But this was a step too far. This response was what Cornelius had expected and he was ready for it. "I apologise for the rather melodramatic demonstration and I am fully aware that I am not in the company of what Tory politicians are wont to call plebs and chavs. I know that all of you have had first class educations. I am equally cognisant that such benefits sadly tend to produce liberal and open minded individuals rather than those who read The Sun. Consequently, I appreciate that what I have told you today is a direct challenge to everything you hold dear. I would prefer it if your response was a considered one rather than something out of proportion. Slope is an authorised killer. He was authorised by me and will need to be dealt with by me. If that is all there was then the problem would not merit two pipes on the Sherlock Holmes scale of difficulty. However, as you are all well aware, the Spriggan connection means that there is more to be considered. You will be aware that Slope has sent his top men into deep cover leaving the minions defenceless. What troubles me, and what troubles me should now be troubling you, is that a straightforward hit however well disguised could cause a pressure release among a whole lot of well placed Spriggans who could be very difficult if they so choose. Accordingly, I would like to buy him off. He might have had enough, though I doubt it. Sadly that is not a viable option. Slope will have plenty of resources salted away and he will know that we can't get at them all. However, a possible solution has presented itself. I have been given an ultimatum in the last hour that I believe we should pursue. Slope has been in touch to offer a way out." This was enough to guarantee the rapt attention of the room. Several jaws dropped as if synchronised.

"Thought that would get your full attention. He contacted me on my secure phone in my office while you lot were nosebagging away on the college's finest sandwiches. The upshot of it is this. He will agree to go into exile for the small price of a watertight guarantee of immunity and £4 million. The money he regards as compensation and such immunities have been issued before. Given the current financial position the money may prove a bit more problematical. In any case my superiors are convinced that this is the best immediate solution and are currently putting a load of pressure on our financial masters to find the cash. That in turn is putting a lot of pressure on me to effect a resolution.

I am not a happy man at the moment so I intend to bring matters to a close swiftly. One more thing. Slope has certain conditions that I am obliged to fulfil."

"I have been silent for some time now," said Loveday in a steely tone. "I'm afraid that it sounds to me that you are suggesting that one or all of us meet with this extremely dangerous couple and deliver the goods. Are you seriously suggesting this, or have I got it wrong? They were bad enough before you casually informed us that they were both trained and skilful murderers. Don't you think that this is a bit too much for ordinary people to deal with, or don't you care?"

"I'm sorry to disappoint you, Loveday," her uncle answered. "I wasn't trained in this job to consider what the army refers to as collateral damage. We have a situation here that needs to be resolved. It must look as if I am not involved. There is, of course, a reason for that. It is the most banal reason of all. There is a leak within the department. It is not within my specialist unit, of that I am certain, but it definitely exists within MI6 which is why they are kept outside the boundary around MI7. Those boys are not quite as clever as they pretend. I want this to be clean and final. If I cannot pull it off it will have to be a 'kill' order. The consequences of that will be considerable. I am doing my best to avoid an extremely dangerous escalation.

"Everybody trembles at the prospect of destabilisation in the Middle East and rightly so, But I wonder how many have considered what could happen if it happened right here on our own doorstep. Potentially it could be a catastrophe. The Jocks are already contemplating leaving the union. If they do, and they might, despite the efforts we are currently putting into preventing it, if that happens what do you think will happen next? The Taffies will be next and what happens then? Three separate countries that have been yoked together for centuries occupying the same space and in general terms loathing each other. Well if I am to be accurate perhaps it is the Scots and the Welsh who dislike the English for their self evident superiority. But whatever we think of each other it would be absolute chaos if we tried to disentangle all the paraphernalia of law and government that binds us together. If you think that Europe is a bloody mess, and it is, you have seen nothing such as will occur if the United Kingdom was to be dismantled. And how long would it be before the Cornish were demanding home rule? Then those bloody northerners would want their own parliament! Great God, this would be an awful place. So in short none of it will be allowed to happen."

The fact that Cornelius was unleashing this level of bile in front of a mainly Celtic audience was testament to the amused tolerance that the original inhabitants of the island of Britain exercised when dealing with their self appointed betters. There was a general belief that if Sir Gawain bloody Cornelius wanted a dirty job doing then he could damn well do it himself, and it fell to Prideaux to tell him so.

"Listen Cornelius, given that you have spent the last ten minutes boring the arses off all of us and that same amount of time insulting us, what is it, do you think, that will persuade us we should risk our lives to help in one of your schemes?"

"Do you really need me to answer that? For fuck's sake, take a look at the minstrels' gallery. And please don't say you can't see anything. You aren't bloody well supposed to. OK boys, give these peasants a light show to convince them that I'm not fucking about here." As he spoke a net of red laser spots appeared on the far wall of the Great Hall. It would have been an impressive enough light show if it had been a bunch of ghost hunters on speed. As a serious show of potential fire power it was terrifying. It had the intended effect.

The Celts were suitably cowed. "OK boys, turn off the light show, we don't want to crash the National Grid, now, do we?" Cornelius had extreme difficulty in not sounding patronising every time he opened his mouth. The positive side of his performance, in instructing half a dozen of the anti Spriggan unit's finest marksmen and trained snipers as though they were kindergarten drop outs, was a potent piece of one-upmanship. It seemed there was little left to do but at least feign compliance if only until a better offer happened along. Piers Prideaux had already assumed the mantle of spokesman so he continued in the role in the absence of any other volunteer.

"OK, Sir Gawain. We are all ears. And as it happens I for one would like to hang on to both of them. Perhaps you could tell us what you expect of us."

"Since you ask so politely then I cannot refuse, Prideaux. Unfortunately the us is not an us, it is a you. Slope insists that you should deliver the immunity document for him and Bennett in person. You will also be delivering the bankers' draft for £4 million as soon as I can arrange it. It might well take a little time. The wheels of Whitehall grind at their own slow pace. I admit that undertaking this will leave you heavily at risk. I can provide cover for you to some extent but Slope is a clever bastard and if he suspects anything it could all get very ugly."

"If I should be mad enough to do this I'd like you to give me a rough estimate of what my survival odds might be. I've already estimated that if I fail to comply they would be pretty bloody thin.'

"Paper thin, old chap," Cornelius grinned. "To be honest they aren't a pile better if you do follow orders, but I suppose any chance is better than no chance. Listen to me, my little ones, and do listen carefully because I really shall say this only once, so you had better get attuned a bit swiftly. I am assuming that Prideaux's avenue of choice will be to meet with Slope and Bennet. He will contact me again with final instructions when I have everything in place. My technical boys are currently establishing means for him to contact me. He will then send through the instructions that you will follow to the letter. You will then present him with his cast iron guarantee of immunity and the £4 million that I hope will be forthcoming from a white faced chancellor. It's not the best plan in the world, I know. In fact it's only marginally better than when the officers told the boys at Ypres that a stroll across no man's land would be good exercise after all that hanging about in damp trenches. It's up to you, Prideaux."

"I shall need to trust you with the money and the pardon, Prideaux. That might just get you off the hook with Slope. Fuck it up and you will all be very much on the hook with me. One more thing. He has insisted that £250,000 of the money should be in cash and should come from you. You will be tasked with the job of convincing Slope that somehow you have come into a significant sum of money. Don't look so worried, we have various ways of getting round tricky obstacles. I suggest that we use the lottery tactic. It has worked for us before. The serfs seem so blinded with the possibilities of greed raised by that particular charade that even intelligent people seem to accept that such mammoth sums are regularly won by quite ordinary folk. Of course they aren't, won by ordinary folk that is. Those who appear on TV and in the local gutter press are government employees who do the usual 'it won't change my life' routine. In my mind they should be bloody shot for coming up with something so predictable. At least it would be more interesting if one of them said publically that he was going to drink himself to death on vintage champagne in the shortest possible time. These characters get paid a reasonable amount together with a strong warning to keep their mouths shut and the majority goes straight to the jolly old Exchequer. Better than income tax and nobody's any the wiser. Now, when you meet Slope and his ghastly companion give them the draft for £4 million. Then hand over the £250,000 in cash that you will have apparently won in a weekend lottery and hope that gets you and your pals off the hook. It might do the jolly old trick.

Up to this point Cornelius had done a sterling job of keeping his personal grief under wraps. The thought of what could happen to Prideaux brought everything flooding back. He choked and turned away so that the group could not see the tears. Lola's face appeared in his mind's eye. He fought to control himself before stalking from the room. He returned to his office to calm down as well as he could. She had suffered. Those bastards had tortured her. They didn't deserve to live. Somewhere down the line they would pay. For now the only option was to remain focused and placate those at the top. There would always be another day.

A successful outcome could buy some time. Slope and Bennett could never be trusted. Perhaps immunity and a sweetener would at least get them out of his hair for some considerable time. It was possible, and for the moment it was all he had. He knew that his sense of personal loss was beginning to cloud his judgement but he had to remain strong.

Cornelius had the air and bearing of one schooled and trained in the higher reaches of the ruling classes. Though no aristocrat he had the air of one born to rule. His every utterance was distinguished by certainty. In his case it was the certainty born of experience. He knew how far his writ ran, what he could get away with and what was slightly dubious. Because he had served his country so efficiently in past crises he knew that he had complete power and all that came with that. Fortunately he also retained a sense of duty that so far had ruled out ultimate corruptibility, but he brooked no opposition. His vengeance was always sudden and complete. If not for the current little local difficulty within MI6 and pressure from above, the mortal remains of both Slope and Bennett would have long ago been tucked away in a country churchyard somewhere. The accident leading to their joint demise would have been sudden and completely unpredictable. It would have been no accident but yet another example of the inventive minds within the anti-Spriggan special unit. They had a guide book full of 'necessary accidents', something the operatives had great fun in adding to. When the unit was first established it had been all tragic car accidents. Brakes suddenly failing or undetected oil spills on particularly dangerous stretches of road did the job, but that had become tedious. This had not been entertaining enough, and some internal rivalry had led to some more imaginative ways of disposing of those deemed, by the state, to be disposable. It began with falling trees, stampeding cows, sudden choking incidents, poisonings, unexpected insect bites, sometimes the result of an exotic spider imported in a shipment of bananas. The list was endless and included death by meteor strike, which really was taking internal competition a little too far. Still, it kept the unit occupied and in their minds it helped to keep democracy safe in a land fit for heroes.

This was what Bones, Prideaux and their group had to contend with, and they were smart enough to realise that there were few options. It was an uncomfortable position to be in. Prideaux for one thought that the plan was paper thin and the likelihood of pacifying two card carrying psychopaths extremely remote. But, as Bones was fond of repeating, 'when you ain't got nothing you got nothing to lose'. So they listened and all absorbed

Prideaux's instructions as if their very lives depended on it. Prideaux would be the one to deliver the guarantee of immunity, the draft and the cash. He had reluctantly agreed. He had little enthusiasm for the task but sometimes when the devil drives... He had at last agreed to take the job on, simply on the grounds that someone had to do it. He had been partly mollified by Cornelius's promise of Unit S back up and support in case things went wrong. After all, there was a great deal of history between Slope and Prideaux so essentially anything could happen. For the time being all they could do was await Slope's further instructions. It was not a happy position to be in.

Never had the old cliché about rocks and hard places seemed more appropriate. Damned if they did, dead if they didn't was not a comfortable place to be hanging around for too long. All they could hope for was to make the best of things, and pray that Slope stuck to the agreement. The possible termination of Slope and Bennett somewhere down the line would be a happy accident. All this would be testing the limits of probability to breaking point. Given their position, though, the group agreed to go along with this the flakiest of plans. For the moment it meant keeping their heads down until contacted by one of Cornelius's men from Unit S. Until then they faced the near impossible job of attempting to live a normal life. But this is what it had come to. There was no alternative. Things must seem to go on as usual in order to deflect any possible suspicion from all of them. It was agreed that the twins and Loveday Cornelius should return to Cornwall. The twins would go back to the farm and, for safety, Loveday would stay there with them until contacted. The odd couple, Bones and Prideaux, really had no idea where would be the best place for them, until an unexpected text solved the problem for them.

35

The hand of God

Having initially ignored the text from Mark Williams it was simple curiosity that prompted Prideaux to look at the message he had received from his old friend. It was a week since the disturbing events at St Jude's had revealed to the old friends the extent of the mess they were in. Neither man felt comfortable in Oxford. Not a peep had been heard from Cornelius or Unit S and life, as it has a way of doing, was beginning to resume its humdrum pattern. There was some comfort in numbers so they had moved into Prideaux's flat together. The text was not particularly enlightening. It simply hinted at some unexpected change in direction that Mark and Ginny Williams had decided to take. It sounded sufficiently intriguing to find out a little more about what the couple were up to. After all anything involving Slope could be important to them, even though they had attempted to distance themselves from the current situation. They would certainly need to be kept informed of recent developments.

With this in mind Prideaux rang Mark. The news was much more interesting than he had expected. Mark and Ginny tended to keep themselves to themselves but the change of direction would put an end to that lifestyle once and for all. They had come into a significant sum of money from an aged aunt who had recently passed away. They had grown bored with Cheltenham and decided that they needed a new challenge. They were the types to take on such tasks with such enthusiasm that they tended to drag others along in their wake. Since they had last been in touch they had invested a good portion of their inheritance; strictly speaking it was Ginny's, but they were sharing types. The investment they had made was in an inn that they had spent no little time bringing up to scratch. They were to reopen it as an inn with rooms and were wondering whether Bones and Prideaux would be interested in coming to stay for a while as they got acclimatised to their new lifestyle. The expression on Bones's face as Prideaux related this news to him was something like that of a child presented with a giant everlasting lollipop. Of course the answer was yes, and in no time both men were flying around the flat sorting out clothing and other necessaries for what they hoped would be a long and bibulous stay. There is a well worn saying that goes, 'If you want to make God laugh tell him your plans'. It wasn't God who laughed at the idea of Bones and Prideaux relaxing in deepest, darkest Wales. It was a much more sinister figure and one with eyes and ears everywhere.

The Hand of God was nestled in one of the most idyllic spots in the UK. Mark and Ginny had long talked of a lifestyle change, and, as both were extremely knowledgeable about food and wine, the idea of an ancient tavern offering top class accommodation and the best cooking available was an appealing one. This idea had crystallised during a short break a few years ago when they had visited the tiny Monmouthshire village of Skenfrith. It was during a time when their marriage was going through a rocky patch and the short break was an attempt at reviving the now guttering flame that had brought them together in the first place. It worked. There was unquestionably something magical about the area. It had all the hallmarks of a romantic dream. There were a few houses in the village and the remains of a fourteenth century Norman castle. The River Monnow, a much overlooked river outside the area, runs through it, separating the countries of England and Wales. The area has seen more than its share of conflict over the centuries, but these days is valued for its silence and reversion to the timelessness of an ancient countryside unspoiled by intrusion. It is shooting and fishing country with most of the old crafts making a comeback, and as one would expect the whole place is steeped in history. For the brief time they were there history took a back seat as they rediscovered each other at a classic fourteenth century inn that had been carefully restored without losing any of its original charm. There were around a dozen rooms, beautifully fitted out with top of the range fittings, all fitting perfectly in with the country inn ambience of the place. The bar featured an open fire place burning logs sourced from the surrounding woods, giving the whole ground floor a necessary whiff of wood smoke. The room at the front of the building where the two stayed looked out over the ancient bridge over the Monnow. The river was angry and swollen with winter rains but the entire perspective was of another time and another world. Occasionally, abandoning the everyday world and inhabiting something other is just the jolt that human beings need to reconsider limping relationships. It was certainly something that worked to strengthen the marriage of Mark and Ginny Williams. Of course, it would be foolish to discount the fact that the chef held a Michelin star with another one on the way. Or that the owner was a connoisseur of fine wines and ensured that he kept a cellar that was the envy of many a top London hotel. Whatever the combination, the overall effect was to make the two stronger than they had ever been as a couple. It also placed in them both the germ of an idea that running such an establishment would be a change of lifestyle that would make the whole process of growing old gracefully much more likely. It was that jointly held belief that had brought them back to this little known part of Wales.

The area is best known as the Marches and historically had formed a buffer between the English to the east and the indigenous Welsh to the west. There are many distinctive features of the area, perhaps the most obvious being the proliferation of Norman castles. Now mainly existing as tourist attractions these castles once served as centres of strength where Norman lords, with the authority of the king, ruled over what were effectively petty kingdoms. There was little if any control over these lords who were not much more than robber barons. The argument as to where discrimination and brutal treatment of the original inhabitants began and ended remains a matter for debate and not just among historians. The area known to the Welsh as Ergyng and Archenfield to the English acquired their new neighbours following the withdrawal of the Romans after four centuries of occupation. One in and one out, that's how it goes. Soon after the Romans left Angles, Saxons and Jutes flooded in. By around the sixth century Ergyng had the dubious pleasure of welcoming the neighbouring kingdom of Mercia, possibly the largest, most powerful and expansionist of the Anglo-Saxon English. The extent to which the newcomers to the area respected the existing population is probably best summarised in one indisputable fact; Welshmen were forced to march with the English army. Perhaps not that telling a fact until the follow up that, when marching into battle, Welsh soldiers were in the van and when retreat became inevitable they were forced to form the rearguard. It was without question a buffer state that existed here and that state did not exist for the benefit of its original inhabitants.

Such history is part of what gives the area its particular qualities and, although the details are largely forgotten, its legacy accounts for the individuality and ruggedness of many of the current inhabitants. The remoteness also has its own appeal and, for those who want something different in a modern era dominated by instant communication, it is one of the few places left to offer a slower pace of life. History is all around in the Monnow Valley and that history had its own appeal to both Ginny and Mark Williams.

It was history that figured strongly in the thoughts of Mark Williams as he took the opportunity of a fine day to put some of the finishing touches to his new venture. He knew more of this area than the average professor of medieval history. He was aware of the markings on the north wall of the inn cum restaurant that he had recently bought. There was a lot more to the area than many people realised and as a history graduate he had an interest both professional and personal. Its very name, The Hand of God, was testament to the origins of the old building that now housed the most exciting adventure of his life. There was no doubt in his mind that the fourteenth century building he had taken so much care to modernise had associations with the Knights Templar. He was fully aware that just over the modern border into Herefordshire lay Garway Church. The Templars had been in the area since the twelfth century and had been given land by Henry II. On part of this land they had built Garway Church. Remarkably, the church still stands today and makes no secret of its Templar connection. The church was built with the characteristic Templar touch of a round nave, the remains of which can still be seen. And as if to emphasise the threat from across the Monnow there stands hard by a massive thirteenth century tower, believed to have been some sort of defence against the marauding Welsh. Williams had a mind full of these ancient groupings, grumblings and grudgings as he whitewashed the walls of The Hand of God. At the front of his mind remained the imminent arrival of Prideaux and Bones. Though they had been close for many years he was unhappy with the chaos that usually followed in their wake. As a double act they made Laurel and Hardy look sophisticated. If Bones and Prideaux came could chaos be far behind? He had more than one reason for wishing them elsewhere, a more compelling one for wanting them to be where he could see them. This last was something he dare not admit even to himself, no, especially to himself. It dated back to his youth and before Prideaux, Bones and Ginny had swum into his orbit. It was something that was bound to have consequences. Mostly he could bury it deep in his consciousness but lately he was aware that the nightmares were coming back. Mark Williams was not a man at peace with himself, neither was he in charge of his own fate, as would soon become clear.

Putting the finishing touches to his new business at least afforded him the sanctuary of committed physical work, which helped take his mind away from some of the concerns that were making him short of temper. Shortage of breath was surely preferable in the circumstances. And in any case the coming Saturday was to be the official opening night. Although familiar with the area he knew how hard it could be to get the locals onside. He was confident that what the inn could offer would catch the attention of the well heeled from all corners of Wales, as well as over the border and further afield. But it was a body of regular customers that would be the mainstay of the now fully restored inn with its small restaurant and half a dozen letting rooms. Williams had learned the best of lessons from staying in the area some years ago. More recently he had done his research before sinking a large part of the windfall into what could prove a difficult venture. It was clear that there was an appetite in the area for quality locally sourced food and that visitors would pay for top quality accommodation coupled with a serious wine list. Accordingly, he had targeted local businesses but with a wider trawl of more upmarket visitors, walkers, cyclists and the more controlled fishing and shooting parties. This was after all among the best shooting and fishing available in Britain. It made perfect sense to focus on what the landscape offered. Pheasants were here in abundance as well as mallard for the more adventurous. The Monnow provided top quality game fishing with trout and salmon on a private stretch of river, the rights to which had come along with the inn. Yet there remained a nagging doubt writhing just behind the Williams forehead. Sadly for him it was not solely the prospect of Laurel and Hardy pissing off his local custom if they contrived to arrive on his official opening night. Finishing his outdoor whitewashing he took a step back to admire his handiwork, which at least brought a half-hearted smile to his face. At least it looked good, nobody could say differently.

The rotten windows had been replaced in hardwood by a local craftsman and fitted the appearance of the front of the inn perfectly. The door, believed to be a fifteenth century addition, had been restored as closely as possible to its original glory. It was made of local oak and double the size of modern doors. It was suitably imposing. His whitewashing blitz had obliterated most of the masonic symbols from the front of the building. This was deliberate on his part. Some years earlier the popularity of Dan Brown's book had made the Knights Templar better known than they had ever been in their heyday. It was not his intention to attract seekers after the Templar legend. He was concerned that it would have consequences that could easily damage the business he was hoping to build. Such seekers would inevitably assume that the Holy Grail could easily be in the vicinity and the ensuing coach loads of aficionados would probably not sit that well next to his best payers, the shooters, fishers and walkers. His awareness of business principles surprised him. Rampant capitalism had been a target of his and of Ginny's when they were students at Oxford. But everything changes and never mind the past, for him the present was another country and it was Mark Williams who was doing things differently. Still, there was that one nagging doubt. The past still retains the ability to surprise. Just at that moment when youthful mistakes seem at their most distant they have the disturbing habit of popping up to bite you on the arse. He had seen it happen before. He had no wish to see it again. His own secret had been buried so deep for so long that he sometimes genuinely wondered whether it was something he had dreamed in the sweat of sleep. Yet every time he woke there it was, nagging at him still. Not even Ginny was party to this stomach churning awareness that he could be blindsided at any time, leaving all his dreams crumbled into dust. She must never know that the husband she loved and respected had once been a killer.

"Why the hell couldn't you hire a car with a sat nav, Piers, you prat?" Bones was becoming frustrated at the prospect of missing so much potential drinking time. This feeling was exacerbated by rumours he had heard of the presence of a free bar. He was also aware of Mark's predilection and, more importantly, expertise in both whisky and whiskey. What a combination; the original Welsh whisky, the newer Scotch whisky and a few bottles of Irish whiskey for good measure. Couple all that with the promise of accommodation with Mark and Ginny in the private area of The Hand of God and it was a heady cocktail that inspired the ageing aristocrat to encourage his more careful companion to greater speed, and preferably in the right direction. Neither man had given a single thought to the persistence Mark had shown in persuading the pair to come along to the new venture. Mark was never the most enthusiastic of men.

There was no doubt that he was keen to get both Bones and Prideaux along. This uncharacteristic behaviour on Mark's part did not register, as both men were desperate to get away for a break.

It was the particular Saturday reserved for the official opening of the inn that Ginny and Mark Williams had worked so hard to establish. They had been open for several weeks to test the water and the signs were very positive. Bookings were coming in from shooting parties and a few fishing friends. The newly employed chef may have been young, but he came with impeccable references from a little further east in the county that, these days, was blessed with a plethora of quality places to eat. A couple of good reviews in the regional country magazines had helped to put a gloss on things and bookings were beginning to look very healthy. All this was known to William Radleigh de Beaune and was indeed festering in his mind as he was driven sedately along the B4521 towards an appointment with a whisky bottle or two. Not that Bones would have minded if it was Scotch, Irish or indeed Bourbon on offer. The amber liquid, as he never referred to it, had rarely failed to put the old boy into tip top form. Prideaux's driving, however, was becoming a bone of contention between the two.

"Hold on, Bonesie, we're nearly there. I'm sure that we are on the right road now. Sorry about the little detour but it's quite a while since I've been this way. Look, it's only six, we can be there by seven. Only I haven't driven for ages mainly because I don't have a licence. I lost it years ago and haven't got around to renewing it."

"That is just perfect," grumbled Bones. "Not only are we going at a speed that would shame the driver of a hearse but at any time we could be pulled over by the polis and end up in chokey. You haven't pinched the blessed thing, have you? Only frankly these days I'd put nothing past you. Here we are with all prospects pleasing and the opportunity of a free stay in a gourmet pub with, presumably, streams of whisky that will sharpen the sinews and loosen the bones, well, this Bones anyway. It is not an opportunity to be taken lightly but grasped firmly with both hands. At last we can forget about Slope, Bennett, the Spriggans and that sarcastic bastard Cornelius, who by the way is supposed to be on our side, and relax for a few days. It's all gone very quiet. Could be the calm before the storm perhaps, you never know. Wouldn't it be great if the blighters had knocked each other off? Save the state a job. I'd be as happy as Larry if that were the case. Put your foot down and we'll take our chances but for God's sake do not antagonise the local gendarmes or all will be lost."

"I am sad that you should think I could be irresponsible enough to steal a car, Bonesie. The fact is I borrowed it from my cousin who just happens to be a police officer. He is in fact a Chief Inspector in the Oxford force. He has told me what I should say if we do get stopped by the local plods. Apparently, it's some sort of Masonic thing. If I get it right then we will go on our way as if nothing had happened. Much like the iceberg in that contretemps with the Titanic. If not then the consequences could be dire and you will need to accept that the streams of whiskey will be flowing without your loving attention and not in your direction. Life can be a right bastard on occasions, can't it?"

The two by this time had established an easy peace. Prideaux's smile widened as he began to recognise some of the villages and hamlets they were passing through en route to their reunion with Mark and Ginny. They were approaching the village of Skenfrith before Prideaux's confidence reached its acme.

"This is it. Left here, down the lane and there it is." He screeched to a halt; a difficult thing to do when travelling quite so slowly, but impressive nonetheless.

"Not seven yet, Bonesie, and here we are. Seems a bit quiet though. Lights on in the bar but no cars around and no welcoming committee. Perhaps they don't come out to play until later in these country areas. Must make for a long evening in their humble cottages while they do their spinning and weaving for the local squire."

"Your socio-political analysis is as ropey as it ever was, Prideaux my old red. You would be hard pressed to find any peasants around here. If you come across any they will probably have been bussed in from the odd local farm that employs such people. They will also, probably as not, be local to Cracow or Warsaw rather than Hay, Cusop or Crickhowell. I think a few are sometimes employed too by heritage organisations, to add a little colour from bygone days. Most of the folk you will find living around these parts will already have made their pile in the city. They'll all be down here avoiding urban foxes, stress and strife and buying up the quaint cottages that the locals can't afford. It'll be more like Surrey, the posh bits that is, than anything else. They will all probably claim some form of descent from local families but it sure as hell won't be from the peasantry. I'm shocked and surprised that an old commie like you is not aware of the modern facts of life. Hey ho! Let us go then when the evening is spread out like a bloody blanket, let us go and pay our visit. And if you spot T S Eliot before I do tell him that the first round is on him."

As the two walked towards the beautifully restored front door a Range Rover typically covered with mud and manure rumbled past, on and up the lane that fronted The Hand of God. There was something that distracted Prideaux. There was something familiar about the driver but the agricultural covering was a fairly efficient screen and he couldn't be sure, but there was something. Could it be? Surely not. It couldn't be all the way out here in the wilds. Could it? His reverie was sharply interrupted by the impact of a small clod of earth, mostly mud, which splattered on the back of his neck.

"Come on Piers, you dilatory bastard. Do keep up. We're going in and if you look up you will see that we will be safe in The Hand of God. What could possibly go wrong? Let's consider wrapping ourselves around some obscure and enticing young ladies while we are at it. This place could well be paradise. Come on."

Prideaux meekly followed his friend through the great oak door and into a vestibule. Satisfyingly there was the distinctive aroma of the country hostelry swirling in the air as they entered. The smell of wood smoke, the wet smell of drying Barbours and the distant scent of drying dog. The floor was old, in fact very old, flagstones. This had been no mere updating job. It was quality work and the integrity of the original had been respected to such an extent that entering really was a step back in time. The only oddity was the silence.

"I don't like this, Piers," whispered Bones.

"Come on, Bonesie. This is right up your street. Shouldn't be surprised if you'll meet a relative or two. You aristos are all interbred, aren't you? An aristo home from home is this. What's not to like? Look, there's a cracking fire burning through there. That must be the bar. Let's go and see where Mark and Ginny have got to."

"There's something about this place. I don't know. It's an aura or something. I just don't feel comfortable. Just take it easy until we get our bearings. I have a bad feeling that I didn't have when we were outside. And don't make that sarcastic face at me. I'm not talking ghosts or spirits from the past or any of that guff. I just don't feel that I can relax."

"Well you had better make an effort, you old goat," chimed a voice from behind the bar as Mark stood up, smiling at the two men. "What the hell are you doing hiding down there, Mark? Where is everybody?" Prideaux regained his equanimity quickly though Bones remained seemingly disconcerted. "I was just checking glasses" said the smiling publican "and as for everybody, everybody and his wife and probably dog will be here in an hour. Don't worry, just walk through and let me pour you a drink."

That phrase galvanised the two who smartly walked through into a long bar that echoed the vestibule. It was all old wood within, with stone floors and a roaring log fire. It was much larger than it had appeared to Prideaux and Bones as they had entered the building.

"Good to see you again Mark, and I'm sure that goes for Bonesie too."

The handshakes were warm though there was some reticence on Mark's part. His original invitation had been warm and effusive. His manner now seemed a little distant. Both men were vaguely aware of the change. "Why don't you go and sit over by the fire and I'll bring you a bottle of the local whisky." The two men were happy to sit in front of a real log fire. The distressed leather sofa enveloped them both and they began to relax. Mark, as he had promised, brought over a bottle of single malt whisky and two crystal glasses. "Now you two sit there for a while and give me a chance to finish off the preparations for tonight. You should enjoy that whisky. It is a new release from the distillery. I think it's one of the best whiskies I have tasted for some time. I'll be back in a tick."

"Shall I be mother?" joked Bones, who had needed no prompting and had already poured himself a generous four fingers of Mark's recommended tipple. "Piers, Piers", he repeated as his friend continued to stare gloomily into the fire. "Come on Piers, what the hell is wrong with you? Here we are sitting on a sofa in front of a log fire drinking an exceptionally smooth whisky from crystal glasses. Better still the whisky is a newly released single malt and there is a party on its way to this very spot. How could life be any better?" Prideaux grabbed the bottle and filled his glass to the brim. He coughed. This was no way to treat a whisky. Bones was appalled with his friend. He also suspected that something was troubling him. They had been friends for too long for him to miss that. It was just for the life of him he could not admit what could possibly be wrong.

Piers, however, had his serious head on. "There's something wrong, I'm sure of it. I've known Mark for years. He is hiding something and I am prepared to bet that it is something serious. You know how he kept pushing for us to come along here. Now that we're here, he's not his usual self. You can see in his face that he's miles away. It doesn't make any sense. If he was so keen for us to come then why isn't he all over us now that we've made the effort? Anyway you were the one who was uncomfortable as we came in."

"That, my 'Beamish boy', was before I spotted this fine and dandy looking bottle of top class malt with the top off. If malt should thus present itself then how can ecstasy be far behind? I expect he's nervous about the new venture. Look around. They didn't get this lot for peanuts. They must have invested a serious bundle in the old place. He's probably terrified that it might not take off. These country sorts can be very unpredictable, you know. What if the local serfs and their masters don't turn out regularly enough to sustain such an upmarket hostelry? We're still struggling with austerity you know, which makes this a hell of a gamble.

"Look, Bonesie, I know that you were uncomfortable, and that is not something I associate with you and your cavalier approach to life. Please do me the favour of taking my concerns seriously. Mark is looking very shifty and that is not his style. Distant, yes, but he's hiding something, I'm certain of that. There is no sign of Ginny and that is not her style either. She knew we were coming and I was expecting her to be at the front door to welcome us. She wouldn't have been able to resist the opportunity to swank about in the sort of pub that you or I would kill to own. So what on earth is going on?"

"Pour me a decent glass of that malt, I'll be over in a second," shouted Mark who was still busying himself at the bar. "Just a few more things to sort out and I can take a break before the deluge."

"Right, this is our chance," said Prideaux to a Bones who was already beginning to list a little to starboard. The effects of good whisky and a ripsnorter of a log fire were beginning to show themselves "If he's coming over to sit with us we have a chance of finding out where Ginny is and what the hell is going on. If we can persuade him to help us finish this bottle then we can also persuade him to be straight with us. I don't see any evidence of people or traffic or anything much else in the area. He said the place would be jumping by eight. Unless half the population of Crickhowell are on the way in a fleet of charabancs, which all seems a bit unlikely to me, then something is seriously wrong. And in case you haven't noticed we are in the middle of nowhere. Apart from a ruined Norman castle, a church and a few houses there is nothing around here for miles."

Thirty minutes later and two old friends still sat in front of the log fire in the bar of The Hand of God. The fire that had burned so brightly was choked with ash. The whisky bottle was empty. There was no sign of Mark. A stranger observing the scene of two old friends who had imbibed just that bit too much would have probably given a rueful smile, recalling similar excesses. That would have been the case without looking too closely at the two. The general state of the two, slumped against each other on the leather sofa, was due to more than the effects of good whisky and too much heat. Both men were pale and completely unconscious.

The bottle had contained more than malt whisky. Prideaux and Bones had been drugged and they had been drugged by a potion perfected by experts over several centuries. It would be a long time before either of them saw daylight, much less recognised it, again. It was midnight. The bar was as deserted as when they first walked in. More so as there was no sign of the throng of revellers predicted to be celebrating the pub's official opening. The lights were out and the front doors locked. There was no sign either of their erstwhile friend Mark Williams. He was, at the moment the clock struck twelve, making his way to the shepherd's hut hard by the church at Garway, just over the border into Herefordshire. He had the gait of a beaten man. His shoulders were slumped and he kept trying to persuade himself that there was nothing else he could have done. If he cooperated there was just the wildest chance that he might see Ginny alive. He choked back a sob as he approached the hut. Two of his best friends could be dead by now. He had administered the final coup de grace. He had been given the colourless, odourless potion and told that if he slipped the Mickey Finn to the two then it would simply knock them out so that they could be dealt with when time allowed. He had persuaded himself that this was true. Yet in his heart he knew that in this area, a place that had remained a law unto itself for centuries, it was highly unlikely that he had been told the truth. There were plenty of people living in the woods who could conjure up potions made from herbs and wildflowers that could go undetected, especially if the victims were not discovered for several hours. He knew that his own chances of staying alive were slim. They no longer needed him. It would be the work of moments to render him unconscious and deposit him in the swift flowing

Monnow. He didn't really care that much. If they had already murdered Ginny then he wasn't sure whether he cared to live in any case. Mark grabbed the rusting handle and pulled open the metal door that made the hut secure. It opened without a sound. As he stooped to walk in his foot caught something and he fell headlong into the hut. It seemed to take an age for his eyes to adjust to the single paraffin light that glimmered in the corner of the hut. As his sight cleared he shook his head. It couldn't be, but it was. Ginny stared down at him with a smile on her lips. Either side of her stood two men he knew well.

The twins laughed as one. "You took your time, Mark. If I were you I'd get up, there's a lot of shit on that floor. Including the foot belonging to the leg of that Spriggan corpse that you just tripped over. Careful, there's another one lying just next to your other foot. Couple more outside too. Sadly Slope and Bennett got away before the cavalry arrived. Come on man. You can see Ginny's OK. You didn't think we'd let those bastards hurt her, did you? We knew that mobile phones don't work at all in this area so we've been on watch in the woods for days, waiting. We expected something but weren't sure what. Give her a hug and let's get back to the pub before anyone else realises that Prideaux and Bonesie are fast asleep. We'll tell you all about it on the way. The boys will have the mother and father of all headaches, but they are both pretty well used to that." As he spoke he lifted one of the corpses as if it were a dead lamb. "I've put in a radio call for a clean up gang. They'll be here in no time. When they've finished there'll be no trace of any bodies and nobody will know they've ever been here. I'd just as soon pop these ex Spriggans in the river just before we reach the bridge near the pub. But to be fair, there are too many of them for that. Just another few of Slope's misguided soldiers. Nobody will miss them, and don't worry, they didn't lay a hand on Ginny. Well one did and that was the last time he laid a hand on anyone. Poor bastard never knew what hit him. Ginny was very brave."

Robert and Bob smiled approvingly at them both and led them out in the dark towards the parked Land Rover. The nameless corpses were piled up like so many dead sheep after a winter storm.

36

What lies beneath

The pub remained in darkness, and as the party pulled up outside the front entrance it was clear through the large front window that Bones and Prideaux were where the drink and its special additives had left them, snoring on the sofa. Of the group it was Mark who was most uncomfortable. Ginny appeared relieved more than anything else, and the twins were seemingly untouched by the fact that one or both of them had so recently had a hand in killing a gathering of Spriggans. Mark, however, had some explaining to do. He had administered whatever the substance was that had been supplied to him and had done so in the full knowledge that it could prove dangerous to those who had drunk quite so much whisky. He was also in the company of men who killed without compunction. It was not a very cheerful position to be in. The saving grace, if there was to be one, was that he had done it out of love for Ginny as he genuinely saw no other option. She might accept that, but whether the others would was extremely doubtful. Still, there was nothing for it. The twins knew the situation, and once they woke up so would Bones and Prideaux. It crossed his mind to make a run for it. It was useless though. He could never outrun the twins. His only hope was to count on Ginny standing up for him. She was certainly her own woman; would his attempt at saving her would be sufficient excuse to get him off the hook? They had been together a long time but there were things in his past that she neither knew nor did he care for her to know.

"Come on Mark. Get that bloody door open. I could

murder a pint," chorused the twins. It sounded hollow and a little threatening, coming from two men whom he had so recently witnessed joking as they piled the bodies of the men they had killed earlier into a heap. Perhaps this was it. He had always known that his membership of the Spriggans could come back to haunt him.

Over the years he had pushed that knowledge, like a lot of mistakes, way back into the recesses of conscious thought. Like everyone, he had made mistakes as a young man. Mostly they hadn't mattered. The Catholics had forgiven that pope who had once belonged to the Hitler Youth, hadn't they? People forgot in time and it wasn't as if he was in a position to be of use to those who sought to overthrow the status quo. It was just that, in his youth, some form of rebellion against the massed ranks of the bourgeoisie was regarded as a cool position to take. The Spriggans were not taken seriously at the time but had just a sufficient edge to them to impress the trendy left. He should have been warned by the fate of one of his acquaintances who had made the mistake of joining a hard line political grouping calling themselves 'atomic Trotskyites'. He thought it made him look a man to be reckoned with. So it did, until it came home to his fairly muddled intellect that their major policy, of fomenting atomic war between America and the Soviet Union in order to build socialism from what was left, was a fundamentally flawed concept. Not only had he left the organisation but made the mistake of publically burning his membership card. When Williams saw him months later he walked with a stick. A year later he read that he had been found hanged in a sleazy Earl's Court bedsit. Some organisations never forgive. It is not the Mafia alone that operate entrance only policies. As the song has it, "you can check out any time you want, but you can never leave". He was currently living at The Hand of God but for him it might just as well have been the Hotel California.

His hands were cold as he fumbled with the keys. He didn't know whether it was the cold or the fear that made his hands shake so much. If he was trying to put on a brave face he was not making much of a fist of it. He felt himself losing contact with the ground as the keys left his grasp. It was Robert this time. "Give me the bloody keys, Mark. We haven't got all bloody night. I could do with a pint. It feels as if my throat's been cut." More panic as Robert held him in the air with one hand, operating the keys with the other. He dropped him just over the threshold. "In some cultures that means we are married now," he giggled, and the attempt at humour swept right past Mark and into the night sky. "Come on you lot," shouted Ginny as she hurried into the bar. "Let's wake these two sleeping beauties before it's too late." The snores coming from the sofa were window rattlers of the first order. These were two very soundly asleep individuals. Ginny's solution was typically forthright. Filling a bucket from the kitchen she threw the contents over both Prideaux and Bones. "Come on you silly buggers. Shift yourselves. There's work to be done. I'm not having piss heads lying about making my bar look untidy. The sun will be up before you two." She had taken the precaution of placing a bucket on the sofa between the two. Next to each man was one of her 'liveners'. Nobody knew for sure what she put in this drink. It looked as if it had tomato juice in it and obviously some spirit but it smelled to high heaven. Short of saying that it was designed to revive corpses she would only claim it as an old family recipe left to her by her Uncle Vlad, who had lived somewhere in Transylvania and had a penchant for sleeping in a coffin.

The results on two apparent corpses involved a good deal of spluttering, and, having managed to get half the contents of their respective glasses somewhere near their mouths, some very clever synchronised projectile vomiting. Throwing the pair a towel each she barked, "Now get to your rooms, clean yourselves up and get back down here quick smart. The coffee is already on and when you have consumed sufficient unto the hour we all need to have a bit of a chat. This last remark was delivered with a sideways glance at Mark, who was looking as sheepish as possible and in total awe of his wife. He had always known that she was feisty but she appeared to have taken charge of this whole business. It was probably just that she was on home ground, or perhaps she was just feeling reassured that she was safely out of the orbit of the Spriggans, for the time being anyway. Either way she did not have the demeanour of a damsel who had very recently been in distress. She had instead a confident air that surprised him, given the circumstances. The twins sat at the bar helping themselves to bottles of expensive lager as if they had just arrived at the start of a night out. Bones and Prideaux had carried out her bidding and were both now alternately sluicing and vomiting in their rooms, but were both reasonably happy to be back in the land of the living even if they were unaware of how close they had been to leaving it forever, or at least until the last trump. This could be one of the trickiest situations Mark had faced in a while.

A weak sun, doing its level best to illuminate the bar, announced to the assembled group that dawn was thinking about breaking. Bones and Prideaux sat together on stools at the bar. The twins were standing behind them, taking turns to ensure that Bones was returned to an upright position when he had leaned too far either to the right or left. Prideaux looked to be in reasonable condition considering what he had put his liver and associated other quite important organs through the previous evening. Neither man was saying much but concentrating strongly on just what the hell was going on and, equally important, what it was that had laid them so low the previous evening that a quiet death might be the preference if they had any say in the matter. They didn't. Ginny didn't.

She did, however, anticipate what was on the minds of both men.

"You were doped, boys, but only a bit. Please don't blame Mark too much. He did what he did out of love for me. And I'm prepared to forgive most things for love and the first one of you who sniggers at that small romanticism should be aware that, having been within spitting distance of death very recently, I am not in the mood to be trifled with. Don't even think about it." The twins seemed well aware of their position in the scheme of things and allowed Ginny the floor. "Mark, I know that you were a member of The Spriggans when you were too young to know which way was up. It was long before we met. I knew that at some time we would have to deal with the consequences and a week ago the problem raised its ugly head. Well, his ugly head actually. I recognised that clown who came into the bar with the shooting party. I couldn't put a name to him, but I was sure I knew the face. Everything suggested he was here on a recce. I know it's years since college but I've never forgotten the demos and the way the Front used to try and infiltrate our meetings. They were rarely successful. They always had a smell about them and I was pretty good at sniffing them out. He thought he had struck gold when you had to leave around one to get back to the house up near Crickhowell because the alarm had gone off. His pals were so pissed they were all in bed half an hour after you left. He stayed at the bar. I stayed with him rather than closing. I noticed that he was hardly drinking at all and around two I suggested he climb the wooden hill so that I could clean up. That's when his mood turned. To be honest my biggest problem was trying not to laugh

319

at him. He pulled a small pistol that might have been a replica. Initially I thought I might be able take it off him and see him off. I wasn't that confident though. In the end I had no choice but to go with him. I thought I'd just let him take me off and overdo the frightened woman pose, although it was more than a pose if I'm honest. All the while I was praying that someone would see us and wonder what was going on. I'd have settled for a poacher, and God knows there's enough of them in the woods on any night.

"When we got near the old shepherd's hut I realised I was in a whole mess of trouble. There was a real gathering of Spriggans there. They were obviously foot soldiers, nasty bastards and pretty pissed. I couldn't see a way out. I'd have tried to phone for help but up there in the woods you can't even text. I was a bit resigned to suffering a lot before the inevitable end. The hut wasn't big enough for them all to get in so three of them dragged me inside. It was clear what their intentions were. They grabbed me and two of them tried to hold me as the bastard from the pub tried to rip my clothes off. He ripped my blouse before I managed to stick my fingers in both his eyes. He screamed like a baby. I really meant it. I knew what was coming so I fought like a wild cat. Managed to get as far as the door of the hut. As soon as I stepped outside I was grabbed by another of the bastards and they formed a ring around me. It was horrible. They were grabbing at my clothes and yelling what they were going to do to me. Two of the biggest ones held me so that I couldn't move. Their hands were all over me and they were getting louder and louder. I could hear a four by four revving up in the darkness. A Land Rover covered in mud swung around the corner of the stand of beech trees and skidded to a halt. Two people got out. It was Slope and Bennett. The silence was palpable when they walked over towards me. The men holding me tightened their grip but none of them made a sound. Slope walked up to me with Bennett just behind. 'So here we have the very lovely Ginny Williams.' He grabbed my chin and twisted my head so that he could look right into my eyes. I could smell his stinking breath. I managed to spit in his face. He didn't say anything, just wiped the spittle off with the back of his hand. Then he did say something that made my blood run cold. "Feisty little bitch I see. Well we have a situation here. Do I leave you with my men, in which case you will undoubtedly be gang raped? Or perhaps Elizabeth here might try another Lola Cutler job on you. What do you think, Liz?"

"She looked at me and began to lick her lips. I don't think I've ever seen a more evil look on a woman's face in my life. I had no idea what a Lola Cutler job was but I was certain it wasn't something I'd appreciate very much. I thought, 'Well you've done your best. Whatever happens next at least you tried.' What happened next was the cavalry arriving. In fact it was more the 7th cavalry on speed. There was the sound of an engine screaming and something flew out of the darkness. The main group of Spriggans scattered as a Jeep headed straight for the shed. I was thrown to the floor. I looked up to see the Jeep smash into the hut. The hut seemed to implode with four of the Spriggans inside. They didn't know what hit them. The Jeep reversed at speed knocking over a couple more Spriggans. Then out jumped the Job twins. I'd heard what they were capable of but I'd never seen anything quite like it. It was men against boys for sure. They just charged the main group without a sound. There were bodies dropping like so many autumn leaves. The only sound apart from the occasional scream was that of skulls being fractured and limbs being snapped. They must have laid out half a dozen of them in a couple of minutes. It was terrifying. They were smiling all the time. The only time they stopped was when they realised that Slope and Bennett had managed to get back into their Land Rover with two of the lightly injured Spriggans and hare off through the woods back down to the main road. They strolled over to me to make sure I was all right as if they had just been out for a night-time stroll in the woods. I'm glad they are on my side."

Ginny's explanation of the twins' intervention brought weak smiles from the two sufferers followed by rather half-hearted attempts at enthusiastic expressions of gratitude. It was a touching scene and one played out in total ignorance of what was currently taking place literally below their feet.

The Hand of God was a fourteenth century tavern built at around the same time as Skenfrith Castle and the Templar church at Garway. The three buildings, all of them built for specific purposes, had one thing in common; they were built to maintain Norman control of one of the most lawless areas of Britain. There was a Norman castle built of earth and timber, on the site of the current remains of the later castle, sometime in the 1160s. A written reference to this includes the two other castles, Grosmont and The White Castle, that complete the powerful triangle of Norman buildings in the area. Obviously major features in the military conquest of the land of Gwent, the castles, initially military buildings, became political sites of domination. These Norman castles dominated an area that was almost wholly Welsh. Something else was needed if any form of control was to work. The village church was constructed around the same time to cater for the spiritual needs of the now occupied area. And to balance this The Hand of God was built to cater for the baser instincts of the local population. History has a way of rearing its head in unpleasant ways. Those who are aware of that history are able to turn long forgotten features to their own purposes. Given the hatred of the incoming Normans that existed in these places, stout defences were essential to the invaders, simply for staying alive. The later stone castles were masterpieces of that combination of defence and intimidation that the Normans were so adept at. The castles inspired fear and awe in equal measure and basic Norman cruelty ensured everyday submission at least. The original motte and bailey castles built of earth and wood, with wooden buildings inside a protective palisade, gradually gave way to the stone monsters that are a major feature of the Welsh countryside in the present day. One other thing that the Normans were skilled at was something often ignored in historical reckoning, and that was the skill and art of tunnelling. Though by nature a warlike breed, being the descendants of Scandinavian pirates who had terrified Britain for years, they were savvy enough to know that it was more than possible to set fire to wooden buildings. As a consequence they realised that there really would be nowhere to run once castle walls had been destroyed by fire. The solution was to go underground. Norman armies had always employed engineers, initially in an offensive capacity. If you couldn't go over or through the enemy's defence you could surely go under. Teams of skilled engineers could tunnel through metres of ground in remarkably short order. It is not recorded who was the first to become aware of the possibilities of using these skills in a defensive capacity, but it was something embraced with great enthusiasm at around the time that stone castles began to replace the original wooden ones. Every castle, as it was improved, employed a team of engineers to fashion escape tunnels as a last resort.

The use of tunnels to avoid capture and detection has a long history, particularly in areas with a reputation for independence and only a loose acceptance of prevailing laws, particularly Wales and Cornwall. There is a long history in both these countries of using tunnels to avoid paying duty on imported goods. Smugglers in both places made good use of tunnels to evade the Revenue men. The Normans quickly adopted the tunnel as the ultimate defence system. With skilful engineers at work these tunnels could run for many miles. They were also built to last, and if you know where to look there are plenty of examples still in good order today. Like the Celts, the Normans used these defensive works to link buildings. In this particular spot the initial defensive tunnel ran from Skenfrith Castle to The Hand of God and thence to the Templar Church at Garway. Those who knew of this network of tunnels had a ready made means of moving unseen around the countryside. One such was Sebastian Slope, a man with unlimited access to the Spriggan archives. He also knew that in this part of the world the Spriggans, far from being the enemies of the Templar Knights, had made alliance with them, sharing their secrets, including the big secret of the subterranean network that still existed beneath the Welsh countryside.

As Ginny continued with her explanations to the group assembled in The Hand of God, Slope was entering the tunnel system through the defensive round tower that stood hard by Garway Church. He was not alone. He was accompanied by two Spriggans who had escaped the wrath of the twins in the battle in the woods. The Job twins were not going to interfere with his plans for Prideaux and company. The group were armed to the teeth. They had been in the Garway for long enough to trace and excavate the arms cache that the Spriggan system ensured would be available near any ancient Spriggan settlement. Just another card that Slope kept up his sleeve for the day of reckoning.

Defence was the last thing on Slope's mind as he switched on the powerful torch he carried. He knew the tunnels had all been built to a strict pattern. Once that pattern was fixed in your mind it would be possible to make your way from one place to another without a torch if you needed to. Accompanying him as he set out along the Garway tunnel heading for The Hand of God were the ever present Bennett together with the two Spriggans from the woods. In a way these two were now captives of their own side. Any Spriggan not quick enough to escape the twins was either dead or had given up the fight. They had been given a small glance at hell and were more afraid of the terrible twins than Slope himself. No help was forthcoming from that quarter. Whatever Slope did next he would need to do it with his current companions. He had no way of contacting reinforcements and in any case word of the rumble in the woods would spread like wildfire. Nobody would be hurrying to queue up to help Slope after that little exhibition.

Silently the group passed the subterranean border between England and Wales. This was to be Slope's concerted attempt at completing his revenge on Prideaux. Any of his friends or acquaintances unlucky enough to be present, particularly the Jobs, would be invited to share his fate. Slope was nothing if not even handed. Why destroy one life when multiple murders would provide an even greater frisson. Psychiatrists would have had a field day with Slope who, had he chosen that particular route, would have outperformed any serial killer whether real or fictional. It is not that common to find real evil and intelligence bound up in a single package. The fault line in Slope's personality was simple; he found murder enjoyable. If he could turn the process into an intellectual exercise then so much the better.

The original engineers who had built the tunnels in this area knew the game. They had made the footways as flat as possible with run offs and gutters to ensure the worst of the dripping groundwater had somewhere to run off. The roof was built on the old Norman principle that ensured a stable roofing system that could, and did, more than stand the test of time. Because of all this now long forgotten expertise, winding the three miles under the ground was little more than a country stroll. Slope and his two pet thugs arrived underneath The Hand of God in short order, hardly out of breath and only slightly damp. For a moment, as they stood under the access point that led to the stairs behind the ancient door that would allow access to the cellar of the pub, a fleeting thought of murdering the pair crossed Slope's mind. They were of use to nobody really and he had only brought them along as cannon fodder, but already the pair had irritated him beyond measure. An irritated Slope was a dangerous Slope and murder was on his mind. What stopped him simply slaughtering the pair like cattle was his proximity to his target. Only very few senior Spriggans would know of the existence of the door they were now approaching, and most of them would have paid with their lives for that knowledge. This was just the way Norman engineers would have been put to death, once their task was over, to ensure that their expertise did not pass into the wrong hands. There was a palpable sense of history repeating itself in the air. Even if someone had been lucky enough to discover a record of the door's existence, looking for it from inside the cellar would not have helped them. From inside it formed part of the cellar wall, and it was not possible to open it from the inside in any case as there was no handle, or lock. It was another clever piece of Norman craft work. It meant that it would always be possible to access The Hand of God from the tunnel without the pub's inhabitants having any idea that they were under threat. "There's the lever. Grab hold of it and force it to your right."

The instructions were directed by Slope at the slimmer of the two piecework thugs. He did as he was told. After much sweating, swearing and an ominous creaking noise from the ancient handle, there was some movement. "Go on you lazy bastard, put your idle back into it," Slope snarled. "It's coming, it's coming," grunted the thin one. Having seemed to be welded shut the lever suddenly gave. It was so unexpected that the thin man ended up on the floor of the tunnel whimpering that he had twisted his ankle. "I'll twist your stupid neck for you if you don't stop whining," snarled Slope. "Sound travels in a tunnel, you bloody moron," he continued. "For fuck's sake," continued Slope. "One just cannot get the staff. Now get up off your knees and start pushing. We need to get that thing open a bit swiftly before somebody in Abergavenny hears you wailing and gnashing whatever teeth you have left. Believe me, if you have alerted those I wish to surprise you'll be a toothless grinning farm boy before I've finished with you."

The fear on the thin man's face was palpable. He had not signed up for this. Approached in a Hereford pub by a Spriggan recruiter he had thought that fifty pounds, membership of the Spriggans and the promise of all the spirits he could steal from the pub cellar was enough to persuade him to sign up for the deal. This wasn't the plan at all. He still had the horrible image ingrained onto his retina of a muddy Jeep parked on top of his good drinking buddy, Dan Enright, which was bloody ironic when he came to think about it. Old Dan made his living lying under cars as a mechanic, now he was lying under one for bloody eternity. And it looked as if that was not the end of it. All of a sudden he felt that he was trapped in a tunnel with a madman. His misfortune was exactly that. Sometimes it is simply not your day.

"Come on then. Get the bloody door open so we can get inside and get started." The thin man put his shoulder against the door and it began to give, emitting a loud creaking noise. It gave enough room for him to slide in through the narrow opening he had managed to establish. "Just fucking ideal," mouthed Slope as the man gave an exhausted sigh and noisily sank to the floor inside the cellar. "What's the use of that, you clown? That gap is wide enough for a string bean like you to get through, but how about me and Fat Boy Slim out here?" As he said that he became vaguely conscious of a metallic sound much further down the tunnel. It could have been anything but it served to galvanise him into more direct action. "Come on farm boy," he directed the fat man. "Get it open and get through it now." This was a definite order. It was barked as if the man was on the parade ground again and he didn't care for it much. There wasn't much choice though, so he set to widening the gap, something he was able to do by using his not inconsiderable bulk. As soon as the gap was wide enough he followed instructions and stepped through to join his compatriot in the cellar. As he did so he heard a grinding sound as everything went black. The fat man never knew what hit him. Slope heard the impact and the thump of a senseless body hitting the ground. This was swiftly followed by the whimpering of the thin man, sounding like a frightened animal, from behind the heavy door.

"I am a bloody genius. I got it right again," he congratulated himself. "Admirable Norman planning. I guessed that there would be a murder hole just inside the door and given, that the century for guards is long gone, I was pretty sure they'd have rigged up a lovely system of delivering a large chunk of limestone via a tripwire to catch the second man in." This is what the Normans had done. It was a sort of murder one, get one free offer. Typical Norman efficiency combined with an unrivalled gift for savagery. The thin man, however, was not dead but sat on the cellar floor, just inside the cellar door, moaning.

"Shut up you cowardly bastard, will you?" hissed Slope to the hired thug who was in the first stages of shock, having witnessed his companion in agonies on the floor of the cellar. There was no answer. Slope forced his way inside to view the carnage. The thin man was past taking orders from anyone and simply sat staring at what was left of the fat man's face. "Want a fucking job doing, you might as well do it yourself" muttered Slope, drawing a killing knife from his belt. Then he hesitated. Replacing the knife in his belt he turned to Liz Bennett, who had a strange smile on her face. "Sorry. What am I thinking? How rude of me. Of course, ladies first, after you with the final blow."

He bowed low in the direction of Bennett whose eyes already glistened with blood lust. Drawing her own killing knife she finished the job a Norman tactician had started centuries earlier. Turning to the remaining thug Slope pinned him to the cellar wall with his hand on his throat and his own killing knife held against his ear. "Listen to me, you low life. Your friend was careless and paid the price. All my lady friend did was to put him out of his misery. Now if you would prefer that I allow you to live out what's left of your pathetic little life, in one piece rather than several, then pull yourself together now or I will kill you." As he finished his threat he thought he heard another distant noise. Again it could have been the ground settling, it might have been an animal, it could have been water dropping. He would not allow himself to believe that he, the hunter, could be becoming the hunted. If anyone knew he was in the area that is all they would know. It was impossible that anyone outside the organisation could know about this tunnel. Distant noises can confuse and disorientate but he was taking no chances. He was so close to his goal that he could taste it. A few more hours then his revenge would be complete. Nothing was going to stop him now.

His movements became more urgent. Through a series of gestures he instructed the thin man and Bennett to assist him in closing the door they had so recently forced open. As they pushed it shut they piled up barrels of beer hard against it so that, in the unlikely event that they had been followed, there would be plenty of audible warning of anyone intent at raining on his parade.

37

Down on the killing floor

Vertically mere metres away from underground murder, Prideaux and friends sat around the log fire in the bar of The Hand of God. Blissfully unaware of what was unfolding in the place beneath, they were gradually attempting to form some plan of action that would bring a solution to the continuing cold war that was blighting their lives. They could be fairly certain that Slope was somewhere close. Just how close this most intractable of enemies was they had no idea. As usual with this group of friends there were plenty of suggestions, though very few of them practical.

"There is a tide in the affairs of men, which, taken at the flood, leads on to fortune," Bones began.

"For the love of God, Bonesie, whatever you may think, we are not in a play here. Even if we were it would not be one of Shakespeare's. If anything it is more a Greek tragedy, but sadly it is what passes for real life," was Prideaux's response.

Bones looked hurt at his friend's riposte. "There's no need to get all teasy, Piers. If that bastard and his minions are not somewhere in the area and planning mayhem and destruction then I'll eat my foot, sock and all. And we sit here with enough assembled brain power to light several light bulbs. It is bloody simple. Either we entrench here and wait for some form of attack or we actively seek out the villain Slope and eradicate the loathsome bastard and all his works. I don't think my nerves will stand any more jumping at shadows."

"We're all in the same boat here, Bonesie," said Prideaux in an attempt to mollify his oldest friend. "We can't just go running around the countryside in search of Slope with any expectation of success. And if we find him, what then? He is most unlikely to be alone or unarmed or even unprepared. He will know where we are but we could spend months searching and find nothing. Now I know we have the twins here if things should turn ugly, and they have recently bested the bugger in his den and foiled his attempt on poor Ginny's life and modesty. He won't take too kindly to that, is my guess, and the last time I looked we were not exactly bristling with weaponry." Piers cast a quizzical eye at the Job twins who both shook their heads, "My vote is that we make an attempt at contacting someone in the ministry and getting some serious cavalry to turn up while we circle the wagons."

"Brilliant suggestion, Piers," Mark joined the conversation with a serious look that foretold some bad news on its weary way. "I don't want to worry anyone, especially Bonesie, but contacting anyone outside this pub is likely to prove difficult. I was conscious that the phone hadn't rung recently, which is never the case. Given the delicate situation in which we seem to find ourselves I thought I'd ring my wine supplier in Abergavenny to make sure there was no problem with the landline. I'm sorry to say that the phone is dead. Now before you technophiles bother reaching for your mobile anythings I'll just remind you that there is no signal in this part of the valley. It is one of the reasons people come here to stay. It is genuinely a place where one can forget that the twenty first century exists and, though a jolly good idea for a holiday, probably not such a good one when the big bad wolf is sniffing around somewhere in the countryside. Now I know my film genres. If we were in a cowboy film we could send a brave soul to try and outrun the Apache. He would be a brave pincushion in a trice and we would have one fewer defender for the old homestead. If we were in one of those stately home detective films someone would volunteer to go and get help. They would get as far as their car before resurfacing with a broken neck floating in the Monnow. The phone is out; it happens. Why don't we just have a drink and relax until the morning when, with luck, we will be reconnected by good old British Telecom. Then we can ring whoever and if we still feel threatened we can all pile into the cars parked where we can see them, I've checked they are all still in the car park, and drive to wherever we choose. Doesn't that sound a more grown up response to whatever ghoulies and ghosties may be haunting our nightmares? If you need any incentive I have rather conveniently remembered that I just happen to have half a dozen bottles of '82 Petrus in the cellar that I have been saving for a special occasion."

The chorus of 'that gets my vote' rang in Mark's ears as he headed through the bar and towards the door leading down to the cellar. Sometimes democracy is the only way, he thought, as he unlocked the cellar door and began to descend some fairly ancient and rickety wooden steps. In the way of such ancient buildings the cellar light was at the bottom of the flight of steps. There was the usual pantomime of groping for the light switch, accompanied by a welter of curses at his own indolence in not getting round to fitting a two way switch, when the cellar was suddenly flooded with light. Simultaneously Mark felt a strong arm encircle his neck and begin to cut off his oxygen supply. He struggled both to release the arm and to focus in the bright light of the cellar. Gradually he was able to make out two blurred figures in front of him, both observing him with complete indifference. In such circumstances orientation can take a while. Mark wondered whether he would lose consciousness before he realised just what the hell was happening to him. "Welcome to your own personal hell, Mark."

The voice was unmistakeable, as was the rasping feel of a touch of pigskin. The combination of touch and voice left Mark in no doubt of the seriousness of his situation. Slope had always prided himself on his voice. He felt it carried authority and had the timbre of a classical actor. Mark had no illusions as to what now awaited him. He had briefly flirted with the Spriggans before leaving, and to Slope that very act would amount to traitorous betrayal. His more recent efforts at repairing the rift by acting as an informer would cut little ice with Slope.

"Now Mark, you already know who I am and you know that technically you are already a dead man squirming. Since I recognise that you are also a man of some taste, I have examined your cellar, I must compliment you. Why on earth you have been wasting such good wine on the hayseeds who must be the only inhabitants of this god forsaken backwater is a mystery to me. As a small reward, since as you know I despise most human beings, I shall allow you to choose the manner of your death. If you struggle I'll simply slit your throat. Stand still while my accomplice secures your hands and I shall present you with a painless death." Mark was no hero and his fate seemed decided. Shouting was pointless. He knew what Slope was capable of and he was aware that he would be delighted to sever his windpipe at the slightest sign of fight or flight. He stood still and defeated as Bennett secured his hands with cable ties.

"Good boy, Mark," his tormentor whispered with evident enjoyment. Just tell me who is up in the bar, tell me where they are, whether they are armed and then we'll just pop up and have a little chat, sitting around the fire as old friends would. Nod your head while it is still attached to the rest of you and then we'll proceed carefully up those rickety old steps. You want to do something about them. What Health and Safety would say I just can't imagine. A man could have a serious accident and that would never do." Mark dutifully listed the residents of The Hand of God who were awaiting his return in the bar. There was no way of warning them and every probability that this was all going to end very badly indeed.

Under his direction they began to climb the steps, emerging unseen around the corner from the bar.

"You," he whispered to the thin man, "I want you to very carefully look around the corner. If you are seen I'll kill you. Come back here quickly and tell me how many of them are warming themselves in front of the fire and whether there are any more standing anywhere in the bar." He did as he was ordered, returning quickly with the information Slope had demanded. "That seems to accord with the information this wretch has already provided," Bennett and the thin man entered first with Slope a pace behind. The group were so engrossed that at first no one noticed the interlopers. Slope pushed his way into the bar, standing to the front and theatrically pushing Mark to the floor. The effect was electric.

"Now that I have your attention, let me assure you that I am very serious, and to ensure your attention remains undivided let me confirm that assertion."

The fireside group were stunned at Slope's sudden appearance, and at the sight of Mark sprawled on the rug where Slope had thrown him. Slope pointed a Glock 9mm at the supine Mark. Casually, he aimed the machine pistol and pumped a single bullet into his knee. Mark screamed and rolled, desperately trying to clutch what was left of his kneecap. "You two," he ordered pointing at the twins, "pick him up and put him on the sofa." He replaced the Glock in its holster, pulling a much more destructive weapon from the bag slung over his shoulder. "If you have any bandages then bandage him up." Still no one moved. "If anyone among you would care to test my aim then feel free. I warn you, though. In my left hand I am holding an Uzi, a wonderful invention that can fire sixty shots a minute, so I suggest you do as I say from now on. Anyone thinking of becoming a hero should realise that you have a better chance of becoming a corpse. I could cut you in half before you managed to lift yourselves off those very comfortable sofas. And please do not seek comfort in my wish to have a conversation with you all before I kill you one at a time. Be assured I will kill you, but I feel that I should explain that while many are called, few are chosen. You bastards are my chosen few. I suppose that you would prefer to have been chosen for something else but in life nobody gets out alive, as I believe Jim Morrison once averred. Worked for dear old Jim, I suppose.

"First of all, my chosen ones, let me express my disappointment that you were prepared to listen to that pompous clown Cornelius that day in the college chapel. I am upset that you should entertain for a moment the idea that I should consider accepting a bribe of £4 million, and be so stupid as to believe that he would secure me a cast iron pardon, allowing me to swan off into the sunset. That is a clear bloody insult. What sort of lifestyle would a paltry sum like that have sustained? That is chicken feed. Did you really think that Cornelius and his Mickey Mouse unit could outwit me? I knew about the meeting before you did. In fact it was one of my men who demonstrated the efficacy of modern sniper rifles by focusing the red dot on your forehead, Bob. Of course I have infiltrated the anti Spriggan unit. I deliberately made it appear that MI6 had been infiltrated just to put Cornelius off the scent. And he took the bait. He was so busy assuming that the weak spot was there that he allowed himself to get distracted. What with that, and all the port, he's not the man he once was. He's not as stupid as he looks but surely you never thought he could be a match for me. He taught me everything he knew, and as soon as I'd wrung all the information I needed out of him I discarded him like a used sponge. Although his lectures have been of enormous help in my management of the Spriggans. I owe him that, I suppose.

"However, I would like you to realise that I am a cultured if unforgiving man, and to prove that Bennett here has carried up three of those six bottles of '82 Petrus that the unfortunate Mark had intended to collect. I had to promise to allow her to strangle one of you as an encouragement for carrying them up those very dangerous stairs. You really should get them fixed before somebody has a crippling fall." The group remained transfixed. Being in the presence of a genuine sociopath who was having the time of his life was outside any experience they had ever encountered. None of them doubted what he said. They had no doubt that Slope held all the aces. Slope knew that better than they did. He was having a lovely time and was going to extend it, as long as he was enjoying himself. Once he got bored he could just execute them in a couple of bursts of fire. For now he was enjoying the control.

"I'll just fill you in on what is going to happen to all of you. First we shall all have a glass of this fine wine that Mark has so kindly provided for us. Bennett will pour a glass for each of you. As you are called you will walk to the bar and pick up the glass. I reserve the right to apply the sanction of death, either instant or painfully prolonged, to anyone who displeases me in any way. Nod if you understand."

The response recalled the production line in a nodding dog factory as the group nodded in unison. Mark Williams, still lying where he had been thrown, did his best, even though he had fallen on his left side and was facing away from the group's arch nemesis. "Excellent. We are going to get along just fine. There are the glasses, one for each of you, on the far end of the bar.

Get up and pick up a glass and sit back down with it. Do not drink until I give you permission. Don't worry about Mark. I'll probably kill him shortly, if he doesn't bleed to death first. We'll see how things go." The situation had taken such a bizarre turn that the Job twins, no strangers to direct action, got up one at a time, picked up their glasses and sat back down without a sound.

"Now I'll explain how this is going to go," Slope continued once they had all returned to their seats. "I don't know whether you are aware of the contempt in which I hold you all so I feel it incumbent on me to clarify it. I have a towering intellect and a low boredom threshold. The person I hate most of all is you, Prideaux, and to be honest you will die most horribly. Next is that fat fraud Bones, who will die equally horribly. As for the rest of you, I shall decide how each of you will shuffle off this mortal coil in order to amuse myself.

"To that end, and because hope takes a long time to die, you are going to answer the questions I ask you. You are all intelligent and well read people. At least you think you are. Compared to me, of course, you are ignorant peasants. However, I'm sure that each of you is already calculating just how long you can stave off death by answering my questions correctly and honestly. You might be thinking you can string me along by drawing out your answers. I also know that you are desperately hoping that some help will come before you make the last mistake or before I get bored and shoot you anyway. That way madness lies." Slope accompanied this last chilling statement with a hearty laugh and, to the horror of the group, he genuinely seemed to be enjoying himself.

"Here are the rules. I shall ask each of you a question in turn. Answer it correctly and I shall ask the next person another searching question. I'll allow each of you three wrong answers. Three lives, you might say. When

I decide that it is time for someone to die, Bennett here will decide the manner of death and the rest of you will watch as you fervently hope that you are not the next one to go. Just a quick assurance to you: don't worry, it's not poison. The wine is far too good to spoil so nobody will be dying of poison on this particular night. People will be dying though. I shall propose the toast which is 'To murder, mayhem, anarchy and torture. May they live forever'. By the way, anyone who feels that they are unable to join in this toast should swiftly think again. There, I knew that would persuade you. Now the first question goes to you, Prideaux and it is this: who else within the college sided with you when I attempted to bring the benighted place kicking and screaming into the twentieth century? I appreciate that the kicking and screaming was of the genteel variety but I am keen to know what sort of support an awkward bastard like you could have had. Think carefully before you answer. And remember I can only take your first answer. Get it wrong and, of course, you will forfeit a life. Not your life you understand, but the life of one of these pathetic clowns that you regard as your friends." Piers remained resolutely mute and his friends exchanged nervous glances.

"I shall insist that you nominate one of them to be tortured to death as entertainment for me and, I suppose, a bit of a horror show for you. And in the spirit of open and intelligent debate, although I hold all the aces, I should tell you that I want to know anything you can tell me that I don't already know so that I can compile something I refer to as my retirement list. You see, despite the best efforts of you lot and various government departments I have done rather well for myself. Once I have cleaned up here I intend to retire. I haven't decided yet which country will have the honour of hosting my declining years. One thing I can confirm is that it will not be this one. However, anyone with an intelligence such as mine, and there are not many, can get a little bored over time. That is why I need a reserve list of people that might be worth my while hunting down and killing if retirement starts to drag a little. The predator never stays silent for long. Since I happen to be right at the top of the food chain such a list as I envisage could prove a nice little distraction for me as I grow older. Please don't think that silence or lies can conceal the identities of anyone who supported you. I know of most of them, particularly those who did their best to hide because they were too gutless to stand up in public. There are a few I am not sure about." Mark Williams moaned in pain and Slope kicked him in his shattered kneecap, eliciting a frightful scream.

"So come on then, let's have an answer."

"I'm surprised at you, Prideaux, so perhaps I'd better ensure that subsequent questions are just a little bit more taxing and get some form of response, otherwise I shall feel that you are not prepared to play the game. Bones, you've spent a good portion of your life pissed so I imagine that you have voluntarily poisoned the bulk of your given brain cells. Give me an answer to the question that your truculent friend has just refused to answer."

"I have no intention of playing your pathetic little game, Slope. You are a bitter and twisted individual with a highly developed, though unwarranted, superiority complex. God alone knows why, because the truth is that you are a card carrying fucking nutter and should have been locked up years ago. It would have saved a lot of people a lot of suffering. So, as far as I'm concerned you can do your worst, but I absolutely refuse to dance to your tune. If you kill us all you will suffer for it. Who the hell let you believe that you could go running around the country arbitrarily killing anyone who displeased you? You are not the government, you know. You have shot your bolt, you sad bastard, and whatever happens here you will pay the price." This response from Bones was so unexpected that the reaction of those in the room seemed to carry a three second delay. Bones was not cowardly but was not known as the man most likely to confront a disturbed megalomaniac, especially one intent on exacting bloody revenge. There was no sound in the room for what seemed a long time before Slope finally spoke. When he did so his voice had dropped a tone and now had that vicious top note that only the true sadist ever achieved.

"I hope you have finished, Bones, because I have taken offence at your little outburst. There is offence and, as Hamlet once mentioned, "much offence" in your response. Judging by the expressions on the faces of your companions you have surprised them as much as you have me. Your problem is that I am the one with the gun. I think that a little penalty is called for."

Bones looked suddenly very weary and very old as he opened his mouth to speak. Slope stopped him with a look and he subsided with a sigh, a beaten man.

"I'm sure by now you have some idea of how much I despise all of you. What interests me is the sheer hypocrisy of some of you. You know as well as I do that if you held the whip hand you would dispose of me in the blink of an eye. The difference between us is that you are not clever enough to gain the upper hand. Even if you did I'll bet that not one of you would have the guts to pull the trigger. Well, there is one of you I suppose. He may have left the organisation and got away with it for a while but I tracked you down in the end, didn't I Mark?" The room became silent as they all turned to look at Mark. He looked drained, his face pale with the blood loss from the wound he had suffered.

"I'm surprised that it never occurred odd to any of

you that I have always had a pretty good idea of what you have been up to. Look no further, Mark is your man, except he's not. He's my man and has been keeping me informed since you two clowns," he glanced at Bones and Prideaux, "fetched up on that cottage doorstep down in darkest Cornwall. As soon as Speight tracked you to Blisland I knew that you would come in handy as an informant. You didn't have any choice, did you? I knew too much about your time within the Spriggans. After all I was the one who supervised your first kill. She was only a young girl and we had already taken care of her parents. She was hiding in the barn on their farm and you were given the job when we found her. Poor thing never had a chance. You cut her throat and, though it wasn't an official Spriggan execution, you took the opportunity to cut off both her ears as she lay dying. I know it's a long time ago now but my recollection is that you seemed to enjoy it. I know I did. Not quite the man you married, Ginny?"

"You lousy bastard, Slope," Mark screamed as he desperately tried to gain his feet, blood still soaking though his wounded knee. His words were drowned in the harsh noise of the Uzi and the fleshy noise as the bullets tore through his body, the impact taking him over the back of the sofa and onto the flagstone floor of the bar. His body arched with the impact as the bullets tore into him and he died without a sound. Ginny, witnessing her husband being slaughtered in such a casual way and desperately trying to digest the information she had just been given, screamed as she ran at Slope. To her credit she made four of the ten metres between the two before a second burst cut her in half. She was already lifeless as her body hit the flagstone floor, her momentum sending her crashing against the foot of the bar with a fleshy thud.

"How do you feel now, Bones, Prideaux? A couple

of old soaks like you must realise that actions have consequences. Now you have two deaths on your conscience. Killing people has always made me feel hungry. I feel hungry now and before I stamp out any more of you insects I think a nice cheese board with some crusty bread, and perhaps some more of that delightful wine, might just do the trick. Satisfy the inner psycho, eh Bonesie? That's probably what you are thinking, if you are capable of thinking anything at all. Here Liz, hold the pistol while I get the cheeseboard from the cool cabinet. Not a bad selection of cheeses here, Mark," he was addressing the twisted corpse of the man he had just shot. "Some really good spelt bread too. Just what the doctor ordered. Liz," he continued, "just pass back the gun, and you," he looked directly at the thin man "do me the favour of popping down to the cellar to pick up the last three bottles of Petrus. If only dear old Petroc were with us now he'd be in his element. I almost forgot. I killed him too, didn't I? In fact since you are all going to die I might as well tell you that he was my first. Well first, that is, if you don't count that boy who made the fatal mistake of bullying me all those years ago. I cracked his skull for his temerity and I must say it felt good. Until then, apart from the occasional animal, I hadn't killed anyone. The feeling with animals was never the same though. I've done my best to make up for some relatively fallow years but this particular event will, I think, establish my position once and for all on the hit list of serial killers."

It was at this point that Prideaux raised a hand. Slope indicated that he would allow him to speak. "Since there is no possibility that any of us will leave here alive, is there any chance that you would at least tell me just why you have always hated me so much? I know that I was something of a thorn in your side in the old days but I always thought your reaction was out of proportion in terms of the nuisance I caused you. That's all; I want to know before I die."

Slope laughed merrily as he turned his full attention to Prideaux. "I'm sure you know the old Mafia adage about revenge being a dish best enjoyed cold; well, I'd like to say that there's something in that. Where you are concerned that is not the case. You are only amongst the quick rather than the dead at the moment because events have demanded my attention rather than allowing me to focus directly on your demise. At last I am in the position to ensure that I shall be free of the turbulent priest that you once were. You undoubtedly think that your opposition to me when I was Master of St Jude's College was justified, as an attempt at protecting conditions of service for you and your layabout left wing colleagues. Of course there was a political element in my approach. After all I was supported by a government that believed in what you liked to refer to as 'old fashioned values'. That was the obvious cause of friction with you, less so with some of the others. The difference was that you chose to make it personal by exposing what you referred to as my dirty tricks and fraudulent use of the college victuals. That made it personal. And people listened to you. But what to you constituted dirty tricks was to me simple expediency. I was in a position where I could direct an Oxford college in a way I felt appropriate. For a start I could ditch this insistence on wasting places on people from that dependency down there in the depths of south west England. They have nothing that we want anymore. We've taken all the mineral wealth and the place is destined to end up as a theme park within a few years. To be honest, look at you, Prideaux, and your idiot friend. Not much of an advertisement for the human race really. What I wanted was an intake that had some form of drive motivating them. Young people without scruples, with no interest in the easy life of education but those who would stop at nothing to get what they wanted. This is what I wanted and I should have got it too, if not for your bloody interference. You exposed what I was trying to do and it took me years to re-establish myself. But when it comes down to it none of that really matters. What does matter is that a worm like you and your various idiot friends stopped me achieving something I had set my heart on. That made it personal. I recognised a long time ago that if I had any flaw in my personality it was an inability to forgive. A personal slight can throw me into a rage. I never forgave nor did I ever forget. As a younger man I used strategy and spite to destroy anyone who thwarted my plans, however minor the plans happened to be. As I matured my hatred had a visceral quality and the only thing that slaked my thirst for vengeance was physical violence.

"Oh dear, I mustn't exclude the helpless female from all this. Take Liz over there," Slope nodded towards his accomplice with a proprietary air, "she is salivating at the prospect of making someone suffer physically and, if I'm honest, it will be quite difficult to restrain her from doing what she does best of all, which is inflicting pain. You have my answer, Prideaux, and it is more than you deserve. Now just before we enjoy the main course I think a drop more of this delightful wine could be just the ticket to help enhance our enjoyment. You," Slope indicated the thin man who looked increasingly a hunted animal, "I thought I told you to get more wine from the cellar." Though he hadn't signed up to become butler to a pair of lunatics, he had little option other than to comply. "Cut away down to the cellar and bring up more of this wine. You should find at least three bottles together on one of the racks just inside the cellar door. Do you think you can manage that?" He moved as Slope had indicated that he should. For the moment there was nothing to be done. In truth both the Job brothers had done well in sublimating their natural aggressiveness. The moment would come, and when it did Slope would regret having upset the twins.

On such occasions time, if not standing still, often makes little effort to do its job, one that essentially involves moving forward. The bar seemed to have entered that dream time where nothing seems real and seconds begin to imitate their bigger brothers and become minutes. Nobody spoke. Prideaux and his companions looked lost and beaten. For them this was a new experience. Neither of the twins was stupid but they also knew that there were times when charging headlong at a psychopath with an automatic pistol could be a poor career choice. Accordingly, they kept their counsel, as the thin man did as he was ordered and descended to the cellar. Robert literally sat on his hands. It wouldn't do for Slope to notice the involuntary twitching as he tried to control his desire to wrap both hands around Slope's neck. He simply sat there staring at the remains of what had been a blazing fire not long before. The bar had begun to resemble the floor of a charnel house. The heat previously expended by the fire had encouraged the blood covering the floor to begin to coagulate. The musty smell permeated the area with a top note of sickly sweetness. Through this Slope stared at the group impassively, pausing only to take a bite of the cheese and artisan bread, the crumbs of which spread out all over the bar. Slope was not a tidy eater. He was draining the final drops of wine from the last of the Petrus when a noise coming from over his right shoulder, distracted him.

"Watch them," he barked at Bennett as he slipped from his bar stool, turning to watch the return of the thin man. Suddenly he was unsure of himself. The man seemed to be hesitating to enter the bar. It was if he was dithering before fully entering the room. Finally he revealed himself. He carried none of the bottles of wine and was not alone. He was in the middle of two heavily armed men, both carrying machine pistols. Behind them two others stood kitted out in the same way, except these men were armed with automatic rifles. One was aimed directly at Slope, the other at Bennett. Slope knew that his chances were so slim as to be non existent and for a moment it looked as though he would surrender meekly.

"You know the drill. Drop the weapon and put your hands on your head," said the taller of the two riflemen. Slope was suddenly thrown further off balance by the fact that the voice of the rifleman didn't quite tally with the appearance; it was the husky voice of a woman. "I have orders to take you both alive, but to be honest I'd be happier if you made a move. I would be delighted to send both of you straight to hell, so it's very much up to you." These were not men to be trifled with, especially the feminine sounding tough doing all the talking. Slope knew this instinctively. He also knew that they would not hesitate to kill him on the spot. But what the hell.

"What we have here is a failure to communica...." Slope began, then raising his Uzi to waist height he got off a burst that hit the thin man in the lower abdomen. The thin man's intestines burst out, twisting and writhing as he screamed and pitched forward. The two armed men to either side of him hit the ground. Before they could rattle off a burst of machine pistol fire the snipers behind fired a single shot each. The first one hit Slope in the shoulder and the second simultaneously smashed into his lower arm, breaking the bone and rendering it useless. The gun dropped to the floor. Slope, though obviously in extreme pain, stood facing the men, his left arm hanging uselessly at his side. "Well go on then. You know you want to. Get it over with." He stared at the armed group with his usual insolence, married with contempt, etched onto a face that was beginning to register the real pain that followed the initial shock. A sudden crash from the fireplace transferred attention to that side of the room as Bob and Robert crashed simultaneously into the unarmed Bennett driving, her several metres backwards into the ashes of the great fire that had now burned out. It was a textbook technique that the twins had regularly used when terrorising undergrads in their college rugby matches. "One high, one low, the bastard has nowhere to go," the two recited with the same immaculate timing with which they had clattered into the unfortunate Bennett, who lay unconscious in a heap of wood ash. "Ashes to ashes, dust to dust, this poor bitch her neck is bust." The mock prayer in solemn tones came from Robert, who was high fiving his brother at the efficiency with which they had disposed of any threat that she may have posed.

"I sincerely hope not," came the riposte. It was the taller of the two riflemen who spoke. "Our orders were to take these two alive and to rescue as many of you lot as we could. I'm sorry that we were not in time to rescue those two," she indicated the bodies of Mark and Ginny. The man removed the balaclava to reveal that it was not a man at all; it was Rosie. The twins looked shocked. It was not what they were expecting. What they could not have known is that their unexplained abrupt exit from Cornwall had alerted her to the fact that something was happening. In the light of recent events she had contacted Cornelius for his advice. He had instructed her to assemble a task force and to follow the twins. It was more than likely that they would be off to help Prideaux and friends which inevitably meant they would be in a mess as usual. She had arrived late at the battle in the clearing but, noting the carnage, realised that to date the twins were in good form. They were now aware that Slope was looking to put his endgame in place and had picked up their scent near the tower, alerting them to the presence of the tunnels. They would have been there earlier but for the difficulty of negotiating the tunnels without previous knowledge of the way they snaked under the surrounding hills.

"I'm afraid that this sort of action is not an exact science. I should explain that we are the business end of the anti Spriggan unit within MI7. We are Unit S operatives. The man who can explain is on his way through the tunnel. He is complaining bitterly because we had to act blind on this one. Our best bet was to use the tunnel rather than try a direct assault. If he'd waited a bit he could have come in through the front door which, by the way, I'd be grateful if one of you could open so that we can load these bastards into the vans we have waiting outside. Could one of you do the honours and open the door?" It was Prideaux who opened the front door of The Hand of God to find himself facing half a dozen armed men, attired similarly to Rosie and the men inside. Instinctively, he raised his hands. "Hang on, I'm one of the innocents in all this."

"It's OK boys. He's with us," said Rosie. "Get a couple of medics in there. One busted arm bleeding rather badly and a suspected broken neck. We've been told to take them alive so I'd be ever so grateful if you could patch them up for me. They have a lot of talking to do and I need them to be ready for interrogation. Make sure you've got some wire ties on them and don't be fooled, they are both murderers and won't hesitate to kill again. Take no chances, I want them trussed up like chickens before they get any treatment. There's one of their lot in there who has been gut shot and I think is beyond help. Let me know as soon as you're done and we'll cart those two bastards off to somewhere where we can all have a little chat about how naughty they have been. I'll just pop down to the cellar to give my status report to the boss. I hope his mood is not too dark, that's all."

38

The cavalry arrives

At the cellar door Rosie shone a powerful torch down the tunnel. She smiled as she heard uncertain steps off in the near distance. There was no mistaking the voice of Sir Gawain Cornelius, nor the juicy imprecations that he was calling down on the heads of everyone alive or dead. The leader of Unit S was not a happy man. He rounded the bend in the tunnel. A tall man, he was bent over as the tunnel both narrowed and lost height as it led up the slight incline to the cellar door. "Put that bloody light out, Rosie," served as his acknowledgement that he recognised Red Leader silhouetted in the doorway. "Are you trying to blind me, or what?" he barked. In the unit the consensus was that his bark was marginally worse than his bite. The woman he referred to as Red Leader was a little apprehensive as he approached. Her team had achieved what they had set out to achieve. Slope and Bennett had both been taken. OK, they were both a little broken, but that was to be expected in this type of operation. He was mildly discomfited, however, by the fact that two of the group they had been attempting to rescue had been killed before the rescue attempt had been launched. It was not the fault of the team. They had been forced to bide their time. Any type of full frontal assault would have led to a massacre that would have certainly included Slope and Bennett. But there was still that nagging doubt.

Having switched off her torch Red Leader could not help a wry smile at a yell of, "Who the fuck put that there?" This was swiftly followed by, "Switch that fucking torch back on, you clown. Where do they get operatives from these days? Point the bloody thing at the floor or the roof, anywhere but directly into my eyes. And do it quickly before I render you unfuckingconscious." Red Leader did as she was ordered. She watched impassively as a dishevelled and royally pissed off Sir Gawain Cornelius unsteadily negotiated the final few metres of the tunnel without further mishap. Red Leader stood to attention as her boss stepped through the ancient door and into the cellar.

"Right then, Red Leader. Status report, let's have it. If I hear a single going forward, blue sky thinking or a hint of some prat thinking outside a box or pushing a bloody envelope then I shall not be responsible for my actions. Come on woman, out with it."

Red Leader was solemn as she informed Cornelius of the state of play in the bar a few feet above their heads. "Sir. Slope and Bennett have been neutralised but a little bit damaged. Slope is currently having medics sort out his arm which took a couple of bullets. Bennett was briefly unconscious and has a badly damaged neck but is reviving under treatment and the damage is not as bad as first thought. She is probably the luckier of the two, having been hit at full velocity in the best double tackle I have ever seen by those two mad bastards from Cornwall. The action, however, was only partially successful. I'm afraid that two of those we were attempting to rescue were already dead when we burst in. Apparently Slope shot them both just to make a point."

"Don't tell me he shot Prideaux and Bones. Those are the two he hated most, I'm well aware of that."

"No Sir. It was Mark and Ginny Williams. They were the couple who ran the pub."

"The poor sods. This whole mess was nothing to do with them. They were minding their own business in deepest darkest Cornwall before Prideaux and Bones fetched up cold and drunk on their doorstep. Ginny was highly regarded in the world of pottery and Mark was beginning to make some impact with his historical novels set in and around Bodmin Moor. Decent people, even if Mark did have something of a past. A bit of collateral damage can't be avoided at such times. Very sorry and all that. I'll get a separate team in to deal with the bodies."

"How are the survivors managing? Have they had time to come to terms with the situation? Slope and Bennett won't be bothering them or anyone else in the future. In fact unless I miss my guess their future doesn't look very promising. From what I know of them both they are unlikely to talk under questioning. We have some very advanced techniques but I still think a bit of unbearable pain often brings the best results. If the boffins have their way they'll pump them full of all sorts of hallucinogenic cocktails. It'll be the sixties all over again. Still, they are two wild animals that will never be a threat to civilisation again."

They climbed the stairs to the bar. Red Leader had relaxed somewhat. She had not been praised for a relatively successful action. But neither had she felt the full fury of the Cornelius tongue, reputed to be able to blister paint if his mood was not a reasonably placid one. In the bar of The Hand of God medics busied themselves with making Slope and Bennett fit to travel. Slope's arm was bandaged. The bleeding had stopped and he had been given medication for the pain. Bennett had been fitted with a collar and was now sedated. Both were secured to stretchers with individual guards keeping them under close observation. The survivors had moved through to the restaurant while a separate team removed the bodies of Mark and Ginny Williams. The body of the fat man in the cellar and the thin man in the bar had also been removed and were heading for unmarked graves somewhere windswept. The small group had reassembled at one of the dining room tables that looked out over the vegetable plot adjoining the pub. This had been Mark's baby. He was convinced that in the era of food from verifiable sources the addition of fresh untainted vegetables that, if you so choose, you could almost hear growing, was essential to attract more demanding customers. It was working too, with diners travelling significant distances to enjoy the freshest of dishes. The plot looked forlorn now.

Cornelius, having given the orders that Slope and Bennett should be taken, in separate armoured vehicles, to high security establishments at least 100 miles apart, knew that any form of debrief with the survivors would be problematical. His task was to put a lid on the whole sorry mess, and somehow persuade Prideaux and the rest to forget their ordeal and allow him the breathing space to organise a complete clear-out of any remaining Spriggans or Spriggan sympathisers embedded in sensitive areas of government. He knew, better than most, how hard it would be to get reliable information from Slope and Bennett. He didn't really care whether the techniques employed sophisticated man-made drugs or good old fashion torture; these two were hard nuts to crack. What he could do without would be the day's events becoming general knowledge and alerting any followers of Slope to the coming purge, allowing them to escape and regroup. That would make his job much more difficult. This was a golden opportunity to destroy the Spriggans root and branch. If he could do that he might be able to negotiate a retirement package that would allow him to realise a long held dream. He was still a relatively young man. When much younger he had fallen in love with the people and the attendant lifestyle of southern Italy. A retirement package would allow him to buy a flat in one of the small towns in the region of Puglia, right down there in southern Italy. He had once toyed with the attractive idea of asking Lola Cutler to join him there. Poor Lola, sadly that would not now come to pass.

Cornelius strode through the bar and through the door into the restaurant. "I am here to offer my apologies to you all. I am so sorry that we were not able to get here in time to save Mark and Ginny. They deserved better. Stopping Slope and that evil bitch he consorts with is small reward for the loss of two such decent people. All four of you, however, have made a major contribution to wiping out forever this vicious organisation that has caused so much death and misery. Rest assured that those two will not be causing any more mayhem in the future. What my organisation needs to do now is to root out and destroy any lingering vestiges of this cult. We must avoid what has happened here becoming generally known until we have had the time to establish just what level of organisation remains, and whether there is anyone likely to emerge as a leader now that Slope has been removed from the equation. I must ask that you cooperate with me on this and say nothing about what happened here until I am able to give you the all clear."

Only Prideaux looked up as Cornelius completed the speech he had prepared as he had walked the twenty or so metres from the bar to the restaurant. "That's all very well, Gawain. We are all just coming to terms with being still alive. But let's not forget that we watched two of our best friends cut down by that sadistic bastard. We had to witness that knowing we were all on that twisted sod's to do list."

"If it hadn't been for me and Bonesie they'd be back in their Cornish cottage painting and writing and generally enjoying life. Instead they left this place, the new love of their lives, zipped into body bags. We need to talk, firstly about appropriate funeral arrangements, secondly, what happens to their properties here and in

Cornwall, and also, about what will happen to the two psychopaths that your medics bandaged up with such care and efficiency. What I do not want to happen is to read in The Times a few years from now that, as a reward for being good children, Sebastian Slope and Liz Bennett have both paid their debt to society and therefore have been freed to continue their lives without let or hindrance. That would not be fair on us and it sure as hell would be a stain on the memory of two good friends."

"I can deal with your concerns in outline, then when the necessary arrangements have been made I shall put you fully in the picture," was the sober reply from a very serious faced Cornelius. "For your own peace of mind you need to know that both Slope and Bennett will never again be in a position to threaten anyone. We could, of course, deal with them summarily, but in the current climate of transparency that is no longer allowed as our first choice. In any case before we can sign this particularly complex case off we need some information that both individuals will be reluctant to share with us. Initially we need to question them, I use the word in its ordinary sense, to ensure that we clear out any remaining sleepers within sensitive departments. That is something that will take time as both are capable of misinformation on a grand scale. We have our methods."

"As to the funerals they will be conducted in a way advised by you. We will undertake and pay for all the arrangements and will ensure that there is as little publicity as you feel appropriate. As for possessions, I have people working for me who will legally transfer ownership of this place and the Cornish cottage into your hands. Once that is done you can do with both properties whatever you choose. Both properties will be legally yours and there will be no concerns that some long lost relative may turn up to claim title to either place. It may sound a little cold but then my section was not established to deal with events in any passionate way. We are all card carrying pragmatists, and with that thought in mind I will make a suggestion that may well suit you and would potentially be very helpful to me." All four nodded their agreement to listen to Cornelius's suggestion, though their expressions indicated that there had better be a justification for anything he said and it had better be good.

"I appreciate that everything is a little raw at the moment so I shan't expect your immediate reply. In any case, what I have to say should give you food for thought if nothing else. Pure and simple, this is the deal. I want the four of you to take over both properties with two of you running this place and the other two living in the Blisland cottage. I don't care which way round you do it and this is not meant to be altruistic. Any followers of Slope that are still around, and no doubt bear grudges, will know that both The Hand of God and the Cornish cottage have connections with the fairly tangled web that we are in the process of destroying. In my considerable experience those with a mindset that allows them to follow Slope are of a type. They are likely to return to the scene of the crime, or in this case crimes, like dogs to their vomit. It would be helpful for me if two of the possible sites that could figure in the immediate future could be monitored by those with a good reason to despise Slope and all his works."

Cornelius was comfortable when dealing with any number of intricate situations, and able to relate to powerful people as well as the dispossessed, but had never felt more on edge that he did at this moment. All four had not taken their eyes off him. They had hung on his every word but their expressions were impossible to read. What he was trying to offer would benefit them all as well as giving his section reliable embedded individuals in two potential problem areas. Effectively it was a no lose, no lose situation so why weren't they snatching his bloody hand off? He had more than enough of the kid glove situation and resolved to voice what he had been thinking all along.

"Look, you lot. All I want from you four is an agreement that the twins will take over the cottage and that you, Prideaux, and your oppo Bones take over The Hand of God and run it as a going concern. That's it. What do you say?"

There was a collective sigh summarised by Bones who at last broke into a smile. Looking directly at Cornelius he responded, "Thank fuck for that. We thought you'd never ask." That was the signal for a muted but general round of handshaking and meaningful nods. "Don't bother to say it, Cornelius old fruit. I realise that the understanding here will be dependent on my not drinking the profits. No doubt you will also have a clause that insists that the twins behave themselves in the cottage. Whatever suits. It seems a reasonable outcome for all for us. Just a shame people had to die to get to this point."

"For once I agree with you, Bones. Now get the fuck out of here so I can get my cleaning squad in to fumigate the place. I'll be in touch when all the arrangements are made, but for now I have to ensure that two very dangerous animals are incarcerated in top security complexes. I also have two funerals to organise, and some legal documents to complete to ensure that title is properly transferred to each of you. Off you go and remember that you all know far too much about both me and my organisation. That means that you have a certain level of intelligence and therefore you can expect to be monitored by my people on a fairly regular basis. You won't be aware of it as they wouldn't be working for me unless they were experts in the field of covert surveillance. I shall drop in from time to time to ensure that all is proceeding well."

"Absolutely crystal. Now would you like to seal the deal with a glass of this country's finest malt?" From nowhere Bones had produced five crystal glasses already charged with Penderyn Red Flag whisky. "Here's to us and what could be the start of a beautiful friendship."

39

These are the Hollow Men

Eighteen months later and Bones and Prideaux are sitting in the back bar of the King's Arms in Oxford. They are awaiting the arrival of Bob and Robert Job who are travelling up from Cornwall for a short break and a reunion. Cornelius was true to his word. He managed the necessary arrangements for the joint funeral of Mark and Ginny with the speed and efficiency so often an alien concept to the country's official servants. It was a sombre affair but a serious opportunity for reflection. The couple had owned a small wood that adjoined their cottage in the village of Blisland. They had always intended to have a natural funeral. Neither of them were believers and there was something comforting about the ceremony.

Bones read from Stevie Smith's The Celts as the degradable coffins were lowered into the earth. Prideaux steeled himself to throw a white rose into the open graves of two of his oldest friends. He still struggled with the knowledge that if not for him the couple would still be alive and enjoying full lives, blissfully unaware of the malign influence of the Spriggans. The small choir from the village sang the Cornish song 'The White Rose' as the assembled friends set to filling in the graves. Prideaux planted a rose bush at the foot of each grave and the twins planted a rowan tree at the head. It was simple, correct and heartbreakingly real.

Shortly afterwards the twins had an extension built for their own accommodation. They had sold the farm and, with more energy than is good for two young men, had thrown themselves into letting the cottage to holidaymakers. With the ardent adaptation so characteristic of the Cornish they had also licensed the copse as an official natural burial site, where those without a faith of any sort could arrange to be buried without benefit of clergy. It had proved extremely popular and the twins were busier now than they had ever been.

Prideaux and Bones too were doing well. The population surrounding The Hand of God were blissfully unaware of the previous events that had taken place in their local pub. The two old friends built on the popularity of the late owners by maintaining the quality of both food and drink. The organic vegetable garden had been significantly expanded and, with a new chef who genuinely understood the importance of fresh food, balanced dishes and innovation, the menu drew customers from throughout the area and many from over the nearby border. For the first time in his life Billy Bones had taken something seriously. It was inevitable that Bones would take an interest in the wine cellar but for once self interest had been sublimated by a real drive to establish the pub as a bastion of quality wines and beers. This is where the dilettante Bones came into his own. Rarely had he spared himself in his search which, in later years, had become a quest for the perfect ale and, more importantly, the most sumptuous claret. Through his efforts The Hand of God stocked local ales that could satisfy the most demanding member of the local branch of the Society for Preservation of Ales of Distinction (SPOAD). In fact so successful had his quest been that SPOAD not only held their regular meetings at the pub but by general agreement had made Bones and Prideaux honorary life members of the society.

As they waited for the arrival of the twins the two couldn't help but reflect on the way their lives had changed. The arrest and incarceration of the two people who had brought mayhem and murder into their lives had removed the dark shadow that had hovered over them for years. The success they were enjoying running The Hand of God had transformed their attitude to everyday life. They no longer had that uneasy feeling that they were being watched or followed. Prideaux no longer varied the times and days of his necessary trips into nearby Abergavenny. Bones had eased so comfortably into his role as host that a newcomer would swear he had been filling the role for his entire life. Ever the pessimist though, Prideaux couldn't shake a small but persistent feeling that this was all too pat. In his experience when things were going as well as they possibly could that's when the sky had a habit of falling in. Perhaps that was entirely due to his Celtic blood, or possibly life and its experiences had taught him that the most dangerous thing in the world is to drop one's guard. Bones had teased him many times about this and was, true to form, teasing him now.

"I wish you'd at least try pretending to be enjoying yourself, Piers," he muttered. "We are becoming rich beyond the dreams of avarice. I am gradually renewing my fortune, once cruelly decimated by those butchers at the Inland Revenue. We are running the best pub and restaurant, I refuse to use that ghastly gastro pub title, in Wales, probably in Britain. We have a lifestyle that very few people can even dream about. And for now we are in Oxford. The sun is shining and the female undergrads are scantily dressed in a fashion that can only allow an ageing roué to praise the Lord for the invention of Viagra. What is not to like? I trust that your Wadworths is up to snuff. So what is it, my miserable little companion?"

"I'm not sure, Bonesie. There's a nagging feeling that won't let me relax. Don't you see, it's all a bit too pat. This sort of thing might happen in real life but not to people like us. And before you ask me again, the beer is as fine as I expected so that is not troubling me. And, before you ask, neither is it my socialist conscience troubling me. Don't you ever think about what happened to Mark and Ginny? It was once all sunny for them then bang! Both of them blown to eternity on the whim of a madman. It seems to me that Fate cannot wait to bring down the hammer and cut short anything that smacks of pleasure."

"For fuck's sake, Piers. I love you like a brother but if you don't buck up I shall leave you to wallow in anticipatory self pity while I tootle off somewhere more enlivening. Now what is it to be? Perhaps, in memory of old times, a perambulation along the Broad or down the High would lift the dark cloud for you. What about nipping into Brown's for a nice cup of tea and a cake, if that's what takes your fancy? Or I suppose we could tool along to the alma mater and see what might be doing there, only for God's sake let's do something to lift the mood."

"I'm sorry, Bonesie," murmured Prideaux, making an effort to brighten, "I don't know what's wrong. I think it's that I've spent most of my life tensed for the hammer to fall and it's a difficult thing to shift. Look, the twins should be here any minute. What say I get you another pint of this delicious 6X and I make a determined effort to cheer up? Once the boys arrive I'll have no choice. You know those two lunatics, if twins arrive then chaos cannot be far behind."

"At last a sensible suggestion. A pint of the good stuff would be more than welcome, and if I'm not mistaken those very lads might be about to make a typically noisy appearance."

The door to the back bar flew open, stopping Prideaux in his tracks as two substantially built six footers careered into the pub, one piggy backing on the other. Both men were red in the face and dripping Cornish sweat profusely. They proceeded to argue with each other, both claiming the record for running the length of the Broad carrying the other. Drinkers paused with glasses halfway to lips as the two seemed to swell to fill a space that had previously seemed quite roomy. The twins had shown this ability to fill a room on their own as undergraduates. Age had certainly not withered that ability. In truth, gaining a few pounds over the years since graduating made them appear more formidable. The bickering stopped as they spotted Prideaux mid-way to the bar.

"Welcome back lads, and two more pints, is it? 6X OK with you, or have your tastes changed since I saw you last? Please don't pick me up and carry me around the bar, I've already had three pints and it wouldn't be a good idea. Go and sit down with Bonesie and I'll bring the drinks over."

Unusually for them the twins did as instructed and sat either side of an apprehensive Bones who, though he thought the world of the brothers, was constantly wary of their boisterous behaviour. Bones was at his most comfortable when sat quietly chatting whilst nursing a drink. Generally this was a challenge to the twins who enjoyed nothing better than to wind the older man up. On this occasion they seemed content to forgo their usual behaviour in favour of warm handshakes and some animated conversation.

Prideaux brought four pints across to their table and placed the tray in front of them. He greeted them warmly and they all started talking at once. As it does in such conversations the hubbub died down after a while and the four sat quietly supping their ale and staring into the middle distance. It was Robert who broke the uncomfortable silence.

"To be honest, Bob and I are a bit bored. The business is doing well, we live in a lovely cottage mere yards from the best pub in the area, but we're bored. We haven't had a decent scrap for longer than I can remember. We have to argue with each other for entertainment these days. I don't want the old days back but a bit of excitement couldn't hurt."

This was not what either Prideaux and Bones wanted to hear. As they had not heard from the twins they assumed that all was right in their world and they had at least begun to settle down. Unsettled twins were a potential powder keg. It had taken Prideaux a long time to come to terms with what had happened when Mark and Ginny were killed. That was perhaps why they now worked and lived in the place where it all happened. Most of the time it was all OK but occasionally it all came flooding back. Bones was much more philosophical. If pressed he would admit to feeling a little uncomfortable sometimes, but generally he was more than content. He would sometimes aver that they owed it to Mark and Ginny to make a success of the project, this being the best way to honour their memory. Prideaux understood but had always thought that what happened on that fateful night was as much violence as anyone would want to see in a lifetime. The twins had other ideas. He thought he should find out whether they had any plans that he could find a way of avoiding. They did have this habit of involving friends, and the twins had become the firmest of friends with Bones and Prideaux, both before and during the events of eighteen months earlier.

"Let me ask you this, boys. When most people I know get bored they take up a hobby or go on holiday or something. With you two, it's likely that anything you come up with will have some small element of the life threatening at the heart of it all. Please tell me what you have in mind so that I can establish once and for all that I am not interested and, whatever it is, will not be taking part. I have no intention of jeopardising the best thing that has happened to me in years. Bonesie and I intend to grow old and grey running The Hand of God and bless the day we were spared from the attentions of the bastard Slope. Incidentally, since that night I have heard nothing about him or any of his acolytes that might still follow his twisted path. That's the way I like it and that's how I want it to stay. I hope that makes my position as clear as a Cornish stream."

"I was convinced that my time had come that night. I thought we were all going to die. We've heard nothing so, on the principle that no news is good news, I can only guess that the bastard, if he is still alive, is in a place where any unpleasant experiences are his rather than anyone else's," said Robert.

"Well, I suppose so," Piers looked at Bones who nodded in assent,

"Now let's get some serious drinking done. Then I'll take you out and treat you to a decent dinner with the best wine we can find. We'll leave that job to Bonesie. He has a nose for such things, as everyone can see."

"Cheeky bastard," riposted Bones, but was secretly pleased to link up with the twins again, always providing that they remained true to their word. "Right then, I'll get them in," Bob motioned to stand up. "Hang on a minute, sit down, will you?"

Bones looked concerned. "Look, I know my eyes aren't that good and I also know that the eighteenth century glass in these windows can distort images, but I've noticed someone who seems to be staring at us from the front bar. Don't look up. I have this feeling that I know him but can't place him for the moment. If one of you can take a look without making a production of it then I'll be rather pleased."

As he said that Bones glanced to both right and left. To his consternation there was no sign of either twin. Boisterous as they could be on default setting, when occasion demanded they could also switch to stealth mode. Bones had been so focused on the face behind the glass that he had not noticed the two silently exiting through the back bar and into the larger bar to the front of the pub that gave onto Parks Road.

If he had not noticed them leaving he was certainly aware of the twins' return. They stood in front of him grinning, holding between them a smartly dressed man with a face that combined looks of fury and concern into a fascinating abstract study.

"If you apes don't put me down there will be hell to pay," stormed Sir Gawain Cornelius.

"I'd be a little careful how you talk to us, Gawain old chap," chorused the twins. "It seems to me you aren't holding many cards at the moment." continued Robert. "Unless there is a very good reason for you interrupting what is rapidly turning into a good session you could find yourself floating in the Cherwell a bit sharpish. Perhaps we'll pop you down next to Prideaux and you can tell us why you are here before you bugger off elsewhere. Only make it snappy, there's a good knight."

The twins deposited an infuriated Gawain Cornelius next to Prideaux and facing Bones.

"Call off your wolves, Piers. I'm here because I need to talk to all of you and I'll make it bloody plain from the outset that I am extremely displeased with the way I've been treated. I wonder whether it's worth bothering to save your worthless necks when it comes right down to it. Now we can't talk here, so if you'd be good enough to come with me we'll go somewhere we won't be overheard."

"Just a minute, Gawain. I'm sorry that the twins got a little over excited, but your presence here does not suggest that you have decided to come on the piss with our little gang. If you have taken the trouble to leave the comfort of your London club it can only be that you have something very unpleasant to tell us. Before you get to worry about official secrets and all that malarkey, nod your head if what you want to say involves an evil bastard. A nod will be sufficient, though I suspect I already know the answer."

Cornelius gave an imperceptible nod. "I fucking knew it. You promised us; you said they would never bother any of us ever again. You bastard. Now before I lose it big style let's go to whichever safe house you have waiting for us and you can tell us whatever story you have concocted. And unless you can tell me that you can fix whatever is wrong then I'm going to be mightily upset."

The words came out in a rush, Prideaux blushing as he realised how pompous he sounded. There was nothing for it but to go along with Cornelius and find out what almighty cock up he was currently presiding over.

Cornelius swept out of the back bar on to Hollywell Street without a backward glance. The four followed reluctantly, the body language redolent of all schoolboys who had been discovered by the headmaster sharing a spliff behind the bike sheds. Cornelius walked purposefully towards the Bodleian, stopping at the gates for the four to catch up.

"Follow me," he ordered, as he turned into an ancient doorway that led to a locked office. There was no name or indication of any kind on the heavy door at the end of the short corridor. He pushed open the door with the four men hard on his heels. The room was comfortable but windowless. Inside were three men who looked as if they came from central casting. Surely someone had ordered three actors to pretend to be undercover agents for Unit S. Except, Prideaux knew, this was not the case. They were as real as it got and their very presence indicated that something was rotten in the state of Britain, and Prideaux had no doubt that a sunny day was soon to end with some seriously dark clouds.

Piers Prideaux's worst fears were realised as he sat and

listened to the explanation offered for his unwelcome presence by Sir Gawain Cornelius. It was an explanation that in tone held no hint of apology or regret, but was simply an explanation with a list of options. Unsmiling and still smarting from his unceremonious treatment by the Job twins, Cornelius outlined what had happened the previous week. "There is no easy way of saying this, but I need to warn you that Slope and Bennett have both managed to escape.

"I have no intention of going into any detail as nobody here has sufficient clearance to be aware of where the two were being held. Suffice it to say that both establishments are miles from each other and their very existence subject to the Official Secrets Act. Some good operatives were lost in both escapes. On a positive note, Slope had been singing like a bird for at least a year and it has enabled us to more or less clear up any remaining sympathisers in any delicate positions of authority. Some low level scum may yet exist but they are no threat to national security and will be too busy trying to save their own skins to trouble anyone here. Slope and Bennett, as I have no need to tell you, are cut from very different cloth, although in my judgement they have both mellowed considerably over the extended period during which we have been asking them some delicate questions. Put your hand down, Prideaux this is not some lecture on an obscure Cornish poet, I am apprising you of the facts of the case as they apply to all four of you. This is what will happen. You will return to your relative businesses and carry on as if nothing has happened. In fact it would be better for us if you were all in the same place, at least for the foreseeable future. If you feel that you need some protection then I can provide you with cover from my people for a month or two. These are austere times so it won't be for any longer than that. I can also authorise each of you to have a hand gun with no questions asked. The local plod will be told to lay off and regard you as outranking them, anyway. Before you whinge about that you will be given shooting lessons by one of my people and I suggest you pay attention so that, should the occasion arise, you will all have some chance of balancing the odds. And you can forget any soft liberal ideas about the evil of guns. I'm not really asking you at all, I'm telling you. I do not want to explain to parliament why I have spent another God knows how much defusing a siege involving most of the same people as last time. It is simple economics.

"Now for the good news, and proof that I'm not really the horrible bastard that you think I am. Until recently I was happy for you all to continue as I outlined immediately following the events of that night. It suited me and I assume that it suited you." All four nodded in agreement.

"The escapes have changed the balance. What I have told you already contravenes the Official Secrets Act under I can't remember how many clauses. However, you can still be useful to me and I shall take an interest in your welfare for as long as I serve. I shall try to persuade my successor to do likewise. For the moment though, you can relax." He motioned his men to leave. When they had closed the door behind them he continued his briefing. "All I can tell you is that we have solid evidence that Slope and Bennett have left the country. To the best of our intelligence they are somewhere in Europe and have no immediate intention of returning to this country. If that should change then we will know, but for the time being there is no need to panic. So things are not as bleak as they might be. That is all I can tell you and I wish you all the very best of British luck."

Cornelius was a persuasive speaker. It was, after all, part of the brief. So why was it that Prideaux could see a large and very dark cloud hovering to the left of his sunny day?

Acknowledgements

I am forever grateful to Tim Prosser for his invaluable support in bringing A Touch of Pigskin to print. As an editor and friend he has been more than helpful. I must thank Rosie for her patience and all the practical help she has provided in what has been something of a saga. My son Gareth has very kindly designed what I judge to be a particularly striking cover for the book. Necessary and welcome distractions have been provided by my daughter Bronwen, my daughter-in-law Sophie and the smiliest of my family, the lovely Etta. I'm hoping that when we get to A Touch of Pigskin the Musical son-in-law Steve will agree to write the music. Thanks too for support from friends ranging from Mumbles to Mount Charles, never forgetting Ebbw Vale. Characters in the book are obviously completely fictional though locations are based on places I have lived in or visited. I have taken geographical liberties where it has suited my purpose. This is, of course, the prerogative of the writer of fiction. I have tried to tell a story that began with a dream. The result of following that dream will, I hope, give some pleasure to my readers.

3250854R00225

Printed in Germany
by Amazon Distribution
GmbH, Leipzig